DATE DUE JUN 2 1 2016

			C𝓑

THE
PERDITION
SCORE

ALSO BY RICHARD KADREY

The Everything Box

Metrophage

Dead Set

Sandman Slim Novels

Killing Pretty

The Getaway God

Kill City Blues

Devil Said Bang

Aloha from Hell

Kill the Dead

Sandman Slim

THE PERDITION SCORE

A SANDMAN SLIM NOVEL

RICHARD KADREY

HARPER Voyager

An Imprint of HarperCollins Publishers

THE PERDITION SCORE. Copyright © 2016 by Richard Kadrey. All rights reserved. Printed in the United States of America. No part of this book may be used or reproduced in any manner whatsoever without written permission except in the case of brief quotations embodied in critical articles and reviews. For information address HarperCollins Publishers, 195 Broadway, New York, NY 10007.

HarperCollins books may be purchased for educational, business, or sales promotional use. For information please e-mail the Special Markets Department at SPsales@harpercollins.com.

Harper Voyager and design is a trademark of HarperCollins Publishers L.L.C.

FIRST EDITION

Designed by Paula Russell Szafranski

Library of Congress Cataloging-in-Publication Data has been applied for.

ISBN 978-0-06-237326-7

16 17 18 19 20   OV/RRD   10 9 8 7 6 5 4 3 2 1

For David Bowie and Lemmy,

both gone too soon.

If I die, I forgive you. If I live, we shall see.

—Spanish Proverb

I don't want to go to heaven. None of my friends are there.

—Oscar Wilde

THOMAS ABBOT IS talking about the end of the world, but I can't keep my eyes open. The inside of my head is all Disney dancing hippos and gators going at each other with knives like candy-colored Droogs.

Ever notice how the more pain you're in, the funnier the world gets? Sometimes it's peculiar funny. Sometimes it's "ha ha" funny, but it's always funny. I remember almost bleeding to death in Hellion arenas and all I could do was laugh. I understand if that seems a little strange. That's what I mean about peculiar funny versus ha-ha funny. It's all a matter of perspective. The more totally fucked you are, the funnier everything gets. Right now the world is hilarious.

What was I talking about? Right. Abbot. The end of the world. At least, I think it's the end of the world he's going on about. Maybe someone just keyed his Ferrari. Whatever it is, I'm not listening. It's not that I'm bored. I'm tired, my head aches, and my eyes hurt like someone's tunneling out with dynamite. It's been a month since I've slept right. At night, my dreams keep me awake. Awake, the daylight feels like someone scouring my skin off with steel wool. I laugh once and everybody looks at me because they're not in on the joke. I'm squinting at the light too hard to explain it to them.

"You have something to add, Stark?" says Abbot.

"Not a thing. I'm hanging on every word. But I might have missed some of the last part."

"I was saying the meeting was over. We've voted on everything on the agenda. I had to put you down as an abstention on, well, everything since you didn't feel like joining in."

The other ten members of the Sub Rosa council—the den of thieves, high rollers, and important families that run most of our little world—stare or shake their heads in my direction.

"I was with you in spirit, boss."

"That's what makes it all worthwhile."

He turns from me and back to the room. People are getting up, gathering briefcases, purses, and jackets. You could feed every refugee in Europe with what these people have in their pockets.

"Thank you all for coming. It was a good meeting. I'll see you next week," says Abbot.

Good-byes to Abbot and general chitchat in the room. It's like my brain is an open sore and their voices are salt. I don't ever remember feeling this way, even Downtown.

"Hang around for a few minutes, Stark."

I nod to Abbot. With my head like this, I wasn't planning on going anywhere soon anyway.

When everyone leaves, Abbot comes over and sits down next to me. He's a handsome fucker and that's always bugged me. All-American boyish looks with all the power of the Sub Rosa at his disposal. We're on his houseboat in Marina del Rey. The meeting room is trimmed in gold and exotic woods.

There's enough video monitors and other electronic gear along the back wall to launch a nuclear war. Abbot's floating pad is like a comic-book supervillain's orbiting death lair. Yet I kind of like the prick. He seems honest. He gave me a seat on the Sub Rosa council. And he hasn't thrown me out for doing a lousy job. But I can't help wondering if I'm about to get a Dear John letter. *Things aren't working out. It's not you. It's me.* You know the routine.

Abbot laces his fingers together and leans back in his chair.

"You don't look so good," he says. "Please don't tell me you're missing meetings because you're hungover."

I shake my head and immediately regret it.

"If only. Then, at least, I'd have had a good time. This, though. It's a Trotsky icepick."

"Have you ever been checked out for migraines?"

"I don't get migraines. I leap tall buildings in a single bound."

Abbot gets up and looks through an expensive leather messenger bag.

"Let me give you my doctor's name. He does great work. You're aware, aren't you, that as a council member you get health insurance?"

"I do?"

"It was in the packet I gave you when you started."

"You gave me a packet?"

He comes back over with something in his hand.

"Maybe you lost it at home. Look for it. You even have a small expense account."

He puts a business card on the table. It has a doctor's name on it.

"Free money? I'll find it. And thanks for the advice, but I have my own doctor."

"Then go see him or her. Doctors are like aspirin. They don't work if you don't use them."

"Speaking of aspirin, you have any?"

There's something else in his hand. He sets down a small yellow prescription bottle.

"Aspirin won't do much for a migraine. But you should try these. I get headaches myself and these clear them right up."

"Your doctor's Sub Rosa?"

"Of course. Why do you ask?"

"I don't know. You're one of the moneyed chosen. I always pictured you with your own hospital or something."

He smiles.

"Just one wing. It's all Dad could afford."

I look at him.

"I'm kidding," he says.

"Just give me the pills, Groucho."

He hands me the bottle and points to the glass of water that's been in front of me the whole meeting. If it had been a snake, I'd be taking a venom nap by now.

I pop the pills in my mouth. They taste like flowers. Like one of those goddamn violet candy bars my mother used to gnaw on with her whiskey. Very classy. Very sophisticated. I want to spit them out, then remember they're medicine, so I don't. Abbot pushes the water to me and I take a long gulp.

"How was that?"

I finish the glass.

"It tastes like the wreaths at a mobster's funeral."

He puts the cap back on the prescription bottle.

"It does, doesn't it? Anyway, you should feel better in a few minutes. I can give you a few extra if you'd like to take them with you."

"Thanks. But I'll bug my doctor for something that doesn't taste like a hobbit's lunch."

"Suit yourself. But if you change your mind . . ."

"Thanks. But I won't."

Listen to yourself. Stop whining. This is your boss you're talking to. He's given you free drugs and is offering more. That's what people do when they see someone in pain. Shut up. Be a person.

"I feel better already."

Abbot gets up, tosses the bottle in the messenger bag, and brings it back to the table.

"I doubt that," he says, "but you will. Is your head clear enough to talk? I want to discuss something with you."

"Is this the part where you chew me out for being bad in class?"

"No. I understand how awful migraines can be. But tell me next time and maybe we can do something about it. No, I wanted to talk to you about the real agenda for the meeting."

"Going to dish about your rich friends? What do you tell them about me?"

He sits back down.

"Nothing. But trust me, they ask. What I want to talk about is the real reason for the meeting. Did you hear anything I said tonight?"

"Something about charities. Climate change. The end of the world."

"You're right about the charities part. What I wanted to see was who was pushing for which charities. I think some of the board members are in bed with Wormwood."

Wormwood Investments. What can I say about that bunch? They're into money and power. And they have a good time getting and keeping both.

Charity doesn't really seem to be their thing, though, so I try to get my mind wrapped around that.

"You think that dicking around with charities will tell you which ones are on the take?"

Wormwood is like a mob-run bank if the mob was a Hellion horde and the bank was the world. They make money when the market goes up and currencies collapse. They make money on where and when famines kill the most people. They make money on who is or isn't damned.

And they make money on me.

Who I kill. Who I don't. Whether I'm a good boy or a bad boy, they make a profit, and it pisses me off.

"Wormwood has a lot of front groups," says Abbot.

It clicks. "And the council can funnel to them through the charity fronts."

"Exactly."

"So, you want to see who recommends which ones."

"You've got it."

Another wave of pain gets me just behind my left eye. I close it and squint at Abbot through the right like I'm doing my best Popeye impression.

"Did you find out anything?" I ask.

"Maybe. I made sure everyone knew there was money to be spent. We batted around the names of a few groups, including two that I know have Wormwood connections. The next meeting we'll vote and see who pushes for which groups."

"How diabolical of you."

"Thanks. I'm flattered."

The wave of pain passes and I can use both eyes again. I get up and go around the table to where there's another full glass of water and drink most of it.

"Listen. I know a guy—Manimal Mike—with a lot of power tools. Why don't you point me at some of the shifty types on the council and I'll show them Mike's saws?"

Abbot raises an eyebrow before saying, "I'd need some proof before I'd let someone called Manimal Mike loose on anyone."

"Point me at the Wormwood creeps and I'll make them sing *La* fucking *Traviata*."

"I hope it won't come to that."

"If it's Wormwood, it will."

"You might be right."

I sit back down again and the light in the room stops strobing.

"Hey. I think your hamster food is starting to do something."

"See? I told you so." He pauses. "There's one more thing I wanted to talk to you about."

He reaches into his bag and pulls out a white folder. He opens it on the table. There's a photo of a young boy.

"A friend's son has gone missing. His name is Nick. He's run away before. Mostly to his father's house in San Diego. Everyone was assuming that's what had happened this time, but my friend hasn't heard anything and is worried. I remember that your lady friend, Chihiro, works for a detective agency. Do you think she could look into it for me?"

Abbot knows damn well that Chihiro is really Candy living with a new name and a new face courtesy of a powerful glamour. I have to give him points for being discreet enough, even though we're alone, to use her cover name.

"I was heading to her office after the meeting. I'll give it to her then."

Abbot's face relaxes. I hadn't registered the worry until it wasn't there anymore. I also notice that he's gone far out of his way to not say who his friend is.

"Thank you. That means a lot to us."

Okay. The friend is someone close, not just one of the council members trying to hide a family scandal. So, who is it? A childhood pal? A lover? Is Abbot married? I can't see his ring finger, but that's also a pretty Judeo-Christian tradition—not so much among the Sub Rosa types.

I focus back on the missing child.

"How many times has this kid run off? He looks like he's maybe twelve."

Abbot picks up the picture, looks at it, and sets it down again.

"Yes. He's always been precocious. With luck, this is nothing. But there's some worry that his father might have abducted him."

I flip the picture over. There's information on the back.

Eye color. Hair. Height. The only contact number is Abbot's. I close the folder and put it in my coat pocket.

"I'll give it to Julie. She runs the agency and decides who gets what cases."

"That's great."

"So, what time are we doing this charity vote thing tomorrow?"

Abbot laughs.

"Stark, it's Friday. We don't meet again until Monday. Take the weekend. Get your head fixed."

"Right. Friday. How about that?"

Where the hell did this week go? I swear, it was Tuesday just yesterday.

"Okay, then. I'll see you next week, boss."

"See you Monday," says Abbot.

I leave and walk back to the dock as sunset comes down over the docks. From here, Abbot's floating Xanadu looks like a burned-out garbage scow. Sub Rosa chic. They love their mansions to look like ten-week-old shit from the outside.

One okay thing about being on the council is that I get a stipend (and apparently an expense account—really need to look at that packet Abbot talked about). Since I can't use the Room of Thirteen Doors anymore, and since the last car I borrowed got burned by a psycho named Audsley Ishii, I got one of my own. A black '68 Pontiac Catalina fastback. Actually bought it. Inside, the previous owner put a rebuilt 455 V-8 under the hood. Outside, it looks like a hearse and a cruise missile had a bullet-nosed baby. I get in, turn the key, and make the monster roar.

THE DRIVE FROM Marina del Rey to Hollywood isn't as hideous as it could be. The 405 tonight is a plodding lava flow instead of a graveyard. Abbot's gerbil-food pill tuned down my headache, but the headlights on other cars still hurt my eyes. I can't believe I almost missed Friday. My head will be shaken back into place soon enough. I swear, having a job is half of what's wrong with me.

I never liked being an employee. I tried it before. Signed on with the Golden Vigil—basically, a government antihoodoo spook force. It didn't work out. The bosses—Larson Wells in particular—and I didn't exactly get along (I fought the law and the law won). Then they threw Candy in jail and would have shipped her to a Lurker Alcatraz in the desert if I didn't get help from a friend. Then they screwed me out of my paycheck. Then I tried playing private detective.

Don't bother asking how that worked out.

Even though the council gig is a pretty cushy job, being a salaryman grates on me in a very basic way. It reminds me of working for Azazel, a Hellion bigwig Downtown. The relationship was simple: he was the boss and I was his slave. Pull the plow or get sent to the glue factory. This job isn't as bad as that by a long shot, but being under the thumb of anyone who can burn down your life with a phone call makes me, let's say, uneasy. Maybe that's why my sleep has been shit.

I can't help wondering what Abbot does and who he talks to when I'm not there. Does he discuss me with whoever his personal friends and advisers are? No, that's not really in doubt—of course he does. The question is what he says and why. I mean, he's the augur. He'll play whatever angles he needs to stay who he is. That means he'll use me against

Date: 8/23/2017

Time: 6:06:44 PM

Total Checked Out: 4

Checked Out

Title: Copperhead, Volume 1
Barcode: 31472400236711
Due Date: 09/20/2017 23:59:59

Title: The perdition score : a Sandman Slim nov...
Barcode: 31472600080433
Due Date: 09/20/2017 23:59:59

Title: Inferno squad
Barcode: 31472400301515
Due Date: 09/20/2017 23:59:59

Title: Copperhead Volume 2
Barcode: 31472400250522
Due Date: 09/20/2017 23:59:59

Carson City

Library

Date: 8/23/2017

Time: 6:06:44 PM

Total Checked Out: 4

Checked Out

Title: Copperhead. Volume 1
Barcode: 31472400236711
Due Date: 09/20/2017 23:59:59

Title: The perdition score : a Sandman Slim nov
Barcode: 31472600088433
Due Date: 09/20/2017 23:59:59

Title: Inferno squad
Barcode: 31472400301515
Due Date: 09/20/2017 23:59:59

Title: Copperhead. Volume 2
Barcode: 31472400250522
Due Date: 09/20/2017 23:59:59

the blue bloods, the blue bloods against me, then he'll turn around and use us all against each other. None of this automatically makes him a bad guy, just a politician. For now, I'm going to assume he's on the level with me. But if I get one whiff of nefarious unpleasantness, I'll dump him in one of the open graves in Teddy Osterberg's cemetery collection in Malibu and bury him alive.

Right now, though, I need to get off the road as soon as possible. The headache wants to come back down on me. It tightens the back of my skull like an anaconda wrapped around my head. But Abbot's flower-power pills keep it at bay. I just need it to work for another hour or so. Then, depending on how things shape up, I'll go to Allegra's clinic or the other place.

The one I really want to get to.

BUT FIRST, MORE work.

Julie's detective agency is on Sunset Boulevard in Silver Lake. I push the button on the front door and get buzzed in.

The office is up a flight of stairs. She's fixed it up a bit over the last couple of months. Built herself an office with a door at one end of the space. I tap the glass gently and she gives me a quick wave. Candy's desk is in the large open space so she can greet potential customers when she isn't working her own cases. Small-time stuff mostly, but she's only been at it for a few weeks. Julie fired my ass after just one case. A case I solved, I'd like to point out.

One more indication of what a great employee I am.

Candy in her Chihiro drag doesn't look like her old too-large-leather-jacket-and-jeans self. She's dressed in a short, tight black dress with skeleton bones printed on the front and back. Her stockings say BITCH on them about a thousand times and her bag is a bloodshot vinyl eyeball. Her only concession to her old look is that she still wears Chuck Taylor sneakers.

Candy is at her desk laughing with a redhead I haven't seen before. Each of them has a Styrofoam tray full of noodles. Candy puts down her chopsticks and comes over to me. Gives me a big kiss and takes me by the arm to her friend.

"Stark, I want you to meet—"

"Alessa," I say.

Alessa, the redhead, opens her eyes a little wider.

"Alessa Graves. How did you know?"

I shrug.

"It's just this funny trick I can do."

"See?" says Candy. "Didn't I tell you he knew cool stuff?"

Alessa nods.

"Cool doesn't cover it," she says.

"Fairuza introduced us. Alessa plays guitar. Like real guitar," Candy says.

"Nice to meet you, Alessa," I say, holding out my hand like a gentleman or a Realtor. She takes it and we shake briefly.

Alessa looks to be in her late twenties. She's pretty. Her red hair falls just below her shoulders. She wears a lot of kohl around her eyes, probably trying to hide the lines at their edges, lines she's too young for. My money says she had drug problems in the past. Meth, I'd guess. Fucked up her skin some, but the addiction wasn't so bad she lost teeth. I can tell by her smell that she's clean now. Her heartbeat kicks up a little when our hands touch, but it's not that she's all excited to meet me. She's here to see Candy and talk music. They're just getting to know each other and suddenly the boyfriend walks in and crashes their guitar geeking. That's easy enough to fix.

"You should hear Alessa play sometime," Candy says. "She's awesome. Her old band toured with Skull Valley Sheep Kill. That's Stark's favorite band," she says, leaning confidentially in Alessa's direction. She smiles.

"What's your favorite album of theirs?" she says.

"*Plan Nine from Fresno.* What's yours?"

"That's a good one. I like *Cannibal Holiday.*"

"That's a good one too."

"Hey, maybe you saw her open one of Skull Valley's shows," Candy says. She turns to Alessa. "When did you tour together?"

"It was just before we recorded our album. About eighteen months ago."

I shake my head.

"Sorry. I wouldn't have seen you. Eighteen months ago . . ." A quick flash of pain in my head. I picture the arena for a second. "I was out of town."

"Well, if you're interested we have some live stuff on You-Tube."

"What should I search for?"

" 'Django's Coffin.' "

I'm starting to warm up to her. "Is *Django* your favorite western?"

She shrugs.

"My old girlfriend loved it. I like it, but I like *The Furies* more."

"Barbara Stanwyck. When she takes away Rip's derringer and points it at him."

"It's a good way to end an argument."

"I've ended a few that way myself."

"You should show me sometime."

"Sure. You, me, and Chihiro can go by the L.A. Gun Club."

She makes a fist and holds it out. I make one too and we bump.

"Alessa plays surf guitar. She totally kicks Dick Dale's ass," says Candy. She holds up an LP that's a bit battered at the edges. "Look what she gave me."

The cover is greenish, with a man holding a guitar case on a long stairway. A pagoda in the background. Printed on the front is RASHOMON. TAKESHI TERAUCHI AND THE BLUE JEANS.

"Early-seventies Japanese surf rock. She knows all about it."

I get it now.

"And you bought her noodles to join your band."

Candy picks up some chopsticks.

"She brought a record, so I brought noodles."

"That sounds fair."

Alessa says, "It's not quite that simple. Chihiro played me a recording of her band rehearsing. They're not bad. They need work, but they're not bad."

Chihiro. Good. Candy's staying safe, using her new identity even while she's trying to lure a professional guitarist into the clutches of her garage band. Maybe Alessa's drug problem was worse than I thought. For a pro to want to work with Candy's group, she must have burned some bridges with the local L.A. players.

I look at Candy.

"That's great. You'll be playing with Skull Valley soon yourself."

"Wouldn't that be great?"

Alessa picks up her chopsticks and pokes at her noodles.

"Let's not get ahead of ourselves," she says. "We need to learn some actual songs first."

Candy sits back down at her desk.

"Yes. Songs first. Then touring. See? She's a total professional."

I nod.

"Sounds like it," I say. Alessa continues poking at her noodles. Even I can take a hint. She's done with me being there. Candy looks at her. She's done with me too for the moment.

"Listen, I have to talk to Julie, so I'll let you get back to work."

Alessa looks up and smiles, glad I figured out what's what.

"Nice meeting you, Stark," she says.

"You too."

I head to Julie's office. The moment I'm gone they're digging into their food, Candy talking excitedly through a full mouth. Alessa laughs at her and hums a staccato surf melody.

I knock on Julie's door. She looks up and nods. I go in.

"How's it going?"

Julie shakes her head.

"I'm glad I got myself a door. The Bobbsey Twins out there have been yammering for an hour."

"Chihiro gets a little nuts when the subject of music comes up."

" 'Nuts' is the nice word for it. What are you up to these days? If this is a social call, I have a lot of work I have to do."

I take Abbot's folder out of my pocket and drop it on her desk.

"Be happier to see me. I'm bringing you business."

She opens the folder and picks up the photo.

"Is he missing?"

"That's what Abbot said."

"Abbot? *Thomas* Abbot?"

I look at her.

"Happy to see me now?"

"Happier. Do you have any background information on the kid?"

"There's some stuff on the back of the photo. His name is Nick, Abbot says. It might be a parent abduction, but I don't know."

Julie turns the photo over and scans the information.

"You don't think he's telling the truth?"

"I don't know that either. I just know that he went out of his way not to say what his relationship was with the kid or his parents. He just kept saying 'my friend' wants me to get you to look into it."

She turns the photo over and looks at Nick's face.

"Normally I'd be reluctant to go with a case with so little information and a cagey client, but—"

"Yeah. It's the augur asking. He's got money and he's got pull. It seems like one to take."

"And so we will. Thanks, Stark."

I always feel funny when Julie thanks me. She's the friend who helped keep Candy out of that Lurker relocation camp so she could become Chihiro. Then she gave her a job. We're both a long way from paying her back for that. Any case I can throw at her, I will.

From the other room we can hear Candy and Alessa laughing. Julie holds a hand off in their direction

"Can you have a word with her? I mean, this *is* supposed to be a place of business."

"Looks like she's on her lunch hour to me."

"Lunch hour and then some."

"Look, you made it clear you didn't want me involved with the agency. I'm not about to go out there and scold Chihiro for a noodle break."

"Point taken. Just do me a favor and look at your watch on the way out. Maybe she'll take the hint."

"I don't wear a watch."

"Right. Well, pretend. Stare at your wrist for two seconds."

I get up.

"I'll wrestle them to the ground and give them detention."

Julie gives me a curdled smile.

"Late at night, if you ever wonder why you don't work here anymore, remember this moment."

I open the office door.

"I'll tell Abbot you're on the case when I see him Monday."

"Tell him to call me. It would be nice to discuss a fee."

"I'll give him your number."

"Good night, Stark."

"Good night."

I walk over to Candy's desk and make a big show of looking at my wrist.

"What are you doing?" says Candy.

"Looking at my watch."

"You don't have a watch. You barely have socks."

"I'm supposed to be hinting about the time. Julie's request."

"Oh."

Candy glances at Julie's office.

"I guess I lost track of time."

"It's cool," says Alessa. "I don't want to get you in trouble with your boss."

She gets up. Candy comes from around the desk and gives her a hug.

"Call me tomorrow?"

"Yeah. Let's figure out a time to get the whole band together."

"Great."

Alessa tosses her noodles into the trash and heads for the stairs.

"See you around, Stark."

I give her a wave.

"You too."

Candy comes over and kisses me hard.

"Isn't this the best thing ever? We might be an actual band with an actual guitarist."

"You're a guitarist."

"I'm a guitar player. I know three chords. Alessa is a *guitarist*. Big difference."

"Well, I hope it all works out and you get to work together."

"Me too."

"You need a ride home?"

She shakes her head.

"I have tons of reports and paperwork to do. I'll be here late."

"Okay. I might stop by Bamboo House myself. I'll see you at home."

She sits down at her desk.

"Tell Carlos hi for me."

"I will."

I start for the stairs and she blows me a kiss. I wink at her. I head for the Catalina parked around the corner and see Alessa smoking a cigarette on the corner. She turns and sees me.

"You need a ride or something?" I say.

"No thanks. I have a cab coming."

"Okay. Chihiro is pretty excited about working with you. I haven't seen her this happy in a while."

"Chihiro's cool. And her band is all right. I can work with them."

"Good luck. They're a handful."

She takes a drag on her cigarette, blows out the smoke.

"So am I."

"I don't doubt it. Well, I'll see you around."

"Good night."

I go back to the Catalina and get in. Candy is working late. My head is mostly better, but not one hundred percent. I can get drugs for it or I can do the other thing. A stab of guilt gets me in the gut. I don't like keeping secrets, especially from Candy, but I don't know if she'd understand this and I need it right now. Just until I can get myself together again. I'll stop by Bamboo House later and bring home some food so the evening won't be a total lie.

In the rearview mirror, I watch Alessa get into a cab. It swings around and its headlights reflect into my eyes. Ice-picks again.

That settles it. I start the car and wait for whoever is hiding in the backseat to do something. When they don't, I pull out and head south.

About two blocks on, I hear a moan and pull over into the parking lot of a Spanish Evangelical church. I don't say anything, waiting for the moaner—it sure sounded like a guy—to show himself. He doesn't and I slip the black blade out of my coat.

"Anytime now, sunshine. Kill me or get out."

Someone rustles around and slowly sits up. I turn halfway in my seat.

He's pale. Thin. Unshaven. Three days or more. He doesn't smell that great either. He leans against the side of the door where his face falls into line with the blinking sign in front of a bodega. There he is, yellow one second, then swallowed in black the next.

"How long did you know?" he says.

I hear it in his voice. Now that I'm looking for it, I can smell it under his stink. "Fuck me. You're an angel."

He purses his lips, half smiling and half embarrassed.

"Guilty as charged."

"Get out."

"You didn't answer my question."

"I'm a nephilim, pal. Half angel and half pissed off. I knew you were there the whole time, but I was waiting for you to do something interesting."

"Why not attack when you saw me?"

"I was bored."

"You wanted me to attack you."

"That would have been more fun than this."

The angel shakes his head.

"You're not what I was expecting."

"How's that?"

"I came looking for an Abomination. A monster that acts violently on instinct."

"You came looking for Sandman Slim."

"Does he still exist?"

I take a pack of Maledictions from my pocket, tap one out, light it, and blow toxic smoke rings in his direction.

"If you came looking for Jack the Ripper, you came a couple of months too late. I'm a solid citizen now. Got a job. Eat my vegetables. Hell, I didn't even steal this car."

"I came here for . . . would you mind rolling down a window?" he says.

"Sure. How rude of me."

I roll down the driver's side, letting the fogbank drift away to kill the weeds in the parking lot. Whoever he is in the back seems harmless enough, but I keep my knife ready.

"What was it you were saying?"

He coughs a couple of times. Winces. Drops his weight back against the seat and looks at his hand. There's blood there.

"If you're going to bleed to death, please don't get it on the upholstery. I just had it cleaned."

He points a bloody finger at me.

"That's more who I came looking for."

"For what?"

He's wearing a dirty trench coat. It looks new, but also like it's been dragged behind a car. Sort of like the angel himself.

"Who are you?" I ask him.

"Karael. I came a long way to find you."

"Why?"

He reaches into his dirty coat and I get the black blade ready. From an inside pocket, he pulls out a small ornate box. He leans forward to hand it to me, then falls back against the seat.

"Have you ever seen one of these before?" he says.

I glance at the box.

"It's very pretty. If it's a hope chest, you're one depressed fuck."

"Look closer."

I hold it up to the light coming in from the parking lot lights. The box is lacquered black wood rimmed with gold and ornate flourishes that I recognize instantly.

"It was made in Hell. That doesn't mean I know what it is."

"Open it."

I set the box on the passenger seat, well away from me. Pop the latch and push the top back with the tip of my knife. Nothing explodes. No poison gas or hungry ghosts. Inside the box is a padded compartment holding a glass vial full of a watery black substance.

"Okay. I found it. What is it?"

He leans forward again, groaning.

"They need it."

"Who?"

"The rebel angels."

I put the vial back in the box and look at him.

"That makes you one of the good guys. How do I know you're not gaslighting me?"

"Listen," he says. "I'm dying. There are many of us loyal angels left, but I'm not sure enough. If we fall, the rebel angels will bar all human souls from entering Heaven."

"What about the ones already there?"

"I doubt they'll last long."

"And this black ink is supposed to mean something to me?"

"Black milk, it's called. No human will enter Heaven as long as they have it."

The angel looks at his hands. They're shiny with blood.

"We're near a friend's clinic. You should let me take you."

"It's too late for that."

I'm not going to argue. Angels don't take it well. "What am I supposed to do with this stuff?"

The angel shakes his head.

"I was hoping you'd recognize it. Find out what it is. Find out how to destroy it."

"How am I supposed to do that? I can't get to Hell anymore. I've lost the Room. I'm as landlocked as any of these other mortal assholes."

He frowns at me.

"You can't travel to Hell. You can't find the secret of the black milk." He drops his head. "We were so afraid of you once. Abomination, we called you. Now look at you. When you were a monster at least you were good for something. What good are you now?"

I ask myself that every night I get into bed with Candy. But I'm not going to tell this halo polisher about it. When I look at him, he's staring straight at me.

"Where are you going tonight?"

"None of your business."

"You used to be an honest monster. Now you keep secrets from your friends. Your lover. Probably from yourself."

"If you know me so well you know I don't take advice from angels."

"Not advice. Merely an observation. Before I came here, Father—Mr. Muninn—wanted me to tell you to follow your instincts. But do you have any left I wonder."

The clown is getting to me. I want to kick him out, but I remember being bloody and ready to die in the arena. And I can't kick an angel out in the street, especially not near a church. For all their God talk, the last people alive who want to meet an angel are church types. Show them that Heaven isn't all gossamer robes and harp recitals and they'll hallelujah their lunch right into the toilet.

"Look. I'll get this stuff checked out, but I don't know what you or Muninn expect me to do after that."

But when I look up, Karael is gone. Angels do that when they die. Blip out of existence like they were never there. I look at the box, close it, and put it in my pocket. Asshole angel that he was, he died to bring me this sludge. *Black milk*. I'll show it to Vidocq tomorrow. Right now I have to get across town. I'm late and I can't afford to miss tonight. It's funny, though. Arguing with an angel, my headache disappeared. Now that he's gone, I can feel it crawling back behind my eyes.

I need the cure and I need it soon.

For a second, I wonder about Alessa waiting for her cab.

Could she be in on this? Was she there to distract me from Karael in the backseat? If there's something more going on with her—more than playing guitar with Candy—I'm going to find out what. Until then, it's time to get on the road. I start the car and head back into traffic, hoping that whatever kind of ectoplasm Karael leaked onto my seats will come off with soap. Heaven might be at war, but that doesn't mean angels get to fuck up my car.

HE COMES AT me low, puts his weight behind the punch, and slams it in under my ribs. I let him do it. I like the feel of the blow, my muscles screaming, the breath rushing from my lungs. I relax into the pain. It's something real and tangible, and unlike the headaches, these punches, elbows, and kicks deliver a completely different kind of pain. The headaches make me weak at the knees. This Hulk Hogan stuff, I can grab on to and choke the life out of.

The guy coming at me is built like a battleship welded together from fat and blind fury. Whatever he does for a living, he needs a new job. Whoever he's married to needs to get a ticket back home to Mom because the SS *Shithead* here is not fit for human company. I guess that's why he was the only one who wanted to fight me tonight. There are a couple of dozen other guys in the abandoned high school, but none stepped up. I've beaten most of the others down here in the fight pit. No one knows who I am down here, but I've laid out enough of them that it's mostly the new guys and the crazy ones who want to go at me. I'm not exactly a big guy—people call me Slim for a reason—but most of the weekend gladiators down here are scared off by my scars. But the ones who step up—the crazy ones—they're the cure for a sane life. My best friends and the only elixir for a Trotsky headache.

The only thing I worry about is my left arm. The Kissi one, an inhuman prosthetic that looks more like it belongs on a Terminator insect than a person. That's a problem.

My buddy Manimal Mike makes mechanical-animal familiars, though. He's good with fake skin and made me a sheath so my freak-show left arm matches my right. As far as anyone here knows, I'm just ugly, scarred meat that, like them, is looking to blow off a little steam.

I let the battleship thunder a right cross into my chin. It's gorgeous. A work of art. For a second, I see stars and choirs of angels. The harder he hits me, the more he loosens the ice-picks behind my eyes.

Unfortunately, right when I'm having fun, the big guy decides to get stupid. I've let him hit me enough that he thinks I'm out on my feet and his mean streak is kicking in. When he punches my face he sticks out his thumbs, hoping to gouge out an eye. I shove him back a few feet to get his attention. He thinks it's just muscle memory. That I'm punched out. I give him one more chance to fight like a human being.

But he does it again. I feel his thumbnail catch skin and tear open a slit over my eye. The sight of blood turns him from asshole into animal and he rushes me, hoping to rip the cut open more so the blood blinds me. It's a decent strategy, but he's too big, too dumb, and too slow.

When he swings, I duck his first punch, then block the jab he throws with his other hand. While he's still surprised I give him a shot in the Adam's apple. Hit there hard enough and you can collapse someone's trachea and they'll choke to death, spitting blood the whole time. But I just hit hard enough so that he won't be able to breathe for a couple of minutes.

The battleship staggers back and I close on him, jamming a fist into his gut, then an uppercut when the first punch bends him over. He falls to his knees and I hope he's going to stay down, but the dumb animal doesn't know he's beat. He pushes himself up and runs at me like a bull with a bottle rocket tied to his balls. I wait until he's almost on me, then jump, slamming my knee up into his jaw. This time when he goes down his eyes are pinwheels and his brain is on a train to Cincinnati. He doesn't get up.

The room is quiet for a minute, then a whoop goes up. Two dozen shirtless attack dogs—the other fighters—cheer me on, except for a few I beat as badly as this guy. The pit boss, the closest thing we have to a ref, comes over and checks the battleship's eyes and breathing. He waves his hand in a circle, signaling that the guy is alive, but he's not getting up. A couple of the boss's flunkies come over and haul the guy off the fighting floor like a pile of bad meat. I don't see where they take him. Supposedly, there's a volunteer doctor down here, but I've never seen him.

The fighting pit is really an empty swimming pool in the old school gym. I climb the few steps up to ground level. Guys pat me on the back and call me "killer," tell me what a champ I am. Who fucking cares? All I know is Trotsky is out of my head and I can look at the gym lights without running into the dark like a bug.

Part of the gym roof is down. The floor is warped in

places, collapsed in others. Filthy clothes and food cans lie scattered around the walls. The place must have been a homeless crash pad before the amateur brawlers took over. For all I know, one of the other fighters owns the property. I've seen some flash shirts and designer shoes around the pit during the fights. Maybe here is the real estate agent for his family's property. What would Daddy and his money think if they knew what junior was up to?

As I put my shirt and boots back on, the pit boss comes over. He's an older guy with a few scars of his own. He has one cauliflower ear and nicotine-yellow teeth. I never did learn his name. He stands there a minute waiting for me to say something. When I don't, he starts in.

"You ever fight professionally?"

"Nope."

"You interested?"

"Nope."

I touch the heel of my hand to my eye. It comes back with a streak of blood and the cut hurts from the salt in my sweat.

"There's good money in it," continues the pit boss. "I have connections. I could put you in the ring tomorrow. Strictly underground, you understand. A grand in your pocket guaranteed. More if you win."

I pick up a piece of broken glass from the floor and check my reflection. I heal fast and the cut is already beginning to close, but I'll have a bruise until morning.

The pit boss is still standing there. I want him to go away before he sees me heal too quickly for an ordinary person. I turn around and give him a friendly half smile.

"Let me think about it."

"Sure," he says. "We can talk about it next time. You can sure handle yourself out there and, if you don't mind me saying so, you look like you could use some walking-around money."

"You think so?"

He comes closer and speaks quietly.

"I know an ex-con when I see one. From your clothes, I'm guessing with your record you can't get a decent job. I understand. I've been there. I can help."

I look at my coat and boots. I'm not a fashion plate, but what the hell about them says con? Or is it just me?

Probably me.

Glancing at my crooked fairy godfather, I say, "Thanks. I'll talk to you next time."

He claps me on the back and shakes my hand.

"Tomorrow?" he says, anxious enough that it's annoying.

"I'm not sure. It depends on when I can get out."

"I understand. I have an old lady too. Well, you know where to find us. See you soon."

He bobs his head and goes back to the fight pit, where men are stripping off shirts and shoes for the next bout.

I have an old lady too. Is that the kind of vibe I'm giving off? An ex-con with a shrew at home checking my breath for booze and my wallet for what little pay I can scrounge? I picture Candy, the very opposite of all that, and feel like more of a heel than ever. I can't keep this up. I hate lying and I hate these people. But this regular life . . .

Sometimes it makes me want to cut my throat and head down to Hell forever. At least I understand the rules down there. But I'm not the suicide type, especially knowing how it would hurt the few people I care about.

I grab my ex-con coat and head out. When I get back to the Catalina, I check under the seat for the angel's box. It's right where I left it. I look at it again. Open it, take out the vial, and shake it. Black milk. It sounds charming. What every good boy and girl needs for a growing body. I put it back and slip the box back under the seat. The cut over my eye has stopped hurting. I run a finger over it and don't find any blood. That's good news at least. I start the car and head back into Hollywood. I need a drink to wash the taste of cheap lies out of my mouth.

A LITTLE EAST of home is Bamboo House of Dolls, the best punk tiki bar in L.A. Old Cramps and Germs posters on the walls. Plastic hula girls and palm trees behind the bar. An umbrella in your drink if you ask nicely. There's also a brilliant jukebox. Martin Denny. Arthur Lyman. Meiko Kaji. I don't think there's anything on there less than forty years old.

Carlos, the bartender, laughs when he sees me.

I sit at the bar and he pours me a glass of Aqua Regia, the number one booze in Hell.

He says, "What happened? The bigger kids took your lunch money?"

I touch my eye.

"It doesn't look that bad, does it?"

He steps back, cocking his head from side to side like he's trying to find the naked lady in a Picasso.

"I've seen you worse. The scab is almost gone, but you've got a nice bruise over your eye."

"Goddammit."

"Let me guess. You ran into a tall midget with an iron hat. Or a small giant carrying a lunch box."

"The truth is more embarrassing, so let's go with that last one."

"Please tell me you at least won the fight."

I sip the drink. It tastes like gasoline and burns just right going down.

"I won, all right. But I shouldn't have been there in the first place."

He picks up and tosses a couple of drink coasters some customers left behind.

"Then why were you there? I thought your looking-for-trouble days were behind you."

"That's the problem. They are most of the time. I want them to be, but sometimes . . . it feels like if I don't hit something my brain will go nuclear and run out my ears."

Carlos gives the bar a quick wipe-down and pours himself a drink.

"I know your problem. Seen it a thousand times before. Before I bought this place, when I was a little *niño*, I bar-backed at a cop bar over by Rampart. The ones still working, most of them had their heads wired on right enough, but the old-timers? The retired ones or the bad ones that were exiled to desk duty? They could chew their way through steel. You killers, you men of action, take you out of the game and you're always a month from eating your gun."

I swirl the Aqua Regia around in the glass.

"Thanks for your concern. It's touching. Really."

"Don't be so sensitive," says Carlos. "Those guys, they didn't have your advantages."

"Such as?"

"The things you can do. The places you can go."

I finish my drink.

"That's the problem. I can't go places anymore. I can still do everything I used to, but I don't have anywhere to do it."

"And you being you, you go looking for trouble and you're going to find it."

"Finding it's not the problem. Not looking like I found it is. Chihiro would hate it, and my boss, he wouldn't be too happy either."

Carlos opens the cooler under the bar, puts some ice in a clean rag, and hands it to me. I hold it to my bruised eye.

"Then it's just me that's amused watching you twist yourself in knots," he says.

"I don't like lying to people, but I'm not built to be, I don't know, a regular person. I was born to break things. Even my father said so."

"A natural-born killer."

"That's what the old man said."

Carlos pours me more Aqua Regia.

"Your problem is you're all *Koyaanisqatsi*. You remember that movie?"

I nod. "A hippie music video ninety minutes too long."

"The whole thing is only ninety minutes."

"Yep."

Carlos uses a finger to draw a shape on the bar in the moisture left from the rag. A little yin yang sign.

"Aside from its virtues as a film, the word *Koyaanisqatsi* means 'life out of balance.' That's you, my friend. You go from crazy hit man to a pencil pusher on some board of directors or something with no steps in between. Of course it's going to make you a little crazy."

"And I've lost the Room. It's not just that I could travel through it. I used to think that was it, but it's not. The Room was always *my* place. Somewhere I could hide from this world, Heaven, and Hell. No one could touch me there. It's the only place I ever felt . . ."

"Safe," says Carlos.

I look at him.

"I don't know."

"Of course you know. You lost your happy place and now you've given up the thing that kept you alive all these years. Your fists. That's not the recipe for a happy life."

"So, what do I do?"

"You got yourself Koyaanisqatsied. Now you have to get yourself unkoyaanisqatsied."

"Yeah, but how?"

Carlos shrugs.

"Take a pill. Get a cat. Follow the yellow brick road. I don't know. I'm not a shrink. But this isn't the first time you've come in with bruises on your face or hands and I've helped you hide them. I'll tell you, though: I don't like lying either. Chihiro is good people. Come to me to talk anytime you like, but me helping you hide your sins? Tonight is the last time. I've cut off drunks and junkies and now I'm cutting you off. No more ice after tonight."

Someone pushes past me and orders shots of bad Scotch. I look at my hands. Some of the knuckles are swollen, but not so much you'd notice if you weren't looking for it. I hold the ice on my eye. No wonder the pit boss thinks I'm an ex-con. I am. Only I did my time in Hell and I came out with exactly the same problems all those cons have when they get out of federal or state pens. Candy and Julie nagged me about PTSD a few weeks ago. I didn't want to listen. I still don't, but maybe they're onto something. Maybe this fighting on the sly isn't fixing anything. It's me feeding whatever is wrong with me. So, what do I do about it? I stop is what I do. No more fights. Carlos is right. I need a dog. I need a doctor. I need something else that doesn't make me a chump and a liar every time I open my mouth.

Then I remember something. I take out the box and put it on the counter.

"Carlos, you're a man of spirits and exotic liquids. Have you ever heard of something called black milk?"

He hands the guy his lousy Scotch and thinks for a few seconds.

"Never. What is it?"

I open the box and take out the vial.

"This. Only I don't know what this is."

He takes the little glass bottle and holds it up to the light. Shakes it a little.

"Where did you get it?"

"It was a gift. Of sorts."

"More secrets? Who gave it to you?"

"No one I can talk about this close to such shitty Scotch. You should be ashamed of yourself for selling it."

The guy who ordered them turns to me.

"Hey, I like this stuff. Who made you king high shithead of Scotch?"

I start to say something, but he backs up a step and his mouth opens like a roast pig waiting for an apple. The guy is slumming it tonight. He tried to dress down because he knew he was coming here, but the manicure and the million-dollar college ring give him away.

"Oh shit," he says. "You're him. I heard you hang out here. Can I buy you a drink?"

Carlos waves the guy off.

"Not tonight, man. Come back at Christmas. He'll be a chipper fucker by then. Won't you, Stark?"

I look at Carlos, not at the groupie.

"Thanks, but I have a drink."

"Then, can I get a picture with you?" he says. "I swear it will only take a second."

"What did I just tell you, *pendejo*?" says Carlos. "Not tonight."

Out of the corner of my eye I can see the guy turn from Carlos to me and back to Carlos. He holds up his hands.

"Fine. Be an asshole. You're not that special, you know. I've met lots more cool people here and what do you call them . . . ?"

"Lurkers," I say.

"Yeah. Lots more interesting ones than you."

I look at him.

"There's lots here that love guys like you. Just be sure to check your wallet before you go home."

He takes the cash for the drink out of his front pocket. He slaps himself on his back pocket, hoping to hit imported hand-tooled leather. By the look on his face I'd say he came up empty.

"Shit," he says, and checks another pocket, coming up

with his iPhone. He looks relieved. At least he can still text his buddies about his night with the wild people on the bad side of town.

He thumbs the phone on and says, "Please. So the night isn't a total loss. Just one picture."

"Get out," says Carlos. "You don't listen, so you can't stay. Move. Now."

I look at Richie Rich.

"Better do what he says or he'll hit you with a coconut carved like a monkey."

The guy gives up. Puts his phone in his breast pocket, sadder but wiser.

"I get it. Sorry to have bothered you. I'm going. Besides," he says, "you look like hell."

"Now," says Carlos.

Richie starts for the door.

Carlos shakes his head.

"Some people couldn't buy a clue with all the gold in Fort Knox."

I hold up my glass, toast Carlos, and down my drink.

"Thank you, Doctor. I'm feeling much better now. How's my eye?"

He looks and nods.

"It's getting there."

Then he looks up past me.

Someone throws his arm around me and clicks a picture. It's Trump and his iPhone. I turn just in time to see him scrambling out the front door with my bruised face in his hand.

Perfect.

So, to sum up the evening. A Sherman tank with the brain of an angry hamster gave me a black eye, and now some college boy snuck up behind me and got my picture without me even knowing he was there. I think this is what's known as a wake-up call. Something has to change. Starting with me.

"You have any food left back there tonight?"

"Some tamales with some beans and rice. You want some to go?"

"Could I get three?"

"No problem."

He disappears into the back and reappears with a packed paper bag.

I sniff the food and smile.

"What do I owe you?"

"You know you always eat and drink for free around here," he says.

"Not for the food. The advice."

"All you owe me is not fucking yourself up anymore. Do that and we're square."

I set down the rag I've been holding to my eye and pick up the food.

"I'll work on it."

"You do that. And tell Chihiro hi for me."

"You got it."

I got out to the car and set the food on the passenger seat. Donald Trump is halfway down the block showing his phone to anyone who'll look. Showing my face to strangers.

I start the car and gun the engine a couple of times. If he moves just a little to his right, I could pick him off without hitting anyone else. The front of this Catalina is solid steel.

He won't even make a dent. I can just hose him off when I get home.

But I don't do it. It would be too easy. Too *Koyaanisqatsi*. Something has got to change and it will start with me not killing a rich kid who'll go on drinking shit Scotch and stealing photos with people because he'll never know how close he came to frat-boy Heaven tonight.

I pull away from the curb and head home.

"I KEEP TELLING you," says Kasabian when I come in. "If you just *buy* the Girl Scouts' cookies, they'll leave you alone."

"That gets funnier every time you say it."

"It'll be even funnier next time."

Kasabian runs things day to day at Maximum Overdrive, the video store where I live with him and Candy. Him downstairs in the back and me and Candy in the small apartment upstairs. This arrangement is best for everyone if for no other reason than Kasabian doesn't really have a body. I mean, he has one, but it's not his. It's a retrofit from a mechanical hellhound body I stole when I could still shadow-walk Downtown.

"Keep going. You're going to talk yourself out of tamales."

Kasabian holds up a mechanical hound paw.

"Witness me shutting up."

The paw creaks a little as he says it. Sometimes he clanks when he walks. That's the other reason he spends most of his time down here and not upstairs in our palatial penthouse. I set the tamales on the counter.

"Smart man. How's business?"

"We're doing all right. Still making bank off the special

stash. But we haven't had anything new in for a while. The requests are piling up."

The special stash are videos a little witch named Maria gets for us through her ghost connections. Movies that don't really exist, at least in this time and space. James Cameron's *Spider-Man.* Sergio Leone's *The Godfather.* Orson Welles's *Heart of Darkness.*

"Do you explain that our movies come from another fucking plane of reality? It's not like we're rifling the bins at the Salvation Army."

Kasabian lifts the edge of the tamales bag and looks inside. I close it and move the bag to the other end of the counter. He gives me a look.

"They're customers," he says. "They know what they want and they want it now."

"Next time someone whines, tell them to fuck off home and watch *Kindergarten Cop* on Netflix."

He slips a DVD into a case and holds it up in my direction.

"And that's why you're not allowed down here during business hours."

"I have my own work these days. I don't have to mingle with you rabble."

He points at my eye.

"Your boss give you that for mouthing off?"

"It's still noticeable?"

"Like a glazed ham at a bris."

"Don't say anything when you see Candy."

I take the bag and head upstairs.

"Hey. What about the tamales?"

"No one eats until Candy gets home."

"I admire her work ethic, but tell her to get a day job. I'm hungry now."

"Didn't someone say that suffering was good for the soul?"

"Only preachers and insurance salesmen."

"We're still waiting. I'll put these in the oven to stay warm."

I go upstairs, stash the tamales, and go into the bathroom. In the bathroom mirror, I stare at my face. Yeah. There's no way she's not going to notice the bruise. It will be gone by morning, but right now I'm fucked. For a second, I think about more ice, look at myself again, and see how stupid and desperate that is.

I take the angel's box out of my coat and put it on the bedroom bureau. Maybe Vidocq will be able to tell me what this is. He's an alchemist. Even if he doesn't know what black milk is, maybe the box will be in one of his books.

What was it Abbot was talking about at the meeting? The end of the world. Climate change. Charities. Blah blah. Then through the memory of the headache it comes to me: Wormwood. Something is up with them. Those Wormwood creeps I met a few months back hinted they had a branch office in Hell run by Norris Quay. He used to be the richest man in California, but he was dumb enough to follow me into Kill City. Now he's the richest corpse.

I go downstairs. Kasabian is still putting returned discs back in their cases. I go over and put a few in myself, but he takes them away when I mix up the DVDs and Blu-rays.

As casually as I can I say, "How's your view of Downtown these days?"

He raises his eyes to me for a second, then goes back to putting away discs.

"You haven't asked about Hell in a while. Since you went white collar, I thought you'd forgotten about the place."

"It's depressing not being able to see the place for myself."

"You're the only person who thinks it's depressing they *can't* see Hell. Why do you care all of a sudden?"

"I met an angel tonight. Karael. He said that Heaven is fucked. If it is, that usually means Hell is double-fucked."

"That's a distinct possibility," Kasabian says.

"You still have access to the *Codex* and the peeper I gave you?"

The *Daimonion Codex* is basically Lucifer's Boy Scout manual on running Hell. Once he let Kasabian look inside, he could sneak looks all over Hell. I gave Kas the peeper. It's a magical eye you can look through and see remote places. Sort of Hellion security cams.

He scratches his nose with a metal claw.

"Your angel is right. Pandemonium is falling apart. Like Berlin after the blitz falling apart. Nothing works anymore but the sewers. The buildings are falling apart. Gangs of ex-Hellion soldiers and some of your less savory damned souls run protection and control everything from weapons to food. Basically, anyone who isn't going *Wild Bunch* in the city is going batshit at Heaven's gates. You said they're supposed to be open, but I haven't seen it."

"I know. Goddammit. I wish I could see into Heaven."

Kasabian raises an eyebrow.

"You never said that before."

"I never had a reason. If I knew Karael was telling the truth and angels were fighting each other, it would make it easier to believe him about other things."

"What do you care what some angel says? They're all assholes."

"I met a couple of okay ones over the years. Not many. One or two. Karael gave me something. And he said no souls would get into Heaven as long as the war lasted."

"What did he give you?"

"No clue. I'm taking it to Vidocq tomorrow. Do you know much about Wormwood?"

"Only what you told me."

"How about Norris Quay? Do you ever see him Downtown?"

"Now, him I've seen," Kasabian says. "He's a real player in Pandemonium. Got himself protection. A nice setup in an office building. Norris is doing fine, making bank on everything that goes down."

"Any new souls hanging around with him?"

"They come and go. You know more Wormwood faces than I do. I just see creeps in tailored suits and limos with Hellion escorts."

I pick a DVD of David Cronenberg's *Frankenstein* and Kasabian plucks it from my hand, slipping it into its case.

"I need to get down there and see the place for myself."

"I need a week in Fiji with Brigitte Bardot, but that's not going to happen either."

"You're right about that."

"I'm always right, but you won't admit it."

"There's no Nobel Prizes around here. Just tamales."

"It's time for you to call the missus. Tell her I'm going to die sorting discs."

"Good. More tamales for us."

"And once again, you're not allowed down here. Go upstairs and stay out of my way."

"Yes, boss."

I go upstairs and pour myself some Aqua Regia.

If Abbot is right and Wormwood is playing games up here and Quay is doing business down there, it makes sense that they're connected. I wonder if he's the source of black milk? But how would he make money off it? And who else could be working with him? Maybe David Moore. He's dead and had connections through a talent agency run by the Burgess family—Wormwood heavyweights. But that wouldn't help Kasabian. He wouldn't recognize Moore. Fuck me. I should have brought more peepers with me when I came back from Hell that last time. Just another in a long series of mistakes. Maybe there's some other way I can see Downtown like Kasabian. Who could help with that? Maybe go back and ask the powers that be in Piss Alley? Maybe not. When they gave me the power to sidestep for a week, it aged me enough that I've got a few gray hairs. Who knows what price they'd want next time?

I go into the bathroom, strip off my clothes, and get into the shower. I need to wash the fight and as many lies off me as I can.

When I get out, I can hear Candy and Kasabian talking downstairs. She comes up and the first thing she says is, "Kas says you have a black eye. Are you all right?"

If Kasabian wasn't already dead, I'd kill him tonight.

"I'm fine. I just bumped my head getting off Abbot's damned boat."

"Poor baby," she says, and drops her vinyl eyeball bag on the kitchen counter.

She comes over and kisses my bruised eye.

"Maybe I can take your mind off all the pain."

Candy opens the eyeball and pulls out the record Alessa Graves gave her. She puts it on the stereo and cranks up the sound. The trembling rumble of surf guitar fills the room.

Reaching under the towel, she begins to massage my cock, then kisses me hard. I lean against her, smelling her hair and neck. She pulls off my towel and pushes me down on the sofa, keeps pumping me with her hand. I pull her on top of me and start to roll her over when she says, "Wait a minute." She throws off her short dress and underwear and pulls me inside her.

"*Fukaku hamekonde chodai,*" she whispers.

I have no idea what that means, but I don't think it has anything to do with tamales. When she wraps her legs around me, I have the strange feeling it's the music more than me that's driving her, but it doesn't seem like the right time to ask.

THE GOOD NEWS is that we don't break any furniture we care about, just a secondhand lamp that was here when I moved in. I know that if I get another lamp, Candy will conveniently lose it and replace it with something horrifying. Something that spins and has talking robots or waving tentacles.

Candy crawls into bed and we divvy up the tamales. I take some down to Kasabian, and when I come back upstairs, she's propped against a pile of pillows digging into her dinner. I take my plate into the room and join her in bed.

"Hey, do you remember me bringing home a folder or packet of some kind when I went to work with Abbot?"

She nods, holds a hand over her mouth, and chews.

"It's on the floor next to the bureau. You put it there and I've been wondering how long it would take you to ask about it."

"You looked inside?"

She nods, looking a little guilty.

"Sorry. A big envelope from the augur. How could I not look? Besides, knowing you, it was a check for a million dollars and you forgot about it."

I mix some beans with rice and swallow a mouthful.

"I guess I don't have a good history with money."

"It's not money. It's authority. Someone gives you a job and you take it, but then they give you an envelope full of stuff to read and it's like homework. You leave it on the floor hoping the dog will eat it."

"And it never does."

"You're mad at the dog we don't have?"

"Can we rent one to clean up my mistakes?"

"It would have to be a pretty big dog."

I poke her in the leg with my fork and she punches my arm. Candy isn't exactly human. She's a Jade, which is kind of like a vampire, only worse. It also means she's strong. Her love taps are like a velvet-covered baseball bat.

"Abbot said there was stuff in the folder about insurance."

"Mmm," says Candy around a mouthful of food. She swallows and says, "Yep. Medical and dental. There's 401(k) stuff in there too."

"Now he's just fucking with me. He knows I don't have any bank accounts."

"He's the augur. He has pull. Just because there's paper-work that says you're dead, it doesn't have to always be that way. Talk to him. Maybe the Sub Rosa can resurrect the late James Stark."

I shake my head and eat my tamales. I'm very hungry and then very self-conscious. We're in bed naked and I wonder if I have any bruises on my body from the fight. I should have checked myself when I took a shower. It's a good thing I'm not a spy. I'd blow my cover story two minutes into enemy territory. I change the subject.

"Did Julie tell you about the kid I brought her?"

"Yeah. He's a friend of the Abbot's or something like that."

"Abbot was cagey. I've been wondering about that, but I don't know what to think."

"There aren't that many secrets men usually have about a missing kid. The kid is dead. The kid was snatched by the mother and he doesn't want to say so. Or he snatched the kid and doesn't want to say. There's another more common reason."

"Come on. Tell me."

"It's his kid and maybe Mom is married to someone else."

I try to picture that for a second. I don't know anything about Abbot's personal life. He could date women, men, or tentacled elder gods for all I know. I look at Candy.

"You're getting good at that detective stuff."

"I know," she says. "That's why I'm with Julie and you got fired."

"Thanks for bringing that up again."

"Blame it on the dog."

When we finish the tamales, Candy grabs the plates, takes them into the kitchen, and ditches them in the sink. She comes back into the bedroom and crawls onto my lap.

I start to kiss her, but she pulls back.

"What's wrong?"

"What happened to your eye?" she says.

I reflexively touch the bruise.

"It's nothing. Like I said, I bumped my head leaving Abbot's boat tonight."

"Sandman Slim walks into doors?"

"Hey, a guy snuck up behind me tonight and sneaked a selfie before I knew it."

"That I can believe," she says, and rolls off me onto her back. "I know there's something wrong with you, but I can't help if you won't let me."

"I'm okay," I say.

"No, you're not. This isn't the first time you've come home bruised. You're usually better at hiding them, but I know your body pretty well, so I notice them even when I don't say anything."

I put a hand down on the bed and she reaches out and wraps her warm hand around one of my fingers. I don't want to look at her, so I look at my hand. Old scars gleam white like I stuck my hand into a metal grinder looking for my car keys.

"I'm still getting used to this new life is all. I'm a little off balance."

She rolls onto her stomach and looks at me.

"Know how we just talked about me being a detective? If you're doing something to hurt yourself, I'll find out."

"Let it go this time, okay? I'm just a little off balance, but I'm getting better."

"Okay," she says uncertainly. "But I reserve the right to bring it up again if I suspect you of asshole behavior."

"Agreed."

She sits up and kisses me.

"You told me I could tell you anything. You can do the same with me."

"I'll remember that. Thanks."

She puts her arms around me and I just hold her like that for a while. I feel something light slide down my chest. She's crying or I'm sweating. Probably both. I feel like I'm fourteen, caught in a lie within a lie with no way to get out.

"Do you want to get a dog sometime?" Candy says.

"Not really."

"Thank God. Neither do I."

See? The truth didn't hurt. Now I need to get out of this particular knot of lies by not going back into the fight pit.

"Get whatever kind of lamp you want for the living room. Flying robots. Naked witches."

"You know I was going to anyway."

"Yeah, but I just wanted to say it."

"Thanks. You know if I find out someone's hurt you, I'm going to eat their fucking heart, right?"

"I know."

"I know you know, but I just wanted to say it."

"Thanks. Can I ask you one more favor?"

"What?"

"Can you turn that goddamn surf record over and play the other side. You've played this one about fifty times."

"This is *my* homework. Alessa is going to teach me surf guitar."

"I bet there are songs on the other side you can learn."

"Your wish is my command," she says, and pads out of the bedroom to the stereo.

When she's gone, I take a long, deep breath. This thing we have. I don't want to fuck it up. I don't want to lie anymore and I don't want a dog. I just want Candy or Chihiro or whoever she has to be next to stay alive. We're in this together and I'll kick the ass of anyone who gets in the way. Even if it's me.

"Did I tell you an angel gave me a birthday present tonight?"

She comes back into the room and flops onto the bed.

"No. Tell me every little thing about it."

So I do. And we're okay.

For a while.

CANDY IS GONE when I wake up in the morning. There's a note on the kitchen counter when I go in to make coffee.

> Jamming with Alessa at her rehearsal space
> after work
> Home late. Be naked.

There are some hearts and she's taped a press-on tattoo of a sleeping cat at the bottom of the note. I lick a spot on my forearm and press down on the tattoo. A minute later I pull it off. No cat. Just a few frayed lines scattered across my scars.

Once again, my stupid body rejects the simplest amusements. So, I make coffee. That's one bit of pleasure that still works.

I don't bother going downstairs and bothering Kasabian. He's even drearier than me in the morning. Before he gets up and turns on the news or does something else to annoy me, I turn on the rest of a movie I started with Candy the other night: *Amer*. It's a deconstruction of Italian *giallo* flicks. The directors tear it down to its essential elements—beats, images, violence, colors, sexual tension—but they do it almost wordlessly, like a silent movie. Just the thing for that time of day when words are still hard to come by.

I sip coffee and smoke, letting the movie run through to its end and one last little shock, then pick up my phone and thumb in Vidocq's number. He picks up after a few rings.

"James, how nice to hear from you at this early hour. Is everything all right?" His voice is deep, the accent relentlessly French.

"Nothing's wrong. Sometimes I'm actually up during daylight hours. I just thought if you were going to be around, I'd swing by and show you something that fell into my lap from Heaven."

"Really? You must come immediately. Do not stop for coffee. I've made some better than your vile swill."

He says it all like the friendliest headwaiter in L.A. See, I always notice the accent because it's such an accomplishment. Eugène Vidocq has lived in the U.S. for around a hundred and fifty years. Any normal person would lose an accent after all that time. But Vidocq holds on to his like some grandma with the family photos. Nothing in the album means anything to anyone except her, which makes her hang on all the harder.

"I need to get dressed. I'll be over in half an hour."

"I doubt that on a weekend," he says. "Let us say an hour."

"Don't rub it in."

I used to walk across town through a shadow and come out by Vidocq's front door in ten seconds. It feels like something that happened in another lifetime, but it's really been less than three months.

I plow through the Hollywood traffic south and get to Vidocq's place in just under an hour. L.A. people are obsessed with addresses, distance, and times between places. I used to worry about the first two, but now I'm just like every other asshole in this town. A clock watcher, knowing the hour I wasted getting here I'll never see again. Everyone in L.A. is like this. It's one of the town's big secrets. Want to know why people drink and smoke so much weed? They want to wipe out the time slipping away from them. Want to know why people do coke and get on the pipe? They're trying to outrun the clock. Like Superman at the end of the movie where he flies around the world fast enough to roll back time. That's all anyone in L.A. wants. To get back the time they lost *just fucking being in L.A.* I can't outrun time. I don't even know if angels or Mr. Muninn can. Gods and regular schmucks, we're all stuck on the same linear run from here to the end of time. Just some of us get to run a little longer. Like Vidocq. He's immortal. He doesn't worry about being stuck in traffic. He could spend a month waiting for a cab and not blink. Me, I have to wait eleven seconds at the bodega to buy coffee and I'm contemplating a murder/suicide pact with everyone in the store.

I take the old industrial elevator up to Vidocq's floor in

his building and knock on the door. He meets me at the door in a robe and slippers, holding a plate of crisp bacon slices. Vidocq has salt-and-pepper hair and a short trimmed beard. I put on actual people clothes and he's just rolled out of the sack.

"I see why you wanted me to come to you."

He looks down at himself for a moment.

"I couldn't bear to dress myself this morning. Do you ever feel that way? One more morning, brushing your teeth, putting on your clothes. It can drive you mad. When I was alone, I went years without cutting my hair or beard. I looked like the Abdominal, Aminal . . . What do you call him?"

"The Abominable Snowman."

"Yes. Him."

" 'Yeti' is an easier word."

"Yes, but I prefer the other. It gives him a sinister dignity whereas Yeti makes him sound like just another animal."

"He probably *is* just another animal. He's got to know by now we're looking for him. Three hot meals and a fresh pile of hay every day has got to beat running away and throwing your shit at hikers."

"I suppose it comes down to who's looking for you. Will the hunters study and appreciate you or do they simply want to dissect you? Likely a smart beast, he will be suspicious of us," Vidocq says.

"Hey, don't knock it. That's how I feel every day."

"As do I."

"Then give me some coffee and let's drink to that."

He hands me a cup full of the black stuff. I hold it up and say, "To freaks everywhere."

Vidocq holds up his mug.

"May you fly, walk, swim, or crawl for all eternity under the noses of our betters."

"And if you can't, at least get your own reality show. *Sasquatch Hoarders*. Or *The Real Housewives of R'lyeh*."

We drink our coffee, satisfied that we're the two cleverest people in the room.

He sips his coffee. Sets down the cup and the plate of bacon on his worktable.

"As I recall, you have something for me."

"That I do."

I set the box on the table near his food. Among his many interests, Vidocq happens to be a world-class alchemist. He was a good alchemist back in the day, but the extra two hundred years since then have given him plenty more practice.

He picks up the box. Looks it over top and bottom, then eyeballs it with a magnifying glass.

"Where did you get it?" he says.

"A dying angel brought it to me. Didn't say what it is. Said he didn't know. All I do know is that some angels like what's inside it. He said the war in Heaven won't end unless someone destroys it."

"Dying angels. Wars. This does not fill me with joy."

He sets the box back on the table and pushes back the lock. When that goes all right, he gets a long steel rod and carefully pushes open the top. I don't blame him. I've been known to bring him things that catch fire.

When nothing explodes, he takes the vial from its padded case and holds it up to the light.

"The fluid is almost opaque, but not quite. As if there is

some shifting something inside. I can't tell what. Some debris? Sediment?"

He looks at me.

"Is it safe to open?"

"I have no idea. But if it blows up I don't think the angel who gave it to me knew it would."

"That will be a great comfort to the other residents if I set the building on fire or fill it with poison."

I hadn't thought of that last bit.

"You have any gas masks?"

He reaches under his worktable and comes out with something rubbery that looks like it's a couple of wars past its prime.

"Just the one, I'm afraid," he says.

"Story of my life. Fuck it. Let's go. I'll hold my breath."

Vidocq gets a small, stumpy candle down from the top of a set of wooden shelves behind the table. He lights the candle with a paper match and the flame flickers a light green.

"As long as the flame stays this color, we're safe," he says, and puts on the gas mask.

I lean in close and shout, "You're still wearing the mask, even though I don't have one?"

He nods vigorously.

"Thanks," I say. "It's good to know you're always there for me."

I take the vial and unscrew the top. "The angel called this stuff black milk."

And suddenly I know why. It smells like the curdled insides of a lizard-skin Hellion bovine with shit for blood and fish guts for bones. Even in the gas mask, Vidocq is choking. I get the top back on the bottle fast. Last night's tamales are seriously considering making a break for it onto Vidocq's nice rug.

Vidocq shakes his head. Takes the vial from my hand.

"No."

He points to the candle. The flame is still pale green.

"See? The smell is unpleasant, but not deadly. We must persevere."

With his other hand, he opens an old medical cabinet on his worktable. The cabinet doors swing apart like bird wings, revealing racks of potions and drawers for instruments.

He takes off the gas mask and pulls some potions from the cabinet. Pours a little of the black milk into a shallow Pyrex dish and screws the top back on. I put the vial back in the box, hoping it will kill some of the smell.

"Mind if I open a window?"

"Mmm," he mumbles, already lost in the experiment, barely noticing I'm there. I crack a window, letting in the smoggy L.A. breeze.

Much better.

Vidocq uses a dropper to add tiny amounts of a purple potion to the black milk. I take one of his bacon slices and wait to see what happens next.

After almost a minute, he says, "Interesting."

I look at the mess on the table.

"What's interesting? I don't see any difference."

"That's what's interesting. Look closer. The two liquids remain separate. They won't mix."

"What does that mean?"

"I have no idea. Yet."

He pours the mixture into a flask that's connected to a

series of glass tubes and other glass receptacles. As the liquid moves through the tubes, it separates back into black milk and the purple potion. He pours out the potion in the kitchen sink and swirls the milk in its flask.

"I would like to test it with red mercury," he says. "But I'm out of it and it's not easy to find these days."

"What are you going to do?"

He sighs.

"Make some phone calls. Ask a few favors."

"Did the test tell you anything?"

He crosses his arms, staring at the mystery goo.

"The potion I used is a very simple one. It separates other potions into their basic elements for study. But instead, the milk repelled it."

"Meaning?"

"As I said, I have no idea. My greatest fear is that being angelic in origin, it might not react properly with any Earthly chemicals."

"It could be Hellion."

"True. But Hellions being fallen angels, the problem remains."

And here we are again. Back to the same problem. I'm stuck in L.A. with no way to get to Hell, where I might find an angel that I could choke long enough to help me. I need to sit Kasabian down for a more serious talk.

Vidocq puts a drop of the milk on a glass slide and places it under a microscope with a PROPERTY OF UCLA sticker partly scraped off.

Among Vidocq's other interests is burglary.

"Anything?" I say.

He shrugs.

"There's movement within the fluid. Perhaps living organisms. Perhaps simply repellent elements. It's too early to say with any certainty. I'm sorry."

"It's fine. I knew it wouldn't be simple. Nothing with angels ever is. For all I know, this whole thing is just a prank. Now that he can't get at us, let's fuck with Sandman Slim. Maybe black milk is just an exploding cigar."

"Please," he says. "Until we know what this is, don't say 'exploding.' It's bad luck."

"I didn't know you believed in that kind of thing."

"I believe in everything. It's what frequently comes with age. We hope for wisdom, but we just end up with more uncertainty."

"Well, you're still the smartest guy I've ever met."

"*Merci.*"

He stands aside and lets me look into his microscope. All I see is black sludge with tiny dots spinning into and around each other.

"I mean it," I tell him. "I don't know if I could make it two hundred years and stay sane."

"Don't underestimate yourself," Vidocq says.

"Are you ever going to tell me how it happened?"

He goes back to the microscope and carefully removes the slide.

"It's a long and not very pretty story."

"My favorite kind."

While he's pouring the milk back into the flask, I reach for my coffee, but bump into his shoulder. The slide slips from his hand onto the worktable. Most soaks into the wood, but a black drop slops onto the side of the plate with bacon. When the strip of bacon comes in contact with another strip, it stiffens and flips into the air, convulsing when it lands, like a fish dying in the bottom of a boat. Each time the bacon touches another strip, that strip starts writhing and twisting too.

Vidocq slams a bell jar on top of the plate, trapping the meat circus underneath.

I look at him.

"Ever seen that before?"

"No. Never. It's fascinating."

"This is truly one of the most goddamned things I've ever seen. What do we do with the little bastards?"

"We wait and see what happens."

"What if they don't stop? What if we just invented immortal bacon?"

"One mystery at a time, my friend."

"We can't exactly Google 'disposing of zombie thrash pork.'"

Vidocq puts his hands on a pile of old books next to the medical cabinet.

"This is my Google. I'll find an answer for you. Don't worry."

"I know you will. But it's going to lead to trouble. I can tell."

He nods. "Profound mysteries have a way of leading to yet more mysteries."

The bacon strips make little *tinking* sounds when they hit the glass dome.

"What do we do now?"

"Normally, it would be lovely to have you stay and chat, but you should go," he says. "I have a lot of reading to do."

"You sure you're safe with that stuff around? Maybe I should take it and ditch it in the ocean or something."

"You'll do no such thing. It's not often an old sorcerer gets to explore angelic puzzles. Leave this here with me. I'll be fine."

My phone buzzes. It's a text from Abbot. He wants me to come over tonight. So much for "Take the weekend, Stark."

"Okay. But call me if things get any weirder. In fact, call me no matter what. If these bastards are still hopping around tonight, I want to know about it."

"Of course. Of course," he says, leading me to the door. "But now you must go and I must look for answers."

At the door I say, "I got some of the milk on your table. I might have wrecked it. I'll pay for a new one."

"Perhaps you did and perhaps you didn't. In any case, I'm the thief, not you. If I need a new table, I will get one like that," he says, snapping his fingers.

"I at least owe you a drink for killing your breakfast."

"That I will accept."

He opens the door and I go out into the hall. I start to leave when something bothers me.

"Seriously, what's the trick to living two hundred years? How do you do it?"

"It's easy," he says. "I'm not two hundred. I no longer believe in the past. Each morning when I awake, I'm newly born. From now until the sun burns out, I will never be more than one day old."

"I'll call you about the drink," I say, and go down to the car, not sure if what Vidocq said was the smartest or saddest thing I've ever heard.

"I'M SORRY TO call you in like this," says Abbot. "But the whole thing fell together quickly."

"What is it? Some kind of emergency meeting?"

Abbot hesitates.

"More of a cocktail party."

"Seriously?"

"I'm afraid so."

"I used to be the Devil, you know. I didn't have to put up with this kind of shit."

"Maybe you should have kept that job, then."

"Nah. I look lousy with horns."

"Is that really what he looks like?"

"No. He looks more like, well, you."

"Should I be flattered?"

"Very."

"Then I'll take the compliment."

Abbot ushers me into the living room area on the boat. I was here once before, when I first met him. The room is impeccably decorated—a Southern California manor house—swaying gently on the Pacific. I have a hard time picturing the boat ever moving much, even in a tsunami. Nature wouldn't dare spill the augur's coffee over something as silly as a volcano.

"No problem. Chihiro is learning to play 'Pipeline,' so I'm all on my lonesome."

"Playing pipeline. Is that slang for something I should know about?"

I put my hands in my pockets, not wanting to touch anything, afraid I'm going to taint his Beach Boys Taj Mahal with my grubby paws.

"Candy is getting guitar lessons is all. And I'm here when I could be curled up with a good western."

He points a finger at me.

"Right. But there's good news. You don't have to talk to anybody or be nice to anyone."

"That *is* good news."

"In fact, as far as anyone at the party knows, you won't even be here. I want to put you in the back with Willem, my head of security. You and he will monitor the meeting on the boat's surveillance system."

"I came all this way to sit in a broom closet with a hall monitor?"

He comes over and puts an arm around my shoulder, leading me down a deck into the bowels of the boat. The decor is simpler down here since it's mostly a utilitarian space for the staff, but it's still nicer than anywhere I've ever lived. He takes me forward until I figure that we're right under the living room. There's a door with a keypad. The sign on the door says AUTHORIZED PERSONNEL ONLY.

As he punches in a code on the keypad I say, "This is a yacht, right?"

"Right."

The lock clicks open.

I look around.

"This thing is huge. Is it a boat or a ship?"

"A boat. As far as I know all yachts are boats."

"Then what's a ship?"

"A very big boat."

"But this is a very big boat. Why isn't it a ship?"

He looks at me for a second.

"I can see how you'd make a good Devil."

"Sorry. Doors like this just make me nervous."

Abbot pushes it open.

"You're not under arrest. You're with me now, remember? If anything, you get to arrest other people."

"Terrific. Now I'm a cop. All of my worst fears have come true."

"You'll do fine."

Inside, the room is dark except for a bank of video monitors that ring the walls. I don't know how many rooms this bucket has, but it looks like Abbot has every square inch of the place covered. I go over to get a better look at the setup.

"You have as many trust issues as I do. I feel so much closer to you now."

A guy sitting at the control console turns around and gives me the eyeball. He has a cop mustache but a tailored shirt. His gold tie clip has three Greek letters on it. This guy hasn't been in college in fifteen years, but he still flies his frat colors. Audsley Ishii used to do that. It isn't love at first sight for either of us.

"Willem, this is Stark," says Abbot. "Stark. Willem."

Willem holds out his hand and I shake it. His heartbeat races a little. It's obvious by his smile that he thinks I'm the scum they scrape off the sides of this boat, but he stays professional and says, "Welcome aboard."

"Thanks, Willem. I appreciate the hospitality."

That confuses him. But his heartbeat slows. The guy is the

real thing. He gets excited, but has enough training to get it under control fast. I can't see where he keeps his gun, so my guess is it's strapped to his ankle and he can get it out as fast as he can corral his heart. He'd be a good guy to have on your side in a fight.

Trouble is, I don't think he thinks we're on the same side.

Abbot goes to the monitors and points to a cluster of six that cover the living room and surrounding corridors.

"This is the area I want you to concentrate on. People are coming over for drinks in a little while. Some of them might be Wormwood. I want you to listen in case someone says anything that might give them away. Some are from the council, so you'll know them. But try to learn as many of the other faces as you can."

I look at the monitors then at Abbot.

"Down here, I'm useless. Up there, I'd be able to tell you who's packing, who's a straight arrow, and who's lying."

Abbot smiles broadly.

"They're *all* liars. I'm the augur and they want to make me happy. Also, they all want to one up each other's family. They'll say anything that suits their interests."

"Tell me again why you need me when you have Willem over there?"

"You've met at least some of Wormwood's higher-ups. That puts you ahead of either of us. Look for those faces. Look and listen for anything familiar. If nothing comes up, then I wasted your evening and I'll send you home with some cake."

"You didn't say anything about cake earlier. I'm completely on board now."

"Good. Willem knows the system down here. He'll be running the electronics. All you have to do is watch the show. I know you like movies. Pretend it's *My Dinner with André* or something."

"I prefer A *Fistful of Dollars,* but I get your drift."

"Good. Okay. I have a couple of things to do. You two should get acquainted. The guests will be arriving shortly. If you want anything to eat or drink, you can have something sent down."

I take the seat next to Willem.

"Very comfy. I love flying first class."

"I'll see you afterward."

He leaves and I watch him go, crisscrossing from monitor to monitor on his way to check on the caviar fountain or corn-dog buffet, whatever it is heavy Sub Rosa clans dine on with their pope.

I turn around and Willem is looking at me.

I say, "You do this kind of thing a lot?"

"Sometimes it's me on the console. Sometimes it's someone else. The work gets done."

"And no one is down here playing Ms. Pac-Man or Tetris while the blue bloods feed at the trough?"

He punches a few buttons, changing angles on some of the cameras.

"No. That's more your speed, from what I've heard."

"Really? Palace gossip about a small-town boy like me? The folks back in Arkansas will be so proud."

He keeps at the console, not looking at me.

"No gossip. Just facts. I have friends on the force."

"LAPD? They practically invented gossip. They're worse

than Hedda Hopper. They're like the mean girls in a high school lunchroom. If they don't know the truth, they'll make something up just to see if they can make you cry."

"That's not true and you know it."

I lean my elbows on the edge of the console. Look up at the screens.

"I don't know what I know sometimes. It's a funny world. I saw bacon dance this afternoon. You ever see that? A whole plate. They could practically do a Busby Berkeley number."

Willem draws in a breath and lets it out.

"What do you say we don't talk for a while? Guests are starting to arrive."

"Is there a red carpet? Will we know who they're wearing?"

Willem ignores me.

THE GATHERING IS exactly what I was afraid of. A CIA torture session of wine, cheese, and tony chitchat. Maybe eating Brie just makes people stupid. I never trusted the stuff myself. Soft cheese is a reminder that all cheese is just milk that crawled into a ditch to die, then some lunatic came along, spread the corpse on a saltine, and invented hors d'oeuvres. Now people pay heroin prices for stuff they could make themselves if they only had the guts to strap a pint of whole milk to their engine block for a few days. Sure it might come out a little greasy, but that'll just shoot the stuff through your system faster. No need to absorb any actual calories. This is L.A., where the food is prettier than the movie stars and twice as untouchable.

I look at Willem.

"How do you sit here like this without committing ritual suicide?"

He adjusts a camera angle.

"It's my job."

"Do you like it?"

"Of course. It's an honor to work for the augur."

I can't see his eyes, so I can't tell if he's lying.

"Sitting in a stuffy room pushing buttons. I get it. I used to talk that way the last time I worked for a bigwig."

He does a sarcastic little snort laugh.

"When did you ever work for someone respectable?"

"Respectable? Never. I used to work for Azazel, one of Lucifer's generals. I guess I didn't really 'work' for him. I was more of a slave. Anyway, I talked the way you do all the time. 'What a great boss. What a great gig. I'm the luckiest boy in Candy Land.'"

He looks at me and says, "Bullshit," but he takes his time about it. Savoring the moment.

I lean into the glow of the monitors to light up my face.

"You think I got these scars playing Jenga?"

"I've seen a hundred cons with faces like yours. You're nothing special."

That's the second time in a couple of days someone said I look like a con. One more time and I'm getting a haircut.

I take the pause in the heartbreaking verbal abuse to look over the guests. A lot of old faces from the council meetings. I can't remember most of their names, but I could find them in a crowd if I had to. A lot of new faces too.

Beautiful people. Perfect clothes. Teeth like CG snow-scapes. Breasts lifted. Jowls tightened. You can tell the Sub

Rosa men from the civilians because the civilians have hair plugs, while the balding Sub Rosa have hoodoo and self-loathing. I know I'm supposed to be listening for Wormwood giveaways, but I'd rather machine-gun the entire room than listen to any more chatter about private jets, vacation homes, or Arabian horses. I'd do it too. Wipe out the whole party, but Wormwood probably has bets on it and a mass slaughter would line someone's pockets, so, for now, everyone is safe. As for why Abbot called me here, I haven't heard one out-of-place word all evening.

"I'd say this whole thing is pretty much a bust. How 'bout you, Willem? Picking up any supervillain vibes from this bunch?"

"That's not what I'm here for."

"What are you here for?"

"To operate the equipment and to keep an eye on you."

"I have been falling asleep at meetings recently. Do you ever have sleeping problems, Willem? I do. Nightmares and migraines. I found a cure, but I'm not sure it's healthy. Not a keeper. What do you do to relax, Willem?"

He takes his hands from the console and wraps them together like he's praying or wants to keep from punching me.

"Stop saying my name all the time."

"Have I been? How rude. Say, Abbot said we could have stuff sent down here. What do you say to a couple of aperitifs?"

He shakes his head.

"Coffee is all you're allowed."

"Ouch. Of everything you've said tonight, that's the most hurtful."

Willem turns to face me. It's the first time since we shook hands a couple of hours ago. A giveaway that this won't be a lasting romance.

He says, "The augur sees something in you, so I've been trying to give you the benefit of the doubt. But you come in here with these games and attitude, and worst of all, this Hell bullshit. Is that supposed to scare me? Am I supposed to be impressed with your lies or, more likely, your delusions?"

"I know some card tricks too."

"See? That's what I'm talking about. You have nothing to say. Nothing to contribute except noise. If it was up to me, you wouldn't just be barred from this boat. I'd keep you out of the whole marina."

"Luckily, it's not up to you, so we get to spend this quality time together."

He turns back to the console.

"Just be quiet and try to do at least a little piece of your job."

I watch the screen for a few minutes. The guests mingle. Abbot presses the flesh. Spends a few minutes with Tuatha Fortune, the wife of the previous augur. Waiters bring in drinks and food and take out the remains. The most exciting thing that happens is when a waiter runs out of shrimp puffs and Charlie Anpu, the graying, liquored-up patriarch of a heavyweight Sub Rosa family, gets bent out of shape about it. Like the poor-slob waiter is supposed to bend over and shoot seafood out of his ass. What a creep. My hoodoo is good enough that I could probably do it, but I hate to show off at parties.

I pull out my phone and check the time. More than two hours down here in Glitter Gulch. The best night of my life.

"So, Willem. How long were you a cop?"

"I told you to stop saying my name."

"It's a simple question. How long were you on the job?"

He shakes his head.

"You don't get to ask about my personal life."

I point to one of the screens. The augur laughs at a billionaire's dirty limerick or maybe the guy does a mean Ed Sullivan impression. Anyway, the laugh looks real, but I can see Abbot's eyes and he's dying inside. That makes two of us.

"Abbot seems to be having a good time."

"He's doing his job. And he's not the one you're supposed to be watching."

"I'm watching plenty. But I can't hear a thing with you talking all the time."

He freezes for a minute, but doesn't say anything.

I take it back. I don't want to machine-gun the party. I want to find the fault line that will drop California into the ocean and toss a nuke down there. No one on this boat, me included, will benefit the human race by living one more day. Let's just blow the whole shebang into the Pacific and give Nevada a shot at some prime beachfront property.

I look at other monitors. Waiters go in and out of the kitchen. Security patrols the walkway to the boat. A seagull swoops low and shits on the deck. Lucky bird.

"Did you know Audsley Ishii?"

Willem nods. "Ishii is a good man."

"And you don't like me because I got him fired."

"I don't like you because of who and what you are."

I swing my chair around to face him.

"Enlighten me, Willem. What am I?"

He turns to me.

"You're nothing but a loudmouth hustler. You have the skills to watch the room? Bullshit. You're some hotshot killer? Bullshit. You've been to Hell? That's the biggest bullshit of all. But it's a nice line to the right people. The kind of unhinged street trash you spend your time with."

I check the time on my phone again. I swear time has stopped completely.

"Ishii wants to kill me. Did you know that?"

"Good luck to him, I say," Willem says.

"But I work for Abbot."

"I know."

"Which means you sort of work for me. I mean, as part of security it's your job to fall on a grenade for anyone on the council."

"I know."

"That means me."

"Unfortunately."

I lean back.

"Still like your job?"

"I like my job fine. I just want you to stop talking."

"You got it, pal."

We watch the party for a while. The monitors hurt my eyes. I'm afraid they're going to give me another Trotsky headache.

"Audsley was a friend of mine," says Willem.

"You need better friends."

"It really would be a black mark on the whole security team's record if he was to kill you."

Abbot looks up into one of the cameras and twirls his finger a little, saying it's almost time to wrap things up.

Willem zooms in on him.

"The thing to remember about security is we're only human. We have good days and bad. If Audsley was to show up . . ." Willem shrugs. "It could be one of our bad days."

He grins at me and I grin back, but his smile is bigger because I know he means every word of it. Some people just can't take a joke.

AS THE GUESTS straggle out, Abbot comes into the surveillance room.

"What do you think?" he says. "Did you see or hear anything?"

I shrug.

"It was all manicures and shrimp puffs down here. Did you pick up anything, Willem?"

"I'm not the Wormwood expert," he says.

"Still, did you notice anything unusual?" says Abbot.

"No, sir."

"Me neither."

I pick a thread off my coat.

"I think you owe me cake, boss."

"No," he says. "Charles Anpu. Did you see him?"

"He tried to strangle a waiter, so yeah."

"At council meetings, he's been pushing us to contribute to Regis International. There's a good chance they're connected to Wormwood, which means that he might be connected too."

"Where did you hear that?"

"I can't say."

"I didn't know the augur had confidential informants."

"Then you don't know much about politics."

"No. I guess I don't."

He leans on the edge of the console.

"Then trust me. I know people who know people and they seldom steer me wrong."

"Okay. Say you're right. Why don't you just have Willem and his boy band grab him?"

Abbot shakes his head.

"It doesn't work like that. Even for the augur, making accusations against a family without solid proof would be dangerous. It could start a civil war."

That sounds about right for the Sub Rosa clans. They're like the Hatfields and McCoys, but with helipads on the roof.

I look up at Abbot.

"What do you want me to do about it?"

"Go. Follow them. Sneak into the Anpu estate and see what you can find out."

"How am I supposed to do that?"

Abbot holds up his hands, frustrated.

"I know you have powers. You can walk through walls and shadows."

Willem does his snort laugh.

"Not anymore," I tell him. "I lost that trick when I saved the world a few months back. Remember when I did that, Willem?"

He plays with his console, ignoring me.

"All right. But you can tail someone. I know *that*," Abbot says.

"Your security can't even handle that?"

"I can't be seen to be directly involved."

I take out a Malediction.

"This is my punishment for falling asleep at meetings, isn't it?"

"You're not allowed to smoke in here," says Willem.

"Don't worry. I'm leaving."

I look at the monitors. Get up. The boat looks pretty deserted.

"They've got a head start. You have any idea where they're headed?"

"Musso and Frank's," Abbot says. "Get there and stay on them. Follow them wherever they go. If you can't get into their home, well, we'll figure something else out."

"What kind of car am I looking for?"

"A silver Rolls-Royce Phantom."

"Lucky Charlie."

I hold out my hand to Willem.

"It's been a little bit of Heaven spending these hours with you. Tell Audsley hello from me."

Willem shakes my hand and says, "I'll give him your regards."

"Now, Stark," says Abbot. "Time to earn your money."

We go upstairs together. The sea air is crisp when we get on deck. I take a deep breath.

"There are worse places to tail someone than Musso and Frank's. I could use a martini."

"Not a chance," says Abbot. "Stay outside and watch from there. Inside, you're a bit . . ."

"Noticeable."

"Exactly."

I head for the walkway leading to the pier.

I call over my shoulder, "You still owe me cake."

"Go," shouts Abbot. "Now."

I wave and head to the parking lot. Slide into the Catalina and sit there for a minute. Charlie might have a head start on me, but if he's going into Hollywood he's going to get stuck in the same traffic I am. That's going to cut his lead pretty thin. Assuming he took the freeway, if I take surface streets, I might just beat him to Musso's.

I point the Catalina inland, away from Abbot, Willem, and all their upper-crust intrigue. They'll be talking about me for a while. Abbot getting an employee report from his guard dog. I know what Willem's going to say, but I wish I could hear Abbot. The guy hasn't done me wrong yet, but sending me after the Anpu family alone, I can't help wondering if I'm being set up for something.

THE MUSSO & FRANK Grill is legendary even by Hollywood standards. It opened in 1919 and has hosted more movie stars, literary types, producers, directors, and starry-eyed wannabes than all the movie studios that have ever existed. Back in the day, Charlie Chaplain and Rudolph Valentino raced horses down Hollywood Boulevard to the grill to see who had to pay. Rita Hayworth, Bogey, and Bacall drank there. Orson Welles wrote there in his favorite booth. Dashiell Hammett, William Faulkner, and Raymond Chandler might have scribbled something, but mostly came to get wrecked. Musso & Frank's has always been big with star-struck Sub Rosas too. For the classier families and the hicks with money, it's their Bamboo House of Dolls, but without the jukebox.

Parking on Hollywood Boulevard is ridiculous almost any night, but it's deadly on the weekends. I dump the Catalina in a white zone across the street and pray the LAPD is too busy chasing jaywalkers to tow it.

Musso's has a parking lot around the back, which is great if you're eating there, but not so great if you want to look for a particular car. If this was any other place in town, I might be able to blend in with the crowd and wander into the back. But being called a con twice in just a couple of days is a reminder that I don't look like most people and would stand out like a pink unicorn if I tried to get back there. Of course, I could always cause a distraction. Use hoodoo to blow something up. But this doesn't seem like that kind of assignment. I light a Malediction and wander by the front of the restaurant a couple of times, hoping I'll get lucky and catch Charlie waiting for a table. But I don't usually get lucky.

Sure enough, I can't see anything but tourists.

With nothing better to do, I go across the street and wait between an army-surplus store and a tattoo parlor, hoping to catch Charlie going into the restaurant or heading home. I check the time and settle in for a tedious wait. No matter how long Charlie sits in his backroom booth swilling martinis, I'd rather be out with the hustlers and tourists on Hollywood Boulevard than stuck watching *Lifestyles of the Rich and Famous* in Willem's man cave.

I smoke a Malediction, then another. Down some Aqua Regia from my flask and start on my third cigarette when who comes staggering out of Musso's but the birthday boy himself. Which is a little surprising. No one goes in there to have just one drink. Unless Charlie teleported here, he can't have been inside very long. Why the hell go to all the trouble of navigating Hollywood on a weekend night just to pop into Musso's if he wasn't going to stay?

Charlie misses a step and staggers against a blonde young enough to be his daughter, but expensive-looking enough to probably be his mistress. When he stumbles, he drops something. Jean Harlow leans him against the restaurant's front wall and goes to retrieve whatever he lost.

That's when I start running. And it's when I stop because of the bus that almost turns me into a human speed bump. But the pause actually works in my favor. When I get onto the sidewalk, Harlow is leading Charlie toward the parking lot and I get a good look at what she's holding. It's a box.

It's just like the one Karael gave me.

Charlie fucking Anpu didn't stop by for a martini. He came here to pick up some black milk. For what? Is he going to do the bacon trick for Jean?

While they head around the side of the restaurant for the parking lot, I run back to the Catalina. White zones are supposed to be for passenger loading and unloading, mostly during certain hours. Me, I chose one that's the twenty-four-hour variety. It doesn't matter. There's a ticket on the windshield when I reach the car. I snatch it off and cram it in my pocket, gun the car, and pull the most idiotic, dangerous, and unsubtle U-turn since Junior Johnson was still a stone-cold rumrunner.

What the hell is a creep like Charlie doing with angel poison? And where did he get it? Are rich Sub Rosas keeping celestial beings in the backyard as pets these days? There's no way I am letting these assholes out of my sight.

I double-park a couple of doors down from Musso's, waiting for the Rolls to emerge from the lot. Stopping does not endear me to the other drivers on Hollywood Boulevard. People shout at me in a fascinating variety of languages. They give me the finger. Threaten to call the cops. I want to shout at the morons that I'm trying to save their souls, but all they want is for me to move my ass.

Without the Room, this is what I'm reduced to: sucking up abuse and dodging thrown coffee cups.

Soon the Rolls-Royce appears from the side of the restaurant, easing its way into traffic. I don't want to close in on Charlie and Jean too fast. I want them to feel safe and anonymous, so I gently lift my foot off the brake and let the car roll forward.

I get about twenty feet when the Catalina slams to a stop. It feels like I hit a brick wall.

I should be so lucky.

Because it's much worse. There's an angel in front of me with one armored boot on my front bumper, and she looks pissed. No point hesitating. I floor the accelerator, hoping to knock her out of the way, but she leans into the car and I just end up burning rubber. I let up on the pedal, throw the car into park, but leave it running. By the time I get out, a crowd is gathering around us. Even on Hollywood Boulevard, a six-foot-plus woman wearing armored boots stopping a muscle car is something people will notice.

She slams her fists onto the Catalina's hood and screams, "Give me the box."

I stab a finger at her.

"Hey, sister. You dent my car, you're paying for it."

She punches the hood again. I look past her. The Rolls is out of sight, disappeared into the general flow of traffic.

"Return it to me," she shouts.

"You want the box?"

I point past her.

"It's going that way in a silver Rolls. Why don't you puff out your wings and flutter after it? You'll love Charlie."

She comes around the side of the car.

"Not that one. The one you stole."

"Guess again. It was a gift from one of your kind. Ain't that a kick in the teeth?"

I shouldn't have said that last part. It gives her ideas. She lunges for me, but even though I'm only half angel, I'm as fast as her. I dodge her and slide across the hood of a Camry aiming for the curb. With one hand, the angel shoves the Camry out of the way, smashing it into an SUV full of kids in soccer uniforms. What sounds like all the banshees in Hell letting loose at once fills the street as the kids in the van completely fucking melt down. The boulevard crowd, who'd been digging the show up until then—probably thinking we were a publicity stunt for a shitty action movie—starts running at the sound of breaking glass and the kids wailing.

I can't outrun an angel, but I'm about as strong as she is, so I can sure as hell hurt one.

It takes a couple of kicks to knock over the parking meter. When she comes for me, I swing it at her head like a baseball bat. She doesn't even try to get out of the way. Takes the full force on the side of her head. The blow knocks her down, but I can tell I haven't really hurt her. When she gets up, her hands and shoulders are shaking, but not from fear or pain. Her eyes are rimmed in dark circles. Her lips and fingernails are cracked. She clicks her lower jaw against the upper, then bares stained teeth at me. I swear, if she wasn't an angel, I'd peg her for a meth head.

She has scars on her cheeks and her armor is dented and battered. She's seen some heavy action, so my parking-meter stunt isn't going to impress her. Before she can come at me again, I bark some Hellion hoodoo and the car she's leaning against explodes in flames, knocking her through a camera-store window. Now the last few hardcore cases in the street abandon their cars and head for higher ground.

When she comes out of the store her face is singed on one side, which doesn't improve her looks or her mood. But the flames don't intimidate her. She sticks her face into the burning car, takes a breath, and exhales a goddamn wall of fire in my direction.

I dive between a couple of parked cars, letting the flames pass over my head.

Who the hell is she? She's sure as shit acting like a Hellion, but fallen angels are trapped Downtown. They can't come up here. That means she's come here from Upstairs, which is infinitely worse. It means that whatever angel war is going on in God's backyard, I'm now part of it.

I'm still hunkered down behind a car when it splits in two in a shower of heat and sparks. With her free hand, the angel shoves the rear end of the car out of the way while holding her Gladius, her angelic sword of fire, in the other hand. I get up and manifest mine. She twitches. Opens and closes her eyes like she's not sure what she's seeing. However, it's not the Gladius that has her vibrating, it's whatever is wrong with her. But that's not my problem. She bellows and runs at me, her Gladius held high. I didn't want to be here before and now I'd like a big fat shadow to disappear into, only I can't, so I bellow right back at her and charge like the stupidest bull who's ever been stuck on a matador's sword.

When her Gladius crashes into mine it sends a shock wave up my arms. She's goddamn strong. Maybe too strong for me. The fiery explosion from Gladiuses colliding blows out the windows on a nearby shop, setting a row of mannequins and Valentine decorations on fire. An alarm goes off. She doesn't notice and comes at me, thundering chopping blows down at my head. I get my Gladius up and hold her off, but she's not stopping, deep into some kind of berserker rage.

I back up under the strength of her blows, but I can't keep playing defense. When she rears back for one last killing chop, I roll out of the way and tag her in the right arm.

But it doesn't do anything.

I only caught her with the tip of the Gladius and her armor deflected most of the blow. Still, she's getting wilder and fighting sloppy. If I can hold on long enough, with luck she'll do something stupid.

The problem is, she's taking her sweet time about it. Neither one of us is landing a killing blow, but she manages to get close to my right arm, setting my coat sleeve on fire. I don't have time to put it out as she charges in again. I aim under her sword arm, hoping that if I can catch her at the right moment, the tightened chain mail will give way. I get the shot in, but the mail doesn't budge. She smiles, thinking she's winning, and I'm afraid she might be right. In the second she takes to gloat, I get to wave my arm enough to put out my burning sleeve. Something is going to give here soon and I'm afraid it might be me.

When she comes at me again, I feel the parking meter under my foot. I kick it at her and it glances off her left knee, slowing her just long enough to pull the Colt Peacemaker I keep in my waistband at the back. Normally, shooting bullets at an armored angel is a bigger waste of time than teaching algebra to cats, but I don't use ordinary bullets. I dip mine in Spiritus Dei, a rare and excruciatingly expensive potion. It can cure wounds when used right, and when it isn't, it will kill pretty much anything that walks, crawls, or flies. I don't know what the bullets will do to angelic armor, but desperate times call for stupid choices and I'm the world champion of those.

I fire three times right into her heart. The bullets hitting the celestial armor sound like someone smashing a church bell with a sledgehammer. The bad news is, while the bullets dent her armor, none get through. She takes a step back, realizes what I did, and laughs at me. I'll admit it. That hurts a little. It also leaves her open, though, so I shoot her where she isn't armored. The first shot rips off part of her right ear. The second goes through her cheek. The third bullet goes straight through her eye. She staggers, goes down on one knee. There's no time to see if she's playing possum. I charge her.

Even hurt, she's still strong and partially deflects my blow, but I spin my Gladius around and rake it across the side of her throat.

I don't know what kind of vitamins they have in Heaven, but even wounded, she looks like the berserker in her is making a comeback. She lunges at me, but she's slow and she knows it. She has one hand to her throat, but she's leaking blood down the front of her armor. I get ready to move in again, but before I can take two steps, she hammers her Gladius into the sidewalk, splitting open the pavement. I go down flat on my ass, but manage to keep my Gladius up to block her next blow, only there isn't one.

The angel staggers back and her Gladius flickers out. Then she does the one thing I've never seen an angel do in front of civilians. She rolls back her shoulders, allowing her enormous wings to sprout from under her armor.

She points a shaky finger at me and rasps, "You aren't part of this, Abomination. Give me the box."

"How about we go to Musso's instead? Martinis are on me."

She flaps her wings and lifts from the cracked street.

"There will be others coming for you," she says.

I nod. "There always are. You should get going. It looks like you're running a quart low."

With her hand still at her throat, she pumps her wings hard and banks over the Egyptian Theatre, disappearing into the starless Hollywood sky.

Like I said, it's usually a bad move for angels to reveal themselves like that on a street in front of dumb-ass mortals, but after our little slap fight, I don't think it matters much. However, with her gone, I'm feeling a bit naked and exposed.

I might be fast and strong, but lousy nephilim like me, we don't have wings. And I can't disappear into a shadow anymore. I let my Gladius go out, dive into the Catalina, and hit the accelerator, using the steel nose of the beast to shove the lighter modern plastic cars out of the way. In a few seconds, I see a clear spot between the abandoned cars and blast through it. I take the corner on two wheels and keep going.

My heart feels like it's gone twelve rounds with Mechagodzilla and my burned arm hurts like part of me has been deep-fried. Why didn't she set fire to my Kissi arm? That thing is pretty much everything-proof. But no, she had to get my meat arm instead. If I didn't know better I'd swear there was no God. But I do know better and the worst I can truly say is that I wish he was better at his job.

I picture the angel flapping into the sky like an armored goose and wonder how many traffic, store security, and ATM cameras caught our square dance. LAPD already has video of me stealing cars. Now they're going to have shots of me playing laser tag with a celestial tweaker. Nothing I can do about it now.

I hear sirens closing in on Hollywood Boulevard.

The worst part of this whole thing is that when Abbot hears about it, I know I'm never going to get that cake he owes me.

I DON'T HAVE the heart to look at the Catalina until the morning.

My burned arm is healing nicely, but it's not pretty. Candy pulls off big flakes of dead skin and piles them on her night table like limp black potato chips.

As she plucks me I say, "What are you going to do with those?"

"Knit you a leather jacket."

"I'm already wearing my skin. I don't need more."

"Then I'll make one for myself and wear you to work."

"How sweet. You'll be sexy Leatherface."

"That's what I'm going to call my new clothing line."

"Carnivorous clothes for carnivorous girls."

She stops plucking and kisses me on the cheek.

"I'm stealing that. It'll make a good song title for me and Alessa."

"My pain is your art. Good thing I like you so much."

"Yes it is, smart guy."

Fortified with a cup of coffee spiked with Aqua Regia, we go outside to survey the damage.

"Good move parking it right in front of the store so every cop in L.A. can find it," says Kasabian.

"Give me a break. I'd just been set on fire."

"Wait till some prick cuts your head off. Then you can tell me about your bad day."

"Play nice, boys," says Candy.

She walks around the car.

"Honestly, I've seen worse."

"Not outside a junkyard," says Kasabian.

"No, really. All it needs is a little Bondo and paint."

"It needs a last cigarette and a bullet in the head."

I look at Kasabian, wanting to say something, but I don't because I know he's right.

The top of the hood is partially caved in where the angel smashed it with her fists. The front bumper is bent into a

V-shape, maybe by the angel's boot, maybe by hitting the other cars. Both headlights are smashed and both front fenders are crumpled back on themselves. There's a puddle under the engine where something is leaking. And the passenger-side mirror is missing. I'm amazed the damned thing held together long enough to drive home.

"I guess that angel was mad," says Candy.

"She wasn't happy to be there."

"Can you get it fixed?"

"In theory. But how much is it going to cost? And how long will it take? I need wheels these days."

"You need a babysitter and a Valium," says Kasabian.

I pull a crumpled piece of paper from my pocket and show it to Candy.

"Oh yeah. I got this too."

"A ticket? You're actually contemplating paying a ticket?" she says.

Kasabian shakes his head.

"What happened to you, man? When did you turn into such a pussy?"

I run a hand over the dented hood.

"The car is in my name. I can't afford to have cops tracing anything back to me."

"Why did you buy this heap, I mean?" says Kasabian. "You're still an asshole, but at least when you were stealing them you had a little self-respect."

"I know."

Candy comes up and puts her arm around my Kissi arm, politely avoiding my raw meat one, but nothing is very comforting right now.

"I'm working for the augur. I was trying to be—"

"A whipped dog," Kasabian says. "Oh, and smart move coming out here with that burned chicken wing out for all the world to see."

"Maybe he's right about the arm," says Candy. "Come on. Let's go inside."

We go into Max Overdrive and Kasabian locks the door.

"This is what trying to be Joe Citizen gets you," he says. "More scars and a shitmobile you can't drive to Fatburger without attracting a SWAT team."

I drop down on the stairs and Candy sits next to me.

I look at her.

"What would you do?"

She rests her arms on her knees and laces her fingers together.

"Well, you can't drive it like that. Maybe you can do like me when I go to work. Take taxis."

"Sandman Slim saving the world from the back of a yellow cab. That's beautiful," says Kasabian. He goes to the till and tosses a twenty at me. "Here. Buy a fucking bus pass."

Candy scowls at him.

I lean back, resting my elbows on the stairs, but my burned arm feels like someone stuck it with a boning knife. I sit back up.

"I'll use the bike."

"Really?" says Candy.

"That's stupid," says Kasabian. "I mean, it shows you've got *some* balls left, but it's stupid."

I shrug and turn to her.

"What choice do I have? Kasabian's right. I can't take cabs everywhere and I can't just run out and buy another car. They cost actual money."

"But the Hellion hog," she says. "It will stand out worse than the car."

"Not if I do some modifications."

"What kind of modifications?"

The Hellion hog is a one-off. A custom monster bike built by Hell's finest mechanics back when I was Lucifer. The wide handlebars taper to sharp points like something you'd normally find on a longhorn's thick skull. It doesn't run out of gas because it runs on pure Hellion hoodoo. The pipes are like something you'd find at a power plant. They'll turn cherry red when I open up the accelerator. I don't know how fast it will go. They don't have speedometers in Hell.

"If I replace the light on the front with a regular one, change out the handlebars, and only ride it at night, I think I can get away with it."

"What about a license plate?" says Candy.

"I'll steal a plate."

Kasabian holds up his metal hands like a preacher looking to Heaven.

"My God. He's back from the dead."

"That's one vote in favor of the hog."

I look back at Candy.

"What do you think?"

She purses her lips, thinking.

"On the one hand, it's really irresponsible and dangerous for you to be running around on something built by lunatics for a lunatic," she says. "On the other hand, you're pretty hot on the bike, and being more like your old self, maybe you'll be a little less depressed all the time."

"I'm not depressed. Maybe a little off . . ."

Kasabian picks up the twenty and puts it back in the till.

"Are you kidding? You look like a kid who nobody showed up at his birthday party."

"He's right," says Candy.

"Then that's it. I'll get some tools, hit a bike shop, and I'll fix it up tonight."

Kasabian says, "And when you move the bike from around the side of the store, drive that four-wheel piece of shit back there and cover it with a tarp."

"That's a good idea," says Candy. "At least until we can figure out what to do with it."

"And take the plates off too," says Kasabian. "If the cops find it, don't make their job too easy for them."

I get up.

"Okay. It's a plan."

"Great. I've got to get to work now," says Candy, and starts upstairs.

I follow her up.

"I'll go with you. I wanted to check in with Vidocq and he said he'd be at the clinic today."

"So, you are going to take a cab?" Kasabian calls up the stairs. "The monster who kills monsters does not take cabs. No good can come from this."

I close the door and Candy and I get dressed for the normal world.

Or as normal as ours ever gets.

ALLEGRA'S CLINIC IS in the same building as Julie's detective agency. Julie upstairs and Allegra downstairs. Allegra worked at Max Overdrive when I first got there. Then she discovered she had a talent for healing and took over the clinic after Doc Kinski was killed. Allegra has patched me together after fights more times than I can count. Perhaps more important than that, though, she and Vidocq are an item and I think introducing them is one of the best things I've done since crawling out of Hell.

While Candy heads upstairs I go into the clinic. Fairuza is in the waiting room doing paperwork for a couple of Lurkers. Fairuza is a Lurker herself, a Ludere. Blue skin and horns, and always in a schoolgirl uniform. She also plays drums in Candy's band. When she sees me, she straightens.

"Hey, Stark. Go right in. You've got the two of them all aflutter about whatever it is you gave them."

"Thanks. Kasabian says hi."

"Hmm," she says, and looks at her papers. She and Kasabian have had an on-again, off-again thing. I guess it's off again.

I go through the waiting area into the exam room.

Vidocq and Allegra are inside talking quietly. Her hair is close-cropped and shaved on the sides. She recently got a tattoo on her right forearm—two snake skeletons wound around each other in the shape of a Caduceus—and the ink looks good on her café au lait skin. She and Vidocq are huddled over an odd device with a lot of stacked lenses, a bit of Kinski's old hoodoo medical gear. Engrossed in what they're doing, neither she or Vidocq looks up when I come in. Allegra just motions me over when she hears me close the door.

"Stark, get over here and look at this."

They get out of the way and I walk over. The device looks like an upside-down spider with brass legs holding the lenses that swing in and out of the way. I have to move the top one around to get a sharp view.

It's no surprise that I'm staring down into a dark blob of black milk. The smell of the stuff fills the room. What's weird is that there's something twitching and moving through the muck like a hairy electric eel. Tiny blue sparks glow along its edges.

I nod.

"Very pretty. Was the wiggler in there already or is it a new pet?"

"We added it just before you came in," says Vidocq.

Allegra stands close to me so she can look through the lenses too.

"This isn't an ordinary microscope," she says.

"No shit."

"It doesn't just see the form of an object, but other characteristics, like its life force. That's what the blue glow along the sample is. It indicates that it's alive."

"But what is it?"

"The leg of a dead roach we found outside," she says. "We put it in a tiny amount of black milk and it sort of woke up. If you look closer, you can even see that where we cut the leg off has healed itself."

I stand up and look at them both.

"You're telling me that angels are using this stuff to reanimate bugs?"

"No," says Vidocq. "Look again."

I watch the roach leg happily swimming through the stinking milk, kicking up sparks. Allegra gets an eyedropper and adds a tiny speck more milk to the mess.

The leg begins to spasm like it's having a seizure. It goes on like that for a few seconds more before it stops moving and the sparks along its edges disappear.

"You murdered it, you fiends."

"Yes, we did," says Vidocq.

"Eugène showed me the bacon you reanimated," says Allegra. "We've been testing different things in the milk all night."

She points at the device.

"Look at the leg now."

I look through the lens. The leg isn't there.

"Where did it go?"

Allegra says, "It dissolved. That's the strange thing about this stuff. In tiny amounts it has restorative powers."

"But if you add just a touch too much, it destroys the tissue. Any kind," says Vidocq.

"It happened with the bacon too. It was still wiggling around when I got home. Then we added a little more milk, and the strips dissolved into a black sludge like the roach leg."

I glance back at the stuff in the device.

"That's all swell, but what is it?"

"We don't know."

"But we have some ideas," says Vidocq. "While Allegra studied the milk itself, I spent the night with my books and papers. I found references to something like it in a twelfth-century treatise on rare hermetic poisons. The document had been suppressed because it references various heretical biblical gospels. It definitely identifies the substance as angelic in origin and said that it's been seen on Earth before. Athanasius Reuchlin, a German mystic, was said to have been given a small amount by a divine spirit and told to guard it. That's not so different from what happened to you, is it?"

"So, what happened to it? And what happened to him?"

"He found results similar to ours," says Allegra. "Microscopic amounts of the milk heal, while larger amounts are toxic."

I look at one of them, then the other.

"Yeah, but what's it for?"

Vidocq says, "Reuchlin believed it was used by warrior angels in battle."

"You mean they went around melting other angels?"

"Here is where it's frustrating. The treatise is incomplete. However, Reuchlin believed that while the base materials of the black milk were of angelic origin, it was refined here on Earth."

This is when I want to be back home drinking.

"How? By who?"

Vidocq shrugs.

"I'm afraid the answer to that is among the missing sections."

"Can you at least say if this stuff is medicine or poison?"

"Both maybe," says Allegra. "Without knowing how the angels used it, we might never know."

She gets all starry-eyed at me.

"Can you get more?"

"Hey, I almost died for this bottle. I don't want any more."

"All you all right? What happened?" she says.

"You two haven't watched the news today, have you?"

"No. We've been working since last night," says Vidocq.

"The short version is, an angel came to see me last night and words were exchanged. She did this to me."

I take off my coat and show them my fried arm.

"Dammit," says Allegra. "Why didn't you tell me? Let me get you something for that."

"Thanks."

While she hunts around for some hoodoo Bactine, Vidocq looks concerned.

"I'm sorry about your injury, but how is it that your angel would be on the news?"

"The spat was kind of public. We broke part of Hollywood Boulevard."

"You fought an angel in public?"

"She started it. That armored asshole about murdered my car."

"*Merde,*" says Vidocq. "James, you are a reckless soul."

"Hey, I'm the victim here."

Allegra comes back with a salve that smells like cinnamon and roses.

"Leave him alone, Eugène," she says, smearing the stuff on my arm. "I'm sure he didn't mean it."

"Yeah, Eugène. Can't you see I'm hurt?"

Whatever supernatural goo Allegra puts on my arm, it cools my skin and cuts the pain immediately.

"That feels great."

"I found it in one of Doc Kinski's books. It smells nice too, doesn't it?"

"Very nice. Something I could give Grandma for Christmas."

I look over at Vidocq and he's frowning.

"Say whatever you're going to say," I tell him.

"If you say that fight was unavoidable, I believe you. But what is your employer going to say?"

"I don't know. I'm going to see him right after this."

"Did the police see you?" says Allegra.

"No, but there were a million witnesses and I'm sure a gruesome amount of video."

"This isn't good," says Vidocq.

"She was out of her mind. If I didn't fight back she would have killed me and everyone on the boulevard. This isn't my fault."

"I didn't mean that. What I meant is that if angels are free to battle in the streets, Heaven must be in extreme disarray."

"That's the impression I got."

"Have you heard from your friend Samael? Or Mr. Muninn?"

"Not a word. I get the feeling they're pretty busy. And it's not like I can go and see them anymore."

"You must watch yourself," Vidocq says. "You're in danger from Earth and the celestial realms."

Allegra finishes with the salve and wraps my arm in gauze. She smiles.

"Maybe we should have tried some of the black milk on your arm. I bet it would have fixed you right up."

I get up as soon as Allegra finishes wrapping me. She helps me put my coat on. I go to the counter and put the milk vial back in its box and put the box in my pocket.

"No one is trying black milk on anything anymore."

Allegra makes a face.

"Can't you leave us just a little? A few drops."

"I'm not having some liquored-up angel come after you. This stuff stays with me until I know exactly what's going on."

Vidocq nods at Allegra.

"It's probably for the best. Things regarding the milk seem to have moved from our world into James's."

"It looks that way," she says. "What are you going to do with it?"

"Hide it," I say. "I don't know where. The augur is smart. Maybe he'll have an idea."

"You can't go to him in broad daylight. You could be recognized," says Vidocq.

"Way ahead of you."

I improvise a quick glamour spell and change from my face to Charlie Anpu's.

"How do I look?"

"Distressing," says Vidocq.

Allegra wipes her hands on a towel.

"Don't let Chihiro see you like that. You're entirely unfuckable right now."

I check myself in a mirror over the sink.

"Perfect, then. Thanks for the help."

I give Allegra a hug and she squirms away.

"Ew. Take that face and go do whatever it is you have to do to fix things."

I head for the door.

"Maybe I'll see you two at Bamboo House later?"

"Not if you're going to look like that," Allegra says.

"Bamboo House is safe. I'll be me by the time you get there."

"Please do," says Vidocq. "And be careful."

I open the door.

"I'm always careful. I'm just not lucky."

I head out. Fairuza lets out a little scream when she sees me. Now I just hope I don't spook all the cabbies. It's a long walk to Marina del Rey.

IT TAKES A while, but I finally get a ride. The fare all the way out to Abbot's place is soul-sucking, but I pay the cabbie off with a wad of the cash I get paid for being on the council.

So, this is how regular people live. They get paid to do a job, then have to spend the money on clothes they don't want to wear somewhere they don't like, then spend even more money commuting. And that doesn't count the years of their lives spent going from home to a desk and back again. Fuck that. At least in the arena in Hell they didn't charge us for our weapons. And we got to steal better ones from who or whatever we killed that day. Sure, we didn't have 401(k)s, but if there was a boss who wouldn't get off your back, we didn't have to go to HR about it. We just cut the fucker's throat. That's job satisfaction.

I go through the locked gate and down the pier to Abbot's boat. There are a couple of security guys on break, just smoking and shooting the shit. They straighten up when they see me. Toss their cigarettes in the water and stand up straight like maybe the Queen of England is behind me. Only it's just me and I'm getting nervous and wondering if I'm going to have to hurt someone when one of them starts talking.

"Mr. Anpu?" he says.

He looks me up and down.

"We didn't know you were coming."

I'd forgotten on the ride over that I'm wearing someone else's face. Seeing Charlie's mug in my boots and ex-con clothes must be frying some circuits in these boys' heads. I can't let a moment like this pass.

"Since when do I have to clear my social calendar with the employees?"

I let that float in the air for a minute.

"Sorry, sir. Of course. The augur is inside. If you'll come this way, we'll see if he's free."

"He better be. I've come a long way to get turned away like a beggar at the door."

I follow them onto the boat.

The truth is, I don't know if this is how Anpu talks and I sure as hell don't know his voice. It just goes to show you that people will believe anything, let you in anywhere, if you show up with a clipboard or an attitude.

They show me into the living room and I make myself comfortable on Abbot's million-dollar couch. One of the security guys goes off to find Abbot while the other stays with me. I don't think he's here because I might steal the silver. Let's see if I can figure out why.

"I'd like a drink. Gentleman Jack. Neat, if you have it."

For a few seconds he looks puzzled. I guess he's not my waiter after all. How am I supposed to know how these things work? No one gave me instructions when I got the job. Or did they? Maybe it's in the envelope with my insurance papers. I need to check that sometime.

"Oh," he says. "I don't know if I'm supposed to . . ."

I wave a tired hand at him.

"Forget it. Wishful thinking. I should have known he'd keep the cabinet locked. Don't want anyone sneaking nips during working hours, do we?"

"No, sir," he says.

I can see the poor guy's eyes and hear his heart pounding. He'd like to shoot me and dump me in the Pacific. I should ease up a little. He can't help it if he chose a shitty career.

"Thank you. For the courtesy. I'll be sure to tell the augur you've taken good care of me."

"Thank you," he says with the slightest hint of hesitation in his voice.

Now I've really confused the poor bastard. Time to shut up. I don't want him to shoot the real Anpu the next time he stops by for tea.

A minute or so later Abbot comes into the room with a big quizzical smile on his face.

He says, "Charles. Did I forget a meeting tonight?"

"No. I just stopped by for a chat. Your men have been taking care of me. This one in particular. Be sure to give him a good performance review."

Abbot glances at the security guy.

"Well, thank you, Charles. I'm sure we're all grateful for your input."

He looks at Mr. Security.

"We're fine now. Thank you."

"Yes, sir," he says. Then to me, "You have a good day, sir."

"You do the same," I say in my most magnanimous voice.

As security hustles out, Abbot sits down. He stares at me.

"This is a new look for you, Charles. Do you have a cold coming on? Your voice sounds a little strained."

"When you get kicked in the throat as many times as I have, it can sound a little funny."

"Excuse me?"

He looks alarmed. No one around here can take a joke.

"Who kicked you?"

I do a little hoodoo in my head and the glamour fades away.

"Every dickless shit heel in downtown Dixie."

When he sees my real face, Abbot drops back against the couch cushions.

"I should have known by the clothes. Charles wouldn't be caught dead in those boots."

"I've been thinking about upgrading my wardrobe. Do you have a tailor?"

"You couldn't afford him."

"Then give me a raise."

He just sits there for a minute.

"You took a hell of chance coming here like that."

"Relax. I walked right by your security guys. The riffraff on the streets aren't going to recognize me."

"The only reason you got on board is because the protective wards recognized you, even if the guards didn't. If they hadn't, you could have been hurt."

"I'm already hurt. Another time more or less won't make a difference."

"I'm glad you feel that way," he says. Then, "I heard about the mess in Hollywood last night. I even saw bits and pieces of it on the news."

"So, they did get video."

"Everyone with a phone recorded you."

"Goddammit. I didn't think of phones."

"How's the arm?"

"You saw that too?"

"Footage of a burning man will get a bit of airplay."

"Then I guess I don't have to tell you that I lost Charlie Anpu."

"I know."

"Does Anpu know?"

Abbot shakes his head.

"We got lucky there. He had a fender bender on the way home, so that would have kept him occupied. And with a reputation like yours, no one is surprised about you having a street brawl with a Lurker."

"Is that what people think? That it was just a Lurker?"

"Wasn't it?"

I look at the handwoven rugs on Abbot's floor. The flawless woodwork and exquisite golden fixtures around the room, and feel like a housefly on a hundred-dollar steak.

"Do you think I could have a drink? If I'm not being an asshole for asking . . ."

"Of course," says Abbot. "And you're not. Relax. I know things went off-kilter last night, but from what I saw on the news it wasn't your fault."

He goes to the liquor cabinet and pours us a couple of expensive whiskeys. Comes over and hands me one, then sits down again.

I actually meant would he mind if I had some Aqua Regia from my flask, but I'll always take free alcohol.

I sip my drink. It's smooth as a newly polished blade. But why did I *ask* him if I could have a drink? Why didn't I just have one? This *Citizen Kane* world is getting to me. I'm like goddamn Oliver Twist begging for more gruel.

I look at Abbot.

"Maybe it's better if everyone thinks it was a Lurker."

"If it wasn't, what was it?"

I take a gulp of his good stuff.

"It was an angel. But I don't suppose Ivy League types believe in spook stories like that."

Abbot fiddles with one of his cuff links.

"I'll admit, an angel wasn't my first thought. But if you say that's what it was, I believe you."

"Just like that?"

"The Golden Vigil believed in you. Why shouldn't I?"

For a second, I want to kiss the son of a bitch.

He looks into his drink.

"The question is, why would an angel come after you like that?"

I reach into my pocket and hand him the box.

"Because of that."

He sets down his drink and looks the box over. Opens the top, looks at the vial of black milk, then closes it again and hands it back to me.

"What's so special about it?"

"It's not the box. The black stuff. The angel wanted it back. She was very clear on the matter."

"I saw. Do you know what it is?"

I could tell him what Vidocq said, but the fewer people who know anything about the stuff the better.

"No."

He thinks for a minute.

"Do you think it was a coincidence that all this happened while you were following Charles?"

I put the box back in my pocket.

"Nope. He has a box like this too. That's why he went to Musso's last night. It's where he picked it up."

"Are you sure? A box like yours."

"He was shit-faced and dropped it on the street. I got a good look."

Abbot stares off into space again, wheels turning in his head.

"Charles and angels. You're the expert. What do you think it means?"

"That it might not be Charles and angels. That you were right and it's Charlie and Wormwood."

"Are you sure?"

"Of course not. But unless Charlie has a secret life, he's not going to know a lot of celestials. Wormwood has contacts in Hell. That means *they* believe in angels, and knowing how they work, it probably means they're in business with some."

I shut up and let Abbot take that in. This time he's quiet for a long time. Then he laughs in a bleak sort of way.

"I don't know what to think about any of this. Mysterious boxes. Angels. Hell." He pauses, then says, "How do you know they're in business with Hell?"

"Because Geoffrey Burgess told me. Norris Quay runs their office Downtown."

"Norris Quay?" says Abbot. "Norris Quay is dead."

"Naturally. How else is he going to have a day job in Hell?"

He shakes his head. "You're telling me to think like the Red Queen."

"Who?"

"From *Through the Looking-Glass*. 'Sometimes I've believed as many as six impossible things before breakfast.'"

"She sounds like a smart lady."

Abbot leans forward, looking intense.

"Let's assume that everything you've said today is true. You were attacked by an angel. Charles is somehow connected to them and that proves he has ties to Wormwood, who also know angels and does business in Hell."

"You're right on the money so far."

"Wonderful. The thing is: What are we supposed to do with this information? I admit, I'm a little lost."

"I spent eleven years Downtown, so I know the feeling."

I finish my drink and set my glass on a nearby table.

"Oops," says Abbot. He reaches over and hands me a coaster.

I put it under the glass.

"Sorry."

"No harm done."

He says it nicely, but I know he's going to check for damage when I'm gone. He probably had this one custom-made in the Amazon. He'll send a flunky to Brazil tonight to pick out a new one.

I cross my legs and get a look at my boots. They're filthy. In all this glamour that makes me happier than it probably should.

"What I think we do right now is what you wanted me to do before. Recon work. I poke around and see if I come up with any new Wormwood connections."

"Do you think it's a good idea to follow Charles? If

something strange happens around him again, he's not going to write it off as a coincidence."

"Not Charlie. Someone else I know is connected to Wormwood. Geoff Burgess. Or Eva Sandoval. I met them with some of the other Wormwood heavyweights. I think I'd rather go for Burgess."

"Why him?"

"I don't like him. And why not? He's as good a place to start as any. I'm just shooting in the dark here. If you have a better idea, tell me."

"No," says Abbot. "I don't have any ideas right now. Fine. Do it until we have a reason to do something else. In the meantime, I'll talk to my contacts and see what they have to say."

"Great."

"I'll also have a word with our contacts in the police department. Let's see if we can push any investigation about last night in the wrong direction."

"I'd appreciate it, having the heat off for a while. And being able to wear my own face."

He sits up. Finishes his drink.

"What are you going to do with the box?"

I scratch my burned arm through my coat.

"Hide it, I guess. Do you have any ideas where? Some supersecret Honeycomb hideout?"

"I know how to make business documents disappear. Family jewels and cash too. But this? I'm stumped."

"Me too. Normally I'd hide it in the Room of Thirteen Doors, but that's off the menu. I'll think of something."

Abbot nods.

"I was hoping we'd find some evidence that perhaps Charles was getting kickbacks or family favors for steering money to Wormwood. We're in brand-new territory now."

"L.A. always throws something new at you. That's why it's fun."

"You think this is fun?"

"Maybe 'fun' isn't the right word. Maybe 'familiar' is better. We're moving from your side of town to mine."

"Where the angels live."

"And the monsters. They're easier to get along with than angels."

"The fact you know that is why I wanted you on my side," says Abbot. He looks at his watch. "However, I have a Skype in a few minutes with some people who might have some additional insight into what's going on. I'm afraid we need to wrap things up."

I get up. Feel the weight of the box in my pocket.

"Good luck with the espionage, boss."

We're walking to the door when he puts a hand on my arm. Happily, not the burned one.

"Before you go, I wanted to ask you something. Have you heard anything about the investigation into Nick's disappearance?"

"No. Aren't you in touch with Julie?"

"Yes, but I was wondering if you might have heard some talk around the office. Maybe something she's not ready to share yet."

"No. But I can ask Chihiro if you want."

"Thank you. I'd appreciate it."

Abbot starts to walk me out onto the deck.

I say, "How hard is it to get a cab around here?"

"What happened to your car?"

"The angel murdered it."

"I'm sorry. I'll have my driver take you home."

"I won't say no to that."

Abbot gets out his cell and makes a call.

One of the two security guys I met earlier is on the deck. He looks at me funny. Right. I forgot to put Charlie's face back on. Too late now. My cover's blown. I stand a little closer to Abbot, just to make sure everyone knows I'm in with the in crowd.

Abbot puts his phone away.

"It's done. He'll meet you at the end of the pier."

"See you at the next council meeting."

"Don't worry about that. Keep up with your investigation. We can get by without you for a session or two."

I head out. The driver is indeed waiting at the end of the pier. He holds the door for me and closes it when I get in. As much as I hate Abbot's world, I could get used to this limo business.

I have the driver drop me on Sunset Boulevard by a bike shop I know. I'm still nervous about being in public in my face, so I put on a new one. The limo driver's.

At the bike shop, I pick up handlebars, a front light, and some tools. It's not that heavy, but it's awkward to carry. I should have asked the limo to wait for me. It's too late now. I hump the gear back to Max Overdrive.

Just an hour ago, I was floating on a custom-made cloud with free drinks and guys whose only job it was to watch my back. Now I'm sweating like a pig and dodging dog shit in the street. It's a hard landing, coming down from Valhalla.

CANDY AND ALESSA are practicing in the storeroom. One of them is burning through "Miserlou" and the other sounds like she's falling down the stairs with a boxful of cats. But she keeps playing. Good for her.

It's after hours and Kasabian has the news on. They're playing shaky phone footage of me getting my ass kicked, then the angel flying away. I change channels. It's the same thing. Me down on one knee, then wings flapping into the sky. Everybody likes the part where I'm getting burned and pounded into SpaghettiOs, but no one bothers to show that I actually won the damned fight. I need a better press agent. Kasabian laughs quietly each time they show me falling, but he's too smart to say anything.

I really hope Abbot can talk to someone about getting my mug off the screen.

Finally, the news gets tired of me and moves on to other local merriment.

Some shitbird shot up the crowd at a food truck selling upscale southern food. Fried chicken, grits, hush puppies, the whole bit. Nine people shot. Six dead. The cops don't think the shooter's connected to the truck or anyone in the crowd. They were just at the wrong place at the wrong time. I wonder who the little creep had a grudge against. It doesn't matter. It's always the same thing with these guys. His girlfriend left him. He lost his job. He ran out of toothpaste. The news show puts up a yearbook photo of the guy's face over the bodies in the street. I don't need to see him. Ninety-nine percent of these guys are the same. They cruise along in a bubble of dude-bro privilege, then can't stand it when the world lets them know they're nothing special. Then everyone has to pay.

However, there's something else that bothers me: I recognize the truck. I ate there once, out at the La Cienega oil fields when I got a note more or less commanding me to come out and meet the Wormwood board of directors. They really rubbed it in too. Made a party of it. Had a circle of food trucks. A dining room table. The works. That was the day where Burgess and Sandoval explained to me how the world really worked. How Wormwood Investments works. That's what gives me a bad feeling about this particular shooting.

Is this a message from Wormwood? Did someone see me on TV and decide to put me on notice? Try to provoke me into doing something stupid? Did they send that fucking angel after me or are they just having a good time, setting up a massacre to remind me that I can't eat a taco without lining their pockets?

Or am I going down a paranoid rabbit hole? Maybe the shooting is just what it looks like. One more asshole with a gun and a grudge having a bloody tantrum?

I'm going to make myself crazy thinking like this. I can't function wondering if everything I do and everything I think is one big Wormwood mindfuck.

What would be hilarious is if I brought the massacre to them. Kill them all in one big Night of the Long Knives dance party. The only problem there is that I don't know how many of them there are. I met a few of the higher-ups, but for all I know they could be like Abbot and his Sub Rosa contacts, meaning they're everywhere there's money or power to be sucked up. That's the only thing that makes sense. How else could they function? They're everywhere all the time, like evil bastard Pinkertons. *We Never Sleep.*

And here I am again. Staring down into a swirling, paranoid rabbit hole.

I go upstairs and check on the box. It's where I left it in my coat pocket. I take it and put it in the bottom drawer of the dresser with my extra guns. It's not any more secure than my coat, but if anyone goes for it while I'm home, at least I know I can shoot the hell out of them.

The worst part of all of this is that every part of my brain and body wants to go back to the abandoned high school and get down into the fight pit with some big bruiser with something to prove and no damned sense. But I made a promise to Candy and to myself, so I light a Malediction instead.

I'm standing by the window, blowing the smoke into the street, when Brigitte calls. We talk for a minute and she suggests something even better to do. I toss the cigarette out the window and go downstairs.

It's quiet in the storeroom when I knock on the door. Candy opens it and smiles when she sees me.

"What's going on, TV star?"

"Please. That's the last thing I want to hear."

"Poor baby. You need a drink. Why don't we go to Bamboo House after we finish practice?"

"Actually, Brigitte is over there with a friend and I'm kind of climbing the walls. I might head over there now."

"Okay. We won't be too much longer. I'll meet you there."

"Great. You're sounding good in there, by the way."

"No, I don't, but I appreciate the sweet lie."

"Anytime, baby."

"But I am getting better, don't you think?"

"I do."

"See you soon."

"Sounds good."

She closes the door and the noise starts up again. This time I really can hear her hitting the melody. It's slow and creaky, but it's there. It's nice to see her so happy.

Kasabian puts on gloves to hide his metal mitts and we head out a couple of minutes later. I look around at the movie posters on the wall and decide to put on Robert Mitchum's face from *Out of the Past.* Kasabian rolls his eyes when he sees the glamour, but, once more, he's too smart to say anything.

THERE'S A DECENT, but not oppressive crowd in Bamboo House. Nobody says hello or bugs me on the way in, which is a nice change. I might have to wear faces more if it will keep the selfie-stick crowd at bay.

Les Baxter is on the jukebox playing "Oasis of Dakhla." Brigitte is standing near it drinking martinis with a woman I've never seen before. She's shorter than Brigitte, with blond hair and the kind of dark eyes that inspire duels. I ditch Robert Mitchum. Brigitte waves when she sees us and Kasabian and I go over.

"Where's Chihiro?" she says when we get close enough to hear.

"A new friend is teaching her some tunes. She'll probably be here soon."

"Hello, Kasabian. How are you?"

"Great, now that I'm with actual people and not stuck in the store with Johnny Buzzkill here."

Brigitte looks at me.

"Are you all right? Are you feeling ill?" she says.

I shoot Kasabian a look, but he's looking at Brigitte.

"I'm fine. Who's your friend?"

Brigitte loops her arm around the other woman's.

"Stark, Kasabian, this is Marilyne. All the way here from the wilds of France."

Marilyne smiles softly and offers her hand. Kasabian and I shake it. She gives him a slightly funny look afterward, but covers it well. His mechanical hands are hard to disguise, even when they're wrapped in suede.

"Nice to meet you both," she says with barely a hint of accent.

Kasabian has had a crush on Brigitte ever since she arrived from Prague, but from the way he's looking at Marilyne, his affections might be defecting.

"How do you two lovely ladies know each other?" he says.

"Marilyne is friends with some of the producers of my new film," says Brigitte.

"How interesting. Are you in the movie business too, Marilyne?"

"Not even remotely," she says.

"She's a doctor," says Brigitte.

Marilyne looks at her.

"Don't be silly. I'm just a chemist."

"But you have a doctorate degree."

"Yes."

"Then you're a doctor," says Brigitte insistently.

Marilyne sips her martini, then shakes her head.

"I just run a small lab, analyzing whatever the true doctors send to us."

Kasabian starts to say something. His pupils are the size of tractor tires. It's true love and whatever is about to come out of his mouth is going to be embarrassing for everyone.

To cut him off I say, "What part of France are you from?"

"Nothing exotic. I was born and raised in Paris. Have you ever been?"

"No. I have a friend from there, but I've never been there myself."

"Yes, Marilyne. You must meet Eugène," says Brigitte. "He's the most French man I've ever met and he's a chemist, like you."

"That sounds lovely," she says. "This is only my second visit to the States, but I liked it enough that I came back and have decided to get my citizenship."

I cut Kasabian off again.

"Good luck with that."

"If you ever need any help studying . . ." Kasabian says.

"Thank you," says Marilyne. "That's very kind of you." She looks back at me.

"And what do you do, Mr. Stark?"

Brigitte touches her arm and aims a wicked smile at me.

"Don't call him mister. It makes him uncomfortable. And don't call him Jimmy. That makes him furious."

"Not furious. But only you and Chihiro get a pass on the Jimmy thing."

"Don't let the tough-guy act fool you," says Kasabian. "He loves being called Jimmy. Isn't that right, Jimmy?"

The jukebox changes to Arthur Lyman doing "Sakura."

"If you ever call me that again, I'm going to recycle you into Max Overdrive belt buckles, Tin Man."

Kasabian is on a roll, though, showing off for his new lady love.

"Belt buckles. That's a great idea. We need to get back into merchandising."

"And what do you do, Mr. Kasabian?" says Marilyne.

"He runs my video store," I say.

"*Our* video store," he says.

"It's mine because you're technically dead."

"So are you."

"No. I'm just *legally* dead. Big difference."

Kasabian shrugs.

"Maybe it's really Chihiro's store."

"I can live with that."

"I never quite imagined you as a shopkeeper, Stark," says Marilyne.

"She's being polite," says Brigitte. "I told her all about you. The slightly tarnished white knight."

"The schmuck who kills schmucks," Kasabian says.

I glance at the bar. This is more talk about me than I like around strangers, even friends of Brigitte.

"I don't do much of that these days. I'm just the monster who falls asleep at meetings."

"Meetings?" says Marilyne. "From what Brigitte told me, I find that hard to believe. What kind of meetings?"

I glance at Brigitte.

"It's all right, James. She's not Sub Rosa, but she knows all about your world."

"In school, my best friend and her family were Sub Rosa," Marilyne says.

I try to get my brain around that for a second.

"You aren't Sub Rosa, but you went to a Sub Rosa school?"

"No. In France, Sub Rosa children go to ordinary school like the rest of us. It's not until *collège* that they're separated from the other children."

"It keeps them from being too insulated," says Brigitte. "Is that the right word?"

"Insular," says Kasabian. "But it sounds good however you say it."

"How very sweet of you."

I can't stand watching Kasabian doing Cary Grant, so I say, "I need a drink. Anyone else need one?"

"I'm fine," says Brigitte.

"No, thank you," says Marilyne.

"Why don't you fetch me something frosty, Jimmy?" says Kasabian. "I'll keep the ladies company."

I head to the bar to keep from shooting him.

Carlos already has a glass of Aqua Regia ready for me. I thank him.

"Can I get a beer for Rin Tin Tin, too?"

He looks past me at Kasabian making his moves.

"Any kind in particular?" he says.

"You have anything shitty in a can? Maybe you forgot it in your car on a hot day?"

"I know exactly what you want."

He goes in the back and comes out with a foamy glass. It doesn't look special to me.

"What is it?"

"Carbonated Alabama swill," he says. "I keep it around for when the frat boys come in. They can't tell the difference."

"Perfect. Thanks."

"You better get over there before he eats one of them."

I weave my way through the crowd and hand Kasabian his piss water. He takes a big gulp and doesn't bat an eye.

"I like your bar," says Marilyne. "I've never been anywhere like it."

I look around the place for a second.

"There isn't another place in the world like Bamboo House of Dolls. That's why we take care of it. Right, Brigitte? The first time I found out who she really is was right here."

Brigitte sighs.

"That's right. We both fought monsters back then. I miss it."

"You fought what?" says Marilyne.

Brigitte gives us both a coy look. I sip my drink, but she doesn't say anything, so I ask, "You didn't tell her?"

"I thought I'd introduce her to you first. After that, anything I said about myself would seem mundane in comparison."

"Mundane is the last thing you are."

"*Děkuji*," she says.

"Brigitte, tell me. What's your secret?" says Marilyne.

"Later," she says. "I'll need another drink first."

"There's Chihiro," says Kasabian.

I look over at the door and she waves to me. She's with Alessa. Grabs her by the hand and pulls her through the crowd.

It's introductions all around when she gets there, then Candy says, "Have you told him about your movie yet?"

"I haven't had a chance," says Brigitte. "But it's a lovely part in a big production. The biggest part I've had since coming here. That's how I met Marilyne, through the producers. Pieter Ligotti and his partners."

That name is familiar. It takes me a minute to come up with it, but finally I do. I was introduced to Pieter by Burgess and Sandoval when they dragged me out to the oil fields. That means Brigitte's movie is being financed by Wormwood.

The angel, the shooting at the food truck, and now this? That's too many coincidences too close together. Now I know that someone is fucking with me.

Candy comes over and puts an arm around me, but I barely notice. I don't hear much of the rest of the conversation either. When I come back to Earth, Candy and Alessa are chatting with Brigitte, and Kasabian is laying on the charm with Marilyne. I go over and tell Candy I'm leaving.

"Are you all right?"

"I'm fine. I just need some air."

I say good-bye to everyone, put the Mitchum face back on, and walk back to Max Overdrive. I'm too restless to sit around or watch a movie, so I haul the bike gear and a flashlight around the side of the shop and go to work modifying the Hellion hog. It's done by the time Candy and Kasabian come home and I've worked off enough nervous energy when they get there that I can act like a human again. But in the back of my mind I know that working for Abbot or not, I'm going to have to start killing people and it's probably going to be soon.

IN THE MORNING, I bring a cold twelve-pack of beer into Max Overdrive and set it on the counter. Not beer like last night's sewage. This is good stuff. Candy is already at work. It's just me and Kasabian.

"What's the occasion?" he says.

"No occasion. We haven't had a drink together in a while. I thought it was about time."

"Okay," he says, more than a little suspicion in his voice.

I open the pack and hand him a bottle.

He pops the top with his metal mitts, but he doesn't drink. He hands me the bottle.

"You first, chief."

"Why do you immediately assume I'm trying to poison you?"

"Because you're you. Now drink."

I hold it up and drain half the bottle. Put it back on the counter with a flourish.

Kasabian looks at me. Waves a hand in front of my eyes. I remain upright and extremely not poisoned.

Finally, he says, "Okay. But I'll pick my own bottle."

"Don't strain yourself."

He takes one from the corner and opens it slowly, like it might be full of snakes on springs. He sniffs and takes a small sip. When his tongue doesn't melt he takes a longer pull.

"Just because it's not poisoned doesn't mean I trust you."

"I don't blame you."

I pick up my bottle and finish it. I'm not really much of a beer fan, but I can handle it if it's the only thing around. Kasabian would get suspicious if I gave him beer and drank Aqua Regia. Kasabian, on the other hand, loves the stuff. He has four bottles by the time I finish two. I'm barely sipping my third when he cracks open his fifth. I can smell traces of alcohol in his sweat and his eyes tremble microscopically, too little for regular people to see, but I can pick it out fine. Kasabian isn't smashed, but he's officially DUI. Now I just have to keep him calm and focused.

"Do you mind if we talk about Hell for a minute?"

He sets down his beer and makes a face.

"Oh man. And I was just starting to feel good."

"I don't want a dissertation. Just a few questions."

"I don't like seeing down there, man. I just don't."

"Someone's got to keep tabs on it."

He picks up his beer again. Sips.

"Great. You do it."

"It doesn't work like that."

"Why am I always the lucky one when you want a weather report Downtown?"

"Because you're the only one that has access to the *Codex*."

"And you stuck that fucking peeper in my head. Don't forget that. I don't. The damn thing keeps me up at night."

I sip my beer.

"Sorry."

He drains his beer and opens another.

"First you leave me without a body, then you replace my eye with a Freddy Krueger marathon."

"I'd trade you the eye anytime if I could use it."

"Then do it."

"I tried."

"Try harder. You're good at making up spells and stuff."

He's starting to slur his words. He's nice and toasted.

"Maybe I can give you a break for a while."

"What does that mean?"

I set down my bottle. At this point, he won't notice if I stop drinking.

"Not a long break, you understand. Give me the eye back for a half hour. I want to try something where I might be able to see Downtown for a few minutes."

"How?"

"I'm going to have to die a little."

"Oh fuck," he says. "You're going to do that blood ritual again, aren't you? Who's going to clean up the mess? Not me. And what if Candy comes home early and finds you passed out. She doesn't need to see you like that."

The Metatron Cube ritual is one where I draw a mystical sigil on the floor, get down in it, and slice my wrists. It lets me talk to the recent dead, especially if they're close by. This time, though, I want to try something else.

"The Cube is strictly a backup. I think I have a work-around."

"What kind? If it hurts, I'm not doing it."

"Relax. It's just a potion called Dream Tea. I used it once when I worked with Ishiro Shonin last Christmas."

"That four-hundred-year-old, walking, talking bag of bones you worked with at the Golden Vigil?"

Kasabian looks suspicious again.

"Wait—how is it you ended up with a Vigil potion?"

"What do you think? I stole it."

"Oh good. You're such a little Mary Sue these days I thought you might have paid for it. So, how does it work?"

"That's the great part. You just drink it and meditate."

"You can't meditate."

"Yeah, but I can have some Aqua Regia and relax into it. It worked last time."

"And there's no blood?"

"Not a drop. There's only one weird part."

He rolls his eyes.

"Here it comes."

"The only time I used it was when I was following a dead man into the Tenebrae. This time I'll be on my own."

Kasabian finishes his beer and opens another.

"And you might not be able to make it back this time—I get it. You're doing this upstairs. If something goes wrong, I don't want your bony ass cluttering up my sales floor."

"That's fair."

So I head upstairs and he follows me, a little wobbly on his feet. He bangs off the walls a couple of times, but makes it into the apartment without too much damage. He drops down onto the couch.

"So what do we do?"

I pour some water into a mug.

"Like I said, I haven't done it this way before. But think of it like pizza delivery. I guarantee to have the peeper out and back in your head in thirty minutes or less."

He shakes his head.

"I don't want to have to pry my eye out of your dead body."

"You won't."

He thinks creaky booze thoughts for a minute.

"I'm getting a bucket of water. If I think you've been gone too long, I'm dumping it on you."

"That's not a bad idea."

"Wait here," he says, and staggers downstairs. While he bangs around down there I get the Dream Tea out of an old suitcase full of other stolen goodies that I keep under the bed.

Kasabian comes in with the filthy bucket we use to clean up downstairs. He fills it at the kitchen sink and carries it back to the sofa.

I put the mug of water in the microwave for a minute. When it's finished, I dump in some of the tea and let it brew or steep or whatever it is tea is supposed to do. When it looks done, I swallow the whole cup. It tastes like Swamp Thing's bathwater.

"If you die, try not to piss yourself," Kasabian says. "The smell is hard to get out."

"Love you too," I tell him, carrying a glass of clean water over to the sofa. "Now give me your eye."

"I hate this part," he says.

"You'll get a lollipop if you're a big boy."

First, I whisper a little hoodoo, pluck out one of my eyes, and drop it in the glass. It floats there like a deflated egg. Carefully, I pop out Kasabian's peeper and put it in my socket. Kas flinches a little when it comes out, but doesn't whine, and I'm grateful for that at least.

With the eye in, I get up and walk around, trying to get it to settle into place. It doesn't take long. As my vision grows clearer, I feel the familiar drunk sensation I had when I first used the tea. I stumble in the direction of the sofa, but don't make it and have to sit on the kitchen floor with my back against the counter. Closing my eyes, I feel like I'm sinking into a bath of warm Jell-O.

When I open my eyes I'm on a wide plain of dry packed

earth. I know that if I walk in one direction I'll get to Tene-brae Station and the ruins of a kind of ghost L.A. where restless souls too afraid to even haunt the crumbling streets hang out. In the other direction is a range of low mountains. I stumble in their direction, and before I'm halfway there, a door opens in the rock face. This is the door to Hell. Souls get a choice at this point. They can go inside, to a freak show designed to torture and torment them for eternity, or they can stay out here in the Tenebrae, with nothing but their shell-shocked brains and other hungry ghosts for com-pany. In their shoes, I'd go inside. I'd rather be someplace than nowhere at all. But that's me.

I want to run for the door, get Downtown as soon as possi-ble, and spend as much time as I can there, but my legs won't cooperate. I feel like I'm drunk, and that didn't happen last time. It might be the effect of coming through here with no one waiting on the other side. Whatever it is, I'm not feeling springtime fresh by the time I step through the door. I throw on another glamour as soon as I get inside. The last thing I want is for anyone to recognize Sandman Slim when he can barely stand and definitely can't defend himself.

For this disguise, I choose a Hellion face. Some Hellions look pretty much human while others look like they just won an ugly-farm-animal contest. Some are more like human-size bugs—even other Hellions don't like them. I go for middle ground and put on a bland, empty-eyed boar's face, complete with cracked yellow tusks. It's the little details that make the disguise. I don't want to look like I got my mask from the bargain bin at Walmart.

It's a shock being back Downtown. I haven't been here in

months and for the first few minutes the smell and sound of the place are hard to deal with. It's all familiar, but drunk like I am, it's hard to ease comfortably back into damnation.

When doomed souls walk through the front door into Hell, they're funneled like cattle into veal pens, where they wait to be sorted. Who gets a holiday in lava? Who goes to the Butcher Valley or the Room of Knives. Me? I'm just another idiot Hellion out for a stroll, so I don't expect any trouble getting past the guards. Turns out it's no trouble at all.

And it's not because I'm dressed like a local.

The new souls aren't being led to the holding pens because they aren't there anymore. Where there were cages is a collection of twisted metal bars and the crushed remains of cages in a shit-reeking mud swamp. I want to get a closer look, but I'm so light-headed I have a feeling that I'd end up flat on my face in the muck. Damned souls mill around the pens not sure what to do or where to go. There aren't any Hellions left guarding them, much less telling them where to go. A few notice me and head in my direction, but I wave them off and head into the Hell's capital, Pandemonium.

I don't make it. I have to duck inside one of the abandoned guardhouses on the outskirts of the city, where I collapse on the floor. I'm drunk and the peepers are kicking in full force now. I can see everywhere, all of Hell at once, and it's making me throw up in my skull.

You know how flies have those funny compound eyes that divide images into hundreds of little pieces? Now imagine one of those compound eyes where each of those hundreds of lenses sees something different. This is beyond information overload. It's a flat-out Hellion acid trip.

I'm back at Lucifer's palace in Downtown's demonic Beverly Hills. I have a watery image of the palace lobby. The grounds outside. The kennels where the hellhounds are supposed to be. Even Lucifer's endless library upstairs.

Ruins everywhere.

Everything trashed. The palace looks deserted. Out front, hundreds of Hellion legionnaires are camped in tents and in the backs of broken-down trucks. There are fires everywhere, fueled with Lucifer's furniture and his books. Damned souls wander the streets—the ones that haven't gone native and joined the roving legionnaire gangs raiding the last of the stores for food, Maledictions, ammo, and booze, that is. There are gang fights, executions, riots, and burning buildings all across the city. And I'm seeing this all at once, through one big sulfurous, spinning kaleidoscope.

I'm cold. I'm sweating. I can't feel my legs. Then my legs come back and I can't feel my arms. My heart bangs around my chest like my ribs are a mosh pit. I'm too dizzy to even get up and head back to the Tenebrae door. All I can do is lie here as drytts—Hellion sand fleas—trampoline over my face and hands.

I see south of the city, all the way to the golden walls around the fortress that opens into Heaven. Millions of Hellions and damned souls surround it. I expect rioting and fights here too, but it's different. The crowd is barely moving at all. It's just miles of hopeless, catatonic bodies, human and otherwise, in every direction. Months ago, God—Mr. Muninn—put out the word that Heaven was now open to everyone, human souls and fallen angels alike. Only the gates never opened. Over the walls of the fortress, I can see flashes of the angel war that's raging to decide who gets into Heaven and who doesn't.

It's too much. I feel like someone parked an earthmover on my head. I can't get enough stinking air breathing through my nose, but if I open my mouth, the sand fleas get inside. Even though I know I'm not bodily back in Hell, that I'm only here as a projection of my soul, everything hurts and everything is horrible and I roll over and throw up as the visions continue.

There are waves of Heavenly angels in the streets of Pandemonium. They're carrying bottles in wooden crates like we use to haul wine bottles. The angels' bottles are dark and whatever is in them swirls with a deeper darkness. I don't need anyone to tell me that this is black milk because around the ones humping the bottles other angels are on guard, their Gladiuses out and ready to murder anything that gets in their way.

Somewhere in Downtown's Hollywood, the leader of this angelic horde is talking to an old human soul, one I only met a couple of times, but one I'll never forget. It's Norris Quay. He's laughing it up like him and the angel are all old Skull and Bones club buddies.

I don't care about any of it anymore. I just want it to stop. For these bugs to get off me and the pounding in my head to stop.

But another vision comes swimming up through the rest. It's Samael with some Hellion generals in the burning ruins of the old street market. They're arguing. The generals close in on him. Fire up their Gladiuses. Samael doesn't flinch. He fires up his twin swords and waits for them, a Zen warrior in a sea of monsters. I want to help him. I try to get up. Instead, I fall on my face back into the sensation of warm Jell-O that brought me here.

"FUCK!"

I open my eyes. I'm back in Max Overdrive, curled up in a fetal position on the kitchen floor. My arm is wet where I've drooled all over it. I wipe my mouth. Kasabian is on the couch with the dirty bucket by his foot and a beer on his knee.

He takes a sip of the beer.

"I take it it worked?" he says.

I roll onto my back.

"You could say that. It was all jumbled together, but I saw plenty. As much as I needed to."

"So, you're okay."

"Yeah."

"Good," Kasabian says.

He walks over and dumps the bucket of water on my head.

I sit up sputtering and coughing.

"That's for calling me Tin Man in front of Brigitte and Marilyne. Now give me my eye back."

I pop it out and hand it to him. He pops it back into the socket, blinking to get it into place.

I sit up, drenched and cold.

"Would you hand me the glass?"

He gives me the glass with my eye floating on top. I pop it back in and gulp down the water.

Kasabian takes the bucket and goes back downstairs. I stagger to my feet and get some towels from the bathroom. While I wipe up the water I yell at Kasabian.

"I'm trying to save everybody's soul, you know."

"And we appreciate it," he yells back. "But you're still a dick."

Honestly, I can't argue with that.

ABBOT GIVES ME Geoff Burgess's address in Beverly Hills and I drive the Hellion hog over as soon as it gets dark.

The place is a gated Tudor behemoth. Something an exiled dictator or a silent-movie star would have. I park down the street between a Land Rover and an Escalade. They're big enough to hide me, but close enough that I can keep an eye on the place.

Around nine, the gate opens and a Bentley Mulsanne pulls out. It's a gorgeous machine and I have to talk myself down from ramming it to avenge my Catalina. But I stay put until it passes. Pull out and get on its tail, keeping my light off until we're out of Beverly Hills and back into normal traffic where Burgess won't notice me.

He heads across town, then north up into the hills. I keep a respectable distance. The streets up here wind around each other and branch off in all directions, like veins and arteries. It would be easy to get lost and starve to death by a millionaire's billion-dollar digs. The coyotes will drag you down into a ravine and the only thing they'll find of you will be your bones. They'll identify you by your dental work and joke about you around the morgue, calling you Coyote Bob or Susie Dog Food. If no one claims your carcass, you'll be burned, and your dust and bone fragments will be buried in the L.A. County Crematorium Cemetery, a place that's prettier than the Mojave Desert, but no less lonely.

The Bentley slows at a curve and pulls up to a gate where a uniformed flunky or maybe low-key security guard speaks to Burgess through the driver's-side window. After a few seconds, the flunky punches a button on one of the brick gate supports and they swing open. The Bentley continues up the circular driveway and I pull a U-turn and park down the hill. Even if I pass by casually, whoever is on gate duty is sure to notice an oversize rat bike prowling somewhere it isn't supposed to be. A Maserati goes through the gate next, then a Hennessey Venom. L.A. is a town that judges you by your car and the crowd tonight is pulling out all the stops. The only thing that's going to top these last few heaps is a solid-gold submarine.

From where I am, all I can see is a twenty-foot wall around the mansion grounds. Maybe I could climb a tree, only what am I going to find up there but bats and squirrels with a taste for Dumpster caviar? I'm way too far away from the mansion to see inside. I should have brought binoculars, but unless they're doing a human sacrifice on the lawn, I still don't know that I'd be able to see anything. It's probably just another cocktails-and-cheese mixer like I sat through on Abbot's boat. I don't need to waste one more evening on one of those. Besides, it's Burgess I'm after and Burgess is behind the locked gates of Fort Sugar Daddy. Which means he's not home and that's good news for me.

I gun the bike and head down the hill, back to Beverly Hills.

Headlights in my eyes all the way, and while they don't bring on a Trotsky headache, my head starts hurting after a while. I should have asked Allegra about the migraines. Bullets and knives I can handle, but these damned headaches are my Kryptonite. Like the one I had when I was Downtown this morning. That laid me out but good. I run through the images again as I drive, each time stopping at the same one: Samael facing off against six or eight Hellion generals. I've seen him fight with a Gladius, but not against a group like that. It feels stupid to hope that he's not hurt. I just hope he's not dead and vanished, one more victim in a cosmic brawl made worse by whatever Wormwood is up to.

In Beverly Hills, I roll the bike back between the Rover and the Escalade. Burgess's place looks empty and quiet. I wonder if he's the kind of guy to have a staff that spends the night? I get the feeling not. During the day, I can image the place being a busy little beehive. But at night, with what he's into, I think he'd want some privacy. I watch the windows for a while. The lights don't change and no shadows pass by.

It's a thin reason to break into the place, but I'll take it.

There's a wall around Burgess's palace, but it's lower than the one back up on Mount Olympus. There's a row of topiary bushes by the near side of the wall. They give me a nice pool of shadow, so I can climb over without being too obvious. When I land I do another glamour. This time I put on Burgess's face. That should confuse any video cameras he has on the grounds.

My skin prickles from all the protective wards he has installed around the grounds. They make my heart race and my throat tighten. I whisper some Hellion hoodoo and my chest and throat loosen up as the wards lose their effectiveness. I've broken into a lot of houses here and Downtown, and the owners almost always go for the same lame protections. Once you figure out the pattern, you can find a way to work around them. The problem is that I can't turn off the wards indefinitely. They're going to start working again soon, so I have to do whatever I'm going to do fast.

That leaves me with one big question: Do I kick the front door in or maybe toss a potted plant through a window and poke around Burgess's linen drawers? I decide against both. They'll give away too much too soon. I want to be able to keep tailing him or come back here again, so I don't want him getting paranoid, maybe doubling his wards and hiring armed guards to prowl the place at night. That means it's just a recon mission. Prowl the grounds and see what I can see. Come back later and rip into the interesting stuff after coordinating with Abbot and whatever he's up to.

There isn't going to be anything interesting at the front of the house, so I head around the side.

Nothing but bushes over there. I can make out the frame of a gazebo at the rear of the place, so I head that way.

It's awfully exciting around back—meaning it's the same giant heated pool, lounge chairs, and tables you'll find in every backyard in the goddamn neighborhood. If Burgess has any secrets stashed around here, they're inside the house, exactly where I can't go yet.

I'm looking over the house's rear windows when my throat starts getting itchy. Maybe I should take off and come back another night when I've had a chance to prepare some better protection for myself. But as I'm moving back to the front of the house, something moves upstairs. In the far right window, the curtains part and a small face looks down at me.

It's Nick, the kid Abbot is looking for.

I start for the rear door when my lungs decide to stop working. My throat tightens and my heart kicks into overdrive. I'm almost to the door, but I'm moving too slow.

Lights come on all over the mansion grounds. I'm pinned under floodlights beaming down from every direction. If the lights are on, it means someone else has been alerted. The cops or local private muscle. There's no way I can break in, get Nick, and get out again. The kid waves at me. I wave back. Then head for the wall I climbed over to get in.

The moment I'm on the other side, my lungs open up and my heart slows down. I feel like shit and know a drink would help, but this isn't the right time or place to administer medication. I run back to the hog as lights come on in other houses. Kicking the bike into gear, I haul ass out of blue-blood country, still wearing Burgess's face. I don't change back until I'm in Hollywood.

Across from the Whisky a Go Go, I pull the bike over and get out my phone. I dial Abbot's number. He takes his sweet time answering.

"Stark? What's going on? I'm in a meeting."

"Fuck your meeting. I found your kid."

"Nick?"

"No. The ghost of Jackie Coogan. Who do you think I mean?"

"All right. Calm down. Where did you find him? Are you with him now?"

"Burgess has him. Geoff goddamn Burgess. I saw him

there not ten minutes ago, but I couldn't get to him. Now the place is going to be crawling with cops."

I can hear Abbot breathing at the other end of the line.

"All right, listen to me. Do nothing. Do you hear me? Nothing. Let me handle this."

A cop car cruises slowly down Sunset Boulevard. I keep the phone up, blocking my face as it goes by.

"Stark, did you hear me?" says Abbot. "If you do something stupid, it could put Nick in jeopardy. Do you hear me?"

"Yes. I hear you. You know everything I just told you is worthless now, right? By the time you can do anything, they'll have moved the kid."

"Let me worry about that. You did a good job tonight. Let's keep it that way. Go home. I'll call you when I learn anything new."

"You told me Nick was with his father in Long Beach. What the hell is going on here?"

"I don't know. Sit tight and let me handle this."

"Sure. You do that."

I hang up and dial Julie.

"Stark. What time is it?" she says with a voice thick and slow. "I must have fallen asleep."

"Well, wake up. That kid you're looking for for Abbot? I found him. He's in Beverly Hills, at the home of Geoffrey Burgess."

"Burgess? Where do I know that name from?"

"He's a heavyweight at a talent agency called Evermore Creatives Group. But trust me, he's into worse stuff than boy bands."

"Right. You went after them before I fired you. Why are you bothering Burgess now?"

"I told you. I found the kid there."

"You were looking for the kid? Dammit, Stark. That's not your case."

"I wasn't looking for anyone. I just found him, which means I solved your case, so do something about it. Burgess is into some weird shit and that kid shouldn't be around it."

"Listen. You stay out of this. After the stunt on Hollywood Boulevard the other night, no one wants to hear from you. I'll call some contacts in LAPD and get them to look into it."

"Look into it. Well, I feel better. I'm sure the kid's parents will be thrilled to know you're looking into it."

"Calm down and go home right now. I'm sorry if I don't sound eternally grateful, but you have a way of making any crisis worse."

"Burgess is in bed with some pretty bad people. They probably have contacts in the police force."

"So do I. Go home. I'll have Chihiro call you later with any updates."

The line goes dead.

I spend all of six seconds wondering if I should go home. Then I kick the bike on and head back to Beverly Hills.

Which is pointless. I can't get within a block of Burgess's house. LAPD and rent-a-cops are all over the neighborhood. It looks like D-Day with palm trees. For a minute, I consider throwing some hoodoo at one of the cars. Maybe set it on fire. But I can't take those kinds of chances with a kid around. I can burn something later if Abbot or Julie's cops don't come through.

I turn the bike around and head back to Max Overdrive.

AT HOME, CANDY sits up with me, waiting for a call from Julie. She even left practice early on account of me. Around two, I carry her into the bedroom and cover her up. Back in the living room, I have a smoke and a drink.

Why am I so twitchy about a kid I don't know or care about? The privileged sprog of some show-biz or corporate master of the universe. Maybe because I've seen what Wormwood and the Burgess family can do to innocents. Lucius Burgess, Geoff's recently deceased father, used to run ghost bum fights in a warehouse off Sixth Street. Innocent idiots who'd signed blue sky contracts to keep their souls working on Earth were tortured and beaten in front of dogfight audiences. The place was run by a particularly lunatic bunch of Nazi fuckwits and all the profits went through Burgess to Wormwood.

What's a bastard like that doing with a missing kid?

Or is there a slim chance I'm reading this all wrong? What if this isn't sinister and is just some kind of *Magnificent Ambersons* family spat? The Burgess family are a bunch of bourgeois pricks, but even they must take breaks from being pure evil to have dinner. I mean, Nick didn't look freaked out. He didn't scream or pound the window. And he waved to me. I had on Geoff Burgess's face and he acted like it was the most normal thing in the world to see him.

Goddammit, I hate this Mike Hammer stuff. Trying to figure out people's dirty little secrets. It's worse when they don't have any good ones. I mean this is L.A., where everyone has a skeleton in the closet. But that doesn't make them all Mr. Hyde. Most people are just idiots, getting bounced around like pinballs by bosses and lousy marriages. They're quiet desperation types, not backyard cannibals cooking the Little League team over mesquite chips.

What if I'm wrong about Burgess? I've been known to make mistakes. I've always been best at hoodoo and hitting things, not at pondering the deep mysteries of life. Maybe I'm just on edge about what I saw Downtown. What if I dragged all that horror back home in my head?

Great. I'm going to end up a hermit like Howard Hughes, sealed up in the apartment with six-inch fingernails and my feet in Kleenex boxes, afraid of people, germs, and my own shadow.

I have another drink and another cigarette and wander downstairs.

Kasabian is counting the money in the till. The final credits for *Until the End of the World* are running on the store monitor, so I switch to the news.

A truck jackknifed on the 405. A gangbanger was shot in a drive-by near Compton. Before the show cuts to a commercial, the newscaster teases a story about an attempted kidnapping in Beverly Hills. I recognize the street. I recognize the tangle of cops and private security cars. I turn off the monitor and go back upstairs. Put on *Them*. James Arness fights giant ants in the L.A. sewer system with machine guns and flamethrowers.

Finally. Something I can identify with.

I fall asleep on the sofa.

I SPEND THE next day locked in the apartment waiting for a call from Abbot, Julie, or Candy. It's a long wait for nothing at all. I watch movies. Alternate spaghetti westerns with old-school Japanese horror and science fiction. *Death Rides a Horse,* then *Matango, Curse of the Mushroom People. The Great Silence*, then *Goke, Body Snatcher from Hell.* No one calls. I drink Aqua Regia, smoke, and sleep all day. By the time I think about eating something, my stomach feels like it's full of battery acid and eels.

In the afternoon, I wander downstairs when there are no customers in the store and ask Kasabian about borrowing the peeper again.

All he says is "Don't make me get the bucket."

I go back upstairs with *Keoma* and *The Human Vapor* under my arm.

Around seven, Candy calls.

"Have you been out of the apartment today?"

"What about the thing last night?" I say, ignoring her question.

"Julie says the kid is fine. She's chasing down leads, trying to find out where he's been and who knew about it."

I take a sip of Aqua Regia.

"It's just like when I worked for her. I solve her case and she's still mad at me."

"She's not mad at you for finding Nick. And she wasn't mad about you solving Vincent's murder last winter. She gets upset about how you do things."

"I solved the case."

"You solved it your way, by breaking in, scaring the neighbors, and getting all of Beverly Hills up in arms about roving packs of baby snatchers. Julie was a U.S. marshal. She's a bit more procedurally minded than you are."

"And what about Abbot? I haven't heard from him either."

"I can't help you there. Why don't we do something tonight? Want to go to a movie?"

"I'm too antsy to sit through a movie where I can't drink."

"Want to drive to the beach?"

"I don't have a car and we don't have helmets. We'd make it about five blocks."

"Fine. We'll go somewhere you can walk to. Let's meet at Bamboo House of Dolls in an hour."

"I've been drinking all day."

"I haven't," she says, "so I need to catch up."

"That's the most reasonable thing anyone has said to me in days."

"See you there."

"One hour."

"Or sixty minutes, whichever is sooner."

I hang up feeling vaguely better.

I put the Aqua Regia away, brush my teeth, and take a shower, scraping off the grit of this frustrating day.

I'll give Abbot and Julie twenty-four hours to call me. After that, I think I'm going to have to do something really stupid.

VIDOCQ AND ALLEGRA are already at Bamboo House when we get there. Candy chats with them while I go to get drinks. On the jukebox, Frankie Carle is playing "Beyond the Reef." Carlos uses one of the potions he's been buying from Lurkers to spritz a civilian clown harassing a young Ludere. The guy's skin turns a pale green when the potion hits him.

"So everybody can see your sorry ass from a mile away," he says.

The harasser doesn't need to be told to get out. He figures it out all on his own. As he hits the exit, half the bar is laughing at him. Usually I'd say the incident was the price civilians pay for playing on our turf without knowing the rules. But how dumb do you have to be to not know to back off when a woman—Lurker or civilian—is giving you the cold shoulder? Fuck him. Maybe Carlos grew the guy up a little tonight. If you go home from a bar looking like a jalapeño in Dockers, it's time to reexamine your life choices.

I bring the drinks back and give Candy hers. The three of them are talking about music. Candy and Allegra get excited about their favorite guitarists. Vidocq has them both beat when he talks about seeing Django Reinhardt in New York in the midforties.

"That's not even a little bit fair," says Allegra. "You've been around too long to play this game."

"Then I'll remain silent," he says.

"Besides, *show-off,* I know Jades who saw Jimi Hendrix at the Monterey Pop Festival," says Candy.

"Alas, I wasn't there," Vidocq says. "But I did see him perform at Madison Square Garden, though I honestly don't remember the evening very well. My friends and I had taken LSD before leaving home."

"Goddammit," says Candy. She looks at Allegra. "We missed everything cool."

"It's true. I never even got to try getting into Studio 54," Allegra says. She holds a hand up to Vidocq. "And if you ever went, I do not want to hear about it."

A small smile creeps across his face, but he keeps his mouth shut.

"Did you ever seen Robert Quine?" says Candy.

"No. That was more James's type of music," he says.

Candy looks at me. I shake my head.

"Quine was the New York scene. I'm an L.A. boy."

"You haven't seen enough," she says to me. "And you've seen too much," she says to Vidocq. "You're both useless."

"We've been put in our place," says Vidocq.

I nod.

"I'm humbled. Do you feel humbled? I feel humbled."

I think just to change the topic, Allegra says, "Have you learned anything new about black milk?"

"Don't talk about that here," I tell her. "And no. I'm still working on it."

"I'd love to have more of it to test."

"As would I," says Vidocq.

I look around the room.

"I never want to see the stuff again."

The crowd mills and flows through the bar. No one is paying any attention to us, even after Allegra mentioned black milk. I haven't been this jumpy since planning my escape from Downtown. I assume everyone is listening, that every kid with a fake ID nursing a whiskey sour is a master spy. I need to stop looking over my shoulder all the time and deal with real things in the real world.

"Have I mentioned that Candy's boss still hates me?"

Candy makes a face.

"She doesn't hate you. She just gets . . . concerned."

"But I'm not invited to her birthday party, am I?"

"Be quiet and stop feeling sorry for yourself."

"Tell her not to worry about me. I'm going back to the Sub Rosa council like a good boy and staying off the streets."

"Really?"

"Not right away. I mean, eventually. Probably."

"How about I don't mention you at all?"

"That might be even better."

Allegra looks past us.

"I think Brigitte came in. Who's her friend?"

I look over. All I see is what might be the backs of their heads.

"Probably Marilyne," says Candy.

The two of them head to a table with a couple of young guys in sharp suits. Film producers probably. They're all smiles and air kisses. If they're the ones financing Brigitte's new movie, are they Wormwood or just show-biz schmucks? Either way, I don't think Brigitte would appreciate me busting up her meeting, so I stay put.

"Marilyne is French," says Candy. "When they're done with the civilians maybe we can get them over and you can compare bouillabaisse recipes."

"Not every Frenchman is a chef," says Vidocq.

"It's sad but true," says Allegra. "He's better at raising the dead than making breakfast."

"Alchemists do not raise the dead."

"And you can't fry a damned egg."

"Je suis désolé."

They go on like that for a while. Friends having a drink and talking nonsense. I try to listen, but I can't. I keep flashing on angels with crates of black milk and Samael being cut to pieces.

Allegra says, "Looks like they're coming over."

Brigitte and Marilyne head in our direction. Vidocq is telling Candy about buying King Oliver a drink in Chicago in the twenties.

"Hello, you lovely people," says Brigitte.

"*Bonsoir*," says Marilyne happily. I think she's a little drunk.

At the sound of her voice, Vidocq stops talking and turns. His face goes slack.

"Liliane?" he says.

Marilyne turns white.

"Eugène?"

Everyone just stands there for a minute, not sure what the hell just happened.

"It is you," he says.

"And you," Marilyne says.

He takes a step toward her, holds out a hand. Lets it drop. Holds it out again.

"You're dead," he says. "Long ago."

"Not so dead after all," she says.

He looks her up and down.

"Your hair was different."

She looks him over.

"So was yours. You look better without those curls and whiskers."

He nods.

"It is you."

"So it is," she says.

He grabs her and they hug for a long time. Too long. I watch Allegra, but can't quite read the look on her face. She's as shocked as the rest of us and also a little uncomfortable watching Vidocq and this stranger stuck to each other like barnacles. Finally, they break the clinch.

He takes the woman's hand.

"Everyone, this is Liliane. A friend from long, long ago."

"She's like you, you mean?" says Candy. "I thought there was only one of you."

"Apparently, immortality isn't quite so rare as I thought," he says.

Liliane puts her hand on Brigitte's shoulder.

"I'm sorry I never told you my secret, but then you only told me yours recently."

Brigitte shakes her head, as stumped as the rest of us.

Quietly, she says, "It's all right."

"So you're two hundred years old?" says Candy.

"I'm afraid so," Liliane says.

"Holy shit."

Allegra puts out her hand.

"Hi. I'm Allegra. Another *friend* of Eugène's," she says a little stiffly.

Vidocq drops Liliane's hand and takes Allegra's.

"Remember, dear? I told you about Liliane."

"I remember. I also remember you said you killed someone because she died. Only it looks like she didn't."

That shuts everyone up. Vidocq's shoulders sag. Liliane takes hold of his sleeve. She says something to him in rapid French. He answers her the same way and they keep on like that for a couple of intense minutes. The conversation goes from grim whispers to quiet shouts, then back down again to smiles and awkward laughs.

Liliane touches Vidocq's face.

Finally, he turns back to us.

"Liliane and I knew each other back in Paris. She worked with me as I delved into the alchemical arts."

"Kind of like you and Allegra now," says Candy, I think trying to remind him who he came with tonight.

The look Allegra gives her is as hard as the six inches of steel I imagine *she's* imagining sticking in Vidocq's back right now.

He speaks French with Liliane, gesturing at Allegra. She crosses her arms. Shifts her weight. I know she must have picked up some French over the last year, but there's no way she's keeping up with Vidocq and Liliane's pillow talk.

I say the only useful thing I can think of.

"You want a drink?"

She nods. "That would be very nice."

"You stay here with her," I tell Candy.

She gives me a look somewhere between abject fear and *fuck you.*

Brigitte follows me to the bar.

"I don't know what to say," she whispers. "I had no idea. Really."

"I believe you. I'm more worried about Allegra."

"The poor thing. Her lover pining for another woman for two centuries and here she is. What can she be thinking?"

"She's wondering if it's cheaper to buy two caskets or one big one."

"I think you're right."

"Should I do something? Drag Vidocq outside by his baguette?"

She sighs.

"It's too late for that. The damage is done. None of them will be getting much sleep tonight, I think."

"If he doesn't keep his hands off Marie Antoinette, he might never get to sleep again."

Carlos gives me an Aqua Regia and a shot of whiskey for Allegra, but Brigitte gulps it down, so I order another.

"I feel so guilty," she says.

"Relax. Everyone has exes. They'll work it out."

"Allegra said that Eugène killed a man. Do you know if it's true?"

"A long time ago, he told me he killed someone over a woman. I'm guessing this is her."

Brigitte stares.

"It's all so impossible. How can something like this happen?"

Now it's my turn to gulp my drink.

"The of-all-the-gin-joints-in-all-the-world part? It can't. Someone set this up."

"Who?" she says.

I shrug.

"I got mugged by an angel the other night. It's been a weird week."

"But why Liliane?"

"I hate to say it, but this might be more about me than them. Wormwood has been playing a lot of games with me lately."

Brigitte pats me on the arm.

"Dear Jimmy, you know I love you, but not everything in Los Angeles revolves around you."

I look over at the three of them. Right this minute, Vidocq, Allegra, and Liliane look pretty far from me and my stupid obsessions.

"Maybe you're right. I'm seeing conspiracies in my cornflakes. But you have to admit, this is fucking strange."

"Maybe it was inevitable. Whatever impulse drew Eugène to Los Angeles, could it have drawn the only other immortal possibly in the world?"

"If you're not coming to L.A. to get famous, this is an easy place to blend in, no matter how weird your past."

"And we do all have pasts here," she says.

"We've been through a couple of things."

"Come. Let's get Allegra her drink."

I hand Brigitte the shot glass.

"You should give it to her. I don't think she wants favors from a guy right now."

We go back through the crowd to our friends' international psychodrama. Vidocq and Liliane alternate between English and French. It doesn't take a genius to see that Allegra doesn't appreciate the parts of the conversation she can't understand.

Brigitte hands her the drink.

"Thank you," she says, and drinks half, looking like she might be saving the other half to throw at someone.

After a few more brutally uncomfortable minutes, Brigitte tells Allegra that she's leaving. Candy tells her the same thing. She's not stupid. I'm sorry to abandon Allegra, but there's no way we're staying alone with this situation.

Outside, we say good-bye to Brigitte and head home.

Neither of us says anything. As Candy and I walk, I wonder what's a stranger life, fighting monsters or trying to figure out how people work? One is a lot more dangerous than the other and it sure as hell isn't monsters.

AFTER YESTERDAY'S DRINKING, I don't wake up until the crack of whatever-the-hell o'clock. All I know is that I hear people downstairs and *Apocalypse Now* cranked up loud. It's our special alternate-universe version with Harvey Keitel instead of Martin Sheen. It's crack to our kind of customers.

I check my phone and find a message from Abbot. I don't bother listening to it, just sit on the sofa with coffee and call him back.

"Stark. Did you get my message?"

"Yes. But I didn't listen. What was it?"

"Why do you have voice mail if you don't use it?"

"I don't like talking to machines and I figure that if it's important people will call me back."

"That's actually a more rational explanation than I expected."

"I'm full of surprises. I once ate a salad."

"That's more the answer I was expecting. What I called you about was Nick."

"What about him?"

"He's all right. From all reports, he's back at home with his mother."

I take out a Malediction. Stick it behind my ear for later.

"Did you find out why Burgess had him in the first place?"

"It was a family situation that got out of hand. Apparently, the father was making demands and everyone thought it would be better if Nick spent some time away from home."

"That's very tidy. Do you believe any of it?"

"As far as I can trust my source—which I do—yes."

"I don't know. Burgess doesn't do anything without an angle."

"But what proof do you have? You're obsessed with the Burgess family because Lucius was involved with the ghost-abuse situation last year."

"For good reason. But that's another thing that bugs me. The Golden Vigil shuts the thing down, but it never goes public. Then daddy Burgess has a heart attack and Geoff takes over the family business."

Abbot doesn't say anything for a second.

"Are you actually accusing Geoffrey of killing his father?"

"Not necessarily. I'm just saying I think he's capable of anything."

"Listen to me. You need to leave the Burgess family alone. I appreciate you finding Nick, but that's enough for now. I want you to come back to council meetings for a while. At least until we can think of a new course of action."

I get up and walk the room.

"I'll do it, but I want one more night."

"To do what?"

"Charlie Anpu. I want to follow him again."

"In the current climate, I don't think that's a good idea."

"Maybe you're right about Burgess and I'm out of my mind. But Anpu had one of the angel boxes. That proves he's up to some nefarious shit."

"Nefarious isn't good enough. We have to link it back to Wormwood."

"So, give me the night."

"Is there any way I can trust you to do this quietly?"

"I'm quiet as a butterfly pissing in whipped cream."

I can hear him sigh.

"See, when you talk like that it gives me pause."

"I promise. No break-ins. No cops. No street fights or explosions."

"One night. And you won't get near him personally."

"He's hot lava. *No tocar.*"

"All right. But call me tonight, no matter how late."

"It's a date."

I hang up and go to the window for a smoke.

I hope I can keep my word to Abbot. I'll do my best. Move softly-softly. But if an angel shows up, I don't care if we're on the teacup ride at Disneyland.

I'm killing it.

OF COURSE, CHARLIE lives in a gated community all the way out in fucking Brentwood. Faux–Southern California charm meets Narnia with storm troopers on the parapets. If someone could bottle artisanal air, the residents of Brentwood wouldn't permit ordinary peasant breezes to ruffle the blades of grass on their emerald lawns.

I should have stolen at least a Lexus to come out here. It isn't easy being inconspicuous on a bike in this burg. Just as I'm about to head out to liberate luxury wheels, a silver Rolls Phantom cruises out of the gates. I recognize the license plate as Charlie's and take off after him. It's just like the other night at the Burgess place. Keep a safe distance. No lights until we're back in the land of the living.

He heads into Hollywood. I wonder if he's going back to

Musso's for another supervillain rendezvous when he turns on Highland Avenue and the only thing up that way is the Hollywood Bowl. Finally, some good news from this guy.

For a minute, I think I'm in trouble when he heads in the direction of valet parking, but like so many Scrooge McDucks, he's cheap when it comes to the small things. He leaves the Rolls across two spaces in the peons' lot. I cruise by him and the blonde from the other night like I'm looking for parking. There are a lot of suits and evening gowns in the crowd. Either it's some kind of symphony show or the blue bloods are expecting a starship to take them to the promised land and they want to look good.

I leave the bike in a space at the back of the lot. Stroll casually back to the Rolls. I get out the black blade and jam it into the driver's-side lock. The knife will open anything, even a snooty wagon like this. Naturally, I take a lot of guff from the bumpkin crowd when they see me pulling out of two spaces, but what's a guy to do? We aristocrats are used to a certain level of asshole luxury. I give them the finger and speed away before someone starts asking why a con is piloting a four-wheel Learjet.

Privacy is the first thing I need for my next move. If I can't break into Charlie's mansion, I can sure as hell spend some quality time pawing through his glove compartment or whatever kind of steamer trunk they use in a Rolls.

I drive across town to Sixth Street, back to the warehouse where Burgess's dad used to run his spook-bum fights. We're far enough from civilization that even winos don't hang around here. It's just us rats by the railroad tracks tonight.

The warehouse is still deserted. There's ragged crime-scene tape and cop KEEP OUT signs stapled to the doors, but I'm not going inside. I pull the Rolls around the back.

I pop the glove compartment and start digging. Which yields nothing but the registration, an insurance card, a pen, and some of his lady love's makeup. I check under the seats, but they're cleaner than a surgery. Charlie might cheap out on parking, but he pays for a good cleaning service, which really pisses me off. Couldn't the scrub and vacuum crew leave me one bullet casing or the guest list for a Black Mass?

I check between the seat cushions in the front and back. The leather padding the Rolls is soft as angel food cake. For a second, I consider keeping the heap for a day or two. Candy and I could mess the interior of this thing pretty nicely. But that's not an option in this invisible man operation.

Outside, I check the spotless wheel wells for hidden keys and, again, come up with nothing. Finally, I go around to the trunk, jam the blade in the lock, and open it up.

You could move a family of four in here and have room left over for a kiddie pool. I know that the trunk is going to be pristine and, honestly, I'm just going through the motions at this point. There won't be anything in the back of this idiot's ride but the smell of soap and money. But I keep at it.

Check the sides of the trunk for hollow places where he might be smuggling out-of-state fruit. Take out the tire and shake it to see if there's anything inside but air. It's just one more disappointment. There's more padding under the wheel because, of course, we can't let the poor tire ride in less luxury than the driver. How else will you impress the tow-truck drivers and car thieves?

I pull up the floor mat and my heart does a samba. There's a compartment cut into the metal body of the car. The cuts are ragged at points and there are small gaps between the lid and the body. No car dealer did this. It's as crooked as a Capone aftermarket mod. I hook a finger in a hole on the compartment lid and pull.

Oh, Charlie, my Charlie. What have you been up to?

The first thing that grabs my jaded gaze are the piles of neatly bundled hundred-dollar bills. I pull out a few. Then a few more. The compartment is deeper than I thought at first. There must be half a million in cash back here. As hard as it is, I put the money back and move on to the other goodies. Bags and bags of pills. I recognize a few. Civilian stuff. Pharmaceutical-quality amphetamines. Vicodin. Dilaudid. Some muscle relaxants and a fistful of blue Viagra tabs. Then there are the Sub Rosa goodies. Akira. Dixie Wishbone. Even some Red Sonja, a combination of dried blood and pituitary glands. Only vampires and their flunkies use that stuff, proof Charlie has been cheating on his Sub Rosa friends with bad kids from the other side of the tracks. There's even a Glock 17 with six loaded clips. But it's what's in the secret compartment under the secret compartment that makes my night.

It's an angel box. Maybe the one he had the other night, maybe another. Who cares? I take it out, then put it back in its padded cubbyhole. If Charlie is carrying it, the car is going someplace and I don't want him to notice it's missing. Instead of stealing the whole box, I open it and take the vial of black milk. Let him explain that to whoever the box is for.

The only other thing in the compartment is a complete

mystery. It's kind of, well, dildo-shaped, but made of a dark, heavy metal. There's a thumb-size recess on the thing's blunt end. When I push it, the body of the dildo retracts, exposing a thin, sawtooth-ended tube. I relax my thumb and the thing snaps back into its original shape. Is it something new that an angel gave him? If it's important, why didn't my angel give me one? I bet if I got Charlie high enough on his Dilaudid and some Dom Pérignon, he'd come around, but Abbot doesn't want me to have that kind of fun.

I'll have to console myself with stealing it instead.

I stuff it in my pocket with the black milk and put everything else back where it was. I even wipe the dirt off the tire from where I set it on the ground. Last thing, I wipe my prints from every flat surface.

Back in the driver's seat, I give the dildo one more look-over, and it confirms my instincts. There's a maker's mark by the thumb recess. I can't read it well, but I know the look. The thing was made by a Tick Tock Man.

I start the engine and ever so gently drive the car back into the city. Park it in the lot of a twenty-four-hour Denny's on Sunset and wipe down the interior. Just as I step out of the Rolls, a couple of L.A.'s finest walk out of the Denny's to their cruiser on the other side of the lot. The only thing more conspicuous than my ugly face next to this high-end car would be my ugly face running away from it. So, I just stand there and light a Malediction, like I do it every night.

The cops glance at me and keep walking. They get in the cruiser, head around the corner onto Gower, and disappear. I start breathing again. The only thing worse than punching Charlie Anpu I could have done tonight is punch a couple of cops. The fact they ignored me makes me wonder if I just got lucky or if Abbot pulled strings with LAPD like he said he would. Whatever it was, I'll take it.

I take a drag off the Malediction. The Denny's is just a block from Roscoe's House of Chicken and Waffles, where Candy and I first went out together. If it wasn't so late I'd call her for a midnight rendezvous. But she's probably still rehearsing with Alessa and I'm not going to get in the way of her music. Besides, I have plenty left to do myself, so I let the thought go.

I walk deeper into Hollywood, where I'll have a better chance of finding a cab. I still need to get back to the Hollywood Bowl and pick up the bike. While I walk I call Abbot and tell him what I found.

But I leave out the part where I stole Charlie's car.

A Tick Tock Man is halfway between a garage mechanic and a true hoodoo artist. He makes mechanical familiars for rich Sub Rosas. Some use them for abracadabra purposes and others just keep them around for show. Manimal Mike is a Tick Tock Man, and a good one. He lives over the hill in the San Fernando Valley. It's a bit of a drive after going all the way to the warehouse, but with luck it will be worth it.

I pull up outside the small auto repair place he runs in Chatsworth. Not that he actually repairs cars. He just keeps a few junkers around for show so that no one will guess what he's really doing inside.

It's late and Manimal Mike has locked the metal sliding gate to the garage. I bang on it and shout until someone opens the door to the back room. All I can see is a silhouette lit from behind, but I can tell it's a big man with an even bigger wrench in his massive mitt. He heads for the gate and I take a step back into the light outside the garage where he can see me. The mobile-home-size silhouette stops for a second and cocks its head. I hold out my arms and give him a stupid little wave.

"Stark!" he says through a Russian accent thick enough that you could chisel it into bowling pins. "How are you?"

"Great, Pavel. Is Mike home?"

"Of course. Of course," he says, tugging at a ring of keys attached to his belt by a thin chain. A second later, he pushes the gate aside and lets me in. Gets me in a big bear hug when I come through. Pavel is one of Manimal Mike's cousins. It's not that Pavel loves me so much. He treats everybody he likes this way. He and his little brother, Ilya, are Vucaris. Russian beast men. Imagine a wolf or bear in human skin. They're nice to have on your side in a fight, but if they're not on your side, you'll want to make sure your life insurance is paid up.

Pavel leads me into the back, where Manimal Mike has his workshop. The place is full of half-constructed mechanical animals. Everything from squirrels to Bengal tigers. It's a beautiful place in its way, part zoo and part mad scientist's lair. Pavel calls to him and Mike looks up. He puts down his tools and comes over.

"Stark. How are you doing?" he says, and we shake hands.

"Just fine, Mike. It looks like you're getting along all right."

It's true. The first time I was in Mike's workshop, not only was it a chaotic grease pit, but he was playing Billy Flinch, a kind of one-person William Tell game where you try to shoot a glass off your head with a ricochet. Aim wrong and you'll blow a hole in the wall. Aim wronger and you'll blow your brains to Fresno. But Mike isn't into that anymore. He's not in the very top tier of L.A. Tick Tock Men, but he's on his way. All he needs are a few more of the right customers.

"Things are going pretty well," he says. "Did you know I'm making a Persian cat for Tuatha Fortune?"

"That's great news. A couple of more clients like her and you'll be setting up shop in Beverly Hills."

He wipes machine oil off his hands with a rag.

"That's why I have to make this cat perfect. Want to see it?"

"Another time. This isn't actually a social call."

He nods. "This time of night, I had a feeling."

I take the dildo from my pocket and hand it to him.

"Any idea what that is?"

He turns it around in his hands. Looks at it from all angles. When he finds the recessed button, he pushes it. The thing slides open and he lets it close again.

"Beautiful work," he says. "Did you notice there was no sound? That's some ace engineering."

"Yeah, wonderful. But what is it?"

He takes it to his workbench and examines it under the big magnifier attached to an adjustable metal arm.

"The metal is cold iron," he says. "High quality. Beautiful workmanship. The teeth at the end of the boring mechanism are in perfect alignment."

"Boring? So, it's some kind of drill."

"It could be," he says, and brings the dildo back to me. Opens it up and points to small clips inside the body.

"They hold something. My guess is it's for seating small mechanical parts in a larger mechanism."

"Any idea what?"

He shakes his head. "It could be anything."

"Maybe a box? Could you use it to make a small box? Something with delicate metal parts?"

"Definitely. If you want to leave it with me for a while, I can play with it and tell you exactly how it works."

I take it out of his hands.

"Can't do it. I liberated it from the car of one of our betters, so you don't want to be caught with it."

"No, I do not," he says, walking back to his workbench.

I follow him over and show him the bottom of the drill.

"What's this?"

"It looks like a maker's mark," he says.

He puts it back under the magnifier and shines a light on it.

In a minute he says, "Damn."

"What?"

He hands it back to me.

"Whatever that is, it cost someone a fortune. Atticus Rose made it."

There's a familiar name. Rose was one of the most famous Tick Tock Men in L.A. At least until me, Candy, and Brigitte busted up his workshop. No one has heard much about him since, but it looks like he's far from retired.

"Do you have any idea where he might be? Any rumors in the Tick Tock world?"

Mike picks up a tiny saw. Plays with it while he talks. I don't need to see his eyes or hear his heart to know he's nervous.

"Nothing. Personally, I think if he's still around—and it sure looks like he is—he's got one full-time private client."

I put the drill back in my pocket.

"Thanks a lot, Mike. I owe you for this."

"If you want to pay me back, forget you were here. I don't need trouble right now."

"Don't worry. I didn't tell anyone where I was going and I won't."

"Cool," he says. Then quietly, "Still, I'd love to see the workshop that came out of. Rose always had the best of everything."

"It would take someone with heavy money to set him up, I bet."

Mike's eyes widen a little.

"The kind of work he does, just his equipment is going to run four or five million dollars. That doesn't include the workshop itself, materials, and maybe an assistant."

"I've got the picture. Thanks again."

"How's the arm skin working out for you?" he says, touching his left arm.

I flex the fingers on my Kissi arm.

"I'm not wearing it now, but it's really come in handy."

"That's great to hear. Let me know if you need more."

"You're a prince, Mike."

I wave to his cousins as I head for the door. Pavel follows me out and locks the gate behind me.

"*Do svidaniya,* Pavel."

He laughs. I put my hand to my heart, wounded.

"I didn't say it right, did I?"

"You say it right for parrot or little sister's talking doll."

"Take it easy, Pavel."

He waves a hand and goes back into the shop repeating *"do svidaniya"* to himself, adding little bird squawks every now and then.

I get on the Hellion hog and head home.

So, someone in town has a pet Tick Tock Man on the payroll, maybe turning out more angel boxes. But who are they for? It has to be Wormwood and some of their lackeys. How much black milk is there floating in L.A.? My guess is not too much. If we were rolling in the stuff, Karael would have mentioned it to me when he gave me the sample. And that psycho angel wouldn't have had to carve me up like an Easter ham. That means whoever has Rose on the payroll is getting ready for more of the black stuff to hit town. That's one problem.

The other is that I still don't know what the hell they'd use it for. Allegra put one tiny drop too many on the slide and it wiped out her swimming meat. No one is getting high off the stuff, that's for sure. And unless someone is doing a magic act teaching pork chops the flying trapeze, no one is using it to reanimate dead things.

So forget the milk for now. What about the drill? If I can figure out who's got Rose on the payroll, I'm sure it will get me the rest of the information. Good-time Charlie is the logical suspect. He's got the money and he had the drill. But Abbot is right. I can't touch him for now. If I'm wrong, going for Charlie will send whoever has Rose underground, and that's the last thing I want.

Shit. This means I have to think and be patient, my two least favorite things.

When I get home, Candy is curled up in bed. I go in and kiss her and she wraps an arm around me.

"You should hear me play now," she says sleepily. "I'm goddamn Rick Derringer."

"You always were, baby."

"Fucking A. I'm the king of the wild frontier."

A second later, she's back asleep.

Elvis has left the building.

CANDY IS BACK at work when I get a call from Vidocq asking me to come over. After the cops' giving me a pass last night, I'm feeling better about riding the Hellion hog and wearing my real face during daylight hours. Glamours are easy, but if you do them too much they get itchy. But it might be time to switch out the license plate on the bike. The owner has probably reported it missing. It's harder finding expensive motorcycles to steal because their owners don't like to leave them on the street. I have a policy of only stealing pricy vehicles because I know the owners will have good insurance. It's like what my mom said: "Only bums steal from bums." I might be a killer, an Abomination, and a thief, but I'm not a bum.

Traffic is light and I make it to Vidocq's in good time.

"James," he says, and hugs me, pulling me inside. I can smell the booze on him from out in the hall. I pick up a bottle of expensive-looking red wine from the coffee table.

"Are we celebrating something?"

He puts an arm on my shoulder.

"The light. The air. The fact we have been through so much and lived to talk about it."

From the kitchen, Liliane says, "We are all little miracles, right Eugène?"

I missed her when I came in. She's as tanked as Vidocq. I hold up the wine bottle.

"Hey there. Nice stuff you brought."

She comes into the living room.

"Oh. You know wine?"

"No. I was just being polite."

She and Vidocq laugh a little too much at that. Liliane takes the bottle from my hand and pours me a glass. I hold it up to them both and take a sip. It's nice. A good excuse to get hammered with your ex while your current girlfriend is at work. I look at Liliane.

"I'll admit I was a little confused at Bamboo House the other night. What should I call you now?"

"For safety's sake, you should probably continue to use 'Marilyne' in public," says Vidocq. "Liliane is only a name for private moments."

"It's true," she says. "In Los Angeles on this day, in this year, I'm Marilyne. The name cost me quite a lot of money. I need to get my money's worth."

Vidocq takes a big swig of wine and settles on the sofa. Liliane sits down next to him. I take the chair across from them.

"We've both had many names over the years. I've lost count of how many," Vidocq says.

"And it gets harder every year. A century ago, with a few pieces of paper you could be anyone you wanted to be. Travel the world and come home again. These days, it's all finger-prints and computer chips in your passport."

Vidocq sighs, drinks.

"It's one of the many reasons I've never returned to Paris. I've simply waited too long."

"It's why I'm applying for citizenship," says Liliane. "Travel is difficult for people like us. It will be even harder in the future. Soon, just staying alive and anonymous will be a nightmare."

Vidocq puts his hand on hers. Gives it a squeeze.

"We will get by. There's always a way. Right, James?"

He points his glass in my direction and mock-whispers to Liliane, "Young James here is legally dead, yet he walks the streets and runs a business. Together, we will all survive."

"Together," says Liliane.

They look at me.

"Together," I say, and finish my wine.

Vidocq pours me another. I look around the place. There are books open and lab equipment scattered across his worktable.

"So, what have you kids been up to today?"

Vidocq sits up, looking excited in that way only drunk people can.

"Liliane carried on my work after my apparent death all those years ago. She became a noted alchemist in Europe."

"Perhaps not noted, but noticed," she says. "It's why I work, and enjoy working, in laboratories now. It feels like home."

"I've been showing her my tools and research materials. It's lovely to have a fellow worker of the way to share things with."

I lean back and cross my legs.

"Like they say, sharing is caring."

They're drunk enough to find that funny too.

"Excuse me for a moment," says Liliane, and she heads for the bathroom.

When she's gone I look at Vidocq. He grins like a lovestruck twelve-year-old.

I say, "What's going on here, man? Did you invite me over to show me some work or to be your alibi?"

He frowns. Starts to pour me more wine. I put my hand over the glass and he sets down the bottle.

"James, believe me. Nothing untoward has happened."

"Yet."

He turns the glass around in his hands.

"I was hoping that you'd better comprehend the thrill I feel being with Liliane. We have a common bond experienced by no one else. Eternal life. Yes, I've spent time with ancient vampires and alchemists who have extended their lives, but those are not the same things as immortality," he says. Then, "Think of it this way. Imagine if you met another person, man or woman, with whom you shared the experience of Hell. Wouldn't you be drawn to that person? The moments of trauma. The moments of beauty. I know you understand what I'm talking about."

He's right, of course. All those years I spent alive Downtown. And then there's the nephilim thing. There's no one in the universe like me, but I never really thought of it that way before. I've always known I was a freak, so it never occurred to me what it might be like to meet someone who'd been through the same shit, someone I could talk to about it. My old girlfriend, Alice, was dead when I came back to L.A., so I never got a chance to talk to her about anything. Even Candy, with as much as she's been though, still has a community. There are thousands of Jades in the world. Plenty of monsters too, but only one of me.

But there's only one Allegra too and Vidocq better remember that or I'll remind him. Hard.

"I get your point. I'd like to have a war buddy too. But just reel it in a little. Okay?"

"Perhaps you're right," he says. "I've been overcome since meeting her. You know how much I love Allegra, but until I met Liliane again, I never knew how truly lonely I was."

"Then see a shrink. Until then, cool it with the prom-night stuff."

"You have a point."

Liliane comes back into the room.

"What have you gentlemen been discussing while I was gone?"

I reach into my pocket and take out the vial of black milk. "This."

"You found more," says Vidocq, a little more focused than before.

"What is it?" says Liliane.

"We're not sure yet," Vidocq says. "It's a substance James calls black milk. Believe it or not, it was a gift from a—"

"A friend from out of town. Neither of us was supposed to have it and she never got the chance to tell me what it's for."

"May I see it?" Liliane says.

Vidocq gives her the vial and she holds it up to the light. Shakes it a little.

"It is dangerous," he says.

"Is it all right to open?"

I politely take it back from her and set it on the table.

"You might want to hold off while you have a belly full of wine."

She gives me a loose-necked shake of her head.

"I work with a lot of odd chemicals in my lab all the time. Some of them don't smell like roses either, but I manage."

"I wasn't calling you a lightweight."

"Good, because you should have seen some of the things that were in Eugène's little dungeon in Paris. The most god-awful smells you can imagine."

"What was it you used to call it?"

"Your perfumed abattoir."

He chuckles lightly.

"That's it. I once experimented with a Hand of Glory, sub-jecting it to an array of chemicals, potions, even electrical stimulation. All in hopes of reviving it."

I look at him.

"You tried to bring a hand back to life? What the hell for?"

He shrugs.

"To see if I could. I was more reckless and ambitious in those days. We all were. They were exciting times."

Liliane nudges him with her shoulder.

"They certainly were."

He gives me a sheepish smile.

Liliane turns to me.

"Speaking of hands, James, what's wrong with yours? If you don't mind me asking?"

I give Vidocq a look. He nods.

"It's all right. She's seen much in two hundred years. She can handle it."

I shrug off my coat and glove. Roll up my shirtsleeve, giving her a full-frontal look at my biomechanical flipper.

Her eyes widen. Liliane puts a hand to her mouth. She looks at me, then Vidocq.

She says, "Would it be all right if I touched it?"

"Sure. I suppose so."

She comes around the table and runs her fingers down the length of my arm, from shoulder to fingertip. She examines my wrist and flexes my elbow, watching the weird gearlike growths and the flat gray-black bands that do the job of muscles.

"Thank you," she says. She goes back and sits near Vidocq. "Wherever did you get it?"

I roll down my sleeve and put on my coat.

"Another out-of-town friend."

"You get so many interesting visitors."

"That he does," says Vidocq.

I get an idea, and take the drill out of my pocket and hold it up to them.

"You've both been around a lot of weird gear. You ever see something like that before?"

They take the drill and look it over together. Liliane finds the button on the end and pushes it. Both smile when the mechanism retracts and closes again.

Vidocq shrugs and Liliane shakes her head.

"No. I'm sorry," she says.

"Neither have I. Do you have any idea what it's for?" says Vidocq.

"A friend who knows about these things thinks it's some kind of precision drill for making delicate objects. Or maybe it belongs to a high-rent Tick Tock Man."

"A Tick Tock Man?" says Liliane.

"They make expensive windup toys for people burdened by too much money."

"That's a burden I wouldn't mind trying."

"You and me both."

Liliane looks at her watch and makes a face.

"Look at the time. I have to get back to work."

She and Vidocq stand. They say something French to each other and both laugh. She kisses him on both cheeks and comes around to my side of the table. Everyone else is standing, so I do too. She gives me a couple of quick air kisses and says, "It was lovely spending more time with you, James. I hope we get to do it again sometime."

"Sure. Sometime."

Vidocq shows her to the door, then drops back down onto the sofa.

He looks at me.

"Are you going to continue your lecture? If so, I'm going to need more wine."

I hold up my hands.

"No more lectures. Just this: if you break Allegra's heart, I'm going to kick your ass."

"And I would deserve it."

"I'm glad you understand. Now—what the hell is the story with you two? What happened back in Paris?"

He sighs and picks up his wineglass, settling against the back of the sofa, looking exhausted.

"I don't think I have the energy for a long tale right now."

"Then give me the TV-pitch version."

He smiles, but he still looks tired. Not tired. More like deflated. He was high on Lilianc and the past and now they're both gone.

"She murdered me," he says finally. "In the spring of—if memory serves—1857."

I look at him, waiting for him to go on. But he doesn't.

"That's it? She murdered you and now you're best friends. What the hell happened back then?"

"It's not something I'm proud of," he says. "I don't really want to talk about it."

"I've killed pretty much everything in this world and the next that can be killed. I'm all out of judgment."

He sits up with a wan smile on his face.

"Liliane and I lived and worked together for many years and were happy. But in the end, she suspected me of an infidelity."

"Was she right?"

He nods.

"With the wife of a police official. She was lovely. And I didn't much care for the police of that time. You must understand that."

"I do. So, what happened?"

"I was old. I felt the years acutely. People died early and often badly back then. There were dozens of patent medicines at the time that promised revivification. But they were all frauds. I experimented with mesmerism. Electricity was all the rage. I experimented with animals. Old ones. Sick ones. To see if I could reenergize them. I experimented on myself with repeated shocks of different voltages to different parts of my body."

"Did any of it help?"

"A few things. In small ways and not for very long. Finally I came across a formula in an obscure British pamphlet on folk medicine. I recognized some of the formulae as coming from ancient alchemical texts. They had been disguised to appear as simple nostrums. One in particular caught my eye. I'd never seen anything like it before, but I recognized most of the ingredients and thought it might make the basis of what I was looking for."

"And here you are. I guess it worked."

He wags a finger at me.

"No. It didn't. But I kept working with it. Modifying it to increase its potency. One particular batch demonstrated a dramatic effect. Overnight, the spots on my hands disappeared. My vision improved and I felt my old strength restored. But, as with my other successes, the effects wore off quickly."

"Something like that could drive a person a little crazy."

"It did. I think that's what prompted my affair. The fear of death. The scent of the grave."

"But you obviously came up with something that worked."

"Never. I was a complete failure. Nothing I tried worked for more than a few hours. A day at most. I was despondent. And the more despondent I became, the more the affair intensified."

"So, who figured out the secret?"

"Liliane. Just before she poisoned me."

He leaves that floating in the air while he pours more wine.

"I had prepared a new potion from my most promising experiments. But it wasn't a fast process. The potion had to age for a few days in a cool, darkened cabinet. I believe it was during those few days that Liliane learned of the affair."

I try to picture him old and dying. I don't like it.

"She spiked your formula, didn't she?"

"Yes," he says. "And created a miracle. I died. Or seemed to. I was immobile for two days. In one stroke of luck, Liliane regretted what she'd done and kept my body at home, not telling anyone what had happened. But I remained dead. Or so it seemed. Finally, on the third day—and this part of the story she just told me today—she wrote a note confessing what she had done and took the potion herself."

"At which point you woke up."

"*Exactement*. And I found her dead. I was heartbroken. But I was also young again. Well, as young as you see me now. My hair was still gray. The lines around my eyes remained. I was no spring chicken, but I felt strong and alive. I was also frightened and my mind remained fogged for a long time. I was afraid people would think that I had killed Liliane in revenge. And if they didn't, what would they make of my transformation? We were long past the legal persecution of witches, but ordinary people had never lost their fear of the unexplained. So, I packed a few bags and disappeared."

"What happened to Liliane?"

"Like me, she woke up. In her case, during her funeral preparations. Her revival caused the exact uproar I had avoided. The police were called. François Grillet, the police official with whose wife I had conducted my affair, arrived first at poor Liliane's resurrection. Unfortunately, he knew about the affair by this time and recognized Liliane as the lover of his greatest enemy. So, he took this woman who shouldn't have been alive and stabbed her in the heart."

"And because she'd popped out of the casket, he could claim anything he wanted."

"You understand these monstrosities so well, James," he says before settling back against the sofa. "Well, after that, no respectable mortician would have anything to do with Liliane's apparently dead body. She was taken to a paupers' cemetery to be interred in a mass grave with the lost and forgotten. But, like me, on the third day she awoke before she could be put into the ground. She understood what had happened and knew that she could never live in normal Parisian society again. She escaped and crossed the continent for decades, using the alchemical techniques she learned from me to pay her way. In fact, she only went back to France as a refugee when Herr Hitler breathed his last. She's been living there ever since."

I flex my Kissi hand, feeling the sheer strangeness of it for the first time in a year.

"It's a nice story, but you're leaving out something."

"Am I?"

"The part where you kill François Grillet."

He laughs.

"See? You do understand."

He takes a long breath.

"The story of *la femme revenante* was everywhere. When I heard about what Grillet had done to Liliane, I surmised what had really happened. So, one night while the gentleman was in bed, I crept in and cut his throat. When I was recognized and men came for me, I killed them too. I'd seen the grave once, thought that I had lost my great love to it, and was not about to be sent to the next world by such curs."

I watch him, sprawled on the sofa, half drunk and with tears in his eyes.

"You're still in love with her, aren't you?"

"Who can say?" he mumbles.

"I do. You're in love with the woman who murdered you."

"It sounds strange when you say it like that. But it was so long ago. Time has healed so much of what happened between us."

I shake my head.

"This is all very sweet. Very *Romeo and Juliet*. Just be careful, man. Don't do something stupid that's going to get you poisoned again."

He sits back up.

"I'm not foolish enough to make that mistake again."

"I'm glad to hear it."

Vidocq pushes back his hair and wipes the tears from his eyes.

"Thank you. I've never been able to tell anyone the whole story before. It's good to get it out."

"Are you going to tell Allegra?"

"No," he says. "Even after all this time, one remains ashamed of the mistakes of one's past. I hope, James, that you will take pity on a very old fool and keep my secret."

He looks at me until I nod.

"Just don't do anything fucking stupid. You're a big boy, so I'm just going to worry about Allegra."

"And bruising my ass."

"Yep."

"Understood," he says.

I look around the room.

"We've all got skeletons in the closet, I suppose. Did I ever tell you about how I helped fake the moon landing?"

He laughs, not so drunk this time.

"No. You must enlighten me sometime."

I'm about to say something dumb when the door opens and Allegra comes in. She looks at Vidocq, then at me, then at all the wine on the table.

"I see you two have had a productive afternoon."

"Your old man was telling me alchemy stories. Tell her how you invented water."

She puts down her coat and bag and sits down next to Vidocq. He puts an arm around her.

"That was you?" she says. She looks at him. "Are you keeping secrets from me?"

"Never, my dear. Never."

I get up, feeling a little uncomfortable seeing her where Liliane was a few minutes earlier. Allegra spots the bottle of black milk and picks it up.

"You brought it back," she says.

"Actually, that's a new bottle."

Vidocq sits up at that.

"James, since you now have two bottles, might we keep this one for a while?"

"I want to say no, but I also want to know more about the stuff. Keep it, but don't let anyone know you have it."

Allegra makes a motion at her lips like turning a key.

"Tick a lock," she says.

We say our good-byes and I take the industrial elevator down to the Hellion hog.

Isn't life one big bowl of what-the-fuck? I was surprised upstairs when Vidocq all but admitted that he was still in love with his killer. At that moment, I didn't understand how he could do it. By the time I get to the bike, I know exactly. Alice and I were together for years. It wasn't until she was dead and I met her ghost that she showed me the skeleton hanging in *her* closet. She'd been sent to spy on me by the Sub Rosa council. Alice was my Mata Hari, passing on our pillow talk to paranoid magicians convinced I was making murder potions with my chemistry set. But in the end, she loved me, and when I saw her after missing her all those years, it took me all of ten seconds to forgive her. I don't know if that makes any more sense than what Vidocq said went down between him and Liliane. What I do know is that a famous dead guy once said, "Life is a bucket of shit with a barbed-wire handle." Maybe that's all any of this love crap comes down to. Finding someone to carry your load of shit with, even when your hands get raw and bloody. No one's ever going to turn that into a love song, but if some lunatic did, I'd be first in line to buy a copy for Candy.

SHE GETS HOME around six, taking the night off from work and guitar lessons.

"We're going to start getting the whole band together soon. Alessa and I have worked out a bunch of guitar parts and they'll sound great with bass and drums."

"I'm sure Fairuza and Cindil will be happy to hear you haven't forgotten them."

"I've been talking to both of them. They know we're working some things out and they're cool with it."

"I can't wait to hear the new songs."

"Me too," she says.

She seems a little preoccupied, but with her rehearsals and a full-time job, she gets tired early. Working on the council doesn't take that many hours a week, and Kasabian hates having me in the store, so normally I have nothing but time. The big skeleton in *my* closet is that sometimes I pray for maniac angels and bastards like Wormwood to come after me. I think I'm a crisis junkie. Between holocausts, I watch movies, listen to music, and work a few hours downstairs. I have no idea what the hell else I'm supposed to do the rest of the time. I'm like a college pothead slacker, zoned out on the sofa, then panicking because I have to write a book report on *Silas Marner*. Candy thinks it's all PTSD blowback. Maybe she's right. I don't know what I'd do right now if I didn't have clowns like Charlie and Burgess to go after. My nightmares have gone away and even the headaches are better. Maybe my best bet for staying sane is to get Jason Voorhees to chase me with a machete the rest of my life.

We order Thai food and listen to some of the records Candy and Alessa have been learning songs from. After we're done eating, Candy settles down against me for a while. I tell her about meeting with Liliane and Vidocq about black milk and the drill, but I don't go into anything of them mooning over each other. It's just too weird and it feels like gossip. Besides, if Vidocq pulls his shit together it won't mean anything in the long run. Candy asks to see the drill. I get it and she plays with it for a few minutes before losing interest and setting it on the table.

"Abbot's got you running around all over the place. I'm glad you could make a few minutes for me," she says.

"Excuse me, ma'am. You're the one who's been missing in action. I'm out chasing international jewel thieves and you're playing bongos with your beatnik friends."

"You know it, daddy-o," she says. Then, "Hey, that thing with Nick and Geoffrey Burgess. That was a big coincidence you being there, right?"

"Yeah. The kid was the last thing I was looking for. Why?"

"It's nothing. I just wondered if it had anything to do with Elsabeth."

"Who's that?"

"She's Burgess's wife."

"Why would I care about her?"

"Abbot told you about Nick. I thought he might have heard about it from his sister."

I look at her.

"You're sure about that?"

"Julie stumbled across it and had me double-check. Elsabeth Abbot has been Mrs. Elsabeth Burgess for three years now."

Fucking Abbot. What kind of games has he been playing with me? I knew I should never trust that blue-blood fuck.

"I need to go out."

I start to get up, but Candy grabs my arm.

"Don't go running off yet. Please. I shouldn't have said anything about Abbot. I don't know why I did it. Maybe I was putting off something else."

I sit back down.

"What have you been putting off?"

She sits back, wrapping her arms around her knees.

"You remember a while back, you got mad when I talked to Julie about you maybe having PTSD?"

"Yeah."

"And then you asked if I was upset about Rinko coming by."

Candy and Rinko got together when I was stranded Downtown last year and everyone thought I was dead. She's never forgiven me because, after an ultimatum, Candy decided to stay with me.

"I remember."

"You asked if I still wanted to go out with Rinko, and I said no. But I also said that I sometimes miss dating women."

"Did you change your mind about Rinko? I told you to do what you wanted. I'm not going to lock the doors or tell you how to live your life."

"It has nothing to do with Rinko," she says.

No, of course it wouldn't. Would it? I'm such an idiot.

"It's Alessa, isn't it? She's who you're talking about."

She bobs her head once and looks at me.

"Are you mad? Do you hate me?"

"I'm not mad and I'm never going to hate you."

"Yes, but how do you feel? What are you thinking?"

"I don't know," I tell her, and it's the truth. "I'm not playing games. I just don't know."

Candy turns around so she's facing me. She puts a hand on my shoulder.

"You can tell me no, you know. Say it and I'll never mention it again."

I blink a couple of times. Scratch the bridge of my nose.

"You know I'm not going to tell you no. Listen, I barely know what to do with myself most of the time. Without a crisis, I don't have much to offer anyone."

She bites her lip. "We haven't done anything," she says.

"It's okay. I know that."

"Is that all? You can say whatever you want."

I shake my head.

"If you're looking for a way out, I'm not Rinko. I don't do ultimatums."

"And that's one of the things I like best about you. You don't play games."

"But let me ask you something: Have you told Alessa who you really are?"

"Of course not," she says.

"Then she only knows you as Chihiro."

"Right."

"How are you going to handle that?"

"What do you mean? I'm not going to say anything about Candy."

"Which means most of what she knows about you is a lie. It's the cover story we made up after Candy 'died.'"

Her eyes go blank for a minute. I think she's getting so used to thinking of herself as both Chihiro and Candy at the same time, she didn't consider how that would affect someone who didn't know her before.

"I never thought of that."

"You can't tell her about Candy. Or that you're a Jade. Not yet anyway. And if you do go for this, you better think about what that means for anything long term."

She sits back against the sofa. Frowns a little.

"This advice thing you're doing right now, are you just trying to avoid talking about what you're really feeling?"

"Probably. But listen, I know you've had other girlfriends. I'm not going to be the guy who tells you you have to live half your life."

She looks at me for a long time, like she's trying to dig her way into my skull.

"Then, if I do this, you're not going to break up with me and throw me out?"

"Only if after all this you still suck at guitar. Then all bets are off."

She puts her arms around me. Puts her head into my neck. I think she might be crying a little.

"Thank you for not hating me for asking."

"You can tell me anything."

"And I'm not going anywhere, you know."

"Me neither."

She moves her head around and kisses me.

"And thank you for trusting me," she says.

"Thanks for being up front with me."

She sits back against the couch. My arm is around her and she holds my hand.

"I'd kill anyone who hurt you, you know," says Candy.

"I know."

"That's why I never want to do it. I'd have to kick my own ass."

"That would be something to see."

"Wouldn't it, though?"

She takes my hand and pulls me into the bedroom.

In the morning, I carry down bits and pieces of the broken side tables and bed frame to the Dumpster. They're going to cost money, but I think the mattress is still salvageable.

I DON'T KNOW what to think about anything as I have coffee and get dressed. The one thing I'm sure of is that I'm a lot more pissed about Abbot than upset about Candy. She's still someone I can trust. Abbot is someone I can't. He's played me for a fool and it's time to do something about that. I get out my phone and text him.

I'm coming over. Be there or I'm burning your boat.

I grab the Hellion hog and hit the freeway as fast as I can, lane-splitting at eighty all the way to Marina del Rey.

When I get to the boatyard, I park the bike facing the street, in case things go weird and I have to get out of there fast. I head through the security gate and down the pier. Lucky me. Willem and a couple of Abbot's security guys are waiting for me at the boat. I brace for trouble, but Willem steps back and ushers me onto the deck.

"Good to see you, Mr. Stark. Right this way."

I stop on the boat's gangway.

"What's that mean?"

"The augur is waiting for you."

"He better be."

I start onto the boat when Willem calls.

"Audsley Ishii sends his regards. He says he's sorry about your friend's car. He'll be more careful next time."

I point at Willem and his cop mustache.

"You're on the list, Willem."

"What list?"

"The haunting list. If Audsley kills me it's going to be moaning and rattling chains every night for you. And I don't take weekends or holidays off."

He looks to his men, then back at me.

"I'll just get an exorcist."

"Then I'll haunt your car. I'll haunt your man cave on the boat here. Hell, I'll haunt your shoes. There aren't enough exorcists in L.A. to keep up with me."

"Big talker, all you cons."

"I have friends in low places, Willem. You have no idea the shit I can get up to."

"Are you two done?"

I look around. Abbot is on the deck in chinos and a sporty shirt. He doesn't look happy. Good.

"Come inside, Stark," he says.

I follow him into the living room area. He offers me a chair. I shake my head. He goes to a table and picks up a drink.

"So, what's this about burning my boat?"

"Elsabeth Burgess. That name ring a bell?"

He looks at his drink for a minute and sits down.

"Who do you think has been getting me all the information about Wormwood?"

"Thanks, but I figured that part out. What I want to know

is why you didn't tell me *you* were connected to Wormwood? And don't fucking lie to me because I'll know it."

That sends Abbot's blood pressure up a little because he knows I'm telling the truth.

He sets down the drink. Opens his hands and closes them again.

"I was afraid you wouldn't work with me if you knew I had family in Wormwood."

"Good guess."

He looks out a window, then back at me.

"Anyway, while I'm confessing my sins, I'll tell you something else."

"What?"

"I was using you a little. See, I was hoping that you'd kill Geoff Burgess."

I take a step forward and stare down at him. He looks uncomfortable.

"I'd feel much better if you sat down."

"I'm fine where I am."

He raps his knuckles nervously on his knee a couple of times. "Understand, Elsa was taking a big risk feeding me information about Geoffrey and the others. I think you're a good person underneath this image you put out to people, but you do have a habit of . . ."

"Of what?"

"Flying off the handle. I couldn't risk my sister's safety."

"You'd have left me out there with all Wormwood after me. You fed me just enough information to hang myself."

"No. I would never have done that."

I check his eyes. What do you know? It looks like he's telling the truth.

He says, "I'm not just the augur, remember. I'm a seer. I saw all this coming. I knew you'd find out. Don't you think I could have done something about today if I knew that you'd be coming to me in this frame of mind?"

"You think you know my frame of mind?"

"You said you were going to burn my boat."

"I suppose I did."

I sit down opposite him.

"If you're such a hot seer why didn't you know where Nick was? Or did you know and waited for me to find him?"

"No. I didn't know about Nick. When I scry I often see multiple outcomes. With Nick it could have gone different ways. There were several outcomes where he ended up dead. And I never saw Geoffrey's involvement. I think Wormwood is being protected against people like me."

"They're working with Hellions and angels. They have a lot of protection."

He makes a fist.

"That's why we need each other. You know that world and I know this. I still want to bring Wormwood down. I understand if you don't believe me. That's one of the outcomes I saw. But I hope you'll stay and see this through with me."

I run everything he said backward and forward in my mind. I've watched his eyes and listened to his heart this whole time and he didn't show any traces of lying. But if Burgess and his crowd are protected from hoodoo, maybe Abbot is too. I don't have a lot of choices here. I have to pick one.

"I'll try it," I tell him. "But don't ever lie to me again."

"Or you'll burn my boat. I know."

"No. I'll kill you. Then I'll burn your boat."

He picks up his glass and takes a drink.

"You'll be interested to know that in every way I saw this conversation, it always ended with that statement."

"Then you know it's true."

"Yes."

"Good. Then we understand each other. So, what happens next?"

Abbot pushes a boyish lock of hair out of his face.

He says, "There's another child missing."

"When?"

"I don't know. Elsa just found out about it."

"But it was after Nick was found."

"It seems so."

"That means the whole story about daddy in Long Beach is bullshit."

"Probably."

"Definitely. Someone had a kid, then lost it. Now they have another kid. Why?"

He shakes his head.

"I don't know."

"Whose kid is it?"

"They're Sub Rosa. You never heard of them—they're not an important family."

"Maybe they want to be."

He looks at me.

"You think someone would give up their child to advance their family position?"

"Some of these families would smother the baby Jesus in the manger if they thought it would get them good seats at the opera."

"I don't want to think about things like that."

"I know. That's why you have me. Don't ask me to take this to Julie. She's going to make a thing out of another lost kid. Bring in the cops right away. It might make whoever has him . . . her?"

"Her."

"It might make whoever has her do something stupid. You're going to have to handle this. Rattle some cages. You're the goddamn augur. Scare some people."

"What will you be doing?"

"I'm working on the black milk. If we know what it is, we might figure out what's really going on. That reminds me."

I take the drill from my pocket.

"Do you know what this is?"

Abbot looks it over.

"No. Sorry. Is that the thing you called a dildo you took from Charles's car?"

"The same. I think it might belong to a Tick Tock Man. I'm going to look for him. You can help with that. See if anyone has any new, expensive familiars."

"I'll do that."

I get up.

"Unless you have something else, I think we're done for now."

He stands.

"Nothing for the moment. Thank you for coming, and thank you for understanding the situation."

I take out a Malediction.

"Things get funny with family."

"They do."

"Tell me something. Are you married?"

He looks at me funny, says, "No."

"Got some kind of significant other?"

"Of course."

"It gets complicated. Doesn't it?"

"Sometimes. But if you're honest with each other, it simplifies things."

I get out my lighter.

"Yeah. Honesty. Like you and me now. Right?"

"Right."

"Okay. I'll call you when I know something."

"I'll do the same."

"Oh. And tell Willem not to threaten me again," I tell him as I walk to the deck. "You I'd have to think about hurting. But him?"

I snap my fingers.

"I'll have a word," says Abbot.

"Thanks."

Willem and his boys are still on the dock when I get off the boat.

I give them a little salute as I go by.

"I'll see you shrimp at the fish fry."

"What does that mean?" Willem says.

"Your boss wants to see you."

I walk away and get on the bike.

Sometimes it's fun taking names when the teacher is out of the room. Willem will complain to Ishii that I ratted him out. Ishii will laugh in his face. Sometimes it's the little things that keep you going.

WHEN I GET back to Max Overdrive, I call Vidocq. The phone rings a few times and goes to voice mail. I'm not in the mood to talk to a device, so I dial Allegra.

"Hi. Sorry to bug you. I'm trying to get ahold of Vidocq. Do you know where he is?"

"Is it about the black milk? Eugène is right here in the clinic working on it with Madame Bovary."

"She's there?"

"In her best little black dress," says Allegra. Her voice is quiet and tense.

"If you don't want her there, throw her out."

"I can't," she says. "Eugène wasn't getting anywhere with his equipment at home, so they're here using some of Kinski's old things."

Allegra doesn't say anything for a minute. I can hear her walking, then closing a door.

"Marilyne or whatever she wants to be called might be a high-tone bitch, but she seems to know her chemistry."

"I'm sorry. They're working on it for me. It's important."

"I know. You don't have to apologize for them."

"Still."

"Thanks," she says. "Hey. You want to get a cup of coffee soon?"

"Sure."

"Tomorrow?"

"I can come by the clinic around noon."

"I'm impressed. That's early for you."

"That's why I'll need the coffee."

CANDY HAS PRACTICE again in the evening. She gives me an extra-big kiss as she leaves. It's nice to see her happy after last night. She really thought I might end things right there over nothing more than words. I know words count for a lot, but we're solid enough that I'm not afraid of much. Even Alessa.

Still . . .

Still I feel the ground shifting beneath my feet. Candy needs something I can never give her. Vidocq is acting like a school kid, reliving fairy tales of gay Paree. And Abbot is a liar. Maybe he had good reasons, but he's still a liar and I'm going to watch my back with him. If it comes down to a choice between me and his sister or being the augur, I know which way it's going to go. Willem and the Backstreet Boys would be happy to do the job for him. Or maybe they'd leave it to Audsley. Then everyone who matters could walk away with clean hands.

Frank Perry's *Doc,* a good western, is playing but I can't look at it anymore. The light is too much. I close my eyes and just listen for a while. But the pain gets worse. I can feel Trotsky inside my head, trying to tunnel out with his ice ax. He's doing a sloppy job of it too. Bone fragments and raw meat pile up behind my eyes, making them ache. I take a couple of aspirin and wash them down with Aqua Regia, but it doesn't help.

When I look up again, the movie is over. I never even heard the closing credits. I turn it off and sit in the dark for a while, but all that does is let Hell back in. Marching angels. Norris Quay's ridiculous face. The barely conscious mob outside Heaven's gates. And Samael, getting sliced and diced. I put on an old pair of sunglasses I find in the dresser and go downstairs. With the shades on I can stand the bright lights.

Kasabian takes one look at me.

"Ladies and gentlemen, it's Link Wray, back from the dead."

He has the news on.

Some politician at City Hall tried texting his cock to an intern and it ended up on Facebook. An old club in Chinatown is closing down. It was the first place I ever saw Skull Valley Sheep Kill. They arrested some high school students in Malibu out at Teddy Osterberg's place. Before he died, Teddy collected old cemeteries like some guys collect model trains. The difference is that Teddy was a ghoul. He dug up and ate a lot of his collection. It looks like maybe ghoulishness is catching. A handful of the kids were eating one of their friends.

The camera pans across the kids' bloody faces. Most are blurred, but they miss one. A handsome jock in a letter jacket. I recognize the look in his eyes. Someone in the group was using Dixie Wishbone. It's a funny drug. It gets the user high, but has a habit of driving anyone around them into a twitching meth-head rage. So, some rich kids go out looking to party at Teddy's abandoned digs. Then one of them drops Dixie. I'll lay you ten-to-one it was the kid being eaten. Now we're left with only one question.

How did these prom kings and queens end up with the stuff in the first place? You don't buy it like weed from Kenny behind the 7-Eleven. These days, you can't even get it in L.A., yet these nobodies got some. And they used it at Teddy's. Teddy wanted to eat me. I saw Teddy die. I'm connected to the place. I get a hollow feeling in my stomach that this is more Wormwood hijinks. Maybe someone figured out that it was me at Burgess's place or with Charlie's car. Maybe this is payback.

Trotsky is really going at it behind my eyes.

Kasabian says something and laughs. I can't hear him. I go upstairs and get my coat. Go out and gun the bike into traffic. It isn't Trotsky anymore. It feels like Death rattling around in my skull. I keep the shades on. It's the only way I can stand the lights.

I don't think. I just point the bike and head across town.

IT DOESN'T TAKE long to get back to the high school. The bouncer at the gym door recognizes me and lets me straight in.

I'm late. The empty pool is surrounded by shirtless, sweating men showing bruises and a few cuts. I don't waste time watching the fight going on in the pit. The bench at the far end of the place is clear. I take off my shirt and boots and head for the other fighters.

The yellow-toothed pit boss intercepts me on the way over.

"It's good to see you back, friend. I thought we'd lost you."

"I've been busy."

"Good. Idle hands and all that. Have you thought more about what we talked about? The offer stands. I can get you a paying fight tomorrow night."

"Like I said, it's a busy time. I haven't had time to think about it."

He pats my arm.

"No worries. We'll talk after."

"Sure."

"Have a good time."

"I plan to."

The current fight ends with a broken nose and a few teeth scattered on the bottom of the pool. The fighters bro-hug it out before climbing from the pit. The pit boss whistles at me and points down. I climb the ladder onto the killing floor.

The guy who comes down with me is a mess. He's almost as scarred as me. Not a big guy. He's more like one of those grim, wiry fucks you see in small-time southern pro wrestling circuits. Mean street fighters and carny brawlers who'll take on all comers. They're not big on technique because they fight like rabid wolves, flat out the whole time.

This could be fun.

We stare at each other from across the ring. When the pit boss gives us the signal to fight, Wolf Man runs straight at me. I sidestep him and he practically slams into the pool wall. It doesn't bother him in the least. He pushes off and comes at me again, this time ducking at the last minute, going for my legs. I get a knee up and he cracks his skull on it. The men around the pool cheer. The Wolf Man rocks back, but shakes it off. He rushes me again and this time I let him grab me around the waist. Thirty seconds into the fight and he's sweating like a pig doing wind sprints. The sweat smells funny too. He's high on something. Angel dust to cut the pain? Maybe this fight will be interesting after all.

I throw a couple of medium-hard punches to the back of his neck. He doesn't even notice. He still has his arms around me, trying to throw off my balance and get me onto the floor. His head is pressed against my belly, exposing one side of his face. I throw a medium, then hard punch into his temple. That loosens his grip. I push him back and give a love tap on the jaw. It staggers him, but doesn't do any real damage. Just pisses him off even more. He comes at me, throwing batshit fists and elbows at my head. I take it all, letting him punch Trotsky right out of my skull.

When it gets boring, I throw two hard shots low into his ribs, doubling him over. Shove him upright and stick a heel kick into his sternum, not hard enough to break bones, but enough to hurt. Then I move in. I was hoping for André the Giant and got a hillbilly tweaker. I don't know what the pit boss was thinking. Fuck them both.

I bounce the Wolf Man off the wall a couple of times and he goes down flat on his back. I stand there a minute; he doesn't move. Stupid me, I think the fight is over. I turn my back on him and head for the ladder, pissed at everyone for setting me up with such a shit fight.

Then my head explodes.

The Wolf Man was playing possum, waiting for me to do exactly what I did. When I turned my back, he grabbed a chunk of broken concrete from the edge of the pool and got me on the back of the head. How do I know? Because he comes around in front so I can see him swing the concrete again. I try to move, but he hits me on the cheek, opening up a nice gash. I feel the blood gush down my chin and onto my chest. He comes at me again and I spit in his face. That stops him long enough for me to get back on my feet.

The damned concrete block is almost as big as his head. When he uses it, it pulls him off balance. I let him swing one more time, and while he's off center I hammer his face. It's a beautiful sensation when I feel the bone around his left eye crack.

He drops the concrete and grabs the side of his head, banshee-screaming. Slipping behind him, I wrap an arm around his neck, squeezing his throat and carotid artery like a two-dollar accordion.

I almost have him unconscious, but he's sweating so hard it's difficult to hold on properly. He moves his head enough to ease the pressure on his neck, then grabs my left arm and bites down. It doesn't hurt, the prosthetic never hurts, but I feel something rip. A funny sound travels around the crowd above us and I get a bad feeling. With a handful of the Wolf Man's hair, I smash his head into the side of the pool until he falls over. He's breathing, but this time he's not getting up.

There are no cheers. No boos. It's dead silence. I look down at my left arm and it's exactly what I was afraid of. The Wolf Man's teeth ripped half the skin off my Kissi prosthetic. There's nothing else to do now. I tear the rest of the skin off and shove it into the Wolf Man's mouth. When I climb out of the pool, everybody backs off. The only one who moves is the pit boss. He comes over, his face wrenched in disgust, like he found his darling daughter banging Gregor Samsa.

"I don't know who or what the fuck you are, but get out of here and never come back."

I reach behind my head, come back with a handful of blood, and toss it on the floor. The pit boss jumps back. Everybody does. It might be radioactive.

I go to the bench and get dressed. No one follows me, but I make sure everyone sees me putting the Colt revolver into the waistband of my jeans.

Quietly, I push through the door, outside into the warm spring dark.

The bouncer says, "Calling it early tonight?"

"You could say that."

I reach into my pocket and take out the sunglasses. Hold them up.

"You want these? I won't need them anymore."

He takes the shades and looks them over. Nods.

"Thanks."

I hold up a hand and walk to the bike.

"You know you're bleeding, right?" he shouts.

"Sometimes you deserve to. You know?"

"I know," he says. Then, "Keep it real, man. See you soon."

"Not likely. Enjoy the glasses."

I cruise into the street and head home.

Well, there it is. An hour ago I was feeling superior to Vidocq and Abbot's bullshit and then I went out and broke my promise to Candy. There's no way I can hide these cuts and bruises from her. I'm not going to try. I deserve whatever happens. Candy was so worried about me leaving her last night. Now I'm the one worried about what she's going to do when she sees me.

At least one thing worked out. My headache is gone.

SHE COMES HOME late. I've showered and the cuts are already healing, but I still look like I shaved with a wheat thresher. Candy stops in the doorway. Comes over and takes my face in her hands.

"What happened to you?"

"I'm okay."

"That's not what I asked."

I look down at her.

"What happened is that I have no idea what's wrong with me. Without action I fall apart. Maybe you're right about the PTSD thing."

"I am and you know it."

"I'm seeing Allegra tomorrow. I'll talk to her about it."

"Promise?"

"I promise."

She looks at me hard.

"Is this about me and Alessa?"

"No. It's me and my shit strictly."

"You better tell me if it's anything else."

"I will."

She lets go of me.

"I'm pretty pissed at you right now."

"You should be."

She crosses her arms.

"If it wasn't about last night, what set it off?"

"There's such a shit storm in my head. Vidocq might be in love with Liliane. Abbot's a liar. I'm a liar. Oh yeah, and some kids ate another kid alive tonight and it might be my fault."

She leads me to the sofa.

"Tell me everything and I mean everything."

So, I do.

And she doesn't leave me.

At the end of it, she leans back and says, "Poor kids. Poor Allegra."

"Yeah."

She takes my hand, still hanging on to the barbed-wire bucket of shit with me. If I came back from Hell for anything, it was for this. Fuck the world. If the whole planet was on fire, I'd stay on this sofa with Candy and let it burn.

"We're in it till the wheels come off, you know," she says.

"Till the wheels come off."

We sit there together like that until she falls asleep against me.

WHEN I GET to the clinic, Allegra is waiting for me outside.

She gives me a quick hug and leads me to a café around the corner. When I was dragged Downtown, Silver Lake was still thrift shops, dingy little corner groceries, working-class bars, people cooking on hot plates in garages, and low-level dope dealers. Now it's Wi-Fi-enabled omelets and gluten-free Vespas.

The café Allegra takes me to has all kinds of local handicrafts on the walls. Handblown glass sculptures. Elaborate ponchos and serapes. Artsy photos of shadows and empty parking lots. In another life I would have pegged the stuff as hippie junk, but the prices are aimed strictly at people who'll pay hundreds for vintage Chuck Taylors and ironic children's watches.

"Not a word," says Allegra when she sees me looking

around. "This place has good coffee and these people are my neighbors. I'd like to keep it that way."

"I'm not saying anything. I was just admiring the hundred-dollar doilies. They'd look charming in my gun drawer."

She looks at me.

"What are you drinking, Stark? I'm buying."

"Coffee. Black."

"I'll get you an espresso. You can play with the little cup when you're done."

"I'll get us a table."

I find one by the window and settle down. Check my reflection in the glass. The bruises are fading and the gash on my cheek is healing fast. Still, you'd have to be on the space station to miss it. The knot on the back of my head from the concrete throbs, but Trotsky is nowhere to be found. I'll take a few bruises for that.

Allegra brings our coffee and sits down, smiling at me.

"What?" I say.

"Are you going to tell me about your face or am I going to have to play twenty questions?"

"It's nothing. I was in a fight I could have avoided, and got what I deserved."

"Mmm-hmm," she says. "No trouble at home, then?"

"Home is fine. What about you?"

She picks up a packet of brown sugar and pours it into her latte.

"I don't know," she says. "Eugène is playing like nothing is going on with his lady love, but I'm not stupid. It might not be so bad if they didn't spend half their time speaking French like they don't want me to know what they're saying."

"I'm sure it's not that. Vidocq just misses jabbering like when he was in France. He'll get over it in a couple of days."

"He better. I'm about to throw him and Madame Defarge out of the clinic."

"They're there now?"

She nods.

"Fairuza is keeping an eye on them for me."

I taste my espresso. It's good. Dammit. How am I supposed to hate people if they make good coffee?

"You can't keep doing this. I know you're trying to be all reasonable, but if they're bugging you this much, you need to say something."

"I know. That's one of the reasons I wanted to see you. Will you come with me when I tell Her Majesty to hit the road?"

"Of course."

"Thanks."

We both drink our coffee. I clear my throat.

"Listen. This PTSD bullshit everyone wants to talk to me about. Hell. I don't know."

"Chihiro told me about your headaches."

"What did she say?"

She sips her coffee like she's thinking.

"Have you ever considered that they're psychosomatic? One of your PTSD symptoms?"

I look around the café, hating it more all of a sudden.

"Even my headaches are crazy? That's fucking beautiful. So what's next? Electroshock. Candy's hoping you can fix me."

"Yes, she is."

"Can you? I'm as tired of this as she is."

Allegra looks surprised, but tries to hide it.

"I know a couple of Lurker-friendly psychiatrists I could recommend."

I lean my arms on the table.

"No shrinks. No yoga or positive visualization. I need something that will actually help."

"There are some medications we could try."

I drop my head onto my arms for a second.

"I was afraid you would say that. Will that stuff even work on a half angel?"

She shrugs.

"Sometimes with psych meds it's like whacking the side of a radio. You have to keep hitting it until something works."

"Or breaks."

"That tells you something too."

I look around the café. It feels stuffy all of a sudden.

"Fuck. I'm like some kid who can't sit still without his Ritalin."

"Ritalin and some other drugs actually help people. Look, if civilian medications don't work, I have some Sub Rosa things we can try."

"I like the sound of that. Let's try the Sub Rosa stuff first."

"You're willing to try then?"

I finish my coffee.

"Yeah. I'll try."

She wipes her lips with a napkin.

"Okay, then. Let's go get you stoned."

"You're enjoying this a little too much."

"I'm usually pulling bullets out of your backside, so, yes, prescribing medication is a welcome change."

We get up.

"Okay, Dr. Frankenstein. Let's go. And we'll give Edith Piaf the boot too."

"I'm more than ready for that," Allegra says.

We go around the corner to the clinic. Fairuza gives me a look when I come in.

"Nice look, Stark. Did Candy whack you with a rolled-up newspaper for not picking up your socks?"

"Go play your drums, young lady. You're not good at comedy."

"I'm playing my drums tonight. The whole band is getting together. You should come by."

"Maybe I will."

Allegra looks at Fairuza and cocks her head at the exam room door.

"They still in there?"

Fairuza rolls her eyes.

"Madame Curie asked me to leave. I was cramping their research."

"Fuck that," says Allegra, and heads for the door. I have to trot to keep up.

We go through and she shuts it again. Vidocq and Liliane turn around. Vidocq grins when he sees me.

"James. I have things to show you," he says.

"Yes. We've learned a lot in the last day," says Liliane.

"Great," says Allegra. "Eugène can tell him about it. You, I want out of here."

Vidocq and Liliane look at each other.

"Allegra. I don't understand," he says.

"No, you don't and we're going to have a serious talk about that when Miss Thing leaves."

Liliane sets down the forceps she was holding. She says, "I'm sorry if I offended you in any way. That was never my intention."

"I don't care about your intentions. I'd just like you to leave."

"But we've made discoveries together," says Vidocq. "We know so much more about the black milk."

"After she leaves," says Allegra.

Liliane puts her hands together.

"Before I go, may I please show you all one thing?"

"No."

"It has to do with James," she says.

"What do you mean?" says Vidocq, looking surprised.

"Please. Let me show you."

Vidocq looks at Allegra.

"Fine," she says. "But then she goes."

"Of course," says Liliane. To me she says, "May I see the drill for a moment?"

I bring it over to her. She takes it and opens the mechanism.

"Stay here so you can see," she tells me.

I look at her working. She puts the top on the vial of black milk and holds it up for me to see.

I nod.

"Now what?"

"Watch."

She takes the vial and snaps it into place inside the drill.

"It's a syringe?" says Vidocq.

"Yes," she says. Then lunges at my arm.

I back up, too fast for her reach.

Vidocq shoves her against the counter.

"Liliane. What is this?"

"Shut up, you oaf," she says, and stabs the syringe into his throat. "Die like you should have died in Paris."

Vidocq collapses, his face turning blue. Allegra screams. While I'm looking at him Liliane comes at me again. I grab her arm and toss her across the room back toward the door. She lands close to Allegra. Liliane swings the syringe at her, but Allegra sees it coming and ducks. She grabs a scalpel off the counter and jams it full force into Liliane's chest.

The syringe hits the floor and Liliane goes down with it. She's hurt, but pulls out the scalpel and throws it away. A stab in the heart didn't stop her before. Liliane throws herself at the syringe, but Allegra steps on her hand. Grabs the syringe and slams it into the side of Liliane's neck. She rolls away, gasps, and pulls the syringe out. But it's too late. She's turning as blue as Vidocq.

"Eugène!" Allegra shouts.

I grab him from the floor and put him on the exam table. His face has gone from blue to black.

I look at Allegra.

"What do we do?"

She scrambles to the cabinets, throwing bottles and boxes onto the floor until she finds what she's looking for. It's a bottle full of a pale liquid. With trembling hands, she takes a long heart syringe and sticks it through the top, drawing out a large portion of the liquid. I tear open Vidocq's shirt and she slams the needle into his chest, hitting the plunger when it's inside. He convulses a couple of times. Breathes once and falls back onto the table. Allegra is crying.

I grab her arm.

"What was that?"

It takes her a second to get it out.

"I put him in the Winter Garden."

The Garden is a kind of hoodoo coma. It stops all activity in a body pretty much indefinitely. It's good for poison and zombie bites. Anything where you don't have a handy antidote in your pocket.

I check Vidocq's eyes. They're all pupil.

"Is the Garden going to work?"

"How the hell do I know?" she says. "I couldn't think of anything else."

I go over and put an arm around her. Allegra holds on to my coat.

The door opens up and Fairuza sticks her head in.

"Your two o'clock is here."

She takes one look at Liliane on the floor, skin turning black and blood on her chest, and almost screams. I grab her and pull her into the room.

When Fairuza can look up from the floor, she sees Vidocq laid out.

"What happened to Eugène?"

I hold her by the shoulders.

"We can talk about that later. Right now you need to be very cool. Go out there and tell the two o'clock they have to reschedule. Can you do that?"

She nods and I look at her hard.

"And try to look a little less like you just saw Darby Crash's ghost. Got me?"

She nods again. Takes a couple of deep breaths.

"I'm okay."

"Good. Go out there, tell them the story, and stay there until I come out for you."

"Okay."

I open the door and push her through.

Allegra is still by Vidocq with her hand on his chest, which is crisscrossed with blackened blood vessels.

Allegra isn't crying anymore. She looks at me. Her voice is raspy when she speaks.

"What the hell just happened?"

"I'm so fucking stupid. Liliane is with Wormwood."

"How do you know?"

"She knew the thing wasn't a drill. Only one way she'd know that."

Allegra looks puzzled.

"They sent her to kill Eugène?"

"No. *Me*. But Vidocq was the way in. She could get to me and use him to find out what we knew about black milk."

She strokes Vidocq's brow.

"She was always going to kill him, wasn't she?"

"She came here for me."

"Then she just did Eugène for fun."

I nod.

"Yeah. A two-hundred-year-old grudge."

Allegra's hands shake. I look at her.

"She would have done you too, you know."

She ignores me.

"I just killed someone," she whispers.

"You saved both of us. Liliane wasn't going to stop."

She looks up at me.

"What do I do? Call the police?"

I go over to her.

"No. Too many cops are on the take. Let me handle the body. You stay with Vidocq."

She looks down at him.

I put the syringe in my pocket. Straighten Liliane's body, then grab some paper towels to wipe her blood off the floor. I pile them on her chest and look back at Allegra.

"I'm going to need some garbage bags and duct tape. Also, your car. Mine is still dead."

She goes to her purse and hands me the keys. I pocket them.

Fairuza knocks on the door. Opens it a crack and sticks her head in.

"Everyone is gone," she says.

She looks at the bodies.

"Can I go too?"

"Of course," Allegra says.

Before she can go, I take her arm.

"No one gets to know about this. You'll put yourself in danger. Understand?"

"Yes," she says.

"I want you to go straight home. You're going to freak out in a while. That's okay as long as you don't tell anyone about this."

She nods.

"Normally, I'd say call me, but I'm going to be busy. You can talk to Candy."

"We're supposed to rehearse tonight."

"Rehearsal is off. I'm going upstairs to get her."

I leave them in the exam room and go up to Julie's office. Give Candy a quick rundown of what happened.

"Tell Julie you have a family emergency or something and come downstairs."

"Right."

I go back to the clinic. I don't want to leave Allegra or Fairuza alone with a body for too long.

Fairuza is standing with Allegra by Vidocq when I get back. She's pale and looks like she wants to throw up, but she's keeping it together.

Candy comes in a couple of minutes later. I go to her.

"Fairuza is in no shape to drive. You're her friend. You should probably take her home. I'll stay with Allegra and Vidocq."

Candy tells Fairuza she's taking her home. Fairuza hugs Allegra before she goes. Then it's just the three of us.

"What happens now?" Allegra says.

"We wait until dark. Then I can move the body."

She laughs a little. "'Move the body.' You're moving a body for me." She looks at me. "Hell of a coffee date, huh?"

"It's going to be a hell of a night too. You ready for that?"

"Guess I have to be."

"I'm going to fix this. We're going to get him back."

"How?"

I go over and put a hand on Vidocq's shoulder. It's rock hard, like rigor mortis.

"We don't know exactly how black milk works, but my guess is regular drugs aren't going to affect it."

"What will?"

"Angel blood. It's the only thing I can think of with those kind of healing powers."

"Can we use yours?"

"I'm just a nephilim My blood might make things worse."

"What are we going to do, then?"

I bring a chair to Vidocq's body so Allegra can sit down.

"I'm going to find an angel. They're going to give me their blood or I'm going to take it."

"It's that simple, is it?" she says, shaking her head. "What's going to happen with Wormwood?"

"You let me worry about that."

"Are you going to hurt someone?"

"I'm going to do a lot worse than that."

She looks at me.

"Good."

Candy comes back an hour later. She sits with Allegra.

It's a long wait for sundown.

THE LA BREA Tar Pits are on Curson Avenue between Sixth Street and Wilshire.

I wait until three thirty in the morning before taking Liliane to Allegra's Prius, where I dump the body in the hatchback and drive across town. I stop for all red lights. I drive the prevailing speed of the other traffic. I'm as solid a citizen as L.A. has ever seen.

I stop the Prius at Curson and Wilshire, out of sight of the streetlights and any security cams at the Tar Pits. After

I whisper some Hellion hoodoo, the lights along the whole stretch of Curson blow out. I pop the hatch and grab Liliane's body. The Prius I leave on Wilshire. There's enough traffic on the street that the car won't look too funny if cops come by.

With the body over my shoulder, I sprint to the Tar Pits. She's heavy. There are a couple of stolen cinder blocks in the garbage bags with Liliane's body.

The fence around the pits is about eight feet high. I toss the body over and climb in. The problem with tar is that bodies sink slowly. You have to toss them far enough out that they won't get stuck on shallow ground and so they'll look as inconspicuous as possible until they disappear.

I spin around like a discus thrower and toss Liliane into the middle of the pit. Before I left the clinic, I sliced a few holes in the garbage bags to let the tar in so the bundle would sink faster. I wait behind a palm tree until only the feet are left showing, then climb the fence and head back to the car. This isn't the first time I've dumped bodies at the Tar Pits, but I hope it's the last. I wish I could have had a few more minutes with Liliane to talk things over. Maybe I could have followed her into the Tenebrae if I had some Dream Tea, but I didn't and I thought all the blood from the Metatron Cube ritual wouldn't be good for Allegra to see. Anyway, I know where I can find more information and it will be more fun to get it that way.

BACK AT THE clinic, Candy and I go upstairs to the detective agency office. I have her run Charlie Anpu's license plate. When I have the address, she goes back down to stay with Allegra.

"How is she doing?"

Candy takes a long breath.

"As well as you think. We can't leave Vidocq here. We have to move him so they can be at home."

"Kasabian can help. He won't like it, but tell him I wasn't asking politely."

"What if *I* ask politely? He can be sweet if you talk to him right."

"I'm not sure if we're talking about the same guy, but do whatever you have to. Have you spoken to Fairuza?"

"She called a couple of times, but I got her to take some tranquilizers, so she's out cold."

"What did you tell the rest of the band?"

"I told them that Fairuza and I were both sick. They believed me." She half smiles. "Alessa wanted to bring me chicken soup, but I told her it wasn't a good time."

"Smart. I have a lot of running around to do before sunup, so I'm going."

Candy kisses me.

"Be careful."

"See you soon."

AT BURGESS'S PLACE in Beverly Hills, I throw some Hellion hoodoo and all the cars on one of the streets explode into flames. The concussion sets off the alarms in all the cars across the street. The security Burgess hired to walk the grounds rush the front of the place. That lets me get around the back. I whisper some Hellion hoodoo to get me through the wards and open the door with the black blade. After looking out the windows for security, I head upstairs.

At least one thing goes right for me today. When I get upstairs to where Geoff is looking out the window, Elsabeth isn't there.

Burgess freezes when he sees me in the room. I point the Colt at him.

"Where's the missus?"

"Gone. I sent her away after the other night. I had a feeling it was you."

"But you weren't sure? Who else did you think it might be?"

"That's none of your business."

I take a couple of steps toward hm. He's too scared or too dumb to move.

"Is everything okay in Wormwood land? No one is looking for a way out, are they? Or maybe a change in management?"

"You're way out of your depth here," he says.

"I usually am. Sit down."

He does.

"What's black milk?"

"Nothing that concerns you."

"It got into a friend of mine, so it does."

"Undiluted? My condolences."

I put the Colt away. I was never going to use it. Too noisy. I take out the na'at, my favorite weapon back when I fought in the arena Downtown. Burgess sits back, not sure what to make of it. I extend the na'at into a whip shape. Snap it a couple of times.

"What's black milk?"

Burgess gets a funny look on his face.

"Are you going to kill me? Torture me?"

"The second thing, then the first."

"My security team will be checking on me soon."

"They're not going to like what they find."

He says, "You know that every second you're here, we're making a profit, right? Just you breaking in here triggers all sorts of wonderfully complex financial and celestial mechanisms."

"Is it all just money with you people?"

"Of course not. It's power. It's eternity. It's fun. In this world and the next."

I snap the na'at at his head. He twitches back from it.

"You've had a good time poking me with a stick lately, haven't you? All the weird shit that's been going on."

He brightens.

"You actually watch the news? Good. We had a bet about that too."

"I'm talking about the massacre at the fried-chicken truck."

He laughs briefly.

"Yes, that was us. I wasn't sure you'd recognize the truck. You were so preoccupied last time you saw it."

"And the kids in Malibu?"

"Of course. Teddy Osterberg wasn't one of us, but he wanted to be. This was our way of bringing him into the fold."

"Where did they get the Dixie?"

"I don't remember."

"Charlie Anpu?"

He eases back into the chair. Crosses his legs.

"Charles does enjoy his pills."

"What's black milk?"

He ticks it off on his fingers.

"Two parts gin. One part vermouth. A dash of bitters."

This is a waste of time.

I flick the na'at once more, putting it straight through Burgess's skull. Leave him dead in his chair and head downstairs.

Part of the security team is already back by the pool, sweeping the grounds.

I go to the front window. Get out the Colt and fire four shots through the glass. The pool guards sprint around the side of the house. The ones in the front burst in through the front door. I'm already headed out the back, not climbing the sidewall this time, but the one in the rear.

I drop into a neighbor's yard and climb out a street over. If they see anything out the window, all it will be is Geoff Burgess strolling across their backyard in the middle of the night.

I keep the glamour on while I circle back to where I parked my bike. I should have known Burgess wouldn't come around. But I know someone who I think will. I gun the hog and head to Brentwood.

BY THE GATES of Anpu's walled community, I wish for the millionth time in a month that I had the Room of Thirteen Doors back. Now I have to do things the hard way.

These gated communities used to have guards at the gate. Now it's all key cards and surveillance. I blow that out with some hoodoo and knock one of the gates loose enough to squeeze through.

Anpu's place is on a cul-de-sac a couple of blocks up from the entrance. I could break in, but instead I ring the front door. And keep ringing it.

A couple of minutes later a voice comes through an intercom.

"Who the hell is it?"

"It's me."

"Who the hell is that?"

There's a camera lens on the intercom. I step in front of it so Charlie can get a good look at Burgess's face.

"Geoff? What's wrong? Come in."

The door buzzes and I go inside.

I wait in the foyer, and a minute later, Charlie comes stumbling down the stairs in a bathrobe.

"My God, Geoff. You look awful. Why are you dressed like that?"

"It's a long story. Let's go to your office."

"All right," Charlie says, and I follow him into a room off the front hall. Inside, he closes the door and turns to me.

"Now. What's the emergency?"

I let the glamour fade. It takes Charlie's sleepy eyes a few seconds to catch on to what's happening.

"Oh, dear God."

"God's got his hands full, Charlie. It's just you and me."

I push him into a chair. He stays put.

I put my hands in my pockets.

"Geoff Burgess is dead. I killed him about an hour ago."

"Oh God."

"Stop saying that and pay attention."

"Yes. Of course. What is it you want?"

I sit on the edge of the desk.

"What's black milk? And be careful. I'll know if you're lying."

Charlie squints, like the question hurts.

"Youth. Freedom from disease and time. Immortality."

This garbage again.

"I know immortals, Charlie. None of them are happy about it."

"They aren't us, are they? We have plenty to do and we'll have all the time in the world to do it."

"Because of black milk?"

"Yes."

"Show me."

I take out the syringe. Charlie holds on to the arms of his chair like it's a lifeboat. I bring it over to him.

"Don't ask where I got it. It's from your car, shithead."

I don't even think he hears me.

"Is that undiluted?" he says.

"Very."

His eyes are wide. I don't think I've seen anyone this scared since catching my reflection in a dentist's mirror.

"Please keep it away," he says. "It's poison."

"I know. What makes it not poison?"

He looks at his lap.

"I can't tell you."

" 'Cause Wormwood will kill you?"

"Something like that."

"What do you think I'm going to do to you?"

He seems stumped at that.

"Besides," I continue, "what do you care? You people are always bragging about your branch office Downtown. Maybe death will be great. Puppies and candy and you on Santa's knee forever."

He looks at me. "It's not death. It's other . . . things."

"They'll go rough on you."

"Worse than you can imagine."

"Worse than when I get bored and stick you with the needle?"

He stares across the room. I follow his gaze and see a liquor cabinet.

"Want a drink, Charlie?"

"Very much."

I take out my flask of Aqua Regia.

"Try mine."

He looks terrified. I unscrew the top.

"It's not poison. See?"

I take a big gulp. Hold the flask out to him.

"You don't have a choice, Charlie."

He takes a sip. Gags. Tries to spit it out.

I put my hand over his mouth until he swallows. That sends him into a coughing fit.

I get down close to his face.

"Good?"

His wipes his mouth with the sleeve of his robe.

"You drink that?"

"Everyone drinks it Downtown. How's damnation looking to you now?"

"No one is afraid of damnation anymore. You fixed that."

"Well, yes and no. There's still some dispute over the matter."

"Yes. The angelic war," he says. "We know everything that happens down there. Whether Heaven opens or not, we'll be fine."

"What does that mean?"

He wipes his mouth again. I slap his arm down.

"I asked you a question."

"I've already said too much."

"What makes you think I won't torture it out of you?"

He shakes is head.

"I've seen your prospectus. Torture isn't on your list of major assets."

"Maybe you're right. But I can be damned clumsy."

I take out the na'at, extend it into a spike, and let it go. It drops through his foot, pinning it to the floor. He tries not to scream.

"Oops."

I pull out the na'at. Wipe the blood on his robe and put it away.

"You're right. That wasn't as much fun as it should have been. You know anything about PTSD, Charlie?"

"No."

"Apparently, I have it. A doctor friend is going to give me pills."

"Congratulations," he says, folding onto his foot.

I pull a cloth off a nearby table, knocking a Tiffany lamp and some other expensive junk onto the floor. Toss the cloth to Charlie. He wraps it around his oozing foot.

"What's the magic word, Charlie?"

He squints again.

"Thank you."

"Good boy."

He rocks back and forth in his chair. His heartbeat sounds like Tommy Ramone with a hot poker up his ass.

I take another hit of Aqua Regia and put it away.

"Speaking of pills, what do you know about Dixie Wish-bone? As your attorney, I advise you not to lie."

"If you've been in my car, you know the answer to that."

"Yes, but what do you *know* about it? Its effects."

"I know it can unbalance some people."

" 'Unbalance' is a nice word. Did you unbalance those kids in Malibu?"

He rocks harder in the chair.

"It wasn't me."

"Who was it? Burgess?"

"Maybe. I don't know. I just gave them the pills. It was Eva's idea."

"Eva Sandoval?"

"Yes. The witch."

"Was going after me a power play? Is she trying to knock Burgess off his throne?"

He looks up at me.

"Who knows what goes on in that woman's head?"

"But you gave her the pills."

"I already said so."

"Just trying to be clear."

"Are you going to kill me?"

"Count on it."

He looks around the office, then back at me.

"Don't and I'll tell you everything. I'm your inside man."

"Great. How do you make black milk not poison?"

He does the pained squint again.

"I'll answer everything but that."

I flick his foot with a finger. He groans.

"I don't have to torture you. I can tie you to that chair and set fire to your palatial estate."

"Go ahead. Anything you can do pales compared to what happens if I tell you more about black milk."

I look at him hard. Charlie gets uncomfortable and looks at the floor.

I crouch so I can see his eyes.

"I think I got it, Charlie. Wormwood's not going to torture you. They're going to kick you out. And when you get to Hell, you'll be just another sucker up to your eyeballs in shit."

His nod is almost imperceptible. I stand again.

"Then I'm not going to get much more out of you, am I?"

That does it. He breaks down crying. Big wet sobs and snot running down his face. Things weren't supposed to go like this for a sharp guy with the inside line on eternity.

"Has anyone set odds for me killing all of you?"

He looks up at me with wet red eyes.

"Y-yes."

"Are they good?"

He shakes his head.

"There are too many of us. You don't know all—" He doesn't finish the sentence because I slash his throat with the black blade.

"I could have killed you quick, Charlie. But you're responsible for those kids in Malibu and I want you to have some time to think about that."

He holds his throat with one hand and the armrest of the chair with the other. It's not going to help. He won't stay upright much longer.

I close the office door on the way out. His keys are in a crystal candy dish on a table in the hall. I have to try several keys before finding the one for the office. Jam it in the lock and break it off. Then go to the garage and get into the Rolls Phantom. The garage-door remote is on the dashboard. I push the button and drive the Rolls gently out of the cul-de-sac. I'll sneak back in for the bike later.

Repairmen and a couple of rent-a-cops are by the broken gate when I get there. The one working gate is open. The cops wave the Rolls carrying Charles Anpu straight through. I wear his face all the way home.

The Rolls I leave on Sunset so the authorities won't have any trouble finding it. Before I get out, I think about all that cash in the trunk. Half a million would buy an awful lot of tamales. But it's Charlie's money and that makes it Wormwood's money.

I go across the street and bark some Hellion hoodoo. The Rolls explodes into a million-dollar ball of fire.

It takes a while to get a cab back to the clinic. I want to say that I feel totally righteous and beatific about what I did tonight. But the sad truth is, a little part of me thinks about the money all the way down Sunset.

TURNS OUT CANDY and Allegra never got hold of Kasabian last night. It's probably for the best. His idea of a crisis is when a customer is a day late returning a video.

Just before dawn, Allegra and I roll Vidocq to her Prius in a wheelchair she had in the back of the clinic. I move him into the backseat, then back into the chair when we get him home.

Allegra and I lay him out in bed. She stays with him while I help Candy make coffee. It's a good way to give them some alone time. We hang around in the kitchen waiting for the water to boil.

"Did you find out anything last night?" says Candy.

"A lot, but nothing that's going to cure Vidocq."

"Is there anyone else you can talk to?"

"Again, a lot, but after what Charlie Anpu told me, I don't think anyone in Wormwood is going to come clean."

She picks up two jars of ground coffee.

"Would Allegra want French roast or Colombian?"

"I don't think she wants anything French right now."

"Shit," says Candy. Then, "What are we going to do?"

"I need to find an angel."

"How are you going to do that?"

I don't answer her right away. I wish the goddamn water would boil.

"Stark? How are you going to do that?"

"I wish I knew how to get back the angel that attacked me at Musso's."

"Let's assume you can't. What then?"

The kettle whistles and Candy turns off the flame.

I brush some bread crumbs off the counter.

"If the angels won't come to me, I'll have to go to the angels."

"You mean Hell. How are you planning on getting there?"

"I have no idea."

She scoops the Colombian into a coffeemaker and pours in water. Hits the on button. I don't know if she's mad at me for bringing up Hell or for making her think of ways to talk me out of it.

She looks at me.

"I'm coming with you."

"I don't even know if I can get there. And you got sick the one time you went."

"A lot of that was shock and being scared out of my mind. I'm over that now."

"I don't know."

"The last time you went down there alone you didn't come back for a hundred days. I thought you were dead. I swear, if you do that to me again, I won't be here when you get back."

I don't need any tricks to know she's telling the truth.

"Like I said, I don't know if I can even do it."

"Yes, you do. You always figure out these things. Take me with you or I'm gone. I don't like ultimatums any more than you do and I'll never give you another, but I mean this one."

I touch the gash on the side of my face. It's almost gone, but it's going to add another scar to my collection.

"All right. But you do what I say down there, including leaving me and getting out if things go wrong. That's my ultimatum for you."

She looks at me hard, hating me right then.

"Okay. I'll leave if you say so, but don't say it to be heroic. Only if there's no alternative."

"Deal."

"How long will it take to get ready?"

"We could do it tonight if I knew how to get there. I have the guns. I have Spiritus Dei to prep the bullets. You can wear some of my old body armor. That's nonnegotiable."

"Don't worry. I like the sound of body armor."

"Then all I have to do is figure out a way."

The coffee machine burbles in the background.

She says, "What about Allegra and Vidocq? We can't leave them alone."

"Brigitte can help with that."

"She's making a movie."

"Then she can come by between takes. Is there anyone else you trust who can handle themselves in a fight?"

Candy frowns.

"You think there might be trouble?"

"I doubt it. After last night, they'll be after me. But we need a killer in place on the off chance I'm wrong."

"I'll call her if you want."

"Tell her anything you want. Just make sure she brings her gun."

Coffee drips from the maker into the pot below.

"I guess this isn't a good time to ask if you talked to Allegra about the other thing."

"You can say it. PTSD. And yes, I did. She said she had some pills that might help. But I'm not sure this is the time for me to get too reasonable."

"You're probably right," she says. Comes over and hugs me. "We need monster you a little longer."

It's a relief to hear. The idea of Allegra's drugs scares me more than anything I faced in the arena. I've had my mind messed with before. Doing it voluntarily is not something I'm looking forward to.

"What are you going to tell Alessa?"

"The same thing I told Julie. A family emergency."

"You think Fairuza can keep her mouth shut?"

She blinks.

"I don't know."

"I think she's going to talk sooner or later."

"What do we do about that?" she says.

"Vidocq has potions that might make her forget."

"No. I don't want to do that to her."

"The good thing is that she doesn't trust the cops any more than we do. That means she's going blab to a friend. Who are her friends?"

"A couple of other Luderes. Kasabian. Cindil. She and Alessa have gotten close too."

I lean against the counter.

"Cindil owes me for getting her out of Hell, so she won't talk. The Luderes worry me, so we need to let her blow off steam somewhere else."

The coffeepot is full. Candy fills three cups.

"Maybe she can talk to Kasabian," she says.

"That's what I was thinking."

Candy hands me a cup. I take a gulp. It's too hot, but I'm grateful for a caffeine fix after a long day and night.

I look at her.

"I'm worried about Alessa too."

"What do you mean?"

"Even if Fairuza talks to Kasabian, if she, Cindil, and you know about this, someone is going to let something slip during a band rehearsal or something."

"What can we do about that?"

I stand there for a minute running the options over in my head. They're all rotten.

"Maybe you need to talk to her."

She puts down her coffee.

"You really think so?"

"Tell her about yourself. Not that you're Candy or a Jade. But enough to let her know that Chihiro is deep in the Sub Rosa world. And that it's sometimes dangerous."

Candy doesn't say anything.

"Can you do that?"

"If you think it's a good idea."

"I do."

She looks at the clock on the wall.

"I wonder if it's too early to call Brigitte."

"It's probably too late. She'll be on the set already."

"Maybe you should call her. I'll talk to Kasabian."

"Right."

We bring coffee into the bedroom. Allegra smiles at it, but sets the cup on the bedside table without drinking any.

Candy stays with her while I leave a message for Brigitte.

"Call me as soon as you get this. And make sure to load your gun."

That should get her attention.

I go in with Allegra while Candy calls Kasabian.

She sighs and looks at me. Lifts her hands. Lets them drop again.

I sit on the end of the bed.

"We're going to fix this, Candy and me."

"I know you'll try."

"You take care of us. Now we're going to take care of you."

She reaches over and squeezes my hand.

"Thank you."

"It might take a couple of days. Will he keep that long?"

She bites her lip.

"I don't know. In theory."

"Then that's the one we'll go with."

"You're still planning on finding an angel?"

"Yes."

"How are you going to do that?"

I look at the bedside table.

"Your coffee is getting cold."

She picks up the mug and takes a sip.

I look at Vidocq.

"Candy and I have a plan. Don't worry."

"Then I won't. Just do it quickly."

"With luck, we'll be moving tonight. Tomorrow at the latest."

I get up.

"You won't be alone. Brigitte will be with you."

She nods.

"I'm glad Liliane is dead, you know. I keep trying to feel guilty about what I did, but I'm just numb."

"You had no choice."

"Is this how it is for you? You look at yourself killing someone and it's not you. It's you watching a movie of yourself."

"I have my bad nights, but the kind of people I kill, I'm okay with."

"But you *do* have bad nights."

"Here and there."

"I want to have bad nights. I don't want to be like that."

"Like me? Don't worry. You're not."

She takes another sip of coffee.

"What are you going to do?"

"First I'm going to buy some groceries. Then, when the sun goes down, I'm going to take a long drive."

"Do what you have to."

Candy comes back in.

"I spoke to Kasabian. He'll do it."

I look at the bedside clock.

"The stores won't be open yet. There's nothing we can do right now. I'm going to lie down. That all right with you?"

Allegra nods without looking up.

Candy follows me out into the living room. We take some pillows off the sofa and lie down. It's a tight fit, but it doesn't matter. Even with the caffeine in my system, I'm asleep in a couple of minutes.

This is where I'm meant to be. I'm Heaven's Abomination. I'm a monster. I'm going to Hell. And I'm completely at peace. My sleep is deep and comforting. No more nightmares for me.

ABBOT CALLS ME around noon. Candy doesn't wake up and Allegra is asleep next to Vidocq. I take the call in the kitchen.

"Elsabeth called. It sounds like you had a busy night," says Abbot.

"Consider Burgess an early Christmas present."

"You'll be interested to know that a lot of powerful people vanished into thin air last night."

"Write their names down. There's your list of Wormwood heavies."

"I'm already on it. Elsabeth is leaving the country," he says.

"You told her I wouldn't hurt her, right?"

"I did, but you did murder her husband. Even if she didn't like him, it's a shock."

"That prick is fine. Probably having piña coladas in Hell with Norris Quay right now."

Abbot takes a breath.

"It's too bad we can't do anything about that. A shock like that could bring Wormwood down."

"Who says I can't do anything about it?"

"You said you'd lost that kind of power."

"There's more than one way to skin a flounder."

Abbot says, "If that means you can hurt Wormwood in their sanctuary, I'll do everything I can to help."

"You said I have insurance in that packet you gave me."

"Yes."

"Does that include life insurance?"

"No. Most council members have their own."

"Guess what. I don't. I'll do what I have to do, but you promise me that if something happens to me—like you never hear from me again after tomorrow—you keep paying my salary to Chihiro."

"I can do that," says Abbot.

"Then we're square, no matter what happens from here."

"When should I expect to hear from you?"

"In a couple of days. After that, consider me in Oz with the flying monkeys."

"Wherever you're going, please come back."

"If I don't, have Willem tell Audsley Ishii better luck next time."

"I'll be sure to pass it along," Abbot says.

"One more thing. For a blue-blood, pretty-boy asshole, you're not the worst person I ever met."

"For a terrifying reprobate, neither are you."

"See you in the funny papers."

I hang up. Candy yawns and opens her eyes. I pour us both more coffee.

BRIGITTE CALLS IN the afternoon. Mysteriously, production on her movie has gone into a "temporary pause." I guess Pieter Ligotti lit out of Dodge on the Wormwood Express like the others. I'm sorry it screws up Brigitte's job, but it works out better for us.

"You can pull guard duty on Vidocq and Allegra?"

"Of course," she says. "Will she want to see me, though? I feel like all this is my fault."

"Allegra knows it wasn't your fault. Wormwood used everyone. She needs her friends right now."

"Of course I'll be there. Where will you be?"

"Candy and I are taking a trip. We'll be back in a couple of days. Kill anyone who tries to get in that isn't us."

"With pleasure."

IT TAKES FOR fucking ever for the sun to go down.

I go to a nearby gas station and hit the little grocery inside. It's all road food, grease, and sweets in here. I pick up a carton of unfiltered Luckies on the way out. The clerk gives me a look. I lost the Hellion hog's saddlebags when I rode it back from Hell, and I don't have a backpack, so I have to use one of Candy's. I stare right back at the clerk and strap on a Badtz-Maru pack. Get on the Hellion hog and head south on the Hollywood Freeway to where it forms a crossroads with the 110.

It's early evening and the road is jammed with traffic. Not the best time to do what I'm about to, but I'm sick of waiting around.

I pull onto the shoulder and get out the black blade. Carve an intricate sigil into the roadbed. Then I light a Malediction. Nothing to do now but wait.

It doesn't take long before I get an answer to my distress call.

She burns down the road, doing ninety in the bumper-to-bumper traffic. Every little space between the crawling cars, every opening where someone changes lanes, she blows through them without a care in the world.

After all, these are her roads.

Mustang Sally is the highway sylph. The queen of the freeways, the surface roads, and the filthy side streets. A spirit that's been around in one form or other since the earliest humans left the first mud trails in the ground. She drives L.A.'s roads 24/7 and only stops when bums like me lure her over with tributes.

Tonight, she's in a Porsche 550 Spyder. The car that killed James Dean and a lot of nameless other morons who couldn't handle the horsepower.

Sally gives me a big smile as she stops. But she doesn't get out of the car. Just fixes her hair in the rearview mirror. It takes me a minute to figure it out. Sally has helped me out plenty, but you always have to pay the toll.

I walk to the Porsche and open the door for her. She gives me her hand as she steps out.

"Hello, handsome. That's a new look for you."

I forgot that I still have Badtz-Maru on my back. I shrug off the pack and hand it to her.

"It's for you, Sally."

She opens it and peeks inside.

"Yummy," she says, and tosses the pack onto the passenger seat. Then she walks past me.

"Love the wheels."

Mustang Sally is the most refined lady you'll meet. Tonight she's in diamonds and an evening gown, but that doesn't slow her down. She hikes up her skirt and settles down onto the bike.

"Custom?" she says.

"As custom as they get."

She runs her hands over the fuel tank and the seat leather.

"It's nice to know that they still do good work down below."

"I don't know about that anymore."

She cocks her head at me.

"Well, you do have a way of breaking your toys."

"What if I want to put one back together again?"

"You want to go back."

"It's the only way to make things right."

She looks at me. Then the bike. Then her car.

"Want to trade? My Porsche for your bike? It would make a lovely tribute."

She runs her gloved fingertips over the handlebars.

"Sorry, Sally. It has sentimental value. How about a '68 Catalina fastback?"

She thinks about it for a minute.

"It's not exactly a vintage Porsche."

I come over and get in front of the bike. She could run me down and take it if she wanted and we both know it.

"It would make a nice second car. You can drive it to church and bingo."

She leans back on the seat and takes off a glove. Spits in her hand. I spit in mine and we shake. She puts her glove back on.

I tell her, "But you can't have it right away. It needs a little bodywork."

"That's all right. I trust you. And you always know where to find me. Now, what can I help you with?"

"I need to get back into Hell. Preferably, without dying this time."

The first time Sally helped me get into the afterlife, the process included me splattering myself on a highway pylon. It was messy and gave me a headache.

She shakes her head.

"Sweet boy, sometimes you come to me with the silliest questions. The way to Hell—the road to everywhere—has been there for you since the day you came home."

"Where? How?"

She puts out her hand and I help her off the bike. She takes a minute to smooth her skirt.

"I can't help you directly, but Mr. Muninn can. Sometimes the most complicated way is the easiest."

I look at her. Perfect hair and diamonds lit by a thousand headlights.

"That's all you're going to tell me, isn't it?"

"There are rules to these things. Heaven and Hell are well off my roads, but if you're determined not to die to get there, it's the best I can do."

She strolls back to her car and I hold the door open for her as she gets in. The backseat of the Porsche is completely full of burger bags, candy wrappers, and empty cigarette packs.

I look down at her.

"I hope the snacks and smokes will hold you until I get back."

She reaches up and pats my cheek.

"Just make sure you come back, Mr. Stark. You owe me a car."

"I'll always come back for you, Sally."

"And I'll always be here for you."

She blows me a kiss, finds an opening in the traffic, and peels rubber out into the night.

I sit there on the shoulder for a while. I'm not a goddess. I can't flit my way through traffic like a heavy-metal butterfly and nobody is going to slow down to let someone like me in front of them.

Muninn is in Heaven. And what the hell does "Sometimes the most complicated way is the easiest" mean?

I just traded away my car for a fortune cookie.

Finally there's an opening. I gun my way onto the freeway and pick up Candy at Vidocq and Allegra's. Brigitte is already there, wearing her pistol in a shoulder holster.

"Are you two going to be all right?" Allegra says.

"Right as rain," says Candy.

Allegra hugs her.

Brigitte doesn't say anything. Just kisses both of us on the cheek. She's a killer. She knows what's what and how badly this could go.

Allegra gives us little waves as we leave.

Candy waves back. I give them a wink. Bullshit confidence on a bullshit night.

We get on the bike and head home. Neither of us is wearing a helmet, but I plan to blast out the tires of anyone who tries to stop us. Knowing I might get to shoot something, and with the warm spring night, it's a nice ride back to Max Overdrive.

THERE'S ONLY ONE thing Sally could have meant about Muninn helping us. There must be something in his old shop that we can use to get Downtown.

We arrive at the Bradbury Building at around ten in the morning. Not so early that people will notice. A good time of day to blend in with the crowd.

We spent the night going through my guns, dipping everything in Spiritus Dei. Candy dipped her black blade in the stuff, so I dipped mine for luck. I packed the Colt and put a handful of speed loaders in one pocket. Put a stolen Glock in an old holster I cut from a leather tool belt. Candy got the Benelli shotgun I took off a dead Nazi piece of shit last Christmas. It fits nicely under the old coat I wore when I first got back to L.A. It's big on Candy, but there are motocross pads in the sleeves and sides, so it should protect her if things get physical.

We're not exactly inconspicuous when we walk into the Bradbury, but enough movies and TV have been shot here that people are most likely going to take us for a couple of eccentric show-biz nitwits location-scouting the place.

It's a few minutes of milling around on the first floor before we can get on one of the metal art deco elevators alone. We take it up to the fifth floor, but when it stops we don't get off. I press the one and three buttons simultaneously and the elevator starts down again.

When it stops, we get off. The thirteenth floor is completely dark. The first time I was here, the shop we want at least had candles in the window. Now it looks like the whole floor has been deserted since Mr. Muninn left.

"Where are we?" says Candy.

I point to a dusty shop ahead that looks like a cross between a Beverly Hills Pier 1 and the back room of the world's saddest auction house.

"This used to be Mr. Muninn's shop. Once upon a time, he was a kind of antiques dealer."

"You're a liar," Candy says.

"Nope. I'll show you."

With only the lights on our cell phones, we get to the shop and I jimmy the lock with the black blade.

Inside is a collection of old furniture. Stuffed exotic birds, some of which bear a strong resemblance to dinosaurs. There's a coin set from Atlantis. A glass cage that once held a Fury, now empty. Strange weapons. Canopic jars.

Candy turns in a circle.

"How are we going to find anything in all this junk?"

"We're not. Muninn kept the good stuff in the back."

Through the back is a door that leads to a steep stone staircase. Lucky for us, lucky for the world, the light switch at the top of the stairs still works. Floodlights flicker on for what seems like miles in every direction. If the collection upstairs seemed out of control, the stuff down here is worse, mostly because of the sheer scale.

Rows of shelves spread out in all directions. I know Muninn had a system for his junk, but I never understood it. Aside from small collections in the shop, the hoard down here he put together over, in his own words, "ice ages." In the distance is the prow of an ancient ship. Part of a silent-movie film set. An old L.A. red car train.

"Double fuck me," says Candy. "Upstairs was bad enough. We could spend the rest of our lives down here."

"No. Mustang Sally said that Muninn could help us and the most complicated way is often the easiest. Something like that."

"Maybe she's talking about a puzzle. You solve it and it'll open a portal or a hot-air balloon will pop out."

"That's what I was thinking. Let's split up, grab anything that looks like a puzzle, and meet back here in an hour."

Candy looks around.

"What if I get lost?"

"Yeah. That."

I look around and find a bag of worn old Greek drachmas. Hand it to her.

"Do a Hansel and Gretel. Drop one of these every few minutes when you go, then you can follow them back."

"Thanks, Nancy Drew. I know how the story goes."

We take off in opposite directions. One row over, I find an old grocery-store shopping cart full of candlesticks and vases.

The vases go on a shelf with no problems, but some of the candlesticks try to squirm away or wrap themselves around my arms. A pair of snake-headed sticks hiss at me. I turn the cart on its side and dump the rest of the sticks. Some crawl away under the shelves.

There are some kids' picture puzzles in the next row and some puzzle boxes on a high shelf. There's a whole carton of those fucking games where you roll a ball bearing around and try to get it on the clown's eyes and mouth. I pile the whole damned box in the cart.

"How are you doing?" yells Candy.

"Finding junk. Nothing that screams 'portal to Hell.' How about you?"

"The same. But I did find a cute pair of velvet Mary Janes. They're perfect for Chihiro. Do you think Mr. Muninn would mind if I take them?"

"He has a million pairs of shoes down here. Take them, and if he gets testy, I'll trade him something."

"Do you think we'll see him?"

"Only if he wants to see us, so bring the shoes."

"There's no way I'm wearing these shoes in Hell."

"That's not the point. The fact you have something of his might get his attention."

"Taking them is part of the mission? Awesome."

"Did you talk to Alessa while I was gone?"

I hear her pawing through shelves from what sounds about half a mile away.

"Yes."

"And?"

"She was confused. A little annoyed. But understanding. And had about a million more questions than I could answer."

"Bring her a present. There must be something down here she'll like."

"Seeing me in these shoes is all the present either of you needs."

"Somehow I believe that."

We dig around for another half hour. I have the cart piled high with complete garbage. Even if one of these puzzles is the doorway to Narnia, going through them all could take years. Goddammit, Sally. You're getting my car. You could have come across with a better clue.

"Stark?"

"Yes."

"What's this over here?"

"I can't see around corners, dear."

"Go back to the beginning and follow my coins, Hansel. I'll wait here."

It takes me ten minutes to get back to the staircase and another twenty to track her down. Her coat and face are streaked with dust. She has a wheelbarrow full of the same crap I have.

"Want to see the shoes?" she says.

"Now?"

"We're going to Hell. Indulge me."

"Fine."

She puts them on the floor and steps into them. I'm no longer annoyed.

"Admit it," she says. "You're picturing me in nothing but these shoes."

"Well . . ."

"I'll take that as a yes."

She steps out of them and puts them back in her pocket.

I look at the shelves.

"Yes, I'm suddenly distracted by impure thoughts, but that's not the only reason you called me over, right?"

"Of course not."

She points into the distance.

"What's that?"

It looks like a broken-down, dried-up cornfield from here.

"It's a corn maze. Muninn has pretty much the entire history of L.A. down here. Corn mazes used to be a big item."

She looks at me like I'm supposed to say something.

I shrug.

"What?"

"Mustang Sally said that the way to Hell has been there for you since you got back."

"What makes you think it's that fucking fire hazard?"

"She also said the most complicated is the simplest. Maybe we just walk the maze and it take us where we want to go."

"Or maybe we'll die of thirst next to some dried-up old jack-o'-lanterns. Those corn mazes were just Halloween hijinks."

Candy crosses her arms. In the oversize coat, she looks like an angry tween who didn't get asked to the prom. But I don't tell her that.

"Then you tell me what it means. Are we seriously going to put every kitten and teacup puzzle together? And open every puzzle box ever made? How many years do we have to spare?"

I look at the maze.

"What if we're wrong? We could get lost in there for days."

"We won't. I know it. Call it Jade's instinct."

I pick up a rusty picture frame. It tries to bite me, so I throw it away.

"Jade instinct? Where did that come from? You've never mentioned that before."

"I just made it up. But it's telling me that going in there is a better idea than jacking around with Rubik's Cubes and crossword puzzles."

"And if it's a dead end? How do we get out?"

"We do Hansel and Gretel again. Leave a coin at each turn."

I look at the shaggy thing.

"Can't we just burn it down and find the exit that way?"

"That's that subtle Sandman Slim thinking that gets all the girls worked up," says Candy. "If we burn it, we'll burn up the magic and probably this whole warehouse."

I look at the hundred puzzles she must have in her wheelbarrow. I probably have even more in my cart.

"I'm worn out. You've worn me out. Just remember that if the world explodes, it's your fault."

"Yeah, but I'm going out in great shoes."

She takes my arm and pulls me to the maze, filled with all the confidence I haven't had since this thing began.

At the maze entrance I say, "What do we do? Just walk in?"

Candy punches me on the arm.

"Didn't you have a childhood? You turn left. Then you keep turning left. That's the best way through a maze."

"Is that true?"

"It always worked on the napkins at IHOP."

"I'm not risking the world on pancakes."

She rolls her eyes.

"Yes. The rule of thumb with all mazes is to go to the left. It's mathematical or something."

"Do you have the coins?"

She holds up the bag.

"Fuck it. Let's try."

She takes my hand and drops the first coin. We step into the maze and take the first left turn.

A FEW MORE lefts. A few more coins. The light changes. The floodlights filter down through the dead cornstalks, throwing tiger stripes everywhere, flattening everything until it's faded and two-dimensional. We're videos of ourselves walking through a video of a place. After too many turns, everything gets dreamlike and I have to remind myself that we're real, this place is real, and what we're doing is just as real.

Shapes form in the shadows. Faces. Animals. Whole cityscapes. Glimpses of Pandemonium. Breaks in the stalks give glimpses into adjoining rows and I swear that sometimes I see figures moving past us in the opposite direction. I wonder if this dream state is an effect of the place's magic or just boredom from looking at fucking corn for what feels like a fifteen-hour *Berlin Alexanderplatz* marathon?

I consider checking the time on my phone, but if we've been walking for hours it will depress me. If we've been walking for just twenty minutes it will depress me even more.

The air in the maze is musty. We brush against the stalks.

Dried leaves break apart and drift into our noses. Candy can't stop sneezing.

I didn't think that bringing down Wormwood would include being annoyed to death. It might be time to turn back.

I watch Candy wipe her nose on my old coat for the hundredth time.

"How many coins do you have left?"

She sneezes.

"I haven't had any coins for an hour."

"Thanks for keeping me up-to-date."

"I didn't tell you because you're a big crybaby and you'd have wanted to turn around."

"I have my lighter. I can still burn the place down. Just say the word."

"What's that up ahead?"

Something flat hangs from the stalks a few yards ahead of us. It's a sign. It says HELL and under that is an arrow pointing back the way we came.

Candy and I look at each other.

"Someone is fucking with us," she says.

"Or it's the maze itself. It's screwing with us. Testing us. Sort a temptation of Saint Anthony situation."

"What was his story?"

"He was a monk who went to play hermit in the desert. Lucifer wasn't impressed and tried to kick Anthony's ass with visions. Animals. Bugs. The seven deadly sins. He probably threw in a few Daleks."

"The seven deadly sins sound good," she says. "Wake me when we get to Gluttony. I could use a ham sandwich."

I look at the sign.

"A pretty lame temptation."

Candy pulls it down and tosses it on the ground.

"I suppose we're going to have to question everything we see, huh?"

"Everything but us."

We continue walking. Left turn. Then another.

Candy says, "How do you know everything but us? How do I even know you're you anymore?"

"We can play twenty questions."

"Okay. What's your favorite movie?"

"The uncut version of *Bambi*. Before they took out all the nudity."

"What's your favorite food?"

"Definitely deviled eggs."

"Your favorite sport?"

"Sumo soccer."

"Who's prettier, me or Brigitte?"

"Veronica Lake."

"What do you like best about me?"

"Your velvet Mary Janes."

"Did your father really try to shoot you or is that another tall tale?"

Another left turn.

A man and woman are waiting for us. The man is in his late thirties, but looks fifty. When she was young, the woman looked like Ann-Margret, but the chemo has left her nothing but bare bones and gray skin in a crooked wig.

"Jimmy," she says.

The man raises a hunting rifle.

I pull Candy back around the corner.

A shot goes off, ripping through the brittle cornstalks.

I get out the Colt. Pull the trigger as I round the corner. But there's no one there.

Candy comes up beside me.

"Was that . . . ?"

"Yeah. Mom and Dad. The human dad who raised me. He wasn't a happy person."

I put the Colt back in my waistband.

"I'm so sorry," Candy says.

I nod.

"Just be careful what you say in here."

We take the next turn. And the next.

There's a pile of bodies. The stink is mind-numbing. Corpses rise high above the stalks. I can't count them all. Burgess and Charlie are fresh on the ground. I see Jan and Korlin Geistwald. Their daughter Eleanor. Azazel. Piles of Hellions and revolting hellbeasts. Nameless vampires. Mason Faim and his enforcer, Parker. Josef. Teddy Osterberg. Cherry Moon. Doc Kinski. Bodies of everyone and everything I ever killed or allowed to be killed.

I just stare.

Candy pulls my arm.

"Come on. Let's go."

"You know what that is?"

"Yeah. Let's go."

It goes on like that. Awful visions and fake salvation. Exit signs. Rest stops with rotten food and pitchers of putrid water.

Around a corner is Heaven. Armored angels throw human souls over the battlements, a nine-day fall to Hell below.

Pandemonium empty, the streets full of bones and sewage.

I'm lying dead in the arena. Starving Hellions eat my raw flesh.

I pull Candy away from that one.

Candy and Alessa are asleep in our bedroom at Max Overdrive. All traces that I'd ever been there are gone.

Candy pulls me away from that one.

Hollywood Forever Cemetery. A year ago when I escaped Hell. Only I can't dig my way out of the grave. I claw at the dirt, but it's hard as concrete. I'm trapped there forever, a foot from freedom, in my own idiot tomb.

Candy closes her eyes at that one and I have to lead her away.

And turn another corner.

It's a few minutes until the next sideshow.

The smell of sulfur and filth is stronger as we near the vision.

The corn row opens on another bleak vision of Pandemonium. The empty street market. Off to the left and not too far away is Wild Bill's bar. A pale light flickers through the window and under the door.

I start to turn left, but it feels wrong.

Leaving Candy in the corn, I take a step into the empty street. The abandoned market stalls stretch in one direction. The short street to Wild Bill's in the other. Nearby is a car repair place where I once hid the Hellion hog.

"I think it's real."

"We made it?" says Candy.

"Looks like it."

I put out my hand.

She takes it and steps into the street. I look back, making a mental note of where the entrance to the maze is. It's through the entrance of a sushi bar that used to sell slices of animals that look less like fish and more like the *Texas Chainsaw* night terrors.

And yes, they have sushi bars, street markets, and car repair places Downtown. The place is a bit distorted and full of murderous shitcreeps, but you can still navigate it pretty well with a Maps to the Stars' Homes.

"I wonder if the maze goes anywhere besides Hell?" says Candy.

"You looking to catch some rays in Maui?"

"I was thinking more like Disney World in Florida."

"You can take a plane to Florida."

She grabs my arm and jumps a little.

"Then we can go?"

"I suppose. If we live."

"Finally. Incentive."

I look back at the sushi bar.

"You're probably right, though. I bet that maze will take you anywhere you want to go. If you can deal with its complete and utter bullshit."

"Where to now, Dr. Quest?" she says.

"Fancy a drink?"

"Always."

We head up the hill to Wild Bill's bar.

Back when I did a stint as Lucifer down here, I had the engineers build me a watering hole that looked as close as possible to Bamboo House of Dolls. I gave the place to my great-great-great-great- (I'm not really sure how many greats is appropriate) grandfather, James Butler Hickok, better known as Wild Bill, the greatest shootist in the west.

It's been a while, though. And because I'm not sure what we'll find behind the door, I get out my Colt and Candy levels her Benelli, ready to fill any crabby Hellions inside with double-O buckshot.

As quietly as possible, I turn the handle on the saloon door. It unlocks easily. I give Candy a nod and shove the door open as hard as I can.

We charge inside, ready to blast at anything with too many heads. Nothing does because there's no one inside . . . except for a depressed one-headed bastard behind the bar. He sets down the Hellion newspaper he's reading and glances over at us.

"If you're looking for trouble," he says, "take it down the street. We're closed."

I put the Colt back in my waistband.

"I thought you were a better businessman than that, Bill. From what I hear, Armageddon is a thirsty business."

He squints through the gloom. Walks slowly to the end of the bar.

"You silly son of a bitch," he says, and comes over. He catches me in a big bear hug, something he's never done before. Times change, even in Hell.

He takes a step back and looks me over.

"Ugly as ever, I see."

"Even got a few more scars since we saw each other last."

"Me too, son. Me too."

He glances at Candy.

"That's a handsome street sweeper you have there, miss. Mind if I have a closer look?"

Candy looks at me. I nod.

She hands Bill the Benelli. He takes it over into the light of the nearest candle.

"This is another one of your fashionable modern shooters with too many shots and no way to keep track of them."

"It's called a Benelli. It's Italian."

He turns the shotgun over. Tries it against his shoulder. Studies it with the interest of a man who appreciates guns and has been bored out of his mind for some time.

"I knew some fine ladies with Italian frocks, but I never took those fellers for gunsmiths. Live and learn," he says.

He hands the Benelli back to Candy.

"Is anyone going to introduce the young lady or am I expected to spend the rest of eternity guessing her name? Not that I have fuck else to do these days. Pardon my language, miss."

That makes Candy smile.

She slings the Benelli back over her shoulder and extends her hand.

"Hi. I'm Candy."

They shake.

"Sweet to the ear and the eye," he says. "Well, come on, you two. Belly up to the bar."

We drag a couple of stools down to where Bill left his newspaper.

The shelves behind the bar, which normally hold rows of liquor bottles, are empty.

"Business a little slow?"

Bill raises his eyebrows.

"You could say that. I ran out of the good stuff a few

months back. Sold it or traded it away for this and that. Mostly, and it shames me to say it, protection. I ran out of bullets before I ran out of liquor, so I had no choice. Bands of scoundrels ran wild in the streets. Looted and banditized the market. Back then, I could buy patrols from Hellion Legionnaires with hooch. Now both the scoundrels and the Legions have pissed off into the wind like everything else."

"I'm sorry, Bill. This is my fault. If I hadn't talked Upstairs into opening Heaven and then the deal falling apart, none of this would have happened."

"Don't fret," he says. "You did your best and with good intentions. That's all a man can do. If the world is determined to go bad, it will find a way."

Candy says, "Stark has told me a lot about you, Bill. You're one of his heroes."

"Is that right? Well, you must take good care of him if he has time to contemplate such things as heroes."

"We take good care of each other."

"And yet you still call him 'Stark.'"

She looks at me.

"It's how I first met him and the name kind of stuck."

"I understand," he says. "Most strangers who met me toward the end of my days only knew me as Wild Bill, an adequate moniker at one time. But tiresome at the end."

"What should I call you?"

"Since you haven't used up 'James' on that obstinate creature next to you, that'll do. Or 'Jim.' Some ladies called me that."

"'Jim' it is, then. Did anyone ever call you 'Jimmy'?"

"Not twice."

"Stark is the same way. Except for some ladies."

I lean on the bar.

"Brigitte picks up bad habits fast. And she enjoys tormenting me."

"Buck up, boy. That means she likes you. The respect of men is important, but women, in my experience, usually have a truer sense of a man's character. They see through the veil of horseshit we build around ourselves. Pardon me again."

"You don't have to apologize, Jim," says Candy. "You should hear Stark at home. One little annoyance and he'd make a pirate blush."

"You must be a good woman to put up with the likes of him."

"She is," I say. "Better than I deserve."

Candy does a theatrical eye roll. Says, "Don't fish for compliments in front of family, dear."

Bill laughs.

"As charming as this reunion is, will one of you explain to me what you're doing in this godforsaken pig wallow?"

"We're here to fix things, Bill. Or try to. There's trouble back in the world and some of it comes from here. If I can stop what's wrong in Hell, maybe it will help both of our worlds."

"Will it get folks into Heaven?"

"That's what I hope."

Bill holds up the newspaper he was reading when we came in.

"You see this? I've been reading this damned thing over

and over again for months. It's a dismal pastime and I'm ready for a fresh venture. So, how can I help?"

"We need to find a man named Norris Quay. Ever heard of him?"

Bill thinks for a minute.

"Can't say that I have. Are you saying this Norris feller is the source of this affliction?"

"No. That's a bunch called Wormwood."

"Haven't heard of them either. Damn. I thought a man would hear every kind of secret running a saloon."

"Quay isn't the source of the trouble, but he's the man in the center. If we can get to him, maybe we can shut the whole thing down."

"Well, I'm game," says Bill. "Where is the son of a bitch?"

"That's the problem. We don't know," says Candy.

"That a bit constraining. Hell's a big place to wander with no sure destination."

A candle at the end of the bar gutters out. Bill takes a box of similar candles from under the bar and lights a replacement. Putting the box back, he says, "This is currently my sole and most prized possession. Some days a little light is all that keeps a body's spirits up."

I take out the Maledictions and offer one to Bill.

"Don't mind if I do," he says.

He lights us up with one of the candles and takes a long puff.

"Like smoking skunkweed. But if skunkweed is what you have, be grateful for it."

Candy looks at us. "You're both going to get cancer from those things."

"I'm beyond that, ma'am. But this young fool, who knows."

I blow smoke rings at the ceiling.

"I'm not a person. I don't get sick."

"How do you know?" she says.

"Jade intuition."

"Very funny."

I look back at Bill.

"When he was alive, Quay lived in an underground mansion in Griffith Park. Maybe we should start looking there."

"I don't know about any underground lairs," says Bill. "But a few months back, a whole load of Hellions built a big house in the park, way up by the barbican."

"Then let's definitely start there," says Candy.

I flick some ash off the Malediction.

"Let's." To Bill I say, "Do you have any weapons at all?"

"I always have a weapon around."

He takes an old but serviceable-looking bowie knife and sets it on the bar. Follows it with a well-worn sapper, a heavy weight the shape of a truncheon wrapped in leather.

"Never without them," he says.

I take the sapper with my Kissi hand and rap it against my human one. Just once.

"You could crack some skulls with that."

"Can and have," he says.

"You're going to need more firepower than that if you're coming along, though. Here."

I take the Colt from my waistband and set it on the bar. He

picks it up, admiring the engraving along the body and barrel, then pops the cylinder. Spins it and slaps the gun closed.
Sets it down again.

"Some admirable iron you have there."

"Candy gave it to me."

He looks across the bar at her.

"I'm liking you better all the time."

"You too, Jim," she says.

I take out some of the speed loaders and set them next to
the pistol.

"These will help you reload faster. You open the cylinder
and—"

"Boy, I was shooting the eyes out of eagles in full flight
before your sorry ass was conceived of. I think I know how
to load a pistol."

"Sorry. And don't worry about the ammo. They're special.
They'll kill anything that comes at us."

"I never doubted it."

"Play with your popguns, boys," says Candy. She pats the
Benelli. "Mine's bigger than both of yours put together."

"I'll drink to that," says Bill.

He kneels and pulls up a couple of floorboards, digs around
until he finds a dirty bottle, and sets it on the bar.

"The last man standing."

"What shall we drink to?" says Candy.

Bill gets three shot glasses from a shelf behind him and
wipes out the dust.

"To the end of tumult and the resurrection of delight."

He pours three shots.

"I don't see much down here to be delighted about," says Candy.

"True. But there's always hope for better days."

Candy holds up her glass.

"Better days," she says.

"Better days," me and Bill say together.

We down our shots. I don't know what the stuff is. It's not quite as rough as Aqua Regia, but just barely. More like sweet red wine and motor oil.

Candy makes a face.

"What is this?"

"Hair of the dog," says Bill. " 'Course the dogs down here are mighty homely."

"Remind me not to kiss any dogs while I'm here," says Candy.

Bill gives a slight laugh and pours himself another.

"Shall we get moving?"

I look back, thinking about what's beyond the door.

"I don't suppose you have any wheels?"

"A motorcar? No. Never cared for 'em. But there's plenty in the streets. Maybe one will work."

"Let's find out."

There are hundreds of abandoned cars along Pandemonium's version of Hollywood Boulevard. Some parked and some just ditched at crazy angles in the street. Any of them that look intact, I try. Jam the black blade in the ignition and turn. Candy does the same thing with her knife. We must try twenty cars without a single engine turning over. Then there's a roar.

Candy got one of the Legion's big Unimogs running.

"Woo-hoo!" she yells from the cab.

Bill and I run over and get in with her.

She guns the engine and I check the fuel gauge. Almost half a tank.

"You know how to drive one of these?"

She gives me a look.

"If you're asking me, 'Can the girl drive the truck?,' you can get out and walk, Tiny Tim."

"You might shut your yap, before you get us both booted," says Bill.

I nod.

"My apologies, ma'am. Drive on."

Candy grinds the gears a couple of times before gritting her teeth and finding first. We lurch forward, then move smoothly, weaving around the abandoned cars.

"Call me 'Tank Girl,' motherfuckers," she shouts.

Bill and I don't dare say a word.

WE TRAVEL WEST for maybe twenty minutes, then north on Los Feliz Boulevard into the park. Back home, they have kiddie pony rides around here. I don't know what they used to keep in the fetid, boiling pits in these ruined Hellion stables, but I don't think it was ponies and I don't think they were for granola-and-kale-fattened L.A. cherubs.

The drive through the park skirts the crumbling 5 freeway, then turns inward, bringing you past the park's famous merry-go-round. The ride is a gruesome thing in L.A., the way all merry-go-rounds are. They're the definition of both staggering boredom and ruthlessly enforced merriment. They're the amusement-park equivalent of sticking your hand in fire as a kid. You have to try it once, just to see what it's like. After that, you never want to do it again. All those prancing, leering horses, with their frozen rictus smiles are most kids' first introduction to Hell. Those horses, they think, must have been some murderous bastards to be captured and displayed in such a humiliating way. The wee ones picture themselves in the horses' place, skewered through the gut by a brass pole and yanked up and down—suspended between Heaven and Hell—for all eternity. Parents who've forgotten or repressed their own terrifying merry-go-round memories snap shots of the kiddies in their torment, passing their traumas on to the next generation. Merry-go-rounds are a great shared lie of childhood. Cruelty masked as fun. Tedium cloaked as adventure. A great spinning vessel of torment getting the tykes ready for the damnation most of them will richly deserve, all because their minds were permanently twisted by this parade of pony horrors. I bet Charlie Manson and Ed Gein loved merry-go-rounds. In some weird way, I bet Wormwood was born around here. There is where all those tots first developed a taste for death, and their crimes were just them inflicting their memories of that eternally spinning Perdition on the world.

Luckily, Candy drives us straight past the ride and I don't have to explain my amusement-park terrors.

From there, it's just a few more minutes to the grounds of the old park zoo.

Bill was right. Where empty leaf-and-weed-filled animal cages once stood, is a sprawling Spanish colonial mansion. The moment it's in sight, Candy pulls the Unimog off the road and into a thick grove of moss-heavy trees. Now we just wait to see what happens.

A smart guy once said that war is boredom punctuated by moments of terror. Stakeouts are like that, only they're boredom punctuated by moments of ennui, monotony, and finally, an utter indifference to your own survival. If death was any less awful than a stakeout, there would be about six cops left on the planet.

Maybe an hour later, something comes over the rise from where we've driven up. Bill takes out a collapsible telescope and aims it at the road.

"Got a whole caravan coming this way," he says.

"Can I have a look?" says Candy, and Bill hands her the telescope.

"It looks like three SUVs. I can't see who's inside them."

The vans spread out across the grounds of the old zoo. Out of the first van, six Hellion Legionnaires emerge with weapons. Three angels step out of the second van. Out of the last van come six humans.

I put out my hand.

"Bill, let me see the telescope."

He gives it to me and it takes a second to adjust.

I don't recognize everyone from the lead van, but I know enough of them.

"See anyone you like?" says Bill.

"Not a single one. But I see a bunch I want."

"Is that Quay feller there?"

"Yeah. And Geoff Burgess and Charlie Anpu. A couple of other men I don't recognize. Probably more Wormwoods I never met."

"I think there's a woman down there," says Candy.

"There is, but I don't recognize her either. She looks cozy with Quay."

They mill around the zoo for a few minutes, then the men go into the mansion. The woman talks to the angels while the Hellions fan out around the grounds.

The jabbering goes on for a few more minutes, until the woman heads inside the mansion and the angels spread their wings and swoop into the sky.

"How about that?" says Bill. "In all my years down here, I've never seen such a sight."

I take out a Malediction.

"Yeah. Someone ought to do a fucking painting."

"What's your problem?" says Candy. "You wanted to see the place and we've seen it."

Bill puts out a hand.

"Maybe you oughtn't spark that right now. There are still guards around the front of the house."

I put the smoke away.

"So? What is it?" says Candy.

"The six Hellions don't worry me. We can handle them. They probably have a few more like them inside, but it's unlikely to be more than what's on the outside."

"And how do you know all this?"

"I used to sneak into Hellion palaces and murder people."

"Right."

"That's twelve guards in total. Anything else we should be worried about?" says Bill.

"They might have wards on the place, but I think that with a setup like this, they won't. They're Wormwood. They own this burg right now and no one is going to fuck with them."

"Then what's got your panties in a twist?" says Candy.

"The angels. Three warrior angels is a lot bigger problem than twelve Hellion mercenaries."

"You'll notice they didn't go inside," says Bill. "That woman talked to them and they flew away, peaceful as doves."

"The question is, how often are they around and how many of them are here at any one time?"

"What you're saying is that we have to stay here and see who comes and goes," says Candy.

"I'm afraid so."

"For how long?"

"I don't know. A day maybe."

"Makes sense to me," says Bill. "But no use all of us staying up, getting in each other's way the whole time. We can watch in shifts. Two hours each while the others rest. With three of us swapping turns, time shouldn't pass too disagreeably. You two rest up. You had a long journey. I'll take first watch."

"Thanks," says Candy.

"Yeah. Thanks."

There's a small storage area in the cab behind the seats. It's just big enough for Candy to lie down. I shift over to the driver seat and lean it back a few inches. Bill scans the grounds with his spyglass. I close my eyes, trying to relax, and eventually drift off into a light doze.

BILL SHAKES ME awake two hours later.

"Your turn, sunshine," he says, and hands me the telescope.

"Did you see anything?"

"Just that woman. She drove away and came back in an hour with maybe some papers in her hand. And she only took two guards with her. I think you were right. These people feel above petty things like bushwhackers."

"That's good news. I'll take it from here."

"That gal of yours is something special," he says.

"She is indeed."

"She's not quite human, is she?" he says.

"Neither am I. Is that a problem?"

"It's not commentary. It's an inquiry into her nature."

"She's a Jade. Do you know what that is?"

He chuckles.

"Oh my, yes," he says. "I met a load of those ladies once on a trip to the Barbary Coast. San Francisco. They were guarding a Chinese merchant ship in port. Six little gals no bigger than her. And no one dared step toward 'em. An old sailor told me that their types guarded Chinese emperors and rode with Genghis Khan and Alexander himself."

He half turns toward me.

"I'm not averse to a tall tale here and there myself, but what those men said had the ring of truth. Those gals were different. Mythological. Fierce and loyal."

"That describes Candy."

"Then we're lucky to have her on our side."

"I tell myself that every day."

"Good. Vagabonds such as we need good sorts, human or otherwise, to watch our backs. If I'd had a gal like Candy with me in Deadwood, things might not have transpired as they did. I can still remember that pair of aces I was holding, and the pair of eights, but I'm goddamned if I can remember the fifth card. The assassin Jack McCall shot the memory clear out of my head. I'd be very pleased to someday have it returned. But I'm not counting the days on that."

"Someday, Bill. Someday, you're going to meet someone who was in the bar and sober and then you'll know."

"And how will I track down this benefactor?"

"I don't know, but you have all of eternity to figure it out."

He curls his lip at the thought.

"Eternity passes slowly when you're alone. That's why you need to be good to young Candy there. I haven't had much luck with that kind of companionship, back home or here."

"Don't worry. I'd kill for Candy."

"Oh hell, boy. She's your friend and companion. That means I'd kill for her too. That's not enough."

"What is enough?"

"If I knew that, I might not be sitting with a numb bung-hole talking to a young fool about the vagaries of love."

He looks at me.

"You do love her."

"Of course."

"Then never let her forget it."

"That's the plan."

From the back, Candy says, "As much as I appreciate you gentlemen declaring your undying devotion to me, would you mind shutting the fuck up so I can go back to sleep?"

"Sorry, ma'am," says Bill.

"Yeah. Sorry."

Everyone is quiet for a minute. Then Candy kicks me through the car seat.

"You loooove me," she says like a little kid.

"Shut up."

"No take-backs. You loooove me."

"Go to sleep."

"You'll make such a blushing bride when we get married."

"Please. I'll take you to Disney World if you'll just stop talking."

She kicks me again.

"Jim, you heard him. You're a witness. We're going to Disney World."

"She has you trapped there," says Bill.

"I know. Now go to sleep."

She lies down and gets quiet. Then, in a tiny singsong whisper I hear, "You loooove me."

Finally, she drifts off and Bill closes his eyes.

It's going to be a long day.

A FEW HOURS later, Candy sits up and says groggily, "Has it been two hours?"

I check the time on my phone.

"More like eight."

"Why didn't you wake me up?"

"It was a long boring night. I got hypnotized by it."

"No, you didn't. You just didn't trust us. You had to see it all with your own eyes."

"Careful. Disney World is slipping away."

She climbs back into the driver's seat and pushes me over.

"Oh, we're going to Disney World. And you're going to get some sleep."

"What's going on?" says Bill.

"Dirty Harry here didn't wake us for our shifts. He's been watching the place for hours."

"Is that true?"

"I just got into a groove and didn't want to break it."

"Well, I don't know what any of that means, but we had an agreement and you broke it."

I nod.

"You're right and I apologize."

"Apology accepted. If it don't happen again."

"It won't."

"What did you learn?" says Candy.

"Lots. Let's go back to Bill's."

"It isn't good news, is it?" says Bill.

"It's mixed. Come on. I want to get out of here."

Candy backs us out of the stand of trees and we move down the hill.

When we get to Bill's place, we park the Unimog by the front door so we can keep an eye on it.

"What's the story?" says Bill.

Candy sits down next to me and lightly butts me with her shoulder.

"Come on. Talk to us."

"Here it is. The person I saw most was the woman. Angels came and went. Some brought boxes and some took boxes away. My guess is they were exchanging raw black milk for the processed, nonpoisonous version. I don't know what the other Wormwood guys were doing, but they were inside most of the time."

"That doesn't sound so bad," says Candy.

"Here's where it gets worse. A lot more Legionnaires

arrived last night. Maybe twenty. So, there's a lot more fire-power for us to contend with."

"Anything else?" says Bill.

"I'm worried about those angels. The woman had a sched-ule, but the angels seemed to come and go when they wanted. If we make a move against the house, we might have to fight not only Hellions, but warrior angels."

"Goddamn," says Candy.

"Yeah."

Bill scratches his lower lip, moves his finger up to brush his mustache into place in one smooth motion.

"What you're saying—and correct me if I've misconstrued the thing—but we're not preparing for an attack. This is a suicide run."

"Not necessarily. But that's a possibility."

"In my experience, not necessarily usually means yes. So, we're preparing to throw ourselves on the sword for king and country."

"Like I said, maybe."

"Twenty soldiers and maybe angels?" Candy says. "I'm with Jim. This is suicide."

"Not if we don't run straight at them. Yesterday I wanted to rush in and kill everyone. That was when there were maybe twelve guards. Now we might be able to do something else."

"What?" says Bill.

"The woman is the one outside doing all the work. And see-ing her with Quay a couple of times, I think they're an item."

"So, we snatch the filly."

"That's what I was thinking."

"How do we do it?" says Candy.

"We use the Unimog to ambush the SUV. Grab Miss America, and get Quay to come to us."

"Which is all a fine plan, unless there are warrior angels about."

"In which case we're fucked. Worse, we won't know if there are angels until we start the ambush because sometimes they ride in the SUV with her."

"Well, this is all depressing," says Candy.

She rests an elbow on the bar.

"I agree with Candy," says Bill. "You folks are alive. The worst that can happen to you is you get killed and end up right back here in the Devil's shitter with me. On the other hand, I'm already a spirit. If I should be cut down . . ."

"It's Tartarus."

"What's that?" Candy says.

I look at Bill.

"It's the Hell below Hell. Hell for the double damned."

"And Jim might end up there?"

"Only if he comes with us."

"I'm coming with you. That's not a point of discussion."

"But you wouldn't have to do the heavy fighting, like in the house. You can stay at a safe distance and be our sniper. Take out who you can."

Bill leans back on the shelves behind the bar.

"I never shirked from a fight back home and I'm not about to start here. I'll not be sitting in the trees like a jaybird."

"Do we have anything going for us?" says Candy.

Bill looks at me.

"Not much. We don't have enough information or enough people. But we really don't have a choice."

Bill lays out the shot glasses.

"We may not have a choice, but we can have a drink. I'll get the bottle."

Three hard knocks come from the front door.

Bill sets down the bottle.

I say, "You expecting anyone?"

"Not a soul."

Everyone raises their gun. I move as quietly as I can to the door. Just as I'm about to grab it, it bursts open.

An angel in glowing battle armor stands there. I recognize her.

It's the angel I fought in Hollywood.

I put the Glock to her head.

She drops to one knee and holds out a piece of parchment.

"Shoot me if you must," she says. "But Samael has sent me to you."

WITHOUT MOVING THE Glock from the angel's head, I call Candy over.

"Keep the shotgun on her. If she even looks up, blow her head off."

"Sounds like fun."

I take the parchment from the angel's hand and get one of Bill's candles so I can read it.

> *Dear Jimmy,*
> *You're no doubt reading this with a gun to my*
> *poor emissary's head. If I say that you can lower*

*it, will you listen? Of course not, so I won't. Her
name is Hesediel and she is a good and loyal ally
in Father's war. I'm sending her to you because
I suspect you could use help in whatever fool's
errand sent you Downtown. By the way, how did
you get there, clever boy? You'll have to tell me
about it sometime.*

*Hesediel is quite the warrior and, like the rest of
us, ready for this inconvenience to be over. She's
as ruthless you, Sandman Slim, so you should get
along like two peas in a barrel bomb.*

*Good luck and try to avoid scars during your
visit. Any more and you'll just be showing off.*
Samael
P.S. Tell Candy she can keep the shoes.

If the note didn't call the war in Heaven anything but an
"inconvenience," I wouldn't believe it.

"Let her up," I say to Candy.

"Are you sure?"

"Her note says you can keep the shoes."

"Okay, then," she says brightly, and lowers her gun.

I hold on to the Glock.

"Get up, Hesediel."

She stands. In her armor, she's every bit as imposing as she
was when hammering me into the ground with her Gladius. It
also looks like the eye I shot out grew back. Neat trick.

"Thank you," she says.

"I just have one question before I trust you: Why the hell
did you try to kill me back home?"

"That wasn't me," she says. "It was my sister, Hadraniel."

"I didn't know angels had sisters and brothers."

"A spiritual sister. We were once as close as any human siblings."

"But she changed sides."

Hesediel nods.

"Hadraniel broke many hearts that day."

"I used to have a friend named Mason. It hurts when they go bad."

"Then you understand."

"You know that I don't have a history of getting along with angels, right?"

She looks down at me.

"Samael remarked on that."

"Plus, I used to be Lucifer."

"That too."

"But you're willing to work with me?"

"Strange times make for strange allies. Samael was once the greatest enemy of all, but he saw the light. If I can ally with him, I can ally with the Abomination."

I put the Glock back in its holster.

"And I guess I can work with a halo polisher. Come on over and have a drink."

She follows me to the bar.

"Hesediel, this is Candy and Wild Bill."

She stares at Candy for a minute. Candy stares right back.

"You going to call me Abomination too?"

"No. We're alike. Inhuman, but fighting a war that will benefit mortals."

"It'll benefit everyone, so don't go putting your war off on regular people. They didn't start it."

"It's not pleasant to contemplate."

"Then let's have a drink," says Bill.

She looks at the bottle.

"Is that a Hellion brew?"

"They no longer deliver champagne down here, I'm afraid."

"I've never had it before."

"No time like the present."

"If I refuse?"

Bill looks at her, the only one in the room tall enough to go eye to eye with her.

"Where I'm from, friends have a drink before going into a fight. Makes sure no one supposes they're above anyone else."

Bill pours and I hand Hesediel a glass.

"It's just a ritual. As an angel, you should understand that."

"If I must," she says.

"It's the polite thing to do."

She looks at the glass like it's full of bear shit.

"Samael said there would be trials and tests with you."

"We Abominations are picky bastards."

"Then we'll drink to that," says Bill. "To as motley a crew of bastards as I've ever partnered with."

Everyone drinks.

Hesediel hesitates, then downs the whole thing. And goes into a coughing fit I'm afraid is going to blow her wings off.

She doubles up and leans a hand on the bar. I lean over to her.

"You okay?"

She chokes out, "Yes."

A few more seconds and she can stand again.

"Is that it, then? If there are more rituals and tests, I'd like to get them over with now."

Bill holds out a handkerchief for her. She shakes her head. I set down my glass.

"No more tests. And if it's any comfort, the first time I tried Hellion booze, I did the same thing."

"Good," she says.

"So, maybe we're not a suicide mission anymore?" says Candy.

"Maybe not. With Hesediel, we might actually survive this."

I look at her.

"You ready to kill some Hellions?"

"I'm here to do whatever is necessary."

"Even if it's killing other Heavenly angels?"

"You mean rebels against Father? I've dispatched many of them already. If more are necessary, so be it. I'll take care of it."

"I can help there."

She shifts uncomfortably.

"I'd rather you didn't."

"Why?"

"It would be distasteful."

"The Abomination thing?"

"Yes."

"If you can handle them, fine. But if they're too much, I'm jumping in."

"That's acceptable."

"Then welcome to the team. Here's the deal: we need to get to a man named Norris Quay. He's the head honcho of Wormwood down here. The problem is that he's protected and we don't want to go charging through the front door without knowing what's inside. So, we're going to kidnap his lady friend and make him come to us."

She wipes her mouth with the back of her hand.

"It's a sound plan. Where and when do we act?"

"Griffith Park and as soon as we can."

I look at the others. "Okay, bushwhackers. Let's get bush-whacking."

Candy gets behind the wheel of the Unimog and the rest of us pile in. It's a snug fit. Bill is squeezed up against Hesediel.

"Sorry about the tight quarters, ma'am," he says.

"I'm a warrior. I've suffered worse."

"I've had whores and drunks in my lap before, but never one of the Lord's own."

Hesediel just stares out the window.

"What Bill is saying is we're glad you're here, Hesediel," I tell her.

"The sooner the battle begins, the sooner it will be over," she says.

Candy starts the truck and we take off.

"I like your armor," she says.

"Thank you," says Hesediel.

"Stark wore armor when he was Lucifer. It was sexy. I called him 'Tony Stark.'"

Hesediel looks at her.

"You know. Like Iron Man. Stark's name is Stark and so is his."

"How interesting."

"You don't know Iron Man? You should come with us to L.A. We have all the movies."

"Perhaps," says Hesediel, staring out the window again.

Candy says, "Angels don't make a lot of small talk, do they?"

"It's not in our nature."

"No shit."

WE HIDE THE Unimog along a bend in the road in Griffith Park out of sight of the mansion. Then we wait. Candy stays behind the wheel with the engine running. The rest of us wait in the trees.

An hour or so later, Bill sees something moving below us. He takes out his telescope and surveys the road.

"One of them vans is coming."

I move up next to him.

"You sure it's just one?"

"My eyes work just fine. It's one."

"Then let's get ready. Remember, we leave one of the guards alive to tell Quay what happened."

"What if there are angels?" says Bill.

"Them we kill. Right?"

I look at Hesediel.

"I'll dispatch the rebels," she says.

"Then it's a plan."

We wait for the van to come up the hill. When it's almost abreast of us, Candy guns the Unimog's engine and plows into the side of the van, pushing it off the road. No one gets out for a minute. Then the passenger-side door bursts open and a Legionnaire lurches out. He swings his rifle at the Unimog.

Bill and I step out of the trees, but Candy blasts him with the Benelli before we can even take aim.

The van's side door slides open and more Hellions stumble into the road, shooting in all directions. There are four of them, and none is in good shape. Bill shoots one and I get another. The other two freeze where they are when Hesediel comes out, her armor glowing in Hell's dim light like it's made of fire. When the two idiots get the idea that maybe it's a good time to shoot, it's too late. Their bullets bounce off Hesediel's armor. She cuts one down with a single stroke of her Gladius. She swings again and cuts the other one's arms off. His rifle tumbles to the ground and he falls against the van, his wounds seared closed by the Gladius's burning blade.

I jump into the van while Hesediel and Bill watch my back.

The woman is pressed against the interior on the far side of the van, her eyes as big as weather balloons. I look her over for weapons and wounds. I don't see any guns, but she has a cut over her left eye.

I aim the Glock at her.

"You can get out with me or let the angel drag you out."

She puts her hands up and slides across the seat. I take her arm and help her into the road. She stumbles, a little wobbly after the crash.

I give her to Bill and kneel by the armless Legionnaire.

"Can you hear me?"

"Yes," he says.

"Tell Norris Quay to meet us at the Hollywood Bowl in two hours. If he doesn't come alone, we're going to barbecue Miss America and serve her with beans. Got it?"

"Two hours at the Hollywood Bowl."

"What else?"

He looks down at where his arms used to be.

"He's to come alone."

"Who said you Legionnaires were all blockheads? Wait, it was me."

Bill taps me on the back.

"We'd best be moving," he says.

We pile back into the Unimog, shoving Miss America into the space behind the seats. Candy gets us turned around and we haul ass down the hill. Franklin is blocked with debris from looted houses, so we speed down Hollywood Boulevard to Highland and head north to the Bowl.

It occurs to me as we go that I don't even know if Hell's Hollywood Bowl is even there anymore. I should probably have checked that out. See? Thinking. It's always my downfall.

The good news is that while half of its dome is caved in, the Bowl and grandstands are basically intact. The stage area is covered with dried blood in a charming variety of colors. A lot of Hellions, beasts, and who knows what else have been killed here for the cheering crowds. I wonder if the old arena is still standing. I feel a weird pang of nostalgia for the place. Sure, it was possibly the most awful place in the universe, but it was *my* most awful place. If it's gone, I'll miss it. I never even got to take a selfie there. Of course, I don't mention any of this to the others, but I make a mental note that if we have enough time, I want to take Candy there. If she's going to make me miserable at Disney World, she can be miserable for a few minutes at my old alma mater.

We stash the Unimog by the road beside the Bowl. Hesediel and I manifest our Gladiuses and hack our way through the fences and trees, clearing a path to the front of the stage. She takes a couple of steps back when my Gladius first comes out. I'm not sure she believed that I had one. Now that she does, I'm not sure she entirely trusts me with it. But she does her job and I do mine.

Bill and Candy bring Miss America, and we climb over stage junk until we're backstage in the Bowl.

Bill looks back at the grandstands and grounds.

"Not a bad place for a meet. Lot of open territory. A road nearby."

He points to the line of black, twisted trees on the hill overlooking the grandstands.

"They could put snipers up there."

"Not if Quay wants Miss America back."

"We're really going to kill her?" says Candy. I can tell that she doesn't like the idea. But I don't want to sound soft.

I look hard at Miss America.

"Maybe. Maybe not."

She looks at our sorry group, terrified.

Candy goes over and puts a hand on her shoulder. The woman recoils and Candy moves away.

"What's your name?" she says.

Miss America looks around.

"Holly," she says. "Holly Cranor."

I lean against a half-burned table.

"What did you do for Wormwood back in the world, Holly?"

"Nothing," she says. "I wasn't in Wormwood."

"Then you joined when you got down here."

"No. I'm not in Wormwood. I'm just friends with Norris."

"You're with Quay, but you're not with Wormwood? That's just a little hard to believe."

"Norris says that people have to prove themselves useful to be in Wormwood."

"And you're not particularly useful yet."

"Oh no. I'm useful. I work with Netzach and the other angels. Norris promised that I'll be in Wormwood soon."

"Sounds like true love," says Candy.

Holly half smiles, not sure if Candy is kidding or not.

I say, "The stuff you do with Netzach, it has to do with black milk?"

She hesitates then says, "Yes."

"They bring the raw stuff and you get them the refined product."

"Yes."

"How does it work?"

"I don't know. Norris is very secretive about it. He promised to tell me all about it when I'm in Wormwood."

Her eyes are steady but she doesn't have sweat or a heartbeat for me to check. I go to Hesediel.

"What do you think? Is she telling the truth?"

"I think so."

"Me too. Which stinks. I was hoping for more from her."

"Mortals will believe many things if they think it will relieve their suffering, if even for a moment."

"We just hate missing *The Brady Bunch* is all."

Not a peep from Hesediel.

Tough crowd.

"Holly sounds stupid enough to hook up with Quay without even knowing what Wormwood is."

Hesediel calls to Holly.

"Did you know the mortal Norris Quay when you were alive?"

"No. We met here. When things were getting bad. You know? He saved me."

"Naturally."

Bill and Candy come over. Bill keeps the Colt on her.

"If she's not in Wormwood, we should let her go, right?" says Candy.

I shake my head.

"She's not in Wormwood but she's doing important work for them. And she'll probably do even worse when she gets in."

"Yeah, but she hasn't done it *yet*. If Quay doesn't show or does something stupid, I don't want to kill her. She's just scared and lost."

"She's in Hell. She did something to get here."

"Still."

I look at Candy and remember what a mess she was when Doc Kinski died. A bit lost and freaked out herself.

"We won't kill her. But we can't let her or Quay know that."

Candy takes a breath.

"Thanks."

Hesediel looks at me funny.

"What's wrong with you?"

"Nothing. I simply didn't expect compassion from the Abomination."

"If you liked that trick, you should see me juggle."

"How long do we have to wait?"

I check my phone. The battery is down three quarters.

"Not long. Everybody relax."

Candy finds a folding chair and brings it to Holly. She's too nervous to actually sit. She sort of perches on it like a bird ready to take off at the slightest sound.

Bill and I have Maledictions. Hesediel moves to the other side of the room to avoid the smoke. Candy keeps an eye on Holly.

"If this all goes askew, it was good seeing you again, son," says Bill.

"You too. But don't worry. We're going to make it."

"You that certain?"

"I am."

"Why?"

"I'm taking Candy to Disney World."

"I hope you make it too."

"I hope I survive it. I hate that mouse."

I check my phone.

"Any minute now."

We toss our cigarettes and everyone goes on alert. I get Holly to her feet and kick the chair away. Take her to the front of the stage. The others keep lookout behind us.

In a few minutes, Hesediel says, "There."

She points at a figure moving through the grandstand half-way up the hill. He's waving a piece of cloth like a white flag.

We wait. Let him come to us. Bill and Hesediel scan the tree line for shooters.

When he finally gets to the stage, Norris Quay says, "Holly, dear, are you all right? Have they hurt you?"

"No. I'm okay."

She touches the cut over her eye.

"Except for the accident."

Quay looks better than the last time I saw him. He was a broken-down old man then. Free of his body, he looks a lot more spry.

"Hell agrees with you, Norris. You look like a young Tony Curtis."

"Don't kid me. I look like an old man who's been taking his vitamins."

"Does that include black milk?"

He shakes his head.

"The black milk isn't for us. But celestials can't get enough of it."

"You always find a profit angle, don't you?"

He moves closer, around some broken stage lights.

"Don't act surprised, Stark. It's what we do."

"What kind of odds are there on me killing you and Miss Cranor?"

"Less than you letting us go."

"Why's that?"

"Because I'm going to give you everything you want. I'll

take you right to the source of black milk. Explain everything. What you do about it after that is your business. That's
if you promise to let me and Holly leave afterward."

"Why would you show us black milk?"

"Because there isn't a damned thing you can do about it."

"You're that sure."

"Quite," he says happily.

"If you're straight with us, we'll let you go."

He points at the stage.

"I want to hear it from the angel. They're a bit more trust-
worthy than a murderer."

I look at Hesediel.

"It's agreed," she says. "If you take us to the source, you
will be free to go."

He slaps his hands together.

"See how easy that was? Well, should we get started?"

When I let go, Candy takes Holly's arm. I point with the
Glock.

"Our truck is over there."

"Yes. I saw it on the way in. A little small for all of us,
don't you think? I have a van out front. It'll be much more
comfortable."

I look back at the others.

"The man has a point," says Bill. "Any closer in the truck
and we'll all know each other in the biblical sense."

I turn to Hesediel.

"He's right."

I call down to Quay.

"Same deal as before, Norris. Any tricks and you both die.
Holly first."

"Of course. I wouldn't have it any other way."

"Norris?" says Holly quietly.

"Relax, my dear. These champions of the oppressed will have what they want and we'll be on our way soon."

"If you say so."

"I do, my dear. Now, let's away, shall we?"

"Stop," I say.

Everyone looks at me.

This whole thing might be the end of every human soul, but I have to know something and now.

"In case I have to shoot you later, tell me about Liliane. I get that she was working for you, but why sic her on Vidocq?"

Quay looks disappointed in the question.

"Do you think your friends are special? That they should be exempt from our work?"

"Is that all it was? Hurting my friends to get to me?"

"It was Liliane's idea actually. We gave her Vidocq as a gift. Hurting you and your Merry Men was a bonus."

"Wormwood should leave my other friends alone."

He flicks something off his shirt.

"We'll take that under advisement."

QUAY LEADS US through the grandstands to where one of his black vans is parked. Holly walks with him. I hold my gun to his head. Candy, Bill, and Hesediel keep a lookout for an ambush. But nothing happens.

We make it to the van and everyone piles in, Norris behind the wheel while the others get in the back. I stay up front with my gun in his side. He starts the van and we drive back down Highland the way we came. Then we keep moving south.

We go all the way down Highland until it turns into South La Brea Avenue. Moving around the debris and burned-out cars, it's a long, slow drive.

"Tell me, Norris. What's black milk?"

"You'll see soon enough."

"Is this where it's manufactured?"

"In one sense, yes. In another, no."

"Don't be cute. I can still shoot Holly Golightly."

"And then you'll end up with nothing but a heartbroken old man for your troubles."

"You said you'd tell us, so tell us," says Candy.

"Are any of you history buffs?" says Quay. "No? I didn't think so. Then you won't be acquainted with the term *Panzerschokolade*."

I keep the gun in his side.

"I know the word 'panzer.' It's German for tank."

"And *chokolade* is exactly what it sounds like. Chocolate. *Panzerschokolade*. Tank chocolate."

"You're feeding angels metal bonbons?"

"In a sense, yes. *Panzerchokolade* was a treat the German high command gave their tank drivers back during the war. It kept them awake for days. Made them brave. Even reckless, but able to accomplish remarkable things and win battles they should have lost."

"You're talking about speed. Black milk is speed for angels."

He glances at me.

"The angel who paid you a visit on Hollywood Boulevard, what was her name?"

"Hadraniel," says Hesediel.

"That's it."

He glances at me.

"Did she seem a bit different to you? Not like other angels you'd met?"

"Yeah. She was out of her fucking mind."

"Oh, she was in her mind, but her mind had been transformed by *Panzerschokolade* into something more formidable than before. You must be acquainted with the word 'berserker'?"

"Crazy fucking Vikings who worked themselves up into a screaming lather and ran straight into a fight. You're saying that black milk turns angels into berserkers."

"Precisely."

Keeping my gun pressed into Quay's side, I look at Hesediel.

"Does that sound right to you?"

"I'm afraid so," she says. "Their strength and courage is unexplainable by any normal standards."

I turn back to Quay.

"You're keeping the war in Heaven going. Why?"

"One secret at a time, Sandman Slim. One secret at a time. Now, you wanted to know how black milk is manufactured."

"Stop stalling."

"The raw materials for black milk are found only here in Hell. Isn't that interesting?"

"Fascinating. Now I'll win next time I'm on *Jeopardy!*"

He steers us around a line of overturned school buses. There are no bodies anywhere. All the dead Hellions and damned souls are in Tartarus.

"We use rebel angels to move the raw black milk to Earth, where it's transformed from a poison into a miracle drug."

"How is it done?"

"Geoffrey Burgess was about to cook us a new batch, but you ruined it."

"I didn't see any potions in his house."

"Of course not. It hadn't been manufactured yet. Think hard, Sandman Slim. I know that's not your best quality, but it's important."

Slow as I am, I don't have to think about it too long.

"It was Nick. Burgess had Nick and I fucked that up."

Quay claps his hands on the steering wheel.

"See? You can put those brain cells to work if you try, try, try."

"What does Nick have to do with anything?"

"Black milk is processed in their bodies. Poison goes in and *Panzerschokolade* comes out."

He looks at me. There's practically a twinkle in his eye.

"We milk the little bastards like cattle. Hence the term 'black milk.'"

"You fucker," sputters Candy. "You fucking fuck."

"You're every bit as eloquent as I would expect Sandman Slim's paramour to be."

I jab the gun into Quay's ribs.

"There's another kid missing back home. She's more cattle?"

"Of course. Her family is nothing. This is their chance to move up in the world."

"And join the immortality club."

"Yes, we keep a small amount of processed black milk for ourselves. Any family that sacrifices a child is admitted to the program."

No one says anything for a minute. We spot some broken down hellhounds. Gears and metal limbs scattered across the road.

"Admit it. It's a bargain," says Quay. "Eternity for one brat. If it makes you feel better, the families are free to produce all the little tykes they want after that."

"Are the new kids immortal too?"

Quay shakes his head.

"I'm afraid not. New kids mean new sacrifices. You see, shared secrets like this bind people together. It's the foundation of Wormwood."

"A ritual," says Hesediel.

"See? The angel understands."

"So I've been told."

"I don't have the words for what a low scoundrel you are," says Wild Bill. "I thought I'd seen the worst in men back home. Clearly I was wrong."

"Thank you, Bill. In Wormwood, we aim for excellence."

I don't want to think about Quay's story. There's no way to prove it from down here. It could all be lies. Then again, why would he tell a lie he knows might piss us off so much that we kill him?

"What about the war in Heaven? Why is Wormwood picking sides?"

"We're not. And I'll explain all that in just a few more minutes. Until then, let's take in the sights, shall we?"

We continue across the I-10 freeway, all the way down to the 105.

On the other side are the ruins of an old water treatment plant. Quay parks the van by the entrance and starts to get out. I move the gun back to his head.

"Hold it. Bill, I'm going around to Quay's side. Keep him covered."

"With pleasure."

I move around the van slowly, looking for shooters or traps. When I get to the driver-side door, I pull Quay out. He doesn't resist. Bill steps out, then Candy—still holding her gun on Holly, though she's not even trying to look like she's serious.

The wind changes direction and the stink from the water plant is blinding. Quay just takes a deep breath and smiles.

"Here we are."

"Are we going for a dip?"

"I wouldn't if I were you."

He heads into the plant and we follow, me with my gun on him.

"Is this what you're telling us, Norris? That black milk is water? I don't believe you."

"Of course it's not water," he says.

He walks straight to the edge of the closest holding pond.

"Come closer, Sandman Slim. Take a whiff of the future."

I have to hold my hand to my face until I get used to the stink.

"What are we doing here, Norris?"

"Here's the story. We're not in a water treatment plant. We're in Hell. Who cares if Hellions have clean water? Yet as awful as this place is, what's the one thing Lucifer, you included, wouldn't tolerate in his streets?"

Holly coughs like she's going to throw up. Candy pats her on the back.

"Effluent," says Bill. "Even these Hellion pig fuckers don't want shit on their boots."

Quay points at Bill with one hand and taps his nose with the other.

"You win," he says. "Behold. The only source of black milk in the universe."

I go up with him to the holding pond.

"Black milk is Hellion shit?"

"Of course not. This is a sewage plant, not a shit plant. There's every kind of Pandemonium trash and runoff in here. It's the complete brew that's the secret. It's Pandemonium itself. But you're right to the extent that Hellion shit is the most essential ingredient. Think of it like saffron. Every squatting, sitting, diarrhea-ravaged fallen angel is leaking the most valuable substance in the universe from their puckering assholes."

I look down into the black, clotted mess. Then point the Glock at Quay's head.

"This is a joke. When I met you in L.A., you were surrounded by all kinds of death totems. You were looking for a way not to die. If you're in Wormwood, why weren't you in the immortality program?"

"I wasn't in Wormwood then. Not until right at the end."

"What changed?"

He clasps his hands behind his back.

"I gave them my son. You didn't know I was married, did

you? One dead wife. One living child. I was in. On my way to eternal bliss."

"Then why did you follow me into Kill City if you were set up with Wormwood?"

"Well," he says, "you were hunting for a mystical object. One likes to hedge one's bets with these things. I died before I could use my dose of black milk. But I was repaid for my good works."

"By making you head of their branch headquarters."

"Exactly," he says, giving me the most beautifully smug smile in history.

I lower my gun. Hesediel is on the other side of Quay listening to everything. She doesn't look happy.

"You sold this filth to my kind. You polluted celestials with the bowels of the fallen."

"They polluted themselves with black milk. And the corrupt blood of poisoned children, don't forget," says Quay merrily.

I tap the Glock against the side of my leg, trying not to use it.

"I still don't get it. Why take sides in the war?"

"I told you. We're not taking sides. We're just working the odds."

"I don't understand."

"Of course not. Hush and let me explain."

"Hush" is a funny word. It makes me want to cut someone's head off. But I let it pass for now.

Quay continues: "Heaven is a closed market without the war. Very little profit to be made there. Hell, on the other hand, is wide open. Think of it as Wormwood's offshore bank account," he says.

"What if the rebel angels lose and souls can enter Heaven?"

"Then Hell will remain a haven for Wormwood. The damned who reject Heaven will stay and the rebel angels will ally with us. Who doesn't want an army of angels on their side? Think of what they could do for us on Earth."

"What if the rebels win?" says Hesediel.

"Then human souls and Hellions will be exiled to Hell forever. And, again, Wormwood will be in charge. And as long as there are Hellions in Hell, we'll have a steady supply of black milk."

I finally get it.

"And Wormwood on Earth stays immortal."

"Exactly."

"They need a steady diet of the stuff to stay alive."

"Yes. It's an unpleasant brew, from what I understand, but immortality is the lollipop one gets after the medicine."

I turn him around to face me.

"That means all we have to do is destroy the source of black milk and your whole plan falls apart. The rebel angels lose. No one in your Boy Scout troop stays immortal. And if Wormwood comes apart down here, how long will it take to fall apart back home?"

Quay gives Holly a big grin, then looks back at me.

"Is that your plan, Sandman Slim? You're going to murder all the millions of Hellions in Perdition?"

"If I have to."

"You really are an egomaniacal child, aren't you?"

I want to say something clever, but nothing comes out.

Quay goes up on his toes for a second, then back down, happy but restless.

"Now that I've kept my part of the bargain, I assume Holly and I are free to go?"

I look at him. Then the storage pond.

"Are you a good swimmer, Norris?"

Hesediel looks at me.

"We gave our word," she says.

"She's right," says Candy.

"A man's word, son. It's all we have in this putrid swamp," says Bill.

I know all this. And yet.

Quay never stops smiling.

And I really want him to stop fucking smiling. Or to see his head rolling into the parking lot. It's tempting.

After a moment, though, I take a step back.

"You and Holly are free to go."

"Of course we are," he says. "The odds were always in my favor, you know. Someone upstairs just made a big profit from your wise decision."

I take the van keys from his pocket.

"We're keeping the van. You can walk back."

"Don't you worry about us. I had my team leave a van for us on the other side of the plant. You're so predictable, Sandman Slim."

He walks over and takes Holly's arm.

"Oh, Geoff Burgess and Charlie Anpu say hi. And no hard feelings."

As they walk away, I call after them.

"If you've rigged our van to explode or something, when I get back to Hell you know I'm going to track you down."

Quay turns to us, but doesn't stop walking.

"Don't worry. There aren't any bombs or tricks. You've done enough damage to yourselves already."

He and Holly walk away and no one says a word because we know he's right.

IT'S A LONG drive back to Bill's place.

We park the van and go inside without a word. Bill lights some candles and uncorks the bottle. Pours three shots.

"I don't suppose you'll be joining us," he says to Hesediel.

"I'd rather not."

"No need. This ain't exactly a celebration."

Bill and I drink. Candy just stares at hers. I don't think she likes the stuff any more than Hesediel.

"What do we do now? Go home?" she says.

I pour me and Bill another.

"We can't. We didn't just come for Wormwood. We came for Vidocq."

"Who is that?" says Hesediel.

"Just another mortal to you. A friend to us. One of Wormwood's people poisoned him with black milk."

"And he lives?"

"He's in the Winter Garden. It's like a hoodoo coma."

"Did you really think that Norris Quay and his kind would help save your friend?"

"No. We came here hoping to find an angel."

She comes over to the bar.

"For what?"

"A little blood. It's the one thing I know of that will cure pretty much any civilian disease."

She picks up the bottle. Sets it down again.

"Bill. Do you have an empty one?"

He finds a dusty pint bottle under the bar. Hesediel takes it from him.

"How much will your friend need?"

"Just a few drops," I tell her.

She stretches out her arm, pushing her wrist just past the edge of her armor. I offer her the black blade.

"Hellion made?" she says.

"Yes."

"I'll use mine."

She takes a dagger out of a sheath at her side. Puts the tip to her wrist and lets blood dribble into the glass until it covers the bottom.

"Is that enough?"

"More than enough."

She puts the cork back in the top and hands me the blood.

"I hope it helps your friend."

"Thank you. This means a lot to us."

She nods. Lets the blood flow a little longer. Some kind of strange penitence.

I give Candy the bottle.

"You should take care of it. I break things."

She puts it in her pocket with the shoes.

"Thank you, Hesediel," Candy says.

"I was wrong before," says the angel. "This thing you're doing, it won't help just mortals, but celestials too. I didn't want to say it before because I didn't want to reveal any weakness on our part. That was foolish. After seeing Norris Quay's secret, weakness is all I feel."

"Me too," says Bill. "Weak, foolish, and low. These Wormwood folks, they've run rings around us."

"What are we going to do?" Candy says. "Just sit here and drink?"

I nod. "For now. We're waiting."

"For what?" says Hesediel. "There are no more of my kind coming."

"We're not waiting for angels or anyone else to rescue us."

"Then what are we doing?"

"We're waiting for old Norris to get home."

I finish my drink.

"Then we're going to go up there and kill every one of them. Send them all to Tartarus."

"Isn't that what they're expecting?" says Bill. "We all saw Norris goading you on."

"I was wrong before when I said we had to go through the front door. I was angry and I was dumb."

"So what do you want to do now?" says Candy.

"Me and Hesediel, we're going to burn the whole damned hill they're sitting on. You up for that, angel?"

She stares into the candle at the end of the bar.

"The rebel angels, misguided as they are, fight for a cause they believe in that's greater than themselves. This Wormwood fights for nothing."

"That's it, then. We go up and set off some fireworks. Kill anyone who makes it out of the mansion."

"What about the Legionnaires?" says Bill.

"They're mercenaries. What are the odds they're going to stick around when we burn the whole damned forest?"

"And we have Hesediel," says Candy.

"Exactly—we have our own angel. That should give some Hellions bad dreams."

Hesediel smiles wanly.

"After Lucifer's defeat, I never thought I'd be fighting my own kind again. Even fallen angels. Each death is a knife to the heart."

"Don't worry. Look at me. I've been stabbed plenty of times. Scars just make you look distinguished."

She looks at the ceiling.

"I don't understand you. One moment you show courage and compassion and the next you're as cruel as the rebels we fight above."

"Because I tell a few jokes? It's how we pass the time on Earth waiting to die. You angels are immortal. Mortal life is just one long square dance in rotting meat."

"That explains nothing. The Abomination isn't a mortal man."

"Maybe if you angels ever did anything but try to kill me, I'd be more like you. From where I sit, celestials are all Eddie Haskell. Pretty lousy role models."

Candy goes over to her.

"He doesn't mean you personally," says Candy.

"She right. You're the only angel that didn't take a dump on my head the moment you saw me."

She turns and stares into the dark.

"What a world we've made. Samael, the betrayer, is now Father's staunchest ally, while my sister Hadraniel is my sworn enemy. And here I am with a damned mortal, an inhuman, and a jesting monster as my companions in battle. It's all so confusing."

"I felt the same way when they changed Darrin on *Bewitched*."

She shakes her head like she's trying to wake herself up. I actually feel sorry for an angel.

"Look, nothing ever makes sense. I've never met a happy angel. Even at the beginning of time when you could pretend it was just you and Mr. Muninn, you knew the Kissi were hiding in the dark. Monsters under your bed. But you pretended like they weren't there. That kind of thing makes mortals crazy too. It's called denial."

Hesediel looks at me hard. I scratch my head.

"Mortals, angels, and Abominations, all we get are moments between shit storms. So, have a fucking drink or have a fucking laugh or go sit in the fucking dark and pout because the universe forgot your birthday."

Hesediel stares at the blood on her wrist.

"No one has ever spoken to me like that before. Not even Hadraniel."

"It's a habit. How do you think I got all these scars?"

She does the universe's tiniest laugh.

"Do you think Quay is home yet?" says Bill.

"Only one way to find out. Let's go light a barbecue."

"Thank the Lord. I thought you'd never shut up."

WE LEAVE THE van on Franklin Street and head up into the park. Instead of taking the nice, smooth, probably-not-going-to-break-your-ankle-in-three-places road, we duck into the vegetation and climb through Hell's little Eden.

Griffith Park back in the world is a lot of brittle scrub, annoying bushes, and thirsty trees covering what's essentially a big rock hemorrhoid looming over Hollywood. Most people go there for the big observatory. Others for the zoo. Still others like the view, though they're the strangest bunch of all. Hollywood in broad daylight is a miserable place. Maybe sixty years ago some vestiges of golden-age glamour still clung to the place, but even then it was less like romance and more like a particularly enchanting strain of tuberculosis.

Now the Boulevard is a parched dump full of tourist T-shirts and mournful bars, with a few expensive restaurants so out of place it's like they crashed to Earth on a meteor. At one end of Hollywood Boulevard, you'll get your pocket picked outside an all-night liquor store, and at the other end, you'll be outright mugged by alcoholics who couldn't get SAG cards, but could afford secondhand Spider-Man or Wonder Woman costumes. They're clingier than lampreys and scarier than ticks, and the only cure is to give them twenty bucks for a shitty Polaroid.

But Hollywood at night is a different story. Hollywood has always been a night city. A place built for vampires and insomniacs. It's all blinking lights, neon, the dully glowing stars on the Walk of Fame, and the outlines of not-so-healthy palm trees, but it's okay because they're as spectral as the rest of the place and more alive because of it. Hell, on the other hand, doesn't have real nights. Just an endless, dirty twilight, perfect weather for a teen goth tea party. Because of this, when we go up the hill, we have to move far from the road; otherwise there might be just enough light to see us.

Of course, Hellion Griffith Park doesn't have the same stupid trees and irritating bushes as regular Griffith Park. No, this park is more twisted, vicious, and thorny than Sleeping Beauty's bastard castle.

There are bushes with poisonous berries that burst if you make the slightest contact. Black, twisted trees drop rotten fruit full of venomous centipedes the size of dachshunds. There are shallow pools of toxic algae and deep pools full of deadly puffer fish that look like balloons covered in tiny chain saws instead of spines. A miasma blows through the forest that corrodes your lungs and stings your eyes. Basically, everything in the fucking place is infectious, malignant, noxious, and lethal.

I fucking hate nature.

We have to go slow to minimize our contact with all the vicious vegetable bullshit. And by "we" I mean everyone but Hesediel. Yeah, the stroll makes her as filthy and foul-smelling as the rest of us, but angels are immune to these Downtown poisons. While the rest of us are hopping around roots and barbed vines like we're in the finals of a St. Vitus dance contest, Hesediel tromps ahead like the world's most annoying Sherpa, blazing the trail, but leaving us in her virulent dust.

I run a few steps to catch up to her, snagging my coat on mustard-gas seed pods and tromping on flowers that smell like an alligator's ass.

"Slow down a little. Goddammit."

She stops and looks back at the others.

"I'm sorry. I simply wanted to begin as soon as possible. You were right what you said at the tavern. We're only afforded mere moments of pleasure. It will be my pleasure to deal with these conspirators and return to Heaven and the pleasures of a simpler battle."

"That's great and I hope you have a nice drive home, but we're losing the others. Let's just ease back a little, okay?"

She looks back, her wings moving restlessly. I don't think angels are used to being in such closed-in places. For all her talk about wanting to get into the fight, I think she wants out of this nauseating, brambled puke garden more than we do.

Bill and Candy are scratched pretty nicely when they catch up. Bill is breathing hard. It has to be toughest on him. A damned soul, this kind of torment is designed to make him as miserable as possible. But Candy isn't looking so great either. I'm glad I gave her my old coat. At places it's ripped all the way down to the motocross pads. She's breathing hard.

"You okay? Want to slow down a little?"

She shakes her head.

"It's just this mist. I can't get a good breath. It's making me dizzy."

I look back at Hesediel.

"Maybe you were right. Getting out of here fast might be the best move. Let's keep going, but take a chance and move a little closer to the road. We'll get better air over there."

No one argues with that. Hesediel cuts over to the right a few dozen yards and the rest of us follow, trying not to fall too far behind.

We hear the sound of a van going down the hill. As it passes, we can just make it out through the trees. I was right.

The air is better over here, but we're still too deep in this shaggy shit pit to be seen. We keep moving.

Finally, there's a break in the tree line ahead. Now we move slowly again, getting right to the edge of the forest. We're to the side of the mansion, almost around back. Hesediel looks fine, even with a couple of scratches on her perfect face. But Candy and Bill are pale and panting.

"Let's rest here for a while. We need to check out the scene to get an idea how many guards are around."

All Candy and Bill can do is nod. They walk back a few yards to a clear patch of filth. Bill slides down the side of a tree, ripping his shirt on some thorns. Candy drops down next to him, landing on some stinking flowers. Hesediel and I follow the tree line to the front of the house.

What we see is just peculiar. Outside the mansion, four Hellion guards don't even pretend to patrol the place. Their rifles are slung low on their shoulders, the muzzles pointed down. They pass Maledictions and flasks of Aqua Regia around the circle like they're on a corporate playdate without a care in the world. Hesediel frowns at me. I shake my head because I don't have a clue what's going on either.

I whisper, "Maybe there are more inside?"

"There are sure to be more, but if they're like these miserable creatures, we won't need a fire or a Gladius. We'll send them running with a sharp rap on the nose."

As we watch, the front door opens. A couple of more Hellions come out, but they just join the others drinking and smoking. Hesediel and I move around so that we have a better view of the front of the mansion. We have a few more boring minutes, but it's worth it, because we find out why

Moe, Larry, and the other Hellion Stooges are in complete fuck-off mode.

A small man dressed all in gray comes outside. His name is Arwan and he and his men saved my life in Kill City.

Back home, people call them Grays or Gray Folk. They're not like the Sub Rosa or Lurkers. They come from a whole different ancient line of hoodoo. No one even knows if what they do can be considered regular magic. The don't use spells or potions or clever puns. They simply will things to happen and they happen. They're like weird little forces of nature. Also, they fight like ninjas with a finger jammed on the fast-forward button. I owe them a pretty big favor after Kill City and I wasn't able to pay it back at the time. I don't know why they're here, but if I can clear my ledger, I'll worry about what they're doing in Hell later.

It takes another twenty or so minutes for the Hellions to stop fucking around. A couple of them go back inside the house and the other four wander off to pretend they're doing their jobs. There's a pretty good chance that Arwan could kick my ass in a straight-up fight, but I hope it won't come to that. He's a warrior, but he's also a hustler, and that works in my favor.

I motion for Hesediel to move back farther into the trees. She gives me a what-the-fuck face, but I wave her off. When she's back far enough, I get as close to the tree line as I dare and sort of whisper-yell.

"Arwan."

He looks around.

"Arwan."

He zeroes in on my voice and stares for a minute. Then he laughs at me. He takes his time wandering over.

"Do my eyes deceive me or is it the welsher come calling?"

"Arwan, what the hell are you doing down here? You look like you're still alive."

"Of course I'm alive, you dolt. And so are my men."

"Then what are you doing in Hell?"

"I told you when we last met and you cheated us out of our bargain, the Gray men go where there's paying work. We're not scrounges like some I could mention. Now you tell me, what is a silly bastard like you and that angel hiding over there doing here?"

"We have a problem with the people inside the mansion."

He looks over his shoulder at the house and makes a face.

"Aye. That, at least, I understand. They're not what one would call a jovial lot."

"Those are blue-blood shit-heel murderous fucks you're guarding."

"That sounds about right. But it's our job to guard them and I get the distinct impression that you and the ravishing winged one are exactly who we're guarding them *from*."

I come a little more out of the trees and show him my hands so he can see I don't have a weapon.

"So, what's your story? Are you in love with them? You and your men are willing to die for those waddling shit bags?"

"Waddling shit bags," he says, and laughs. "And yes, since they are our employers, we are in a sense laying down our lives for them."

"But you don't like them."

"They're pompous, grandiose, puffed-up dogs. But their money is good and it comes in large, lovely piles."

I look around for the other guards, but they're off merrily skipping stones with the other loafers.

"What if I can pay you a lot more? Would you stand down? I'm not asking for your help. I just want you and your men to walk away."

"That would be dishonorable," he says. "But what are you offering?"

"Look at me. I'm in Hell and I'm alive. There's another mortal right back a few yards and she's alive too."

"Yes. You could always do your traveling tricks. That's why you were supposed to take us back to our homeland. But you didn't, did you?"

"I couldn't back then. But I can now."

"How?"

"Stark," someone calls.

I look around and see Wild Bill.

"It's Candy. She's sick."

I turn back to Arwan.

"Don't go away."

"Run off, then, like you always do. You know where to find me."

Me and Hesediel follow Bill through the trees. When we get back to where we left them, Candy is on her back coughing. There are flecks of blood on her lips.

I lean over her.

"You're being melodramatic."

She opens her eyes.

"I couldn't find a fainting couch, so I thought I'd just take a nap here in the Shire."

I take one of her hands. It's cold and there's a long gash along her middle finger.

"She must have pricked herself on one of those damned poisoned begonias," says Bill.

"Stay with her."

I take Candy's hand and squeeze it.

"I'm going for burgers. You want chili fries or onion rings?"

"Waffle fries, dumb-ass. You always get it wrong."

"That's 'cause waffle fries make the baby Jesus cry. I'll be right back."

I pull Bill aside.

"Stay with Candy. I'm getting her out of here."

"How?"

"By pissing off God."

"If anyone can do it, it's you."

"Be ready. With luck, the next people you see will be considerably shorter, but just as dangerous, so be nice."

"That don't sound the least bit ominous."

Hesediel and I go back to the edge of the trees.

Arwan has wandered over by the door again and is smoking a pipe.

"Arwan."

He looks up and, again, takes his sweet fucking time wandering over.

"Look who's back. The big talker."

"Listen to me. I know that you don't like those people any more than I do."

"Like doesn't enter into it. Pay does."

"I'm going to make you the deal of your lifetime."

"Are you, welsher? Do tell."

One of the poisonous centipedes strolls across my foot. I start to step on it. I'm fast, but Arwan crushes it under his boot and goes back to smoking almost before I can see it.

"I can get you home. And I can make you rich."

"And pray tell, how will you accomplish these feats of legerdemain?"

"A friend of mine a little down the hill is sick. If you take her with you, I'll tell you how to get home."

He thinks about it for a second.

"I don't think so. But it was lovely seeing you again. Feel free to attack anytime."

"Wait. There are riches."

He stops and turns.

"What kind of riches?"

"There's a cave under the city where I live. The person who used to live there has been collecting gold, art, magical objects, and every other kind of mad shit you can imagine. You can have as much as you can carry if you'll take my friend out of here. You'll go home richer than even you ever dreamed of."

He cocks his head.

"We Grays, we dream big."

"Well, dream bigger and multiply that by ten."

He puffs his pipe.

"Why should I believe any of this?"

"Because the woman you're carrying out of here is the only thing in this whole fucking universe I care about. And I'm trusting her to you. That's how you can believe me."

He looks at Hesediel.

"Lovely armor."

"It's not for trade," she says.

"Pity."

He looks back at me.

"How big is she, this woman of yours?"

"Not big at all. Two of you could carry her."

He looks back at the mansion.

"I truly do not enjoy the company of our current employers. And I do like the sound of fabulous riches." He turns back to me. "You know if you're lying we'll kill you *and* the woman, right?"

"I wouldn't have it any other way."

"How do we get home?"

"There's a maze. You take her through it and you'll get to the cavern. Take everything you want. Take it all. Then go back through the maze, keeping in mind where you want to go. You'll see some scary shit along the way, but they're just illusions. Just keep turning left and you'll get home."

"It's that simple, is it?"

"Just that simple."

He finishes his pipe and taps it on his boot.

"And there's enough treasure for us all?"

"More than enough."

"What about the owner of this vast fortune? Will he or she be coming after us once we help ourselves?"

"The owner only knows me. I'm the one he'll come after."

He raises his eyebrows.

"Vicious, is he? Cruel?"

"The worst."

"I do like the sound of you having to explain us to a big heartless bastard."

"He won't be happy. And I have nothing to repay him with. Who knows what he'll do to me?"

Arwan grins down at me.

"Look at you now. Selling your soul for true love. It's like a sonnet."

"Yeah. I'm goddamn Shakespeare. Do we have a deal?"

"As long as you understand, and not to belabor the point, that you're dead if we're disappointed in the least."

"And I'll dance a jig while you're doing it."

"Careful. Don't tempt me."

He stares at the ground, thinking. His boots are looking a little threadbare. He glances back at the house.

"Wait here," he says, and walks into the mansion.

Hesediel says, "Are you mad? Trusting these brigands with Candy and our whole scheme?"

"We don't have any other choice. Just be cool. This is all going to work out great."

"He doesn't seem to like you very much."

"I grow on people. Sometimes it takes a while."

"It truly does."

Arwan comes back a few minutes later, trailed by a dozen small men dressed in the same gray cloaks and jerkins as him, all carrying bows and swords.

Hesediel starts to stand. I wave her back.

When he comes to the tree line, he nods.

"It's a deal. Where's this woman of yours?"

"Won't your bosses notice that you're all missing?"

"I told them that we're buggering off into the woods for a

look around. We were each delighted to be rid of the other."

"Come on."

I lead them to where Bill is sitting with Candy. She's paler than before.

Arwan gets close and looks her over.

"She's not so big for us to carry."

"I told you."

"And she knows the way to the treasure?"

"She'll lead you straight to it."

"All right, then."

"Give me a minute."

I kneel next to Candy.

"Change of plans. Remember the little guys from Kill City who saved my bacon? They're taking you home."

"What? No. I want to stay with you."

"You're sick. You need to get out of here. And someone needs to take Hesediel's blood back to Vidocq."

She grabs my sleeve.

"What if you get lost again down here?"

"I'm not getting lost. Me, Bill, and Hesediel are doing this one thing. Then I'm heading straight home. I'll be right behind you."

"Promise?"

"I'll get Abbot to advance me some salary and take you to fucking Florida. How's that?"

"Will you wear one of those hats with the mouse ears?"

"You're a horrible woman, but yes. I will."

"Okay, then."

She looks at Bill and Hesediel.

"Thanks, guys. I'm glad I met you both."

"Me too, ma'am," says Bill. He leans over and kisses her hand.

"Go with God," says Hesediel.

I look at Arwan. He motions to his men. A couple come over and easily lift Candy between them.

As they start down the hill, Arwan comes over.

"Well, I hope for both our sakes that this is a fond farewell. If it's not . . ."

He draws his thumb across his throat.

I point down the hill.

"Take care of her."

"She's as safe as a goose chick tucked under its mother's belly," he says. Then walks away. It's only a few seconds before he and the other Grays disappear into the trees.

I get out my na'at.

"What might I ask is that?" says Bill.

"A Hellion weapon."

"Huh—never seen one of those before."

"You'll get a good look at one now. Once we're done with the guards, I'm using it on Wormwood."

"Then let's get to it."

"Let's," says Hesediel.

BILL STAYS UP front while me and Hesediel go into the forest around back.

She starts the party by manifesting her Gladius and sprinting through the woods torching everything like a pyromaniac who got a gallon of high octane for Christmas. I bark some Hellion hoodoo I haven't used since the arena. The tops of the trees along the far edge of the woods explode in flames, sending burning tree limbs onto the roof and through the windows at the rear of Wormwood's playhouse.

As the first Hellions run out to the woods, Bill steps into the clearing and blasts away with the Colt. Cuts down three before they know what's happening. The rest, maybe ten in all, come out of the trees firing wildly. A few at the rear of the pack are burning when they run into the clearing. Hesediel strides from the inferno and downs them all with her Gladius. That gets their attention. The rest make a break for the mansion. Bill hunkers behind one of the vans and fires. The guards open up in his direction, pumping automatic rifles into the side of the van. This really pisses me off, but gives me a chance to get into the fight.

While they're all looking in Bill's direction, I come out of the trees, firing and throwing more hoodoo. I wound a couple, and when the rest fire in my direction, I bring down one of the burning trees on top of them.

It barely misses the group and I'm left with my ass hanging out in the open. I hit the deck, firing blind as bullets kick up clods of dirt around my head. That's fine, though. Really, Bill and I aren't even trying to hit them anymore. We're just keeping them interested in us and not the sky.

A few of the real hard-ass Hellions stand their ground, firing, reloading, and firing again. The rest look around for somewhere to run that isn't on fire or full of flying bullets. It never occurs to them how fucked they are.

Graceful as a feathered torpedo, Hesediel swoops from the sky, her Gladius slicing and dicing the guards in the back. She lands and the hard-asses empty their clips into her armor. The sound is deafening, but doesn't last long. Bill and I take out a couple of pricks with our last bullets while Hesediel beheads the last two in one smooth motion.

Hesediel stands guard with her Gladius while Bill and I reload. If there are any guards left in the woods, they're Kentucky fried. Not a problem.

The grounds of the mansion, the hillside—everywhere we look—is a wall of flame. Sparks arc onto the mansion's smoldering roof. The back of the place is already on fire. All we have to do is wait for the scared dummies inside to decide they want to be dead dummies outside. The light from the flames is weirdly beautiful. It illuminates everything in a wavering, liquid pattern of reds and yellows.

A shadow streaks across the flickering light.

Hesediel's armor rings out again. A hundred church bells clanging at once. Something slams her onto her back, leaving a deep, scorched dent in her breastplate. A few yards away Hadraniel drops lightly to the ground, the glare from her Gladius brighter than the blazing forest. She looks every bit as crazed as she did on the boulevard. Her angelic flesh is dry as sandpaper. Black lines ring her eyes. She's so tweaked she can't even hold her Gladius still. But it doesn't make her look weak. It just reveals her true face, the grimace of a celestial berserker ready to burn down Heaven, God, and every mortal soul there ever was.

Hesediel rolls easily onto her feet. I start toward her, but she holds up a hand to stop me. Hadraniel looks from her to me, then back to Hesediel.

"Is this your new lord, sister? The Abomination? How desperate your God must be."

"He's still your father too, Hadraniel."

Hadraniel looks at the sky.

"Not mine and not yours anymore. But you're too senti-mental to see it."

"Better to have a heart than a twisted soul."

"Better a twisted soul than no future."

Hadraniel flicks her Gladius through the air. Ash and burning cinders fall on the angels' armor. On their faces and hair.

"I know better than to ask you to come with me again," says Hadraniel.

"It would be a waste of both our time."

"So be it."

I thought I was fast. Hell, I thought Arwan was fast. But with their wings outstretched, the charging angels are just a haze of fire and flashing armor.

They fight on the open ground in front of the mansion and in the burning forest. Swoop around each other above the flaming treetops. Their armor clangs and peals when they slam into each other. Shrieks when they glance off each other, metal sliding across metal.

It's hard to tell the two apart. High in the air, one of them spins, catching the other flat across the back. Burning feath-ers explode into the air like skyrockets. The injured angel tries to stay aloft, but can't. She weaves uncertainly, clearly groggy. Tucking in her wings, she dive-bombs just beneath the attacking angel's killing blow.

She comes in low for a landing, but misjudges it. Hits the ground hard and slides across the road almost to the mansion door, tearing up tarmac, soil, and concrete. Hesediel staggers to her feet and takes a fighting stance but the armor on her back is burned open, like someone took a plasma torch to it. A lot of her hair is singed off and half of her face is black. But she doesn't back down. Neither does Hadraniel.

She turns slow circles in the sky above us. Taking her time. Letting Hesediel's injuries do their work, tiring and weakening her.

Hesediel stumbles. Catches herself. Her Gladius flickers.

Hadraniel swoops like a falcon in free fall, and batters Hesediel's Gladius with her own, knocking her off balance. Hesediel staggers back a few steps. Her arms shake like the Gladius is suddenly too heavy to hold. I run through the falling embers to her. Bill fires shot after shot at Hadraniel, who doesn't even bother to acknowledge them.

Hesediel is trying to stand when I get to her. I pull her to her feet. She pushes me away. Her speech is slurred, but I can understand her.

"Get away. This is not your fight."

I manifest my Gladius and stand beside her.

She pushes me again.

"No," she says. "No."

Overhead, Hadraniel laughs at us.

"A lovers' quarrel, is it?" she shouts, turning slow circles.

"Stark, please," says Hesediel. "Let this go. Let me go."

"I don't leave friends behind."

"If I'm your friend respect my wishes. *Go.*"

I hesitate for a moment, but I get it. I let my Gladius go out. Hesediel can't even stand up straight anymore, but she manages to say, "Thank you."

I want to give her my gun. My knife. My na'at. Something.

But I know she won't take any of them. So, I press the only thing she might take into her hand.

And walk away, leaving her there in the open ground.

Bill comes running over.

"What the hell are you doing?"

"It's what she wants."

"You're going to stand there and let her die?"

"It's her fight. She doesn't want me."

Bill looks up into the sky, sputters, "Shit and damnation."

I take his arm and pull him away.

"We're not going anywhere. If things go wrong, I'm perfectly happy to stab Hadraniel in the fucking back."

When we're clear, Hesediel manifests her Gladius again.

Hadraniel makes a couple of more turns in the sky. Then drops. I can barely see her.

When she hits Hesediel, she knocks her twenty feet, through the side of a van. Hesediel stumbles back into the open, but her Gladius is out. She takes a few steps. Collapses onto her back.

Hadraniel lands and lets her Gladius go out too. She takes a knife, like the one Hesediel used at Bill's bar, from a sheath at her side. She doesn't rush. She savors the moment. Yeah, she's gloating, but she also wants to see if Hesediel is playing possum. It goes on like that, with Hadraniel circling Hesediel, for several more minutes. They talk, but I can't hear them.

Finally, Hadraniel steps over Hesediel. Drops her full weight onto the other's damaged armor. I can hear Hesediel moan all the way across the yard.

Hadraniel holds her knife so the fire dances off the blade.

"Are you watching, Abomination? I want you to see this."

"Fuck you, Almira Gulch. You and me. We're next."

"Glorious. I so hoped you'd say that."

She raises the knife and, in a blur, drives it through Hesediel's breastplate. Holds it there while her sister screams.

Hadraniel leans back and looks over at me and Bill. Opens her arms, giddy at the kill.

Lowers her guard.

Hesediel's arm moves. Just a few inches. Into a tiny space where Hadraniel's armor has shifted, revealing a sliver of skin.

Hadraniel jumps up, pulling at her armor. Trying to get to where Hesediel hit her. She runs her hands over her skin. Looks at the palms and holds it up for us to see. No blood.

Hadraniel goes back to Hesediel and pulls out her knife. The blade breaks off in the armor. She throws the hilt into the dirt and walks our way.

She gets about ten paces before she falls over, choking.

Hesediel sits up, but can't get to her feet. Bill and I run over. Get on either side and lift her up. When she's standing on her own, she loosens the buckles on the sides of her armor, letting her ruined breast- and back-plates fall to the ground.

She puts a hand over her chest wound and comes back with only a little blood. She smiles at us through her burned face.

"It's good armor," she says. "And I'm a better actor."

Bill and I help her over to Hadraniel, who's tearing at the ground, trying to crawl away. Hesediel slips a foot under her sister's belly and flips her over.

Hadraniel's face is going from blue to black. She gasps for air. Clutches at her throat.

Hesediel unbuckles Hadraniel's breastplate and pushes it away. Takes out her knife. Hadraniel is barely breathing. Her arms are limp. Hesediel bends and kisses her forehead.

She says, "Forgive me, sister." And drives her blade into Hadraniel's heart. The fallen angel lurches just once. Hesediel stands and slides the knife back in its sheath. When she looks again, Hadraniel is gone. Vanished like all dead angels, good and bad alike.

Hesediel looks at me. Hands me the syringe with the raw, poisonous black blood I gave her earlier. I wasn't sure she would use the thing.

I toss the syringe into the fire.

"Guess I interfered after I told you I wouldn't. Sorry."

"It was my choice. Black blood made Hadraniel what she was. It's fitting it was her downfall."

"You were her downfall. Not that rotgut," says Bill. "In this world and the other, I never saw anyone fight like that."

"I hope you never have to see it again."

Me and Bill help her to one of the undamaged vans. We get her into the back, where she slumps against the seat.

The top floors of the mansion are roaring. A lot of panicked faces I recognize peer out of the windows on the bottom floor.

"Stay here with her," I tell Bill.

"I'll keep her safe."

I get out my na'at and go into the burning house.

I come out a few minutes later, alone. Except for Holly. That's how Candy would have wanted it.

With the black blade, I start the only other undamaged

van and leave it for her. She stands by the house and watches it burn like she's expecting Norris, or Jesus, or Santa Claus to come out of the flames and make it all better. But no one does. After a while she gets in the van and puts it in gear.

Bill closes the door of our van and I turn us back to Hollywood, letting the mansion and hill burn itself to ashes behind us.

Hesediel dozes for a few minutes, then wakes with a start. She looks around the van, not sure where she is. When she sees Bill she relaxes back into the seat.

"Where are we going?" she says.

I look at her in the rearview.

"Back to Bill's. Unless you want to stop for chicken and waffles."

She stares back at the burning hillside for a minute.

"I have a thought. We have to go back to where Norris Quay took us."

"What are you thinking?"

"Do you trust me?"

Something I never thought I'd say to an angel comes out of my mouth. "Of course."

"Then drive."

THE VAN SPUTTERS and coughs as we make our way back down Highland. Everyone is bone goddamn tired. It makes the drive feel even longer than before. Eventually, though, we cross the 105. I pull us up to the gates of the treatment plant and the van shudders to a stop.

Bill opens the side door and we help Hesediel out of the van. Back on flat ground, she can walk again, but she's slow and moves with a bad limp. The skin is cracking under the burned part of her face so that the black is cut through with thin streaks of livid red.

We enter the plant and head to the treatment tank Quay took us to earlier. The place doesn't smell any better on a second visit. She goes to the tank.

"Think of it. A whole war over this," says Hesediel.

I walk up beside her.

"It's going to go on for a lot longer, isn't it? If all the bad guys fight like Hadraniel?"

"Forever, possibly."

"Now there's a pretty thought," says Bill.

Hesediel turns back to us.

"But if we, now, could destroy the source of black milk, it would end sooner. Correct?"

I shrug.

"Of course. But like Quay said, we can't exactly execute several million Hellions."

"Maybe we don't have to," Hesediel says. "*This* is the source of black milk. We must destroy *this*."

"But those Hellions are just going to keep shitting and shitting," says Bill. "Destroying this batch won't stop that."

"I misspoke," Hesediel says. "Everything all of us have done and seen and learned comes together here. Your return to Hell. Bill and Candy's offer of help. The destruction of Wormwood down here. We have a chance. A single moment to destroy it all."

She looks at me.

"And perhaps kill Wormwood in the mortal world. Without them, black milk will be useless."

"But how do we do it?" says Bill. "You two incinerated the hell out of that forest back there, but I don't think effluent even this vile will burn."

"Not burning," she says. "Befoulment."

Hesediel takes a few steps away from the holding tank back toward the van.

"I'm glad I met you both," she says. "I've defended mortals, but I never truly thought much of them, Bill. Thank you for opening my eyes."

"Well, I think a lot more highly of angels 'cause of you. Thank you for that."

She turns to me.

"And you. Abomination incarnate. I wasn't pleased when Samael asked me to help you."

"I can imagine."

"But you're a fine ally and companion."

"Same to you."

She looks past us into the distance.

"Who is that?" she says.

Bill and I turn. Find ourselves launched through the air all the way back to the van. Bill comes to a skid by the bumper. I crash into the windshield. Blood runs down my forehead into my eyes.

I try to get up, but my legs won't hold me. The best I can do is crawl onto my hands and knees. Bill moans and rolls over, in as bad shape as I am.

I look around for Hesediel. Can feel a lump rising on the back of my head from where she hit me. Finally, I see her by the treatment tank. She has her knife out and is cutting a long slit from her wrist up to her elbow.

"What the fuck are you doing?" I yell.

She looks back at me, as happy as I've seen her.

"Saving us all," she says.

I manage to get to my feet and stumble like a drunk to the gate of the plant.

Bill pulls himself up on the van's bumper.

She holds her arm over the sewage.

"You said it yourself, Stark. My blood is the cure for disease. What is more pestilential than war?"

I push myself off the gate and head for her.

"Stop this shit. You're in no shape for this."

"But I am," she says. "Clearheaded. Happy. I thought for so long that the war would consume us all. Now I can finally see its end."

My head clears a little and I can stand upright.

"Let me help. Cut me too."

She slices into her other arm.

"That's noble, but clever as you are, this is something half an angel cannot do."

Bill staggers up beside me. Pushes away and starts for her. I follow him.

Hesediel stands on the lip of the tank, her arms covered in flowing blood.

"Tell Samael thank you for opening my eyes to so much. Take care, my mortal. And my little monster."

She draws the knife across her throat and falls backward into the tank.

Bill and I run to her. But we're too slow. Too stupid. Too late.

She's gone.

We get on our knees, scrabble around there like fools, waiting for her to bob to the surface safe and sound, her sacrifice just another ritual, and when it's over, we can pull her out and take her home.

But she doesn't come up. There's no sign of her. Not even bubbles.

Bill and I stay there on the lip of the tank for a long time, breathing in the stink, neither of us wanting to move in case we're wrong.

Finally he gets up. Taps me on the shoulder.

"Come on, son. It's been a long day. I need a drink. So do you."

It takes me a while to get my legs working.

What did I do wrong? What did I miss? Why did Samael send Hesediel to us? Did he know Hadraniel would break her heart? Did he know this is how it would end?

Is he that big a bastard?

"Please don't be," I say out loud like an idiot. "Please be as surprised as us."

"What are you talking about?" says Bill.

"Nothing."

We climb back in the van and I jam the black blade in the ignition. The engine coughs a couple of times, but won't turn over. We get out.

It's a long walk back to Bill's bar.

IT DOESN'T TAKE long to finish the bottle.

I wonder if Candy is through the maze yet. If she isn't, if the Grays didn't keep their part of the bargain, I'll find them wherever they are. Part of me wants them to cheat. I've never wanted to hurt someone—anyone—more than I do right now.

When Abbot puts the Wormwood member list together, I'm getting it, even if I have to take it from him. I wouldn't mind facing off with Willem. Which probably isn't fair. In the larger scheme of things, he's nothing. Not a good guy or bad guy. Of course, he doesn't see it that way, but Willem isn't a big-picture guy. Just another dog in the pack. Sit. Fetch. Bark. Bury a body if his master needs it. He's the kind of guy who thinks he has a grip on good and evil because he made some big busts and got a few commendations. In the end, I don't really want to fight him. I want to show him the locked doors of Heaven. All those damned souls and pitiful fallen angels stranded between the pearly gates and Hell's scenic vistas. I want him to hear the rebel and righteous angels fighting it out for his future. I want him to know that the difference between salvation and damnation is small and getting smaller. Maybe he'd understand and maybe he wouldn't. Maybe people like him and assholes like me are built to butt heads. But if an Abomination and an angel can get along for even a little while, who knows? I don't want to be his friend, but it would be nice if just once, someone like him understood that I'm not his enemy.

Wormwood, on the other hand, is done. No one is innocent. No one walks away. No more clueless spouses. No more deals, car rides, or stories. No more dead kids.

I'm done with words.

They're dead, every one of them. And when they're in Hell, I'll make it my job to send them to Tartarus. But not before they go for a nice, long swim in Quay's sewage tank.

Those fuckers want black milk? I'll give them all they can choke down.

But not right now. Right now I picture Arwan and his crew carrying Candy through the sushi bar that leads to the maze.

Please make it home, Candy. I can't lose you too. Allegra will fix you. She can fix anything. She'll even fix Vidocq with what you're carrying. Everyone is going to be all right. They have to be.

I've been fighting Heaven's battles for so long.

Seriously: listen. You bastards forgot about me when I was in Hell. Please remember me now. Give me just this one thing.

I take out a couple of Maledictions. Hand one to Bill. He lights them both with a candle. I puff mine until it's red as a poker. Hold it to my wrist until it blisters.

"What the hell are you doing?" says Bill.

"It's where she cut herself for Vidocq. I owe her this much."

"Hurting yourself won't bring her back. You've got to gather your strength for what's coming next. In a funny way, we're lucky."

"How's that?"

"It isn't often that vengeance and a righteous fight coincide so completely. But it's not over. We both have work ahead."

"You're right there."

I rub the knot on the back of my head.

"You take care of those Wormwood pig fuckers back home," says Bill. "Send 'em down to me. I'll handle them from there."

"I might have to come back and help you with that."

"I wouldn't object. Just don't let thoughts of revenge blind you to your responsibilities to those you love."

"Don't worry about Candy. She'll be right with me when she finds out what happened."

Bill looks under the counter for another bottle. Looks frustrated when he comes up with nothing.

"Send me some souls soon. Bereft is not my natural state. I fear I'll go a little mad without a useful task to occupy me."

"It won't be long, Bill. I promise."

He gets a rag and wipes off the top of the bar. It doesn't matter that there will probably never be another customer in here; nervous energy has to go somewhere. Even the smallest things can help.

"Any chance there's more Wormwoods down here that we missed? If there's tracking to be done, I'm ready," he says.

I blow on the blister. Watch it bloom on my skin.

"I think we got them all for now."

"Pity," he says.

"Yeah."

"Maybe it's time for me to get out of this hovel," he says. "I was a lawman once. Maybe I could make myself useful down here."

I set the Glock on the bar, along with all the ammo left for it and the Colt.

"Keep both guns. I have more."

"The Colt was a gift."

I stack the bullets in rows.

"Candy will understand. She likes you—she'd want you to have it." I think for a moment. "We should go back up the hill to Quay's place. Pick up some of those rifles and whatever ammo is left."

He puffs the Malediction. In the candlelight he looks older than his Earthly years.

"That's a good thought. But later. It will give me something to do after you leave."

"Let me show you how the Glock works."

He picks it up. Weighs it in his hand and gives it to me.

"I never thought this would be the time or place I'd modernify myself."

"Life is funny."

"And death is riotous. So, show me how your toy pistol works."

I pop the clip and take out the bullets. Show him how to load the gun and rack in a shot. Playing teacher feels good. Gets me out of my head for a few minutes.

When we've run through it enough times that Bill can do it smoothly, he pulls a crooked smile.

"I guess this ain't such bad iron after all."

"I hate to tell you, but there's not much iron in there."

He sights down the barrel.

"Iron enough for my purposes."

I look around the bar for a clear spot. Over by the wall there's a long table where we served food when I was Lucifer.

"You mind if I lie down for a while? My head hurts, and like you said, it's been a long day."

He hooks a thumb over his shoulder.

"I have a cot in the back. You're welcome to it. Don't use it much myself. I lost the habit of sleep when I came to this elegant burg."

I shake my head.

"Thanks. The table is fine."

I take off my coat and shoulder holster. Set the black blade and the na'at on a corner of the table. Wad my coat into a lumpy pillow.

"Good night, son."

"Night, Bill."

MAYBE LYING DOWN wasn't the best idea after all. In my dreams, I'm drowning. My lungs fill with black, stinking muck so thick it pulls me down like there are cinder blocks around my ankles. I dream of the Tar Pits back home, only I'm not throwing Liliane into the black lake. I wade in myself. First, to my ankles and then my knees. By the time I'm up to my waist, it's hard to move, but by then it doesn't matter. The sticky stuff pulls me down like some dumb bear who didn't watch where he was going. I pass through the preserved branches of trees. The skeletons of small animals. Birds and runty gazers. Tangle myself in a forest of wolves and saber-toothed cats, their ribs folding around me like I'm a bug in a venus flytrap. Then there are the big bones. Pool-table-size mammoth skulls. Legs the size of filing cabinets. I come to rest on the tip of a long tusk. The tar weighs me down so that the sharpened ivory goes all the way through me. I float there for years, a *Flintstones* shish kebab.

Hands reach down and grab my wrists. Pull me up through the muck.

I want to look around when I hit the surface, but my eyes are gummed tight by the tar. Someone holds my face. Uses their thumbs to wipe it away. When the hands let go, I cough up gallons of the thick black stuff, until my lungs work again.

Eventually I can get up on my knees, I grab hold of the

tusk and pull it out of my stomach. Another bad idea. It's like I'm back in the arena, where some fucking hellbeast has sliced me open. I have to grab my abdomen. Only the tar and my hands keep me from falling apart.

I'm not at the Tar Pits anymore. I'm by the other black filth at the treatment plant. I look around for Hesediel. She's the only one who could have pulled me out, but I'm alone.

I stumble out of the plant and head north, crossing the freeways, then up Highland. Turn east and begin the long walk into Griffith Park.

Everything is on fire. The tar on my skin bubbles and burns as I follow the road up the hill.

By the time I make it to the mansion, the boiling tar has sealed my stomach closed. When I can use my hands again, my first instinct is to pull my gun. I reach back for the Colt, but the tar has fastened it to my body.

Shadows circle overhead.

In the sky, two flying things claw at each other. There's so much smoke, I can't tell if it's angels or eagles.

I try to pull the Colt free. Turn round and round in a frantic moron dance. The gun won't budge.

A golden, angelic knife falls blade first into the ground.

I get it now. I can help. I can make things right.

The knife sticks to my tarry hand, but the blade is clean enough to use.

I draw it through the tar and flesh holding my insides in place. It hurts so much I have to laugh. When the hole is big enough, I force my hand through the opening and cut a hole in my back. As the skin parts along my spine, I throw the blade away. Reach through my body and pull the Colt out through my stomach.

Free now, I point the pistol into the sky and shoot. Fire all six shots, but the gun keeps going. I pump round after round through the burning treetops.

One of the angels falters. Spins and nose-dives to the ground. I run to the body. I was so set on using my gun that I didn't bother to see who I was aiming at. My heart is going a million miles an hour.

The body is Hadraniel. Her armor is twisted. Her wings broken.

Hesediel lands a few yards away in the circle of burning trees. Her armor is new and perfect.

I point with the Colt to Hadraniel. Try to say something, but my lips are sealed by the tar. I find the knife and cut through the stuff until I can open my mouth.

"It's okay now. See? *I* killed her. Not you. None of this is your fault. It's mine. You can come back now."

She smiles at me. It's all so perfect and beautiful.

"My little monster. Do you really think it's that simple?"

"Yes. It's over. I fixed it."

She takes out her knife.

"You can't fix things that haven't broken. Some things just are, even if we don't like them."

"Please."

She draws the blade across her throat and falls back into the tank.

The forest is one solid sheet of flame reaching to the sky. The tar boils and bubbles on my skin.

I put the Colt to my head.

And pull the trigger.

I WAKE UP on Wild Bill's table. He's standing over me.

"Bad dreams?"

"You could say that."

He walks away and sits on a barstool.

"That's why I gave up on sleep. The visions are acute. Never had a lie-down that didn't end with me shouting like a fool at ghosts."

"I talked to Hesediel."

"Did you now. What did the lady have to say?"

I rub the back of my head.

"Stay away from rodeo clowns. They're drinkers."

He straightens his mustache with the knuckle of his index finger.

"Sound advice from anyone."

I roll off the table still feeling the gun barrel against my head. It takes me a minute to get my balance. When it comes back, I put on my coat. Slip my knife and na'at back into place.

I sit next to Bill at the bar.

"Now that the thing's been done, how long do you reckon until those rebel angels and Wormwood feel the pinch?" he says.

I pick at a splinter on the barstool.

"We don't know how much refined black milk there is. It could dry up tomorrow or it could take a year. All that matters is there's an end."

"Amen to that."

I look at him.

He nods.

"A funny thing to say down here, I know. But I think apt."

"I wasn't going to argue with you."

Bill looks into the dark.

"I suppose you'll be heading home."

I rub my human arm. My hand comes away wet.

"Huh."

"What?"

"I think I got shot."

Bill gets up and comes around me.

"Let me see."

I shrug off half the coat and he tears open my shirtsleeve. Holds up a candle and shakes his head.

"It's not a shot. More like a bugbite or prick from one of those damned bushes in the park."

"Good. I'd be embarrassed taking a bullet from one of those Hellion mercs."

Bill helps me put the coat back on. Now that I've noticed it, the bite or whatever itches.

"As I observed earlier, I suppose you'll be wanting to get back home."

"I do. But there are a couple of things I need to take care of."

"You feel up to going back out there?"

" 'Cause of the arm? I'm fine."

"You're a little white is all. With them scars, your face is a bit like an ice-skating rink."

"Are you saying you went ice-skating, Bill?"

He shakes his head.

"Me? No. But I saw it once on a lake. All these kids and

ladies twirling around. I thought it must be what Heaven looks like."

"If we do our work right, maybe we'll both find out."

He gets up. Dusts off his pants.

"I didn't think you were too keen on getting to Elysium."

"I didn't say I wanted to stay. But if I can stand Disney World, I can handle an afternoon with halo polishers."

"Where are we headed?"

"To Tartarus."

He frowns.

"Why there?"

"Because it's the right thing to do. And because it's what Hesediel would have done."

"Then let's get moving. The sooner we're done, the sooner we'll get you home."

Bill heads for the door. I blow out the candles and we go outside.

"First we're going to need another car."

He drops his head a little.

"Try to pick a better one than last time. I don't want to spend eternity walking home from one of your damn errands."

There are vehicles abandoned by the outskirts of the old street market. I get out the black knife and start testing ignitions.

It doesn't go well.

I CLEARLY DON'T have Candy's luck when it comes to cars.

It takes a couple of hours to find one that starts. A rusted-out Corvair with seats that are mostly springs. That's bad enough, but the fuel gauge is almost at empty. After some looking, I find a length of hose and bucket in one of the old market stalls.

Did you ever siphon gas from a car by sucking on a hose? It's pretty much the worst thing you can do with your mouth. To make it more fun, Hellion fuel tastes even worse than regular gasoline. It's like gas that's been filtered through a bloated whale carcass and served with a side of overcooked broccoli. I have to hit a dozen cars to fill the damned Corvair, but after another hour it's done. Bill was a big help throughout the ordeal, smoking and shaking his head at me from the back of an old pickup truck.

"You anywhere near a conclusion? You're making damnation boring."

I give him a thumbs-up. Then go behind a VW Bug and throw up.

Bill hands me a handkerchief when I get back to the Corvair. I spit and wipe my mouth.

"Thanks."

"Don't bother giving it back," he says.

I toss it away and we climb into the car. It's a tight fit, but we manage it after Bill figures out how to push his seat back.

"Where to, Magellan?"

"Tartarus."

"I should have stayed at the bar."

"You'll love it. There's a river view."

"It sounds rapturous."

"That's exactly the word I was thinking of."

TARTARUS, THE HELL below Hell, a Holiday Inn for the double damned, is a place of eternal darkness. A stinking cattle car crowded with all the suckers unlucky enough or stupid enough to die a second time. Then there are the Hellions. Unlike Heavenly angels, the fallen don't blip out of existence when they die. No, they get to fall a second time.

Bet Lucifer didn't mention that on the job application.

The entrance to Tartarus is through the river under Hell's creaky version of the old Fourth Street Bridge. The landscape is a wasteland crisscrossed with old railroad tracks running beside a blood-filled tributary of the Styx. I bet all those dead L.A. real estate developers are tortured by dreams of condos and shopping centers as they're sucked down into the dark.

A year or so ago, I broke out of Tartarus, releasing the schmucks below. Then I sealed it again as the final resting place of Mason Faim. A shitty move, I know, but cry me a fucking river. I thought that would be the end of the place, but now it's full again and that's rotten for so many reasons, one of which is visible from half a mile away.

"What in the Lord's name is that?" says Bill.

"It looks like Jurassic Park."

"Boy, this is not the time for riddles."

"You know I used to fight hellbeasts in the arena, right?"

"Of course."

"And you noticed the Griffith Park Zoo was empty."

"I ain't blind."

I stop the Corvair on a frontage road by the railroad tracks.

"I've been wondering what happened to all those animals."

Bill stares into the distance.

"You silly son of a bitch. What have you brought us to?"

"A hellbeast buffet."

The entrance to Tartarus might be through the river, but the exit is on dry land. And at the moment it's surrounded by a wandering, snarling, crawling, slithering herd of the ugliest hellbeasts I've ever seen.

"They must smell the souls."

"May I point out to you that *I'm* a soul?" says Bill.

"Don't worry. They won't even notice you with the hot lunch down below."

"Am I to assume you have some blockheaded idea to take them things on?"

I tap the steering wheel.

"I don't know. Maybe."

"Is it too late to disown you?"

"Calm down. Let me think for a minute."

I look at the bloody river. It's low along the banks.

I look at the hellbeasts. They're moving slow. I bet they're starving.

There's not much around us except for a train yard to the north.

"Fancy a train ride, Bill?"

"That's not a real question, is it?"

I start the Corvair and we head across the wasteland to the depot. We take it slow. Nothing to see here, monsters. We're barely a morsel. Not worth your time.

Eventually, we make it to the yard without being eaten, a good omen if there ever was one. I wish I believed in omens.

"What now?" says Bill.

"How do you like the look of that train over there?"

He squints through the windshield.

"It looks like Lucifer's iron cock."

I see his point. A lot of machines down in Hell might work like Earthly machines, but they're not exactly based on the same aesthetic. The locomotive is a hundred-ton tube with steam pipes that look more like bloated arteries stretched across diseased and pockmarked flesh. The front of the train is a leering skull with smokestacks recessed into the eyes. About fifty freight cars stretch out behind it.

I look at Bill.

"Ever drive a train?"

"Every Sunday after church."

"You're being sarcastic and that's okay. I'm nervous too."

"Thank you for your permission. Now, what are we doing here?"

I get out of the car. Bill follows.

"I just said it. We're stealing a train."

"You plan on driving it by those brutes?"

"Nope. You are."

"Like hell I am."

"Not right away. After I distract them."

"Going to dance a monster can-can, are you?"

I head for the train.

"Let's see if we can get it started."

Bill and I climb up into the engine.

"Do you know anything about trains?" he says.

"Nope."

"Then how are you planning on running it?"

"Magic, Bill."

"Show me."

The train's drive panel looks like the interior of a rocket to the moon. There are enough gauges, dials, and knobs to make Neil Armstrong blush. With a little luck, I don't need 99 percent of them.

I point to a lever on the side.

"That's probably the throttle. Help me find something that might be a brake."

Bill looks over my shoulder.

"All these buttons and whatnot are labeled in Hellion gibberish."

"Fuck it. I'll stop it with hoodoo too."

"Not if I'm driving it."

"It'll be fine."

"You'd be more convincing without all them scars."

I look out the side of the train at the Orc party over Tartarus.

"Okay. Here's what's going to happen. You're going to stay here in the train. I'm going back to Monster Island and get them to follow me. When they do, you drive the train right up to Tartarus. I'll open it and let the souls on board."

"What if the beasties don't all follow you?"

I look around the cabin and spot a button.

"See that? That's the air horn. Push it a few times. Maybe it will scare the rest off."

Bill looks at the button.

"I'd prefer a cannon."

"Me too, but it's what we have."

Bill looks out the window.

"You know, if I get eaten, I'll be down with them others in the dark."

"If I can't pull the hellbeasts off or they come back or won't leave, you just hit the throttle and keep going."

"And leave you behind?"

"Exactly."

He takes a breath.

"Damned stupid thing to say."

"Well, none of this is going to happen if I can't start the train."

"Try it now."

I look at the control board. If I use Hellion hoodoo I'll probably blow up the whole thing. But I've always been pretty good at improvising spells. Good, but not perfect.

"Here we go."

I whisper a few words. Nothing happens. A few more. Some of the panel lights come on. Another little whisper. The panel lights blink a few times and the engine rumbles to life.

"Dammit," says Bill.

I pat him on the back.

"Remember. You don't do anything until you see them back off."

He points. "That's the throttle thing and that's the horn. Where's the brake?"

"I think it's this thing."

"You think."

"If it doesn't work, just pull back the throttle all the way. You'll stop eventually."

He stares at the controls.

"How do you plan on getting them beasts to follow you?"

"Dance a can-can."

"Lord preserve us from your brilliance."

"See you soon, Bill."

I go back to the Corvair and manifest my Gladius. Slicing the roof off is easier than I expected. Once it's out of the way, I get in and fire it up. Gun the Corvair and head straight for the herd. The trick isn't to find the head of the pack. I need the one that's *dumber* than me.

I hang back far enough that I can make a run for it if things don't work out, but I have to get close enough that one of the morons can see me. The problem is, they're all concentrating on the tasty treats below.

Fine. I've got to do everything myself.

Hanging around the edge of the herd is a sort of giant crab/spider creature. A full-grown adult male. About twenty feet tall and dumb as a sackful of pudding. They're fierce bastards in a fight, but I've killed their kind before. Of course, I've almost been cut in half by those claws, so that's on my list of things to avoid.

As quietly as I can, I pull the Corvair right under its belly and honk the horn.

The thing quivers and its big armored legs scuttle around so that it can see me with all five of its black, hairy eyeballs. I'll admit it. My fight-or-flight instinct kicks into full run-home-to-mommy mode. But mom is dead and I don't have enough gas to get to L.A., so I throw the car into reverse and floor it before I get skewered by one of those legs.

I have mixed feelings at this point. On the one hand, the plan seems to be working, and on the other, I'm being pursued flat out by around thirty tons of angry stupid.

I head straight for the riverbank and stop. Honk my horn again to make sure it can find me. No problem there. It heads straight in my direction. I hop out of the car and start running, waving my arms and shouting.

This is where I *really* start to have mixed feelings. Before they were only *kind of* mixed feelings. But once I'm running, everything comes back to me. The smell of the arena. The screaming crowds. Multicolored blood pools in the dirt. Sometimes other hellbeasts and sometimes other fighters around me. I've imagined being back in the arena so many times since I crawled out of Hell, and here I am, my wish finally fulfilled. And part of me is enjoying it. I swear, if I could import a few of these hungry freaks back home, I'd never get a Trotsky headache again.

But that's not what I should be thinking about. Right now it's all about looking delicious without letting them find out if I am.

Crab Cakes follows me along the river to where an enormous drainpipe dumps blood into the tributary. The pipe is a few feet below me. I jump and slide down the riverbank, landing right next to the metal inlet.

Behind me, my new best friend runs at full speed.

Interesting fact: Most crabs don't have even a basic grasp of physics. I don't either, but I know that thirty tons running at full speed is going to have a lot harder time stopping than me.

Sure enough, Crab Cakes sprints right to the edge of the river, skitters, and falls, rolling onto its spiny back before sliding into the flowing blood. Its legs wave in the air as it tries to right itself, but it's wedged in tight.

From the pipe, I climb up onto Crab Cakes' belly and look for one particular break in its shell. It's midway between its front set of legs and its moving mandibles. When I find it, I extend the na'at to its full length and plunge it as hard and as deep as I can between the armor plates.

It bellows like a foghorn and its legs twitch like it's running the hurdles in the Olympics. With luck, the bellow got the attention of the other hellbeasts. All I have to do now is make sure they don't lose interest.

Wet with river blood, I climb back up the bank. Shout some Hellion hoodoo while I run for the car.

Crab Cakes' belly explodes in a foul-smelling shower of fish guts. Some thumps on me and into the car, but this isn't the time for tidiness. I jump into the Corvair and peel out as the other hellbeasts get a whiff of the jumbo fillet-of-fish sandwich waiting for them in the river.

A moment later, the herd turns and lumbers and slithers toward the river.

I fucking hope Bill sees what's going on. Revisiting the arena for a few minutes was fun, but like the fight pit back home, I don't want to like it too much. I made and broke too many promises to Candy to let myself drift back into old habits.

When I'm far enough from the feasting dino bastards, I pull up near the train yard. The area around Tartarus is almost clear. Only a couple of extra-slow and dumb beasts remain, pawing at the ground.

The train starts to move. Picks up speed as it heads straight for Tartarus. Steam billows from the skull on the front of the train. Bill lays on the air horn. The last beasts turn toward the sound, but stumble back as the giant metal fire-breathing monstrosity thunders toward them. One of the beasts runs off into the train yard while the other heads for brunch at the river. Tartarus is clear.

I hit the accelerator and speed along the tracks, bouncing over ruts and tracks. The Corvair creaks and grinds as I completely fuck up the undercarriage. I'm never going to get my deposit back.

I reach Tartarus just after Bill hits the brakes and the train screams to a stop.

Guess he found the right lever.

The exit to the pit is a circle of Hellion steel, sort of like a big manhole cover. I manifest my Gladius and cut away a section big enough for people to get through, but not too big for me and Bill to move.

The crowd below must be pretty shocked. Most haven't seen even Hellion daylight in a while. It takes a few minutes before the first faces nervously appear in the hole.

We help about ten of them out, then give them people-pulling duty while I run around asking everyone if they happen to know how to drive a train. I get a lot of funny looks, but most of them are so dazed and happy that they don't waste time asking stupid questions. While I play Alex Trebek, Bill hustles the crowd onto the train.

We get several hundred people out of the ground before I recognize the first Wormwood face. I don't know his name, but he's one of the pricks I killed back in Griffith Park. He gets it that he's persona non grata when I wave my Gladius in his face. Other souls and Hellions come out while he crawls back into the dark.

I must have asked a couple of hundred damned souls about trains when one of them says, "I can."

"You can drive a train?"

"Sure. When I was alive I was a conductor on the Norfolk Southern line."

"Congratulations. You just got your job back."

He looks at the Hellion engine.

"I don't know if I can run that."

"Sure you can. Anyway, you're not going far."

"How far?"

"Around Long Beach. Basically, you keep going south until you see a shitload of souls and Hellions. It's like Woodstock, but instead of a stage, you'll see Heaven."

His expression brightens.

"You mean we can get in?"

"Not quite yet, but you'll want to be there when the gates open, right?"

"Oh yes."

"Then get up there, Casey Jones. Once we get everyone out, you're in charge."

He seems a little confused by the whole thing, but he heads for the train engine and that's all that counts. Me, I hang around Tartarus, happily kicking every Wormwood face back into the pit. It takes hours to clear everybody out.

Me and Bill are pushing the metal slab back into place when one last face appears.

"Hello, James."

"Hello, Mason."

"I don't suppose . . ."

"No."

"I didn't think so."

"You always were the smart one."

"Who are my new roommates?"

"They're from a group called Wormwood. You're going to love them."

He looks past us at the train, then back into Tartarus.

"Well, lovely seeing you."

"Good-bye, Mason. Enjoy eternity."

"Eternity is a long time, James. Who knows? Maybe we'll meet again."

"Nope."

We shove the metal back into position and I weld it in place with the Gladius.

The conductor runs back to me and Bill.

"I can do it," he says. "The controls are a little different, but I can handle them."

"Then get moving. Those hellbeasts are going to be finished eating soon."

He looks at the river.

"Shit."

"Yeah."

"Good-bye," he says. "By the way, who are you people?"

"That's Wild Bill Hickok," I say, hooking a thumb at Bill.

He points at me.

"That's Sandman Slim right there."

Casey Jones looks at me.

"Funny name," he says.

"Tell me about it. Now get going."

He runs back to the engine. The air horn howls twice and the train starts moving.

I stand there watching them go. I know I did the right thing, but I'm still not entirely happy.

I wish there was time to tell them about Hesediel and how she sacrificed herself for them. But none of these people will have heard of black milk or probably the new war in Heaven. Hesediel's death would just be an abstraction to them. A Sunday school homily you tolerate because you know there's juice and graham crackers later. Hesediel deserves more than that.

Sometime down the road, when the rebels are gone and Heaven's gates finally open, someone will tell them about her. They'll get it then. And someone better build a statue and have a holiday where the banks close and some asshole does a movie about her and it plays all day like *It's a Wonderful Life* at Christmas. If they don't, I promise to make my one and only trip to Heaven and put my boot severely up someone's ass.

As the train disappears Bill says, "We should get going. I think some of them behemoths are still hungry."

He's right. A few of the hellbeasts are wandering back in our direction.

"You sure you don't want to hop on that train, Bill? I think I can still catch it."

"Don't ask fool questions. Take me home."

We get back in the Corvair and speed back to the city.

The bugbite doesn't itch anymore. Now my whole right arm is numb. But I don't tell Bill that.

WE FIND AN abandoned liquor truck on the way. Bill selects a bottle of good Hellion whiskey and we head to the bar. The Corvair runs a little rough on the way back. Something is out of alignment and we're leaking oil. Still, it gets us back to Bill's before coughing its last.

He leads the way in and uncorks the whiskey while I go around lighting candles. When I sit down, Bill has laid out several shots in a row.

"What all we drinking to?"

"First, making it back to hearth and home in one piece."

We down a shot.

"Second, to a good day's work, even if you smell like the innards of a trout."

We have another.

"Third, to a fine angel and friend."

Down it goes.

"Last, to seeing the backside of you for a while. *Vaya con Dios*."

I raise my glass, hoping he's not going to keep pouring.

"Same to you, Bill."

We drink.

He leans his elbow on the bar.

"Is there anything left for us to do down here? Any demons to smite? Bears to wrestle?"

I cork the whiskey.

"Can't think of a thing, except wondering what you're doing next."

He thinks for a minute.

"I might wander south in a bit. That is, unless you think you'll be sending some Wormwoods down here soon."

I flex my arm a few times, hoping to feel something. There's nothing at all.

"It will be a while, I think. They've run off in a dozen different directions. I have to find out where and then get to them."

"Tell you what. I'll wait a little while, then. Maybe set up camp at whatever's left of the house in the park. If no one wanders up in the next week or so, I'll take it as a sign to be moving on."

I scratch my arm.

"Sounds like a plan."

He straightens his mustache.

"That bite still bothering you?"

"Just itches a little."

"Be sure to get it looked at. Don't go playing a hard-ass."

I nod.

He holds up the bottle.

"One more for the road?"

I hold up a hand.

"I'm done for now. I have to walk a straight line if I'm getting home."

"Then let's get you started."

We take our time walking back to the sushi bar.

Bill frowns at it.

"I don't think I want anything to do with fish for a good long while."

"Do I really smell?"

"I'm afraid so."

I take off my coat. Hang it on a loose nail outside the restaurant. Maybe it won't stink when it dries and some wandering soul can use it.

The na'at I put in my back waistband where I usually keep the Colt. The black blade I slip into my boot.

I turn to Bill.

"You sure you're going to be okay on your own?"

"I've been in Perdition a good while, son. I know how to take care of myself. And thanks to you, I have plenty of firepower if anyone gets ideas."

"Okay, then."

I hold out my hand.

Bill grabs me in a brief bear hug. Nods as he steps back.

"Safe travels. Be sure to give Candy my regards."

"I will. Bye, Bill."

He holds up a hand.

I go into the restaurant. Keep going until the light changes.

And walk right into a wall of cornstalks.

Great. The maze. I'm halfway home.

Now I just have to figure out the other half.

A HALF HOUR in here and I'm sweating. My right arm has gone from numb to throbbing.

Wait. Has it been a half hour?

I get out my phone.

The battery is dead. No chargers in Hell. Got to remember that the next time I go down.

The next time . . .

That won't be for a while, not if I have to haul my sorry ass through this hayseed labyrinth. I keep waiting for Minotaurs or Victorian floozies to come running by, high on ether and absinthe. Now that I mention it, I wouldn't mind some of that myself. It would make the time pass faster. Or pass at all. How long have I been here? Right. No phone. No clock.

I'm really starting to feel a little ragged. Maybe I should have crashed at Bill's a little longer. No. That's dumb. If this bugbite is anything, then I have to get home and see Allegra.

Man, it's hot in here.

Candy and I got to Hell by turning left the whole way. Logically, I should get back by turning right. Wait. Does that make sense? You turn left to get through a maze. Maybe right is wrong. Ha. That was funny. Right it is, then.

Are the rows narrower going back? I swear they are. I keep bouncing off the sides.

Shit.

Just fell through one of the walls into a different row. Does that mean I turn left or right from here?

Right. Keep turning right. I'm sure of it.

Fuck.

Look for something familiar.

Hey, it's more corn. That helps.

Shut up and keep turning right.

Is my leg getting numb too?

I get out the black blade and poke my calf a few times.

Yep. Can't feel a thing. And I think I'm bleeding.

Is it hot in here? I'm really thirsty.

I turn another corner and start up a steep hill.

That doesn't seem right. Still. Nowhere else to go but forward.

It's a long way up and the ground is slippery. I look down at my feet. The road is covered in those centipedes from the park. I crush them with every step. Pale green guts explode on the road and my boots. There's nowhere to stop now and I can't go back the way I came. Got to get out of Deadwood with my head in one piece. That's the most important thing.

How long have I been here? It's really hot.

At the top of the hill is the Wormwood mansion. Which

is bullshit because I saw it burn. Great. I'm hallucinating. Or was the other time a hallucination? Wait. Was I really in Hell at all? Maybe I've been in the maze this whole time. I wasn't bitten by a bug. I just feel lousy because I haven't had any food or water for a while. That means I'm lost, right? Or maybe the maze is just longer than we thought.

Wait. Where's Candy? If we're still going through the maze, she'd be with me. Unless we got separated back at the mansion. Was there a mansion? I remember one, but maybe it was just that place I broke into in Beverly Hills. Where was that? Beverly Hills. Right. I just said that. Concentrate.

Stop falling. And stop going up the hill to the damned mansion. It wasn't even real. You're in the maze. Still. The mansion looks awfully real. As I go past, I look at the upstairs windows. See Nick's face staring down at me. He waves. I wave back. Good news. Beverly Hills. I'm almost home.

My leg really hurts. Maybe I poked it too hard with the knife. Maybe I ought to look. Can I do that without falling over?

Nope. Ow. Fuck my head. I can't see right.

Along the cornstalks are playing cards. They're all aces and eights. But there's a fifth card ahead, skittering along the floor in a breeze. I get up and follow it.

Funny. I think my leg is bleeding. Or is that another hallucination?

That must be it. Anyway, I lost the card. Damn. I'd like to know what it is. It's important, but I can't remember why.

Is it hot in here?

I'm on the ground. That's the first thing I've been certain

of in a while. Face in the dirt. It doesn't smell that bad. Like corn and earth.

A centipede runs by.

Time to move, only I can't. My head is funny and my leg is numb.

Someone reaches down and helps me up. I limp as I walk.

"Why did you send her to us?" I ask Samael.

"You needed help. I thought she'd be a good ally. Was she?"

"The best. Did you know she was going to die?"

"Of course not. I wouldn't waste a good warrior like that."

"No kidding?"

"No kidding."

We walk for a while.

"You're not here, are you? You're a hallucination."

"Probably. But I'm not sure how to tell."

"Can you see all those bugs in the corn?"

"No."

"Then you're a hallucination."

"How do you know they're not the hallucination?"

"Don't fuck with me."

"I'd never do that."

"I know. How's the war in Heaven?"

I look over and he's gone. I turn.

There's my father with a hunting rifle.

I duck.

A shot goes over my head.

Now I'm definitely hallucinating. Good for me. Confirmation. Wait. Hallucinating is bad.

Goddammit. I fuck everything up.

Turn right. Again. And again.

I think maybe I should have been turning left. Is it too late to start over?

Was Samael just here? He's the angel of death these days. He can be a lot of places at once. Does that mean I'm dead? Maybe I should stick myself with the knife again to see if I feel it.

I reach down for the knife. My leg is covered in blood.

Let's forget the knife and just assume I'm alive.

There's someone in the corn ahead of me. I think it's Candy. She's back to her old self. No Chihiro glamour. Leather jacket and Chuck Taylors over black jeans. It's wonderful to see her again. I run to catch up, but my legs don't want to cooperate.

If I had the Room of Thirteen Doors back, I wouldn't be lost in this Kansas weed patch. I'd be me again and everything would be all right. I've got to get it back. No matter what. All right. Start a list. First action item, get the Room back. What's the second thing I need to do? Get home. Maybe that should be first? I don't know. I just work here. You'll have to ask the manager.

I turn a corner and I'm home. There's L.A. spread out before me. The Hollywood sign on the hills. Capitol Records building over there. The Chinese Theatre there. Musso's in between. I should catch up with Candy. See if she wants to go for chicken and waffles.

Thinking about food wasn't smart.

I fall on my knees and vomit. It's full of thorns and bugs. I get back up and head for L.A.

And bump into another goddamn row of corn.

I'm starting to think I'm lost.

I look up.

Mr. Muninn's floodlights are overhead. That means I'm back in the cavern. Have I been here the whole time? I don't want to be in the cavern. I want to go home. The maze took me to Hell. Why won't it take me back to Max Overdrive?

Maybe I'm going in circles. Let's stop and think.

I'm in a maze. Candy and I walked through it in a few hours. The maze fits in Muninn's cavern, so it can't be that big. Of course, it's magic, so maybe it's bigger on the inside than the outside. Still. If I go in one direction long enough, I have to come out or to a wall or something. Right? There's no such thing as an infinite maze, is there?

Only one way to find out.

I reach back for the na'at, but have to use my Kissi arm because my right isn't working too well. Extend the na'at into a sword. Then hack at a row of corn.

It comes down exactly like dead cornstalks should. I step through into the next row and hack again. And again. The dry corn falls in heaps before me. This is such a good idea. I'm really smart. I'll be home in no time.

The only downside is that each time I cut through a row, it sends dust and pieces of corn into the air. After a few rows, I'm in a corn snowstorm. And I'm pissing off all the bugs. Wait. Are the bugs even real? I can't remember. A lot of this has been real and some hasn't. Or the other way around. Fuck it. Keep cutting.

I plow through row after row after row, looking back every now and then to see if I'm moving in a straight line. It gets harder as I go and the corn dust gets thicker. After a while

I stop looking. There are too many insects and it's starting to freak me out a little. Also, the corn is growing thorns. It cuts my hands and arms as I slice through the rows. The corn keeps changing and the light grows dim. I'm hacking through the woods leading up to the Wormwood mansion in Griffith Park. Only now I know it's a hallucination. I'm in the corn maze. Just keep cutting. Just keep going.

How long have I been in here? I take out my phone. It's dead. No chargers in Hell.

Man, I'm thirsty.

I look back the way I've come.

Centipedes. Spiders with Nick's face. A tentacle thing sprouts heads as it moves. Burgess. Quay. Charlie Anpu. Their teeth are little hatpins that the insects cling to like the cornstalks.

My legs get weak. I'm hot. Then cold. The insects mass around my feet.

I smash headfirst through the next couple of corn rows. Get up the na'at and slice through the rest. But I'm not going fast enough.

The insects are on my legs. I feel them crawl inside my leg where I cut myself. They're moving through my veins and arteries.

I run.

Someone is up ahead.

If it's my father, I'm going to punch him in his fucking face.

It isn't my father.

Hesediel slits her throat and falls into the tank.

I jump for her.

And land on concrete. I roll. Smash into the side of a parked car.

I pull myself up on the bumper and look around.

This feels real. I smell the exhaust fumes. Feel the too-hot sun on my back.

I turn and look behind me. No bugs. No dead angels.

Maximum Overdrive is just across the street.

I want to run, but all I can do is limp.

I stumble into the shop. It's full of customers. They look at me. Is this real? It could be a movie. But which one?

"Oh, my ears and whiskers," I say. "How late it's getting."

"Fuck me," whispers Kasabian. Then he yells, "Candy!"

It's definitely too hot in here.

I THINK I'M asleep for a long time.

Allegra comes by a lot. Vidocq comes by too.

"Hey old man."

"Hey yourself," he says. "Look at you. Always getting in trouble. Always worrying people."

"A born drama queen," says Allegra.

"You have to admit, when you get sick it's always something exotic," says Candy.

"Next time, *you* get bitten."

"I did."

She holds up her hand. It's wrapped in gauze. I didn't notice until now.

"You all right?"

"I'm fine. Just a little sore. I was counting on you being my houseboy for a while, but, well, that's not going to happen is it, Camille?"

I look at Allegra.

"What did that bug get me with?"

"Some kind of Hellion neurotoxin. Nasty stuff. Between that and the fever, we were amazed you made it home."

"Thanks for fixing me up."

"Thanks for getting medicine for Eugène. Candy told me about the angel."

I look at the blister on my wrist. It's already gone, but there's a new circular scar.

Candy sits down next to me.

"You need a shave," she says.

"How long was I gone?"

"Six days."

"I left a day after you. I was in the corn for five days?"

"You didn't turn left, did you?"

"I thought I had to turn right to get home."

"It doesn't work that way."

"No shit."

I sleep some more. My arm and hand are bandaged. The leg hurts more. I must have dug in deep. Remind me not to do surgery when I'm high on neurotoxins.

I can hear people in the store. Then it's quiet. Later, I can hear people again. That's how I count the days. People in. People out.

Kasabian comes up one afternoon with a bag.

"Apple fritters from Donut Universe."

I take one.

"Thanks."

Take a bite and limp to the bathroom, where I throw it up again.

Kasabian helps me back into bed.

"Don't tell Candy," he says on the way out.

Later, Candy and I are in bed.

"I thought I'd lost you again," she says.

"I told you I'd come back."

"And you didn't bring me a thing. Not a T-shirt. Not a bumper sticker."

"I gave the Colt to Bill. I hope that's all right."

"It's okay. We'll find you something else. Maybe one of those pink Charter Arms revolvers."

I sit up and Candy puts another pillow behind my back.

"Did I tell you what happened to Hesediel?"

"Yeah. You seemed pretty broken up about it."

"I need to find Samael and have a word."

"When you're better."

"If I died, the fucker would be here in a flash."

"Don't even joke about that."

I put my arm around her. It feels good to have it sort of working again.

"Sorry. I'm not going anywhere."

"Good. You haven't even heard the band yet."

"Have you been practicing?"

"Not while you were gone, but we're back at it."

"I want to hear."

"Soon."

A FEW DAYS later, I can actually walk out of Max Overdrive on my own. I get a new frock coat and new boots entirely free of bug juice. I know that the bugs were probably a hallucination, but I still can't look at the coat or boots without seeing centipede guts.

I'm still weak for a few more days. It's pissing me off. I want to call Abbot, but I lost my phone.

Some days, I help Kasabian in the store. Mostly I shelve returned discs. Nothing that requires a lot of brainwork. At night, the band practices in the storeroom. I know they'd rather be at Alessa's rehearsal space, but Candy still doesn't want to leave me alone for too long. They sound really good. One night, I manage to make it to Donut Universe and back on my own. The band devours the whole bag while they take a break.

I think about Bill a lot. It's been a few days. He's probably headed south by now. I hope the train made it to Long Beach. It wasn't fun seeing Mason. He's good at mind games, but I know we're not going to be meeting again. From now on, people only go into Tartarus. No one comes out. Ever, ever, cross my heart.

Oh man. I killed Muninn's maze. And I told a bunch of little guys to loot the cavern. I have a feeling that there are going to be consequences. But what's he going to do? Send me to Hell?

Wait. Maybe he will. He can always have some angels round up the wandering hellbeasts and put them back in the zoo. Then make me the zookeeper. I don't want to shovel monster shit until the end of time. I've got to make it up to him. Maybe one of those fruit bouquets. It will probably cost extra for delivery because of the exotic address, but it will be worth it.

How am I going to pay? Where's my money? In my wallet? Do I even have a wallet? Maybe I'm not ready to see Abbot yet. Give it a couple of more days. Maybe sleep a little longer.

CANDY CALLS ABBOT, and in a couple of days, he sends a limo for me.

That bugbite must have been special high-octane stuff. I don't get sick like this. Now I'm not sorry I burned Wormwood's hill. Maybe clearing out the forest was a good thing. Nothing worse can take its place, I'm sure. I don't want to think about it too hard.

I have the knife and my na'at in my coat, not because I think I'll need them, but because I feel naked without them. My back doesn't feel right without the Colt pressed against my spine. I tried a SIG P220, but the smooth body felt funny after the roundness of the Colt. Guess I'll have to get used to it. I'm not likely to find another revolver I like as much as that Peacemaker. In the end, I put an M&P Shield 9mm in my pocket. It's a little walking-around gun, but the bullets punch regular-size holes in things. Armed up, I feel more like myself, but still not right. And it's not the poison.

It's something else I can't put my finger on.

The afternoon ride to Marina del Rey doesn't take long. The gate to Abbot's boat is already open when I get there. A guard waves me through. Another guard motions on board the boat when I reach the gangway.

Willem is on the deck looking as Eliot Ness as ever.

"Hi, Willem. Is the boss home?"

"He'll be up in a minute."

"Thanks."

He gives me a look. I'm talking to him like a person and it makes him nervous.

"I hear you're back from a trip," he says.

"Been back a few days. But I picked up a little bug and didn't want to spread it around. You know?"

He nods.

"People say that you went down to Hell."

"Is that what people say?"

"You know what I say?"

"Bullshit?"

"Exactly."

I look around the deck. It's nice here by the water. Smells better than dead corn. I still dream about that crap.

"That's okay, Willem. I forgive you."

"Don't talk to me like that. I don't want anything from you."

"I know. But I'm tired and I don't want to fight with you anymore, so I'm just going to stand here quietly and think deep thoughts."

He gives me a look and goes into the cabin.

A minute later he and Abbot come out.

Abbot gives me a big smile and shakes my hand with both of his. We go inside.

"I thought for a while we'd lost you," he says. "I'd already started the paperwork to transfer your stipend to Chihiro."

"I had a feeling I could trust you. It was unsettling."

"Don't worry. I spent most of your time away eating babies and overthrowing third-world governments."

"So, you admit it."

"Guilty as charged."

He gets us drinks. I haven't touched liquor since I got home. The whiskey tastes good.

He crosses his legs. His pants have a crease you could cut diamonds on.

"So, did you finish what you set out to do?"

"Mostly. We rounded up all of Wormwood Downtown. More important, we destroyed their entire supply of black milk. I don't know how much there is up here, but they won't be getting any more of the raw product."

"That's great news. How did you do it?"

"Do you really want to know? I mean this is Wormwood we're talking about and what they were up to in the toilet of the universe."

He sets down his drink.

"We're in this together. I want to know everything."

"Well, I didn't use the word 'toilet' a minute ago just to be colorful. It pertains to what I found out."

I tell him everything. About finding Quay and Wormwood and *Panzerschokolade*. I tell him about how they use kids and about the souls sitting outside Heaven's gates because of the war Wormwood prolonged. Abbot might be a blue blood, but he's Sub Rosa and a scryer. He must have seen some strange things over the years. It takes him a couple of minutes to absorb it all, but he seems to take it pretty well.

"You'll be happy to know that we found Abigail."

"The other missing kid?"

He picks up his drink.

"Yes. She's back at home with her family."

"That's great news."

He looks at me.

"I have the awful feeling that you're holding out a little on me. Maybe there's something you don't want to say. Something you think I won't be able to handle?"

"Do you really believe the things people say about me? That I've been to Hell and back. That I was there again and I saw the dead members of Wormwood?"

"I told you that I do."

I swirl the whiskey in my glass.

"Yeah. But there's believing with your head and believing with your gut."

"I'm not sure I know the difference, but I trust you and what you tell me."

"Good. Then you need to know that I killed them all. Didn't just kill them, but sent them somewhere worse than Hell. And I was able to do all that because of an angel. Her name was Hesediel. I want you to remember that name. It's important. She's the one who did the worst part of the work. Not me."

He writes it down on a pad on the table.

"Hesediel," he says. "It's a pretty name. Would it be possible for me to thank her?"

"She's dead."

"You seem bothered by that."

"I am."

"But I thought you didn't get along with angels."

"I'm not big on kids either, but I saw one do a pretty good card trick at a party once. It was kind of like that."

"The exception that proves the rule."

"There you go."

A flunky in a suit comes in with a loose-leaf binder. He gives it to Abbot and goes out.

Abbot drops it on the table.

"I had a feeling you might not be the computer type, so I printed out the list of suspected Wormwood members we put together."

"All of them?"

"Council members, Sub Rosa families, and their civilian associates all of whom have left the country or disappeared since the deaths of Geoff Burgess and Charles Anpu."

"That book's for me, is it?"

He pushes it to me.

"You said you wanted to be part of the cleanup team. Unless you've changed your mind, it's yours."

I pick it up. It's heavy. I flip through it. Names. Addresses. Work histories. Known associates. Where they were last seen. I weigh the binder in my hand.

"It's like a goddamn phone book."

He cocks an eyebrow.

"That's why most of us prefer the electronic version."

I drop it back on the table.

"Maybe it's time for me to buy a laptop."

"I know someone. I can get you a deal."

"I bet you can."

Abbot opens the book and flips through it.

"I've put together a small team to help with this. We're meeting here in a couple of days. I'd like for you to be there."

"Good. I will."

"I'll text you the details."

I sit back in the chair.

"I don't suppose you can get me a deal on a new phone too? I lost mine somewhere between Hell and L.A."

"That sounds like a long walk."

"Five days when you get lost."

"That's a long time."

"Well, it could have been ten."

"Days? I'm not sure I understand."

I shake my head.

"Sorry. It's a joke they tell Downtown. The fallen angels fell for nine days into Hell. So, when everything is fucked up, you say, 'It could have been ten.' "

He stares at me, smiling.

"Funny. Do they have a lot of jokes like that in Hell?"

"No. That's the best one. Most Hellion humor is just a notch above junior high fart jokes."

"I learn more and more from you every day."

"Just trying to be useful, boss."

"Good job so far."

I look around, a little uncomfortable.

"Tell me. When does the actual Wormwood manhunt start?"

"I thought we'd discuss that at the meeting. Is there a problem?"

"It's just that I need a few days to take care of some things."

"Anything I can help with?"

"Do you know any travel agents? I sort of promised someone that I'd take them to Disney World."

He opens his eyes wide.

"You are full of surprises."

"It's not my idea. In fact, the whole thing is blackmail. But I promised."

He nods.

"It will take us a while to get the logistics worked out. After the meeting, you can have a few days to see the Mouse."

"Thanks. I appreciate it."

"What are friends for?"

He holds out his glass and I clink mine against it.

It feels like I've been drinking a lot of toasts in the last few days. If I can trust my life to an angel, I guess it's no stranger than partnering up with Abbot and some Sub Rosa 007s. It might even be fun. Maybe they can find me a new Colt.

Abbot and I shoot the shit for a few more minutes, but then he has to get to a meeting.

I take the binder and head back to the limo.

Willem is on the pier with some of his men.

"See you around, Willem."

"Have a nice drive home."

"Thank you."

"Watch your back."

"Love you too."

We hit traffic on the drive home. While we're sitting bumper-to-bumper, I thumb through the binder. I'm a little disappointed when I don't find Willem's name among the Wormwood suspects. I know it's kind of a dickish thing to hope for, but I'm not used to this forgive-and-forget thing yet. Maybe Allegra's PTSD pills will help. They still scare me, but what the hell? I'll give them a try. But no yoga.

That's a deal breaker.

IT'S ANOTHER DAY before I get on the Hellion hog. I wait until Candy's at work, of course. No need to worry her. But if I can deal with Abbot's whiskey, I think I can keep my balance long enough to make a couple of runs. My first stop is Griffith Park and Quay's mansion.

Unlike his Hellion digs, Quay's pied-à-terre in Earthly L.A. is underground. He might not have been Sub Rosa, but he was rich enough to afford a Sub Rosa mansion. Not many civilians can say that. I was only there once, but it was a memorable meeting.

The entrance to the place is in Griffith Park's abandoned zoo. Through a graffiti-covered cage big enough for a bear or tiger. The mansion's entrance is controlled by a hoodoo code you have to punch into a crack in the floor. I only saw it used once, so I never got a chance to memorize it. I should have brought Vidocq with me. He's good at breaking into things. But I wouldn't want to get him involved with this kind of trip, so it's up to me. I might be able to blow the place open with Hellion hoodoo, but that would make the kind of awful racket guaranteed to attract a crowd. I could get in through the Room, but, well, you know. I can't think of any way in that doesn't wreck something, so I decide to do it fast and dirty.

I manifest my Gladius and cut a hole in the floor of the cage where I sort of remember the entrance is.

And get it right after just a couple of tries.

There aren't any lights on in the dead man's digs and I can't find a switch, so I keep my Gladius burning and use it like a torch.

The place is just as I remember. A kind of faux-Greek palace full of sculptures and death charms. Not the kind that cause death, you understand. These are the kind that the user hopes will chase death away. The collection didn't work out like Quay planned, but it left him with a nice assortment of morbid tchotchkes.

I wander the marble rooms checking out every flat surface. I'm looking for something very specific.

It doesn't take long to find his office. The door is covered in wards and charms to keep prowlers exactly like me out. Only, none of this backwoods magic can stop a Gladius. I cut straight through the heavy oak door and kick it off its hinges. Now I need to pick up the pace. The charms might not have been a problem, but there's a better-than-even chance that Quay still has a civilian alarm system running down here. He's the type to want to protect his toys even after he's gone. I probably have just a few minutes before hired goons come speeding up the hill.

I go for his desk first. Pull out all the drawers. Check underneath and along the sides for hidden compartments. Nothing. Next, toss all the furniture and pull up the rugs to check for a floor safe. Again, nothing. Pull all the paintings off the walls and the books out off the shelves. I still can't find anywhere he might hide his most valuable possession.

Next, I head for his bedroom. Yank the drawers out of the bedside tables and check under his bed. Pull down more paintings and kick up more carpets. Not a goddamn thing.

Where would a fucker like Quay hide his ticket to immortality?

On a stand in a corner of the room is an interesting object. I turn to the frontispiece to make sure I'm right, and bingo, I am. It's a Gutenberg Bible, dated 1452. Now why, of all his death charms, would he keep this one in his bedroom? Quay never struck me as a sweet-blood-of-Jesus type. I turn a few pages looking for markings, ciphers, codes, anything that might lead to a secret hiding place. Naturally, I'm overthinking the whole thing. That's why people like Quay get away with so much. Those of us trying to guess their supervillain moves get so clever with ourselves that we miss the most obvious answer. The smart guys like Quay expect that, so while we're looking for Dr. Moriarity puzzles within puzzles, they go with the simplest solutions possible. And Quay's is wonderfully simple.

I flip to the end of the book, wondering if maybe he'd get a giggle from writing his clues in Revelation, and find that he's outsmarted everyone, especially me.

At one time, Quay was the richest man in California. He probably has a whole stack of Gutenberg Bibles lying around this dump. It wouldn't be a big deal for him to sacrifice one.

Sure enough, the whole last half of the Bible is gone. What's left is a compartment carved out of the heavy pages. Lying inside is a little 1908 Colt .25 pistol and a vial of black milk. But poor, poor Quay didn't live long enough to get one of the syringes. He was that close to immortality, but because he wanted to hedge his bets by following me into Kill City, he was never able to use the one potion that might have saved him.

I pocket the pistol and take the black milk to a bathroom off the bedroom. Pour the vial down the sink, then burn the rest with the Gladius so there's nothing left for anyone to scrape out. That's one less dose of black milk in the world. One baby step toward ending the war in Heaven.

There's an adorably gruesome little bronze Kali on one of Quay's bookshelves. I pocket it with the pistol. On the way out—partly to keep his other trinkets away from Wormwood and partly because it seems like fun—I drag the Gladius across Quay's bed so it bursts into flames. Do the same thing to the paintings and drapes on the way out. The sprinklers kick in while I'm going up the marble stairs to the zoo. That's fine. I never intended to destroy the place, just char it up to mess with the snoops whose job it is to figure out why someone broke in.

On my way to the bike, a whole gaggle of private security storms past. None of them looks at me twice, just another asshole having a cigarette by the FIRE HAZARD signs.

I get on the bike and make one quick stop before heading out of Hollywood. The drive down Highland is a lot faster than it was with Quay or when me and Bill had to walk home. I blow past the I-10 and the 105 in record time.

Security around this treatment plant is just a wee bit tighter in L.A. than it was in Hell. There are no guards, but a lot of security cameras and KEEP OUT signs. That's okay. I don't need to go inside.

I leave the roses between the links in the hurricane fence by the gate. A couple of guys in vests and hard hats give me funny looks, but none of them bothers coming over. Good. I'm not in the mood to explain the situation. "An angel died in here to save your shitty souls. Touch the roses and I'll come back and saw your arm off. Have a nice day."

That's what's been bothering me since I got back. The final good-bye I never got to say Downtown. It's stupid and pointless and sentimental, and if anyone I knew saw me doing it, I'd say it was a gag. But sometimes we have to do pointless things because that's all that's left for us. It's a ritual. Something an angel would understand perfectly.

When I'm sure the roses won't blow away, I kick the bike into gear and head back to Max Overdrive.

It hasn't been a long day, but I'm tired all the same. Not like I was when I was sick. It's more like the weight of what happened Downtown is back on my shoulders. But it won't be there for long. With that last good-bye, I'm done with this part of the story and ready for the next. I wonder if Abbot will fly me first class when I James Bond around the world, strangling Wormwood hotshots in their sleep. I like those little airline liquor bottles. They're like the fun-size candy bars you get at Halloween. I'll be treat-or-treating at six hundred miles an hour and eight miles high.

Made it, Ma. Top of the world.

IN THE EVENING, I take Candy to Musso & Frank's for martinis. I feel a little guilty for drinking somewhere that isn't Bamboo House of Dolls, but there will be a lot of nights to make up for it.

I can't remember how many drinks we have, but it's too many, which is just the number we came for. We even find a cab to take us home. Maybe Heaven has been keeping tabs on me after all. Decided to throw me a bone when they knew I was disastrously incapable of walking home in a dignified manner.

Thanks for the ride, Mr. Muninn. I'll be seeing you around, but not for a while, okay?

Back at Max Overdrive, me and Candy tear each other's clothes off on the way up the stairs to the apartment. We make it as far as the sofa, fully intending to wreck a lot of furniture, but we're too drunk and ridiculous to get very far.

We wake up around ten in the morning still on the sofa, with gin headaches and surf music blasting from the stereo. Our clothes aren't piled by the door so much as they've been hurled with great force, no doubt by Kasabian when he found the evidence of our indiscretion while opening the store. Candy makes coffee while I carry our wrinkled rags into the bedroom. I think I fall asleep again because when I sit up, the coffee by the bed is cold and Candy has gone to work. I take about fifty aspirin and head downstairs to shelve discs. It's the least I can do after forcing Kasabian to handle our delicates.

"You planning to pull that stunt often?" he says when the there's no one in the store.

"Sorry for the inconvenience. But we were suffering from an acute case of martini poisoning."

"Just make sure to clean up after yourselves next time. I'm going to need psychiatric help after finding all that crap on the stairs. I thought you'd done some of your half-assed magic and disappeared like the Wicked Witch of the West."

"I'm melting. I'm melting."

"Yeah. That."

I carry a pile of discs to the racks. The most famous movie David Lynch never made, *Ronnie Rocket,* has been a popular new title this week. I haven't even had a chance to watch it yet. Maybe tonight.

"I'm starting to feel guilty about not paying royalties on all these movies. We need to send some anonymous money to the AFI."

"Sure. Bankrupt us. Good plan."

"I'm serious."

"I'm ignoring you."

I go over to the counter.

"Are you and Fairuza talking?"

"Yeah," Kasabian says. "Thanks for scaring the holy hell out of her, then throwing her at me. There's nothing better than your ex calling you at three in the morning with night terrors."

"Sorry. But you're still getting along?"

"It seems that way. It's been nice having the band around, you know? Her and Candy having fun. Like old times."

"I hope things work out for you two."

He stares at me.

"Wait. Did you just say something nice? Call Allegra. Your fever is back."

"Nope. It's just me. I'm turning over a new leaf. Saving the shit for Wormwood and those that deserve it and keeping things low-key at home."

"So, we have to choose between you being an asshole or a hippie? I vote for asshole."

"Be sure to put that in the suggestion box."

"I'll leave something for you in the box. But trust me, it won't be a note."

THE BAND FINISHES rehearsing around ten. I've never heard them sound better. They're moving back to Alessa's place tomorrow, where they'll have more room. And she and Candy will be going on their first official date. I take this as a vote of confidence in my recovery since it means Candy will leave me alone at night with no one but Kasabian to babysit.

The four of them pile out of the room, sweaty and excited. Fairuza heads over to Kasabian and doesn't seem freaked out at all anymore. It looks like she just enjoys being with him. Good for her. It takes a while to get over seeing your first corpse, but since Kasabian has been a corpse, I knew he was the guy to send her to.

Candy and Alessa chat with Vidocq and Allegra while I go around checking the doors and turning off lights. When that's done, I order everyone out and lock the front door.

I'm putting my keys in my pocket when I remember something.

The rest of them are already down the street, heading for Bamboo House. I take the little statue out of my coat.

"Candy! I forgot to give you something."

They turn and look at me standing in the doorway holding Kali. Oblivious to the fucking world. I head over to them when Candy points at something.

"Stark! Behind you!"

I turn around, but it's way too late.

Where the hell did he come from and how did he know we'd be here? We never close this late. Maybe he's been hiding by the corner of the store all night. Maybe he floated down in a gauzy bubble like Glinda the Good Witch. Whatever it was, I don't see Audsley Ishii until the last minute and his knife is already halfway into my heart.

Kali hits the ground and I go down flat on my back.

Whatever Audsley stuck me with, it isn't a normal blade. I've been knifed plenty of times and I know what it feels like. This time it's all electric sizzles and paralysis. Down on the ground, I can't move a goddamn muscle.

Which gives me a great view of my friends. Candy is half-way to me and Audsley when I hit the deck. As she runs she transforms. Her nails curve into claws. Her mouth is full of white shark teeth. Her eyes are red slits in black ice. Audsley doesn't stand a chance.

As she's tearing him apart, I see the shock on Alessa's face. I guess Candy didn't tell her about being a Jade after all. She's going to have a lot of explaining to do.

Allegra kneels down next to me.

"Stark. Can you hear me?"

All I get out is "Only got me one time. It could have been ten."

And then I'm dead.

No, REALLY. I'M dead. I've been dead before and I know what it feels like. Except this is weird.

The last time I died, the angel half of me—the immortal Heavenly bit—broke away and ran off to play Robin Hood without human me. That doesn't happen this time. I feel around for him and he's there, at the back of my skull, and he's as pissed off and puzzled as me.

I was right. That sure as shit wasn't an ordinary knife. Wish I'd gotten a better look at it.

I'm flat on my back on parched ground, but at least I can move now.

I sit up and look around.

Gravestones. A dried-up fountain. A big iron gate out front. I know exactly where I am.

Hollywood Forever Cemetery. My home away from home. Only, this isn't *my* Hollywood Forever. There's only one place this ragged, broken-down version can be. The Tenebrae.

I get to my feet. Nothing to do but what I always do. Walk out the front gate and head for Hollywood.

I don't get far before I notice Samael next to me.

He's in an immaculate suit. I'm in my usual ex-con finery.

"I sort of feel like I'm dead. But I can't be dead."

"Sorry, but I'm afraid you are."

"But the angel half of me is still here."

"I didn't say it was a natural death."

We turn up Gower Street. I stop and jab a finger at him.

"I have some serious questions for you about Hesediel."

"No. I didn't know she was going to do what she did. But, let's walk as we talk."

We take our time getting to the Tenebrae's open plains.

"I wonder why Abbot didn't mention the possibility that Ishii would come after me? He's a scryer. He must have seen the possibility. Did he rat me out?"

"You're always looking for enemies. Maybe it's simpler than that. Think."

I light a Malediction.

"Want one?"

"I can't. No smoking during working hours."

"That stinks."

"Another reason I never wanted to be the angel of death. All the protocol."

"Maybe you can shake the job up. Loosen your tie. Wear a tracksuit."

"And have people think they're being taken to the afterlife by an Eastern European mobster? I don't think so."

We turn east on Sunset.

"Have you thought more about Abbot and Ishii?" says Samael.

"Yeah. Maybe Abbot didn't set me up. Maybe Audsley threw in with Wormwood. Abbot said they were protected from his seeing. Shit. That means they might come for him."

"That's not your problem right now."

"Yeah, but they might go for Candy too."

Samael stops. Looks at me.

"There's nothing you can do about any of that at the moment. You really need to concentrate on your current situation."

"The one where I'm dead."

"Yes."

"Well, fuck me."

We walk out onto the Tenebrae's endless cracked plains. On one side are the ruins of the ghostly L.A. where I woke up. On the other side are the mountains. Decision time. I have to choose to be nowhere or somewhere.

"Any wisdom you care to throw my way would be much appreciated."

"Just be yourself. It's what you do best."

"That's it? You sound like a high school guidance counselor."

Samael sighs.

"Death has never stopped you before. Why should it stop you now?"

The door to Hell opens in the side of the mountain.

Nowhere or somewhere?

My Malediction went out on the long walk over. I take out the pack to get another one.

It's empty.

I ball up the pack and toss it away. Samael watches it roll to the horizon on the light breeze.

"Littering. What a classy way to start eternity."

I look at the mountains.

"I guess I'll be seeing you around."

"You're going in, then?"

I shrug.

"Can't spend eternity without smokes."

"I'll walk you over."

It always takes a while to reach the mountains.

I look at Samael in his suit.

"Just the two of us walking along like this, it would be a perfect time to make a *Casablanca* joke."

"Please don't."

"'Louis, I think this is the beginning of a beautiful friendship.'"

"I take back what I said. Don't be yourself. You'll make everybody else in Hell miserable."

"That's the idea. And when they're good and sick of me, they'll kick me out and I'll go home."

"See? You always have a plan."

"Death can't hold me."

"I never said I could."

Samael gives me a sympathetic pat on the back and I go inside.

The door to Hell rumbles closed behind me.

Home sweet home.

Only it isn't.

Where are the sorting pens for new souls? For that matter, where are the other new souls?

And where the hell is Pandemonium?

I turn in a slow circle, looking for familiar landmarks, but come up empty.

Where did Samael leave me? Is this a favor? Mr. Muninn's punishment for wrecking his playpen? Or is it someone's idea of a joke?

Cupping my hands, I yell, "Olly olly oxen free."

Nothing comes back, not even an echo.

There's nothing but jagged lava peaks overlooking a dusty valley. My boots crunch on razor-sharp stones as I walk around the ledge where I came out.

Something hisses behind me.

I whirl around, my hand going under my coat for my na'at. But it's not there.

Right. I'm dead. All of my weapons are back with my body. It doesn't matter. The sound behind me was just a fine rain of black stone slipping down the face of the mountain.

I pull up my left sleeve. My Kissi arm is gone too. It's all me in here, just one more asshole soul out for a stroll in paradise.

Far across the valley, a dust plume rises into the dim sky.

My hand goes in my pocket for my phone, but it isn't there either. Dumb move. A stupid reflex. I'll have to watch that if I'm going to be here for a while, and I have a bad feeling I'm going to be.

To my left are the remains of an old trail cut into the lava stone. It looks steep and slick and dangerous, but from what I can see, it's the only way down.

Unless my eyes are playing tricks on me, the dust plume is heading in my direction, which raises all kinds of fun questions. Is it a storm? A lost pack of stampeding hellhounds?

Maybe it's the damned souls of old Rockettes rehearsing a new show.

Yeah. Let's go with that.

A couple of steps in the direction of the trail, my foot comes down on something soft. It's a pack of Maledictions. I pick it up and put it in my pocket. Now I know someone is fucking with me. They left me smokes, but no way to light them since my lighter is back with my na'at in L.A. Nothing I can do about it now.

I head down the trail.

The dust plume is definitely moving toward me. It looks less like the Rockettes and more like a hurricane with every passing second. Nothing else moves. Everything in the valley is dead except for that roiling dust. It's hypnotic. Kind of pretty in an End of Days kind of way. I suppose I could stay up here on this peak and be nowhere or take another chance and be somewhere. Maybe I'll get lucky and the wind will carry me home to Dorothy and the Tin Man.

I walk down the mountain, heading straight into the storm.

ABOUT THE AUTHOR

New York Times bestselling author Richard Kadrey has published eleven novels, including *Sandman Slim, Kill the Dead, Aloha from Hell, Devil Said Bang, Kill City Blues, The Getaway God, Killing Pretty, Dead Set, Butcher Bird,* and *Metrophage*, and more than fifty stories. He has been immortalized as an action figure, his short story "Good-bye Houston Street, Good-bye" was nominated for a British Science Fiction Association Award, and his novel *Butcher Bird* was nominated for the Prix Elkaban in France. The acclaimed writer and photographer lives in San Francisco, California.